DEVIL'S VENDETTA

TRACKDOWN V

Michael A. Black

MICHAEL A. BLACK

ROUGH EDGES PRESS

ROUGH EDGES PRESS

Devil's Vendetta

Paperback Edition
Copyright © 2022 Michael A. Black

Rough Edges Press
An Imprint of Wolfpack Publishing
5130 S. Fort Apache Road, 215-380
Las Vegas, NV 89148

roughedgespress.com

Paperback ISBN 978-1-68549-070-6
eBook ISBN 978-1-68549-069-0
LCCN 2022933122

DEVIL'S VENDETTA

DEDICATION

For Chicago Police Officer Ella French
Killed in the Line of Duty
August 7, 2021
Rest in Peace

We are such stuff as dreams are made on,
and our little life is rounded with a sleep.

The Tempest
Act VI, Scene 1
William Shakespeare

CHAPTER 1

3000 BLOCK OF TROPICANA STREET
LAS VEGAS, NEVADA

Wolf replayed every blow of the fight as he ran.

It had been two days, but his body still bore the bruises and he still felt the pain.

Ricardo Sabatini had been as tough as his reputation. The Brazilian had come out in a southpaw stance, right side extended, and soon Wolf figured out why. The man's right leg was like a trip-hammer, smacking first into the inner side of Wolf's left thigh, and then seeming to magically swing upward in an arcing motion to the face.

Luckily, Wolf kept his guard high, and Sabatini's instep smacked against Wolf's right glove or forearm. It was the first of many that evening.

The key to fighting a southpaw, Wolf knew from his time in the boxing ring at Leavenworth, was to keep circling to the right, staying away from the opponent's left side—his power side.

At least that's how the theory went.

Sabatini was proving to be somewhat ambidextrous, switching stances and cutting the ring off with alacrity.

It's not really a ring, Wolf remembered thinking as he absorbed a snapping front kick to his abdomen. It's an octagon.

But then again, a four-sided square was hardly "a ring" either.

A thudding right hook smacked against Wolf's left shoulder.

Damn, this guy was good.

"Offense! Offense!" Reno was yelling from the sidelines. "Don't let him bully you."

Easy for him to say, Wolf told himself, but he also knew his coach was right. Plus, he had an idea. If he could time Sabatini's shifts, he might be able to step in with a straight right lead. Throwing that punch was considered anathema to boxing purists, but Wolf figured it might just work because nobody would be expecting it.

That's when the Brazilian surged forward and delivered a thudding combination of a kick to Wolf's thigh, followed by a one-two punch to the head, the second of which landed hard against Wolf's temple.

He was sure the lights went out for a second as he found himself going down.

Black lights, he thought.

What every fighter sees at that crucial moment you get clocked so hard that you're separated, however briefly, from your senses.

Luckily, he landed on all fours and was able to spring away before his opponent could mount him.

Slamming into the cyclone fencing along the perimeter, Wolf was jerked out of his stupor. He lifted his arms just in time to absorb the onslaught, letting the blows land on his forearms, biceps, and shoulders. Then he did the smart thing: he seized Sabatini and took him down to the mat.

The Brazilian was known to be a fearsome striker, but his wrestling and Jiu-Jitsu skills were supposedly less impressive. He and Wolf exchanged arm punches on the floor, which did little in the way of injury. As Wolf tried to press the other man to the mat, his sweat-slick body slithered away like a retreating python and then Sabatini was on his feet again, beckoning Wolf to rise and meet him.

As Wolf scrambled to his feet the air-horn blast signaled the end of the first round. He walked back to his corner trying not to show the weariness that he was feeling after the first five minutes.

Four more rounds to go, he thought. Twenty more minutes of hell.

Wolf was jarred out of his current reverie when a car honked at him as he shot over Valley View and kept going straight on Tropicana, past the early morning cluster at the McDonald's, and the next backup at Starbucks.

"Love that smell of grease and coffee in the morning," he muttered in his best imitation of Robert Duvall from *Apocalypse Now*. "Smells like victory."

The image of the helicopter assault, as phony as it was in the movie, brought flashbacks of Iraq and Afghanistan. Afghanistan was now in the process of falling... Folding up quicker than a hustler's tent. He wondered what was going to happen to all those who'd helped the U.S. Forces during the twenty-year war.

Best not to think about that, he told himself. I've got too many of my own problems.

Trying to gain a few minutes away from the gnawing pressure of reality was one of the reasons he'd chosen to get up and go for the run. But try as he might to forget his problems, he could almost see imaginary images of them standing along the way grinning at him as he ran. Grinning and waiting as if to say, "Yeah, we're still here. And we ain't going nowhere soon."

He went over the bridge spanning I-15 and could see the off-white castle crenulations of the Excalibur Hotel and Casino. Las Vegas Boulevard was right beyond it, and he made a quick left and ascended the long set of stairs leading to the pedestrian bridge. Coming down the other side by New York, New York, after dodging a couple of slumbering homeless people on the bridge, he glanced farther down and saw that the steady flow of cars beneath him was starting to pick up. It was Monday, but it was still lighter than a normal weekday's traffic. He crossed over to the MGM and descended the stairs, and then bounded up the next staircase to cross back over Tropicana. His body was still a bit sore, but it felt good to sweat. And from the feel of the climbing temperature, there was plenty more sweat yet to come. It was still early, only a little after six, and already around eighty degrees. The hazy taste of drifting smoke from the California wildfires was slightly noticeable, but not yet problematic. Wolf wondered what it had been like for those old-time fighters who had to compete in those smoke-filled arenas of the bygone eras.

Glad I don't have to find out, he thought.

"You're letting him be the aggressor," Reno's screaming voice filtered back to him. He was massaging Wolf's arms between rounds. "You gotta start letting your hands go. Your feet, too, dammit."

Wolf knew Reno was right as they helped boost him off the stool at the ten second, seconds out, mark. The minute's rest had done the trick. He felt that he'd gotten his wind back. Or at least some of it. He danced out and touched gloves with Sabatini, trying to project confidence, and then the brutality began anew.

This time Wolf was ready for the switching. He danced nimbly away from the prehensile right leg, smashed a front kick into the underside of his opponent's thigh, and then moved in close and managed to deliver a solid punch to the Brazilian's side. Sabatini winced.

The ref stepped in and cautioned Wolf about hitting to the kidneys. Wolf heard Reno screaming in protest.

"Oh, come on, ref. That was a legit body shot. You forget your glasses?"

Good old Reno… Always trying for that psychological edge.

Wolf was past the Tropicana and the Oyo Hotels and Casinos on his run now. Koval was little more than a block away. His usual morning jaunts took him all the way down to Paradise, where he'd normally do an about-face and head back. Today he was feeling like he was finishing up round ten of a twelve-round fight. Still, he pressed on to the stop light and then grabbed it with his left hand as he swung back around. Another pair of homeless guys eyed him with alarm. Their pungent odor was noticeable from even three feet away.

Wolf started his return, and his mind took him back to that fateful third round. Although he'd held his own in the second, the Brazilian had still maintained his aggression. Reno had told him he'd lost the first two rounds. The image of Reno's frantic expression hovered in Wolf's mind's eye as if he were right back in the octagon that night.

"If he wins this one, all he'll have to do is coast the next two rounds and they'll hand him the fucking decision. And your championship belt."

And winning the third he was… Another combination of a leading right roundhouse followed by a right-left combination had Wolf seeing the black lights again, but only for a second. Then he felt a pinch along his left eyebrow. He brushed at it with his glove, and it came away red.

He was cut.

The question was, how bad?

He danced away, making sure he didn't go straight back, and felt the warm flow down the side of his face. Red droplets dappled the canvas beneath his feet. He hoped the ref might step in to examine it, but no luck. That meant no reprieve, but also that it might not be as bad as he'd thought.

Sabatini seemed to notice it as well and became invigorated by the sight of the blood. He threw another roundhouse kick, double punch combination. But this time Wolf noticed something. The other man's movements had somehow lost a step. He was a bit more sluggish when he shifted stances... Like an old pickup truck with a worn transmission missing a beat as it struggled to climb a steep hill.

Wolf absorbed the blows on his arms and danced away to the side.

"Offense. Offense," Reno was yelling.

Sabatini's corner was equally loud, but Wolf couldn't understand the Portuguese. The Brazilian moved forward, throwing another combination. There was no quit in this guy.

This time, however, when he shifted from southpaw to orthodox after throwing that right leg roundhouse kick, he dropped his hands ever-so-slightly.

And Wolf was there, stepping in with that overhand, straight right he'd been waiting all night to throw, putting his whole body behind it, blasting it into the Brazilian's jaw, watching the man do a little jerk, like he'd received a sudden electric shock.

His eyes rolled up into his head.

When he dropped to the mat Wolf knew there was no need to follow him down, no need to keep punching, no need to punish him further, despite Reno's voluble urgings to do so.

The ref, already sensing that Sabatini was out cold, was moving in and waving Wolf off.

Wolf did his customary walk-away victory strut, trying to look nonchalant, but in reality, he was too tired to even raise his hands in celebration.

Now his wet fingers momentarily traced over the row of black stitching over his left eyebrow. A couple more days and he'd have to get them taken out. But where would he be then?

He did his best to bask in the remembrance of the glory of the knockout win as he made his way back toward the Princess Budget Rooms, where he had his month-to-month apartment. After ending with his customary last-hundred-yards-sprint, he slowed to a walk as he left Tropicana Street and walked slowly through the parking lot. His breathing was ragged, and he took in the copious gulps of the morning air which had not yet acquired the heat of the day. It was his favorite time in Vegas—the early morning, before the conflation of the traffic and the tourists and all the rest of it. His beat-up old Jeep came into view in the parking lot, and beside it a scarlet-colored Escalade.

An Escalade?

It couldn't be, he thought.

But it was.

He saw the familiar figure with his left haunch settled on the front fender of Wolf's Wrangler.

Big Jim McNamara, his arms crossed on his big chest, grinned at him.

"What the heck are you doing here?" Wolf managed to ask, still not quite back to normal after the finishing sprint.

"Hell," McNamara said. "You're acting like you ain't glad to see me."

"I am. Just curious."

Mac's grin faded slightly as his lips tightened.

"Your mama called me," he said. "We've got to talk."

***

SPENCERLAND RECYCLING FACTORY
NEW SPENCERLAND, NORTH CAROLINA

James, "Jimmy" Wolf was sweating profusely inside the protective vinyl suit, full-face respirator, and thick rubber gloves that Sheridan always insisted they wear. The Hell Suit, Jimmy called it, but it was better than getting sick or dying, which the chemist had told him would happen if they didn't wear them.

And I'm too young to die, he thought with a wicked grin, thinking about how much money he was going to make.

But that was a little ways away.

As usual, during the cooking sessions, his duties were mundane and simple: make sure the big fans were on and blowing the fumes toward the hood, holding some of the huge glass beakers in his gloved hands while the other man poured some of the hot, liquid shit into them, picking up discarded junk, like used coffee filters, and taking out the foul-smelling byproduct mixtures and dumping them in the weed patch on the side of the building. He also had to stuff all the discarded trash over to the big incinerator on the other side of the building. The place was like a huge castle and this part was the dungeon. All the windows had been boarded over and the overhead fluorescent lighting shone down with a subdued artificiality.

Keep the light exposure to a minimum, Sheridan always said.

The big fans continued to blow the fumes toward the hood, which sucked them outside, further polluting the air, which was already foul with the smell of incinerated garbage.

"Let them smell methane," Bobbie said. "It's better than smelling what you're cooking."

That was him, Bob Spencer, Jr., perennial smart ass and lately always talking about his extraordinary network of family and friends.

To Jimmy, he was just another rich prick. Son of the mayor, and the little boss who now wanted to become the big boss. Jimmy was willing to go along with the plan, so long as he got his cut.

But there was still a lot to do, and not all of it in this dungeon.

Jimmy glanced around at this walled-off section where they'd installed the lab. He sometimes wondered what it had been like back in the day when this place had been the biggest textile mill in the state of North Carolina. Back before the bottom fell out of the textile industry, at least around these parts, and a whole lot of people were put out of work. Now, thanks to the rich prick mayor, it was a garbage and glass recycling plant... And the crystal meth lab that nobody, except a few choice individuals, knew about. The garbage trucks kept coming and going on the other side of the huge facility, while on this closed off section him and Sheridan cooked meth. Outside, GEM, Willard, and Craig stood guard. Jimmy wished one of them could take a turn in here, but he knew that wasn't in the cards. GEM was too big and clumsy to risk it, Willard was too fucking stupid, and Craig couldn't move that well due to his leg.

So it's up to me, he thought. The dumb Indian.

His breath was fogging up the inside of his gas mask now, and the claustrophobic nature of the mask and the suit made him want to scream. It was hotter than hell inside the fucking monkey suit, and his face and head were sweating so much that a small pool of liquid was floating around inside the mask, periodically slapping his chin.

Pure sweat. He could feel it running down to his toes, too. When he finally got to take this thing off, he knew he'd have to pour out a gallon of perspiration.

August in North Carolina was hotter than hell anyway but doing work inside a rubber suit was the Devil's own torture.

"We almost done?" he asked. "I'm dying for a smoke."

Sheridan didn't answer. He seldom did when he was embroiled in the cooking or heating some junk up on a hot plate. It looked like it was warming to a nice red color. Pretty soon he'd pour in the liquid and then drain it through the paper filter into another beaker. Then he'd give the discarded shit to Jimmy to go dump.

Yeah, they were almost done for the day.

After fitting the coffee filter over the glass tube, Sheridan did the pouring. He moved in slow motion, careful not to spill a drop. His movements were steady and without any tremors. The man was a drunk, but at least he stayed off the sauce when he had cooking to do.

"Dump this stuff, Jimmy," Sheridan said when he'd finished his careful pour. "And be careful."

"I will," Jimmy retorted, feeling angry at the constant reminders from the other man.

I ain't in school no more, he thought, then mentally added, and neither are you.

The felicitousness of his unspoken retort pleased him, even if Sheridan never heard it. But besides once being related to him, in a half-assed sort of way, Jimmy did feel a grudging kinship for the disgraced, former high school chemistry teacher. Jimmy hadn't made it all the way through high school, dropping out in his senior year, and even when he was there, he'd never even considered taking something as complex as chemistry. But he'd known Mr. Sheridan quite well back in the day. For one thing, Jimmy's big brother, Steve, had been married to Sheridan's sister. For a while, that is, when Steve was in the army. It had lasted a couple years, until he got bounced and went to Leavenworth. Then Darlene divorced him.

The bitch.

Back then he'd talked to his brother on the phone, and Steve had seemed all right with it.

"It's better this way," he'd said. "No way I can provide for a wife while I'm in here."

And he'd left it at that.

It had been a couple of years ago now, and it was also the last time he'd spoken to him. He was out now. And doing good... Real good... A fucking MMA champ.

Damn, Jimmy thought. I hope he makes it back here one day.

"Move it," Sheridan said, his voice muffled but stern, coming through the respirator. "And don't drop anything."

"Yeah, yeah."

Don't drop anything. As if he had to be reminded all the time.

Jimmy had to laugh at that. Funny words coming from a high school teacher who'd gotten dropped himself after he'd knocked up one of his students.

***

THE FALLOTTI ESTATE
LONG ISLAND, NEW YORK

After Robert Bray and Jason Abraham were admitted through the gate, Bray drove the BMW down the long asphalt drive toward what could only be described as a mansion. It was two stories high and had a smattering of black colored bricks mixed in with the brown and reddish ones. The result gave the walls a somewhat artful sweep, but it still had the look of a fortress. Two men patrolled the expansive lawn carrying 12-gauge shotguns. Another had a pair of mean looking Dobermans on a long leash.

"I thought the word was that Don Fallotti had stepped down from his position as *Capa di tutti I Capi*," Bray said. "The Boss of All Bosses."

"He has," Abraham said. "But he's still held in high regard. He isn't in the best of health, but he still has a healthy dose of paranoia. Made a lot of enemies over the years."

"I'll bet. What has there been? Three attempts on his life back in the day?"

"Five, but who's counting?"

Bray imagined the Don was, but he didn't say so.

They drove by an impressive looking fountain spraying water into the air from some kind of massive concrete statue. Bray saw a man standing in front of the house directing him to pull the car into a vacant spot. As soon as Bray had stopped, he glanced toward Abraham in the passenger seat and dangled the keys.

The lawyer shook his head.

"Keep them for now," Abraham said. "You can drive us back, too."

Suit yourself, Bray thought, thinking that it wasn't often he got to drive something like this. His own car, and the ones he used for surveillance, were all pretty much non-distinct models. A beamer attracted too many glances.

No sooner had they gotten out when three men, all tough and capable looking, appeared out of nowhere and approached the two of them.

The one leading the two bigger guys, was about five-eleven and lean looking. His dark hair was swept back from his forehead, and a wide grin stretched his lips taut. He held out his palm and said, "Keys."

Bray handed him the BMW's keys.

"Okay, *goombas*," the lean man said. "You guys packing?"

"I am," Bray said, pointing down to his side where his Glock 41 was housed in a nylon pancake holster.

"You must be the private dick," the lean guy said. "Bray?"

"Right."

The lean guy turned toward the lawyer. "So you're

Abraham?"

"That's correct."

"*That's correct*," the lean guy said, intentionally raising his voice to mimic a whining, effeminate voice. He smirked then lowered his voice to its normal pitch. "I'm Geno Valentino. Now lift up your arms and let my good friend, Luigi take charge of that piece."

One of the big gorillas moved forward and Bray did as he'd been instructed. The gorilla grabbed the Glock, stuck it in his coat pocket, and then proceeded to do a thorough pat-down of the rest of Bray's body, including his crotch, which elicited a grunt from Bray.

Valentino laughed.

"Sorry, tough guy," he said. "But this ain't TSA."

"You're telling me," Bray said, flashing his own grin. He'd expected the routine, considering where they were going and whom they were going to see. The gorilla also removed Bray's extra magazine. He stood off to the side.

"Your turn, counselor," Valentino said, turning toward Abraham.

The lawyer raised his arms as well and the second gorilla performed the pat-down. When he came to Abraham's groin area, the lawyer let out a sharp gasp.

"Jesus Christ," he muttered.

Valentino laughed.

"Like I told you," he said, "we take no chances."

Abraham blew out a hefty sigh and nodded.

"Okay," Valentino said, "you're clear to go in."

"What about my gun?" Bray asked.

"It'll be in the trunk of your car."

This is just like being dropped into *The Godfather*, he thought. But after all, Sylvester Fallotti was the last of his breed… An old-style gangster… A dinosaur. And from what Bray had been told, the old man was about to become extinct.

Valentino walked to the ornate, solid wooden door and opened it. Inside the place looked pretty much like the standard, run-of-the-mill, millionaire's house. The carpet underfoot was soft and cushiony, a huge portrait hung on the wall above an ornate mantel, and several chairs were strategically placed. Valentino led them to a closed door and knocked.

After a low muttered exchange, the door cracked open. Valentino grabbed the knob and stepped in front of Bray and Abraham.

"The Don will see you now," he said. "He's not feeling so good today. What you see and say in this room must remain in total confidence."

His expression changed, the flashy smile vanishing, being replaced by an expression of pure menace.

"*Capisce?*"

"Of course," Abraham said. "I was his brother's close associate."

The lean man shifted his gaze from the lawyer to Bray, who also nodded.

As the door opened wider Bray saw the room itself was faintly lit. Thick shades were drawn over the windows, and in the middle of the room a hospital bed took up much of the space. Two large metal tubes of oxygen, both with hoses attached, stood beside the bed, which was elevated at a forty-five-degree angle. A pretty woman in a nurse's uniform sat in a chair in front of the tubes. On the other side two more big men, both looking like candidates for the New York Giants' defensive line, stood next to the bed. The man lying on the clean white sheets looked puffy and haggard. His head turned toward them as they entered, and Bray could see the resemblance between the Don and his late brother. Sylvester Fallotti had the same thick, coarse hair, obviously dyed jet black, but now graying at the roots. His mouth was framed by a mustache and goatee, also ebony.

"Jason," the man on the bed said in a reedy tone. "Good to see you. I assume you bring me news?"

"Yes, Don Fallotti," the lawyer said. His tone had the practiced reverence of all in his profession. "This is my associate, Robert Bray. He's a private investigator used by our firm."

The Don arched an eyebrow. "Bray... What kind of a name is that? English?"

"American," Bray said.

The old man's cheek twitched, and then he snorted a laugh.

"Good answer," he said. "Now what have you got for me?"

Abraham took over, giving a quick summation of the incidents that had occurred down in Belize which had resulted in the deaths of Anthony Marco Fallotti and Dexter Von Dien.

"As far as we've been able to find out," Abraham continued in his most lawyerly tone, "their deaths were the result of a helicopter crash." He paused to let the information sink in a bit. Bray saw no emotion coming from the Don.

"At the time," Abraham said, "Mr. Von Dien and his associates were trying to obtain a valuable artifact—"

"Von Dien," the Don broke in. "Marco told me about him. Said he was a fat cat that was really loaded."

"True on both counts," Abraham said. "To do this, they'd stretched things a bit. They were holding a young woman, as a guest of course, while those close to her brought the artifact to them."

The Don frowned.

"Quit with the bullshit, will ya? Give it to me straight."

The lawyer emitted a short sigh.

"All right. From what we, or rather Mr. Bray gathered—"

"*Chooch*," the Don said. "I told you to give it to me straight, didn't I? You shut up. Bray, you went down there?"

"I did."

"Then you tell me. What did you find?"

Bray took in a deep breath, wondering how to phrase things. He decided on a straightforward approach.

"Von Dien had an operative, a former government man, CIA, grab one guy's daughter. The guy, McNamara, was supposed to bring the artifact down for an exchange. Instead, he brought a bunch of his cronies. He's an ex-Green Beret. There was some trouble. Von Dien and your brother tried to escape in a helicopter, but it went down."

The Don held up his hand, his head drooping now. Bray thought he saw a solitary tear drop from the old man's eye.

"A Green Beret," he said softly. "Like in the army?"

Bray grunted an affirmation.

The Don took in a deep breath, emitted a wheezing cough, and began to pant a bit. This seemed to attract immediate attention from the nurse. She stood and gently fitted an oxygen hose into the old man's nostrils.

When he spoke again, his voice was a whisper. "Those fuckers shoot the helicopter down?"

"That's inconclusive at this time," Bray said.

"Inconclusive?" The corners of the Don's mouth twisted downward into a frown. "What's that mean?"

"We don't know."

"Who's got the fat man's money now? Marco said that the son of a bitch was rolling in dough."

"A lot of Von Dien's assets were frozen by the feds," Abraham said. "Due to the discovery of some stolen artifacts."

"Those fucking feds," Fallotti said. "They can't keep their hands offa nothing, can they?"

"But," the lawyer continued, "he also had substantial holdings in foreign markets."

"Where? Europe?"

"Among other places," Abraham said. "His heir was his sister's son, a nephew. His name's Edgar Von Tillberg."

"Another wooden shoe?"

"Wooden shoe?" Abraham's brow wrinkled.

"A Dutchman," Bray said.

Fallotti smiled. "You know. I like this guy here. Him and me, we speak the same language."

He cackled a laugh that quickly degenerated into a hacking cough, which necessitated the nurse who was standing next to the bed to remove the tube from his nostrils and slip a full oxygen mask over the old man's face. He took in a couple of deep breaths then snapped his fingers ordering her to leave. She left, and he stripped off the mask and replaced the tube.

"I want to talk to this nephew," the Don said. "The least he can do is set up Marco's family. For life."

"It may be a bit problematic," Abraham said, "Contacting him, that is. At the present, he's still living on St. Francis Island. We have been in contact with him, and he's expressed some interest."

"St. Francis Island?" the Don said. "Where's that?"

"It's a Caribbean island where Von Tillberg has a special place."

"What kind of place?"

Abraham's mouth curled into a lascivious looking smile. "Ostensibly, it's a special resort for the rich and famous. Informally, it's known as Lolita's Palace."

The old man's face crinkled a bit. "Hookers?"

Abraham nodded, then added, "Of the young variety."

Fallotti shrugged. "How young?"

"Some are very young," Abraham said. "From what I've heard."

The Don's face wrinkled. "*Il bastardo.* I don't like dealing with scum like that. Who's his clientele?"

Abraham glanced at Bray.

"Movie stars, big wigs," Bray said. "Even rumored that some of our most prominent political figures might have stayed there."

"So he's into putting the squeeze on people?"

Abraham shrugged. "He's already rich, so it's not like he needs to. But you know how it is. Power is better than money, if you need it."

"So he can call in some favors when he needs to?"

"Let's just say, he probably has a lot of friends in both high and low places."

"I want to see the little prick," Fallotti reiterated. "And find them other two jokers, too. Find out what happened exactly, and if they had something to do with it, kill them. Blood for blood. What are their names again?"

"Steve Wolf and James McNamara."

"McNamara." The Don's mouth formed a frown. "Fucking Irish. Wolf? What the fuck kind of a name is that?"

"He's half Indian," Bray said.

"No shit?" The Don laughed. "Where's this son of a bitch, Wolf from, anyway?"

Abraham canted his head to look at Bray, who

consulted his notebook.

"He's from someplace that used to be called New Lumberton, North Carolina."

"Used to be?" The Don's brow furrowed. "What's it called now?"

"New Spencerland," Bray said. "They changed the name."

"Huh? What the fuck for?"

"Apparently the mayor's got a lot of clout down there. His name's Spencer. Named it after himself."

The Don snorted, almost causing the twin-junctured oxygen tube to jump from his nostrils.

"Like I told ya, find this guy Wolf. And that other fucker, McNamara, too."

"We can do that." Abraham arched an eyebrow slightly as he turned to look at Bray, who wondered if Abraham was going to mention the recovered laptops.

"If they had anything to do with my brother's death, anything at all, I want them both dead. *Capisce?*"

While not exactly a hit man, Bray had dallied on the dark side more than once. But still, from what he'd heard, these two ex-military dudes were a little bit out of his league, and he said so.

"What you saying?" the Don mumbled, the space between his eyebrows forming twin creases. "You telling me you're a chicken shit, or something?"

Bray sensed that this was not a man to whom you told the word no.

"What I'm saying, Mr. Fallotti," Bray answered, choosing his words carefully, "is that I have no problem finding them, but you're going to need to recruit some heavy hitters if you want more than that done."

The Don snorted out a sharp breath, started coughing again. The enormous goon on the Don's right exhibited an expression of concern and motioned for the other one standing by the door to get the nurse, but the Don waved at him dismissively. After a few more spasms, he took a deep breath, drew his lower lip up over his upper, and gave a curt nod. He extended an index finger at both Bray and Abraham. The man's dark eyes centered on Bray for several seconds, the Don's expression was stern, then softened into what Bray took to be an approving glance.

"I like this guy," the Don said. "He ain't afraid to tell it like it is. I tell you what. You find them and report back to me. Find out what really went on down there, and if I decide something needs to be done, I know just who to call."

Bray felt a slight wave of relief. He'd apparently passed some kind of test and now he'd made it into the old *capa de tutu's* good graces. And that's where he intended to stay.

***

PRINCESS BUDGET ROOMS
LAS VEGAS, NEVADA

It was taking a minute or so for the hot water to circulate through the pipes, but Wolf was enjoying holding his head under the ice-cold spray for the moment. It reminded him of dumping water over his head after doing a patrol back in the Sandbox or Afghanistan. The prospects of an ignominious withdrawal from the latter weren't sitting well with him, and he imagined he wasn't the only vet who felt that way.

Leave no man behind, he thought. I hope they don't.

The water suddenly grew hot, and he stepped out of the spray, grabbing the soap. Mac's sudden appearance and cryptic pronouncement, *'Your mama called me. We've got to talk*,' made Wolf both curious and wary. It also reminded him that he hadn't spoken to his mother since his release from prison. He felt a sudden wave of shame sweep over him. But finding the words to talk to her had been next to impossible.

Maybe she feels the same way, he told himself. That's probably why she called Mac instead.

And then he realized he hadn't even given his mother his new cell phone number.

The feeling of shame intensified.

After spending an inordinate amount of time lathering up and rinsing off, Wolf still felt reticent to leave the wet comfort of the shower. It was almost like an artificial womb, but he knew reality was waiting for him once he shut off the water and pulled back the shower curtain.

He heard McNamara curse loudly.

"What's going on?" Wolf yelled.

"I can't figure out how to use this fancy damn coffee maker thing," McNamara yelled back. "Why the hell don't you get a regular one?"

Wolf chuckled as he toweled off. His machine made one cup at a time from specially packaged K-Cups.

"I'm down to about one cup a day," Wolf said. "I don't need a bigger one."

"Then get your ass outta that shower and over here in this excuse for a kitchen and make me that one cup."

The apartment was very small—barely two-and-a-half rooms, apart from the tiny bathroom. The kitchen was separated from the bed and three-by-six living room by a small, three-and-a-half-foot wall. The other room held a bed and dresser. A table was situated in between the living room and kitchen. The sink was set into the far wall next to the stove and was piled with dirty dishes. Wolf finished drying off, hung the towel over the shower rod, and walked naked over to the dresser.

McNamara whistled and flashed a grin.

"Man," he said. "Looks like that last guy left his mark on you. I hope you kicked his ass, but good."

Wolf glanced down at the purplish-black bruises that decorated the outside of his left leg and over his washboard abdomen.

"You didn't watch it?" he asked. "I'm crushed."

"Of course, I did," McNamara retorted. "But it's hard to tell how hard you're getting hit on TV."

"Take it from me," Wolf said, grabbing some underwear, socks, and T-shirt from the dresser drawer, "it was hard enough, all right."

McNamara snorted a laugh.

"So, is that the excuse you're giving for that sink full of dirty dishes and an unmade bed?" He frowned. "Didn't they teach you better than that in the army?"

Wolf didn't reply. He knew his current living arrangement left a lot to be desired, but it was temporary. Or at least that's what he was fond of telling himself.

"Hell," McNamara said. "If I would've known that things were this bad for you, I'da invited you back to stay at the ranch again."

Wolf reflected on the time following his release from Leavenworth. He'd lived in the apartment over Mac's garage for several months, helping him with his bounty hunting business. It was a time of getting his life back in order, and he knew he'd be forever grateful to this man, his father's friend from the service, who'd extended a hand to Wolf in his hour of need.

He dressed quickly and then walked over to the sink's extension and stuck one of the plastic packets into the coffee maker. It made a hissing sound and Wolf placed a cup underneath it. The dark liquid flowed into the cup, and after the stream ceased, he handed it to McNamara.

"You like it black, right?"

McNamara winked. "At least you remember that."

Wolf started to jam another of the packets into the machine but then stopped and went to the refrigerator instead. He needed something cool, not hot. After grabbing a bottle of Gatorade, he twisted the cap off and drank copiously. McNamara had his shirt sleeves rolled up exposing his massive forearms, which looked even browner than usual.

"So," he said, "how'd you get here so early? You drive all night?"

"Nah," McNamara said. "I got in last evening. Spent the night at Miss Dolly's. We're meeting her and Brenda for breakfast, by the way. Maybe Yolanda, too."

At the mention of that last name Wolf felt a twinge in his gut. Yolanda Moore, his former lover and now member of the Las Vegas Metro Police Department, still held the key to his heart. They'd grown apart of late, owing mostly to her new job on the PD, and his checkered past being an ex-con with a dishonorable discharge. Miss Dolly Kline was Yolanda's ex-employer and leader of the P Patrol, a squad of female bounty hunters.

Mostly female, he added mentally, since Miss Dolly had been regularly employing him to accompany her and Brenda Carrera on some bail-enforcement duties of late.

Wolf took another swig of the Gatorade.

"I still don't see how you let that special little gal get away," McNamara said, shaking his head.

"It's complicated. We decided to take a step back for the time being, at least until she's off probation."

McNamara took a cautious sip of his coffee and then frowned.

"You call this coffee? What is this?"

Wolf smirked as he picked up the punctured packet.

"Colombian Hazelnut," he said.

McNamara's frown deepened.

"I've had better from straining horse piss through a tube sock." He ran his tongue over his teeth and took another sip. "Aw, never mind. I'll get me some real coffee at the restaurant. I told Miss Dolly she's buying since she stole my number one man away from me."

"That's hardly accurate." Wolf took another long drink and recapped the plastic bottle. "So, what did my mother want?"

"Well…" McNamara drank some more of his coffee and raised both eyebrows. "What kind did you say this is?"

"Colombian Hazelnut. The urine of a dozen thoroughbreds and a pair of compression socks."

Mac chuckled. "You know, I guess it ain't so bad, once you get used to it."

Wolf waited, saying nothing. He could sense that it was Mac's turn to move.

McNamara swallowed and heaved a sigh. "So why ain't you called your mother? She says she doesn't even have your damn phone number."

The shame edged back into Wolf's psyche. He compressed his lips, shook his head.

"Aw, hell," McNamara said. "Never mind. It's your business."

"I've been meaning to," Wolf offered. "But I was

waiting until I heard back from Oz."

McNamara's eyebrow twitched. "That's that high-priced fancy lawyer you got working on things?"

"That's the one."

Maxwell Ozmand had been recommended to him by Miss Dolly herself. He had a sterling reputation and had defended Wolf and Mac in a previous run-in with the law. He was supposed to be the best of the best. He also charged extremely high rates.

"He doing you any good?" McNamara asked.

This time Wolf shrugged. His last session with the attorney had gone pretty much the same way as the previous meetings had. Ozmand, or "The Great Oz" as he liked to be called, said he was "working on things."

"He says we had a solid basis for an appeal."

McNamara snorted. "Ain't that what he's been saying for the past couple months?"

"I'm supposed to call him back."

"Yeah? When?"

"Soon, but we're getting off topic. What did my mother want?"

McNamara took another long drink and then stared at Wolf directly in the eyes.

"She said your little brother Jimmy's been messing up." McNamara's eyes reflected sadness. "Hanging with a bunch of ne'er-do-wells, staying out all night, drinking, smoking, getting into fights..."

Wolf frowned. A vision of his younger brother's face, dark, boyish, and with a perpetual smile, flashed in his memory along with the title of a novel that he'd had to read in one of his English Lit classes. "Nobody loves a drunken Indian, huh?"

McNamara grunted something between a laugh and an affirmation, then added, "She wants you to fly back there and see if you can straighten his ass out."

That had actually occurred to Wolf already, but could he do it?

"Hell," McNamara said, "if I didn't have this new gig, I'd fly back there with you. Between the two of us, maybe we could carry him to the recruiting office. I'll bet that's what he needs."

Wolf wasn't so sure about that. Growing up, Jimmy had always been very impressionable. He'd followed Wolf around to the point of being a nuisance. When Wolf had enlisted, Jimmy, who was eight years younger, hadn't even graduated grammar school but said he wanted to be Green Beret, just like his dad and older brother. Wolf had only ended up as a Ranger, and then he'd gotten bounced. Forfeiture of all rank and privileges, four years of hard labor, and a dishonorable discharge. Wolf wondered if his own fall from grace, like their father's alcoholism and subsequent tragic death, had been too much for Jimmy.

Where do you look when your heroes fail you?

"She say anything else?" Wolf asked.

"Just for you to head back there." McNamara reached into his shirt pocket and took out a piece of paper with a phone number written on it. "Here. Call her, will ya?"

Wolf took the paper and placed it in his wallet.

"So, you been making out all right without me?" he asked.

"Yeah," McNamara said. "Things been kinda slow lately, with all the courts operating at half-assed capacity due to this COVID bullshit. And there's talk they're gonna end all cash bonds nationally, and that'll be the death knell for bounty hunting for sure. But so far, I been getting by. Reno's actually been trying to get back into the business."

"With his leg?" Wolf recalled the last time he'd seen Reno at the fight he'd still been using a cane.

"Yeah, well, mostly I got him driving the War Wagon." The War Wagon was Reno's specially outfitted Hummer, replete with an iron cage between the front and back seats and metal O-rings, for securing prisoners, welded to the floorboards. McNamara drank the rest of his coffee and set the cup on the table. "Funny, about a year ago him and me were vicious rivals and mortal enemies. Now he's gone and sponsored you as a fighter and he even nominated me for the Bounty Hunter of the Year Award."

Wolf picked up the empty coffee cup, took three steps, and set it in the sink.

"Life's strange sometimes," he said. "So, what's this other gig you got going?"

McNamara's face twisted into a wide grin.

"Policing some rich ranchers' properties down by the border," he said. "They're being overrun by illegals and the Best in the West has been hired to provide extra security and I been working with them.

Damn border's wide open. People, drugs, you name it flowing right across."

"Sounds kind of messy," Wolf said.

McNamara snorted. "No messier than bounty hunting. Or the army, for that matter. Lots of similarities, too. We got Ron Corbin flying overhead in a helicopter scouting, and me, Buck Mason, and Big Joe Barnes on the ground scooping them up." Wolf heard Mac's deep chuckle. "I borrowed Reno's Hummer and we're giving it a workout."

"I'm sure he'll be glad to hear that."

"Hell, I'll make sure and clean it up before I give it back to him," McNamara said. "But we're so damn busy we're even thinking of calling Pete Thornton and telling him to close up shop and join us."

Pete was usually left back in Arizona to run the warfare tactics school, the Best in the West. He also was missing a leg, but at times you'd never know it. He was into overcompensating, doing a five-mile run every morning.

"What do you do with the ones you grab?"

Mac shook his head. "That's the sad part. We just turn 'em over to the Border Patrol, and they just end up processing and releasing them. It's either that, or shag 'em back over the Rio Grande."

Wolf considered this and then looked McNamara directly in the eye.

"So, you just came to Vegas to see me?" he asked.

"I needed some R and R." McNamara grinned. "And to see Miss Dolly."

Wolf grinned too, but it intensified the void that his not being with Yolanda had brought to his life recently. It seemed that he was always losing the things he valued the most.

"Well," McNamara said, "originally I was thinking about seeing if you wanted to come and join us." He paused and took in a deep breath. "But then your mama called me and asked me to relay her request."

"I see. What did she say exactly?"

McNamara was about to reply when his cell phone rang. He pulled it out of his pocket, glanced at the screen, and then smiled. When he answered with a "Yes, darlin'," Wolf knew from the tone and expression that it was Miss Dolly. Mac murmured something more into the phone and terminated the call.

"They're waiting for us down the street," McNamara said. "A place called Marie Calendar's."

Wolf picked up his keys.

"I guess the dishes and the bed can wait," he said.

"Suit yourself, slacker." McNamara clapped him on the shoulder. "But if you want to call your mama on the way, I can drive."

Wolf shook his head.

"I'll call her later," he said.

As soon as I figure out what to say, he added mentally.

CHAPTER 2

**DEAGAN'S MIXED MARTIAL ARTS
NEW SPENCERLAND, NORTH CAROLINA**

Jimmy Wolf watched as George Earl Mess, or GEM as he liked to be called, continued to pound away at the heavy bag. He was six-five and around three hundred pounds. Plus, the big, shirtless monster had just ingested a tiny bit of the latest concoction that Sheridan and Jimmy had cooked up, and it was having the desired effect. GEM was a wild man. Each punch was accompanied by a hooping yell, followed by a grunt of effort. The big bag bounced on its suspension chain like a balloon in a windstorm.

Don't mess with Mess, Jimmy thought, repeating the favorite phrase chanted by GEM's fans at his fights. I hope the son of a bitch don't burn himself out before the fight tomorrow night.

Robert Spencer Junior, or Bobbie, stood off to the side, a wide grin on his face. His jet-black hair was brushed back from his forehead in a big, sprayed pompadour. He was of average height, a little bit shorter than Jimmy, with a block-like physique.

'Don't call me Bobbie,' he always said. He didn't like it. He preferred Spence. But Jimmy called him Bobbie anyway. They all did, only not to his face. Like it or not, he was the boss, the man in charge, and the guy who was going to make Jimmy and the rest of them rich very soon.

Next to Bobbie were Craig Langford and Willard Gibbons. Willard had a face like a mongrel pooch, with prominent, round-shaped features and a hefty pot belly. Craig had remained rail-thin since his return from the army. He leaned on a metal cane and wore a matching set of expensive running shoes on his one real foot and over his prosthesis. All three of them were clad in gym attire, with Bobbie's being top quality designer duds. Cadillac sweats, he called them. Compared to him, the rest of them looked like a trio of homeless bums. Jimmy wore an old pair of worn-out sweatpants and a dirty blue T-shirt.

But that would soon change, once this big payday came in. Each of them had his own dream of what he was going to do with the money. GEM would probably blow it on cars, motorcycles, and chicks. The same with Willard and Craig. Jimmy intended to buy some stuff too—a good electric guitar, so he could pursue his music career, and a real big Harley.

And, yeah, maybe he'd give some of it to his mother so she could get out of that lousy little trailer. But, hell, she could always go live with Pearl. Uncle Fred, too.

"Looks like you and Tim whipped up some good shit," Bobbie said. "GEM's going non-stop."

Jimmy did an automatic glance around. Nobody was within earshot, which was good. Not that Bobbie had any worries. His father was the fucking mayor, the guy who was running just about everything in New Spencerland, and Craig's old man was the chief of police. Him, GEM, and Willard, had come there on motorcycles. Bobbie had driven his canary-yellow Corvette, and Craig, who was missing the lower portion of his left leg, had driven his Ridley Auto Glide Trike. It was a specially modified three-wheel motorcycle with an automatic transmission that Bobbie had purchased for him. Jimmy surreptitiously eyed the disabled veteran, and then his thoughts turned briefly to his big brother, Steve.

I wonder what he's doing now? Jimmy thought. And what he'd think if he knew what I was doing?

He decided to push that kind of stuff out of his mind and concentrate on the goal line. Bobbie had assured each of them that they would all walk away from this close to being millionaires.

As GEM drove a pile-driving left hook into the bag

the sweat flew off his big, hairy arms and shoulders. The roll of fat also jiggled a bit around his waist. He slammed a left-right into the bag again and something metallic snapped up above and the whole rigmarole came crashing down to the floor, bounced once, then fell forward against the big, sweaty figure. GEM grabbed the bag and twisted under it, flipping the seven-foot stuffed vinyl container over his hip and onto the floor.

"Hey!" Bobbie yelled as the bag slammed down in front of him with a resounding thud. "Watch it."

The four of them scampered back, with the exception of Craig, who almost stumbled due to his prosthesis. Jimmy reached over and grabbed his arm, steadying him. Craig gave him a sharp glance.

This all seemed to amuse big GEM. His lips curled back exposing a set of ragged, mostly broken teeth.

It looked to Jimmy like the man's meth problem was getting the better of him. But it wasn't like anybody gave a shit. Soon this would be over, and they'd be going their separate ways, each with a payoff beyond their wildest dreams.

GEM raised his foot and stomped down on the fallen heavy bag. He repeated the kick several more times. Finally, he stopped after apparently seeing that he'd managed to cause a rupture in the uppermost part of the bag, spilling some of the internal stuffing.

"Aw, Jesus H. Christ," Lem Carter said, sauntering

over. "Ain't it bad enough you ruined another of my clasps, but you gotta go making more of a mess, too?"

"Fuckin' A," GEM shot back. He puffed up his big chest and arms and did a ferocious looking muscle pose.

The gym owner backed away.

"Relax, Lem," Bobbie said, flashing his dazzling smile. "Now you know who to put your money on for the fight."

"Yeah," GEM said, his voice almost a roar. "I'm gonna kill him."

Lem's mouth twitched, and he said, "Don't do no more kicking on that right now, okay? I gotta get it cleaned up."

GEM repeated his muscle pose and growled. Then he tore off his bag gloves and dropped them on the floor.

"I'm gonna go lift some weights," he said, and went over to an Olympic-sized barbell with four big 45-pound plates on it. He gripped the bar, swung it upward with the aplomb of an experienced weightlifter, and cradled it on his chest.

"Watch," he said, and proceeded to press the bar upward, managing five reps before he began to grunt with effort.

"Looking good, GEM," Bobbie shouted. "But now let's hit the steam. We got things to discuss."

The big man flipped the bar down to his thighs and

then opened his hands and let it fall. It crashed onto the floor with a loud crash.

"God dammit," Lem shouted. "I told you before. Don't drop them weights."

GEM raised his hand and gave the gym owner the finger. The five of them headed toward the locker room, with Jimmy and Craig bringing up the rear. Jimmy had an affinity for Langford due to the man being a veteran, just like Steve, and having lost his leg in Afghanistan. The recent turn of events over there had seemed to make him even more embittered than he already was. Jimmy wondered how Steve was holding up with all this bullshit coming down. Craig was forever going on about how the government and the army "betrayed" him, and how he lost his leg for nothing.

Jimmy could hardly blame him.

After sending GEM into the steam room to clear it out for a special meeting, Bobbie turned to them and said, "We ain't gonna be long."

GEM was pushing three men clad in towels out through the door. He'd fashioned a fearsome-looking sneer onto his face so none of the retreating steam bathers was offering any protest.

"Business meeting, fellas," Bobbie said to them as they passed. "Come back in ten."

Jimmy watched as the trio shuffled by, one man almost slipping because of his bare feet. None of them dared to say a word.

As they entered the steam room Jimmy caught a whiff of GEM's pungent body odor.

God, he stank.

Jimmy figured the smell must have been exacerbated by the meth GEM had ingested. It seemed even stronger than usual and sure had made him a wild man. Jimmy wasn't looking forward to standing in the small confines of the steam room with the pungent-smelling giant.

I hope Bobbie's not kidding about this being a short meeting, Jimmy thought.

As the door slid closed behind them wisps of steam swirled in the air. They felt so hot and moist, looked so tangible, that Jimmy wondered if he could reach out and grab them. GEM positioned himself in front of the door, effectively blocking any view from the outside and preventing anyone else from entering.

"All right," Bobbie said. "First of all, this is just between the five of us. Got it? Nobody else is to know the details, especially not Tim Sheridan."

He looked at each man's face and held the gaze until he'd received an acknowledging nod.

"Okay," he continued. "The new batches that him and Jimmy just cooked up this past week will be packaged and ready to go on Friday for our regular delivery day and pick-up. Pike's already on his way up here."

It didn't sit well with Jimmy that Lucien Pike, the big biker dude from Atlanta, would be going down and coming back with them again, but that was always the way that Batton wanted it. Pike was easy enough to get along with, but there was something about him that Jimmy didn't like. There were a lot of things, actually, ranging from the huge, nickel-plated Colt Anaconda with the six-inch barrel that he carried, to the guy's silver Harley Road King Classic. He was a big bastard, too. Almost as big as GEM, but smarter. A whole lot smarter. So smart, in fact, that Jimmy was worried that he might just catch on to what the five of them had planned.

"Pike's gonna be going down with us and coming back too?" Jimmy asked.

Bobbie frowned at the interruption. He turned his head and glared at Jimmy.

"Of course," he said. "Same as always."

The tone of his voice made it obvious that he was talking down to an underling. Jimmy felt a surge of resentment for being treated that way, but for the moment, he knew he had little choice. After this was over, once he had all that cash in his hands, that would be the time to tell Bobbie to fuck off. Still, he felt compelled to voice his concerns.

"What if Pike suspects something on the way back?" he said. "Or when we get here and make the switch. I mean the guy ain't stupid."

"Then I'll kill him," GEM said. To emphasize his words, he smacked his big right fist into the open palm of his left hand.

"Hopefully, there won't be any need for that," Bobbie said. "It'll all go down like clockwork if we play our cards right. So, let's go over it again." He pointed both index fingers toward Jimmy. "Recite."

Oh, Christ, Jimmy thought. He's going to make us go through those rigmarole bullshit recitations again.

It was better to get it over with.

"I drive the Rent-n-Haul truck down to Atlanta with the shit inside," he said. Bobbie had made them all memorize their parts in the plan, and they all recited it aloud upon command. They'd done it so often that he could practically do it in his sleep.

Bobbie nodded and switched the double pointed fingers to GEM.

"Me and Pike ride escort down and back," he said.

Bobbie indicated it was Willard's turn.

"I go get by the duplicate ride—"

Bobbie snapped his fingers.

Willard compressed his lips momentarily before starting again, "I go get by the second Rent-n-Haul truck and pretend I just backed it in."

Bobbie's face scrunched up and he shook his head.

GEM reached forward and slapped the side of Willard's face, causing the other man to yelp.

"What?" he asked with a plaintive whine.

"You forgot about the façade," Bobbie said. "And the pictures. We got to make sure I know which duplicate suitcases."

"I know that," Willard said, rubbing his temple where GEM had slapped him.

The big man reached over and swatted him again, a bit harder this time.

Willard grunted in pain.

"Come on, cut it out, will ya."

"The façade," Bobbie repeated.

Willard took a deep breath and said, "Me and GEM drop the façade when we unload at Batton's."

Bobbie shot a glance at Jimmy.

"On the way back, I take the picture of the suitcases and email it to you," he said.

"We make sure the suitcases are the same in the second Rent-n-Haul truck," Craig chimed in.

"I make sure I take my sweet-ass time opening the front gate," GEM said. "When we get back."

Jimmy took in a deep breath and then said, "And I drive through and go around to the other side of the plant."

Bobbie winked and glanced toward GEM, who said, "I keep the front gate blocked until Jimmy's out of sight."

"I drive out and go to the mall," Jimmy said. He was getting bored with this constant repetition of the tasks to be.

"And?" Bobbie asked.

"And," Jimmy said, taking in another breath. The hot steam was hurting his lungs. "I wait in Berglander's till you come."

Bobbie made a clucking sound and directed his finger toward Willard again.

"I pull the curtain away from the duplicate truck and get out."

Bobbie Junior's head rotated back toward GEM.

"Me and Pike go into the locker room to change into our security guard clothes," he said.

"I make sure the charges are set," Craig said, reciting his part.

"And I set off the charge," Bobbie said, swiveling his finger in the air. "While GEM and Pike are in the locker room changing into their uniform clothes."

He clapped his hands so loudly that it almost sounded like a gunshot.

"Okay, good," Bobbie said. "We've got it down." He looked over at Jimmy again. "And while you're on the road make sure you stop for gas and email me a picture of those suitcases so I can make sure I have exact duplicates."

"I will." Jimmy tried to keep his tone upbeat but was in truth a bit worried. There were a lot of "what ifs" to this "foolproof get-rich quick plan" that Bobbie had come up with. "But like I said, that guy Pike ain't stupid."

"And like *I* said," GEM added, "he makes any trouble for us, and I'll rip off his head and shit down his neck."

The big man tensed his neck muscles, causing the cords and tendons to stand out in bas-relief.

"We time it right," Bobbie said in a placating tone, "and Pike ain't gonna suspect nothing. Besides, he'll be too distracted about the fire and his precious Harley. He's gonna be crushed to see that fucking bike of his blown up."

Jimmy pursed his lips. It was a risk all right, but the rewards were great... More money than he'd ever dreamed of... But was it all worth it?

"I still don't know," he said. "Batton ain't nobody to fool with."

"Fuck Batton," GEM said. "That nigger gives us any trouble and I'll rip off his head and shit down his neck, too."

Bobbie uttered a barking laugh.

"You'd better get another line," he said. "I'm getting tired of hearing that one."

GEM stood there in silence.

Even as fucked up as the big ox was on the ice, it was obvious that he knew better than to talk back to Bobbie. No doubt about it, he was in charge.

The leader of the pack, Jimmy thought. But why's he doing this? The fucker's already rich.

Jimmy thought about asking him but didn't. He'd

already said too much. Way too much. GEM was looking for an excuse to pound somebody, and Jimmy didn't want it to be him. Besides, it was hotter than hell in here, and GEM's foul odor was making the whole room stink.

It must be more about power and dominance for Bobbie, Jimmy thought. And emerging from the shadow of his wealthy father by showing that he's his own man.

Sort of like what I want to do, Jimmy told himself, even though his father was long dead. But would be a chance to show his mother, his uncle, and the rest of the world that Jimmy Wolf was somebody after all.

"Like I said..." Bobbie smiled as he jerked his index finger toward the door. "We just have to make sure we time it just right, and we'll all walk away millionaires."

"Fuckin' A!" GEM shouted as he stepped away from the door. "It's gonna be great."

Jimmy forced himself to grin, but his thoughts were about Pike and Batton.

Especially Batton.

***

30,000 FEET
SOMEWHERE OVER THE MIDWEST

What's past is prologue, Wolf thought, pausing in his reading of the paperback version of *The Tempest*.

He'd taken a shine to the Bard's work and had even signed up for another online Shakespeare course at the college. Appropriately, *The Tempest*, the play-wright's last work, was the last one Wolf had to read. He didn't know when he was going to find the time to do the paper, though. Everything depended on how things went with straightening out his younger brother. He wished that McNamara had been able to accompany him, not only to help bridge the unfor-tunate neglected gap between Wolf and his mother, but maybe Mac would be better at reaching the kid than he could.

The kid, Wolf thought. Not anymore. He's twen-ty-one now, and old enough to make his own deci-sions. And his own mistakes.

He wondered what kind of trouble Jimmy had been getting into. It had to be something fairly significant for his mother to reach out to McNamara to request a visit from big brother Steve.

His last memories of Jimmy were of a young teen, short and slightly built, black hair long and covering his ears, maybe a hundred and twenty pounds soaking wet.

How much trouble could a kid like that get into?

But that had been almost six years ago, and, as he had just noted, Jimmy was now twenty-one. A legal adult, capable of making his own decisions. And mistakes.

Wolf suddenly regretted that he hadn't seen him in so long. Since before Leavenworth.

A lot had changed. Apparently, his kid brother had grown older, but not wiser.

He looked down and another line jumped out at him from the play's text:

I weep at mine unworthiness, that dare not offer what I desire to give, and much less take what I shall die to want.

Unworthiness... It was Miranda's line, but Wolf felt it was meant for him. Feeling unworthy crossed gender lines, that was for sure.

Gender lines... He then thought about Darlene. It would the first time he'd seen his ex-wife in almost six years as well. Certainly, she'd moved on with her life. At least Wolf hoped she had. He also hoped he could make this a quick trip.

In and out.

He gazed out the window and saw nothing but an expansive blue sky and groups of white clouds. He loved flying commercial, which he'd done once before on a quick jaunt from Vegas back to Phoenix. This one was a bit longer—around five hours, plus he was losing three hours due to the time zones. They'd taken off at eight-thirty in the morning and would be landing at about three-thirty p.m. Fifteen-thirty in military time. Still, it was nothing like his trips over to the Sandbox or the Stand when he was in the army. On those long jaunts he'd never been able to appreciate the view on his trips overseas. Those military transports were always jammed and about as comfortable as being crammed into the luggage compartment of a Greyhound bus. And the flights were a lot longer, too.

On her last pass through, the flight attendant asked him if he wanted anything else.

Wolf smiled and shook his head, and then realized she couldn't see his lips due to the mask he and everyone else was required to wear. It conjured up the image of the women in Afghanistan now being forced to cover their faces in public once again. He wondered if some of the interpreters he'd known had gotten out during this latest debacle. He hoped so, not wanting to think about what was going to happen to them if they didn't.

Leave no one behind. Yeah, right.

"Excuse me," the woman sitting next to him said. "But I couldn't help but notice you're reading Shakespeare."

She was older, with chin-length brown hair and very light blue eyes. The rest of her face was concealed under a black mask.

"Yeah," he said. "I'm taking a class."

"*The Tempest* is believed to be his last work, you know," she said. "And it contains some of his best lines."

"What's past is prologue," Wolf said, smiling again and then realizing it was moot. He couldn't tell if she was smiling either, but the corners of her eyes tightened slightly, and he figured she might be.

"We are such stuff as dreams are made on," the woman said. "And our little life is rounded with a sleep."

"I don't think I've gotten to that part yet."

"Prospero," she said. "Act four, scene one."

"Sounds like you know your Shakespeare."

"I used to be a college professor. English."

Wolf considered asking her for more information about the play, so he could knock out that final paper and be done with it, but then his mind turned to another former professor, Garfield Bellows, who'd helped him out with that once. Poor Garfield had been murdered by a psycho named Dirk who'd been stalking Wolf.

Better not get too close to me, lady, he thought. It could be contagious.

"Are you going into teaching?" the woman asked, breaking him out of his reverie.

"No," he said. "I'm actually a bounty hunter."

Again, with the lower portion of her face concealed, it was hard to determine the extent of her reaction.

"Bail enforcement officer," he added quickly. "Bounty hunter is kind of an antiquated term."

She laughed. "But an interesting one." Her eyebrow

arched. "And dangerous as well. Is that how you got that injury?" Her finger brushed her own eyebrow.

"No. I'm also a professional fighter. Mixed martial arts. I forgot to duck."

The woman laughed again. "Jack Dempsey, right? The quote you just used."

"I believe he did say that. You know your boxing."

"And the man who beat him, Gene Tunney, liked to read Shakespeare," she said. "It seems we have come full circle."

The words had a strange familiarity to him. Then he got it.

"*King Lear*, right? Coming full circle?"

"Very good." She smiled again, or at least he assumed she did. "I really wish I'd had you as one of my students."

Before he could return the compliment, the pilot's voice intruded, coming over the intercom. He advised that they were now beginning their descent into Fayetteville and requested that all seats and tray-tables be returned to the upright and locked positions.

Wolf flipped his tray up and jammed the paperback into his carry-on bag at his feet. He had no other luggage. Traveling light, just like the army. He didn't anticipate being there more than a couple of days, and only brought changes of underwear and T-shirts. The shirt he was wearing had a collar, and he figured one was enough.

As the plane banked right and then left, a hushed silence fell over the cabin. He glanced out the window once more and saw the expanses of greenery becoming more and more discernible. He estimated they were still at about fifteen thousand feet but descending fast. He took out his cell phone and decided to check his messages as soon as they touched down. Before he'd left, he'd tried to get hold of his lawyer, with little success. It was almost eighteen-thirty here, which meant that back in Vegas it was three hours earlier. Fifteen-thirty... Time enough, hopefully, for The Great Oz to be out of court. If that's where he'd actually been when Wolf had called before. He reflected on the futility of that conversation.

"I'm sorry, Mr. Wolf," his secretary had told him, "but Mr. Ozmand's still in court."

"He's always in court when I call. Will you please tell him I called?"

"Yes, sir, I'll be sure to do that." After which she hung up.

So much for customer service.

He'd seen the woman before, and she was a babe. He also recalled seeing Ozmand surreptitiously ogling her and waggling his tongue for Wolf to see. He wondered if the Great Oz was doing her on the side.

Maybe it's time to find a new lawyer, he thought, and then mentally added up the substantial amount of dough he'd already paid out.

It was turning out to be an exercise in frustration, and in an arena where Wolf was totally dependent on someone else calling the shots.

That wasn't easy for someone who liked being in charge. But he also knew in the courtroom he was totally out of his element. Chances were slim regardless.

Chances were probably slim as far as being able to straighten Jimmy out, too. But he knew he had to try.

And then there was Darlene.

The plane was only about five hundred feet now and would be touching down in about a minute or so.

Wolfe said you can't go home again, he thought. I guess I'm about to find out if that's true or not.

***

DEAGAN'S MIXED MARTIAL ARTS
NEW SPENCERLAND, NORTH CAROLINA

Robert Spencer Jr. slid behind the wheel of his canary-yellow Corvette and shoved the key into the ignition. Before starting the big eight-cylinder engine he gazed through the windshield and watched the four members of his team as they meandered to their raggedy assortment of motorcycles—GEM and Willard on their Honda Rebels, trying to masquerade as Harleys, until you heard the pathetic puttering of those 500-cc engines; Jimmy on his beat-up Yamaha V Star 250; and poor Craig on that red Ridley three-wheeler with the automatic transmission. They all drove shit motorcycles that he'd gifted to them. He found it amusing that a few pieces of metallic crap could buy absolute loyalty among those idiots. But there was also the hint of greater rewards to come.

Spencer, or Spence as he liked to be called, watched them start up their bikes and take off. GEM shot out in front them all and Spence frowned at the sight.

The big idiot was high again. No doubt about it.

Even if he was only taking a small taste of the meth, it increased the risk factor. And it was almost a given that stupid Willard was dipping in it too. And Craig popped his prescription painkillers like Tic Tacs. Jimmy seemed to be the only semi-straight one of the bunch, and that was because Sheridan kept a continuous and strict eye on the dumb Indian while they cooked the stuff up.

Tim Sheridan keeping the boy on the straight and narrow...

The very idea of that made him chuckle out loud. Sheridan's little dalliance with the Gilbert girl, his prize-A student, would have landed him in prison had not Spence's father intervened. The old man had foresight, you had to give him that. He saw the potential of recruiting the disgraced high school chemistry teacher to be his new meth cook.

Spence shook his head, knowing his father had

gotten the idea from watching that ridiculous cable TV series, *Breaking Bad*. His dad was already involved in the money laundering business with Batton in Atlanta, so when this opportunity to be both supplier and launderer cropped up, the money really started pouring in.

The TV show had never appealed to Spence, but it had given him his own idea.

Why keep dancing to Batton's tune, taking all the risks for only a sliver of the real dough, when he could take the money and run?

Well, not really run, per se. His plan, to remove the money and make it look like it got burned up in an unfortunate explosion, seemed foolproof.

He was resigned to the fact that one of his team members, Sheridan, would bite the dust, but that was a necessary part of it. None of the others knew about that part yet, but he didn't think that would be a problem. Sheridan was older and the three of them remembered him as the teacher from their high school days. And that wasn't a halcyon memory for any of the three of them. Plus, cooking up meth is a risky business. Very risky. And if nobody died, Batton might doubt the veracity of the presentation.

The presentation—that's what he called it. And he was proud of the intricacies that his imagination had spawned.

He was the quarterback, the coach, directing his

players. And when he pulled this off, it would be like leading a ragtag team to the Superbowl.

It was ironic that Jimmy, the runt of the litter and youngest of the bunch, seemed to be the most squared away. If you could call his sloppy appearance and low level of accomplishments being squared away. He was a high school drop-out, drank like a god- damn fish, and was on a fast track to nowhere.

All four of them were, until he brought them together with his new idea of hitting it big with one enormous super score.

Dealing with drunks and addicts, no matter how small or controlled their habits were, was always a bit tricky. That's why Spence had talked to all four of them about the importance of strictly adhering to the plan—thus, the constant oral recitations. Just like Lee Marvin making his group of army misfits recite their roles in that old movie.

And I'm a hell of a lot better looking than Lee Marvin, he thought.

Cook it, bag it, transport it, and then bring the money back to be laundered at the casino.

And then… Boom!

Batton was going to be highly pissed that his drug profit money never made it to the laundry machine, but such is life.

The price of doing business.

He'd just have to make sure to keep the money

stashed for a while, until he could get it transferred safely to his father's offshore accounts in the Caymans, and that none of his surviving team members got antsy and wanted to go on a spending spree prematurely. But they were all mouth-breathers with room-temperature IQ's. He'd give them something to spread around, but nothing substantial.

And who knows, he thought. Maybe a couple of them, besides Sheridan, won't survive the explosion.

That prospect didn't trouble him. Not in the least. In fact, it might enhance the believability of the unfortunate turn of events.

Spence smiled and took out one of his intricately folded packets and his truncated straw. After a quick look around, he undid the chemist's fold and spread the white powder into two lines. Then he used the straw to snort it up, pausing to grip his nose and draw it in deeper. The rush came very quickly, and he enjoyed the wave of euphoria. The heightened alertness was a pleasant byproduct. Sure, it was a bit old fashioned these days, but he had no inclination to try the crystal meth Sheridan and Jimmy cooked up after seeing what it did to GEM's teeth. He was willing to bet that if one of his opponents caught him square in the jaw, the big fucker's mouth would probably collapse.

And it's not like I've got a habit or anything, he told himself. It's just recreational.

He leaned back in the seat and enjoyed what was left of the immediate ride. He could afford to indulge a little before lunch today.

Things wouldn't get serious until the day after tomorrow.

***

PHOENIX INTERNATIONAL AIRPORT
PHOENIX, ARIZONA

As the plane touched down, Robert Bray looked out the window and wondered what the day's high temperature was on the other side of the metal barrier. They'd gained three hours traveling west from New York, but he was certain that it was going to feel like an oven once they left the airport. The flight attendant's announcement asking that they lower the window shades before deplaning to keep the cabin temperature down made him even more wary.

But at least it was better than traipsing around down in Belize.

He turned to the two operatives whom he'd brought with. As long as the Don was footing the bill, they might as well go first class.

"We've got three separate rental cars booked," Bray said. "That way we can cover more ground."

"What exactly are we looking for again?" Jack Powers asked.

Bray had brought him along primarily as muscle, just in case they happened to run into trouble, and trying to ferret out guys like Wolf and McNamara could always mean trouble. Despite his formidability, Powers had a big mouth and a definite lack of discretion. But he did have some uses.

Maureen Cistero slapped the man's arm and shushed him.

"Too many ears," she said in a hushed tone.

Bray smiled. Beauty, brains, and discretion—an excellent combination. He silently complimented himself on having chosen her for this assignment. She had other uses, too.

Actually, their assignment was rather vague. The Don wanted to know the exact circumstances of what had happened in Belize regarding the helicopter crash that had killed his brother. The late Anthony Marco Fallotti had been equally vague in keeping a detailed record of his association with the dead rich man, Dexter Von Dien. After Fallotti and Abraham's law firm had been dissolved, at least on paper, the official file of the case representation had disappeared. Bray had spent what amounted to a small fortune down in Belize trying to recover the dead lawyer's missing laptop computer. Von Dien's mansion had been looted by the group of Guatemalans he'd employed. Once Bray put the word out down there as to what he was after, he'd been inundated with a bunch of black marketeers claiming to have the item he sought.

He'd returned with a suitcase full of laptops, twelve to be exact, hoping that one of them would be the genuine article. Abraham had a bunch of computer whizzes back in the Big Apple working on cracking the passwords. In the meantime, he had the same sketchy details he'd told the Don.

Von Dien and Fallotti had been running a game on McNamara and Wolf to try to get them to deliver some ancient stolen artifact. To force their hand, an ex-CIA operative named Soraces had been hired to tighten the screws. Soraces and his boys abducted McNamara's daughter and taken her down to Belize. The exchange was supposed to be done down there, but apparently Wolf and McNamara, both combat vets, had come out on top. As far as what had happened to the helicopter, it was anybody's guess, but given that the rich son of a bitch had made numerous attempts to take the two of them out before, sending in some pretty heavy-duty talent, it was a good bet that the crash was not accidental. Soraces and his crew were all dead, so no leads could be followed up there.

Even with all the money he'd spread around to the Guatemalans, nobody was saying squat. One did mention something about McNamara holding one of the rich man's guns, but he held his hands together to indicate a blunderbuss-sized barrel, which Bray took to either mean hyperbole or bullshit. Another trip down there was probably in the cards regardless.

As long as he had some more money to loosen

some tongues. And hopefully, one of those damn laptops would turn out to be the real deal.

But the FBI was also involved, which could mean complications down the road, especially if the Don ordered a hit on somebody. Bray now realized it was going to require some insulation. He couldn't afford to run afoul of the feds or get mixed up in some kind of murder case vendetta. The three of them would have to be very circumspect. Plus, they needed a cover. Luckily, he had an idea.

After they'd procured their luggage and taken a shuttle ride to the car rental facility, Bray gathered them all together and went over the game plan.

"Okay," he said. "Our focus out here is simple. Find these two jokers and get a fix on them."

"And then what?" Powers asked.

"And then we report back and wait," Bray said.

"Can't get much simpler than that," Maureen added. "Can it?"

Bray smiled. He was beginning to really like her. "Nothing is ever as simple as it seems."

***

FAYETTEVILLE REGIONAL AIRPORT
FAYETTEVILLE, NORTH CAROLINA

Wolf made his way to the car rental place rather quickly since he didn't have to wait at the luggage carousel. After filling out the usual paperwork, and showing his Arizona driver's license, the clerk handed him forms.

One of these days I'm going to have to get that license changed to Nevada, he thought. But it can wait.

The way things were going he was seriously considering taking Mac up on his offer to move back to the ranch. They hadn't discussed it further and Wolf had been so preoccupied at the breakfast wondering and hoping that Yolanda might make an appearance that he'd neglected to even ask McNamara how the new arrangement with Kasey being married and out of the house was working out. Mac had mentioned that she was still running the ops center, as he called it, for Trackdown, Inc. during the day when her new husband was at work.

Her new husband—none other than Special Agent William Franker of the FBI.

What an unlikely union that had been.

Franker had been on the original flyaway team that investigated Wolf and McNamara's first foray south of the border down in Yucatan. The FBI always investigated the suspicious deaths of American citizens in foreign countries. McNamara had mentioned that now, due to the marriage, Franker had been transferred off the investigation of the original shootout in Mexico that Wolf and Mac had been involved in due to what the Bureau classified as a "conflict of interest".

What a fiasco that had been. While he and Mc-Namara and Reno had never been classified as suspects, or even persons of interest in the deaths, Wolf was sure they'd come close. The three of them had been interviewed numerous times by the feds, and both Mac and Reno had been wounded. A whole lot of dead bodies, both Mexican and American, had piled up.

It had also started the ball rolling with the stolen Iraqi artifact that the rich bastard, Von Dien, had been after, and had caused nothing but one problem after another. Wolf was glad to be able to put that all behind him. No more stolen artifacts, no more mercs trying to kill them, no more Von Dien, no more crooked lawyers… And Franker, who'd sneaked down to assist them in Belize, had received some nice federal accolades upon his return for recovering the two priceless Iraqi artifacts and turning them over to the FBI stolen art division. He'd scored major points for that and might even be up for a promotion.

Figures, thought Wolf. The grunts like me and Mac do all the work, and some desk jockey like Franker gets all the glory.

But he'd sort of grown to like the FBI special agent. Plus, the guy had married Mac's daughter, Kasey, who'd been a major thorn in Wolf's side since he and McNamara had started working together.

Maybe it was time to revisit the McNamara ranch,

but this time he'd work out a fair rental agreement with Mac. No more freeloading, even though his previous stay there was at Mac's behest. And Wolf had contributed a substantial amount of the money he'd recovered to Mac's business. He'd helped put Trackdown, Inc. back in the black before he'd left, and was in a lot better position than he'd been in when Mac had picked him up that day he was released from Leavenworth. All he had to do was worry about clearing his name, and seemed a few steps closer to that.

Now if I can straighten Jimmy out, he thought, things will be good.

He came to the numbered aisle with the row of freshly washed Toyotas. His Camry was silver and sitting about halfway down the row. He hit he button on the remote just to be sure and saw the flicker of the light and heard the accompanying beep.

Easy enough.

As he headed down the aisle, his cell phone chimed, and he glanced at the screen.

His heart leapt when he saw it was Yolanda.

"Hey, babe," he said.

"Hey back."

After a moment of awkward silence, he asked how she was doing.

"I'm good," she said. "Still in field training. It's going well, though."

He pictured her in that tan police uniform riding

around the Strip, and longed for a glimpse of her.

"Send me a picture of yourself in uniform," he said. "When you have a chance, that is."

"I'll do that."

"Unless it's against the rules," he added quickly.

Some irritation crept into her voice. "What did I tell you about saying stuff like that?"

Wolf let it ride. It had been his decision more than hers that they let their hot relationship cool a bit. Just starting on the police force meant an extensive background investigation and having a romantic relationship with an ex-con with a DD would most likely be a red flag.

"Sorry I missed you at the breakfast," she said after a few moments of awkward silence. "I had to go in early."

Wolf wondered about the veracity of her excuse, but figured it was better not to say so.

"You didn't miss much. Although Mac was there."

"I know," she said. "Miss Dolly told me you're going out of town. Back home to South Carolina, or someplace?"

"North Carolina," Wolf corrected. "And I'm there now."

"You there to see your family?"

"Yeah," he said slowly. "Among other things."

"Other things?"

"I haven't seen my mother or my uncle since I got

out. My sister or my younger brother either." He hesitated and then added, "He's been messing up, from what I've heard."

"Yeah, Miss Dolly told me that."

This struck Wolf as odd. If Miss Dolly, who'd apparently been briefed by Mac, had then told Yolanda about Wolf's family discord, why was she calling?

More silence, then she asked another question: "So, you coming back, or what?"

Wolf felt a simultaneous surge of curiosity and hope. Why was she asking that now? Did it mean she missed him? That maybe, despite his checkered past, there was still a chance for them?

It has to, he thought as he longed for the comfort of her warm embrace.

"I'm planning on it," he said with a chuckle. "After all, I've got something very valuable in Vegas."

"Oh?"

"Yeah," he said. "I left my car there."

She laughed. It sounded like musical chimes to him.

"Well, I hope you do," she said. "Even though I ain't so crazy about that car."

Wolf laughed again, too, and promised to keep her apprised of his situation here and when he'd be back.

"Hopefully I'll be out of field training by then and you can meet me for lunch or something," she said.

Or something, he repeated mentally.

After a few more pleasantries, she ended the call. Wolf felt a bit encouraged by the way the conversation had gone. Maybe all was not lost.

Feeling renewed by her call, Wolf was rather comfortable under the coolness of the cement ceiling in the massive rental car enclosure. The afternoon looked sunny beyond the shade. He glanced at his watch. It was now nineteen hundred, four in Vegas, which meant that the Great Oz might very well have returned to his office from court. Wolf decided to give it another try and scrolled to the number on his phone.

The same sultry voiced secretary answered and to Wolf's surprise, she told him that Mr. Ozmand would be right with him.

Wolf couldn't believe his good fortune.

After about a minute's wait, the lawyer's deep baritone voice came on the line.

"This is Oz."

"Mr. Ozmand, this is Steve Wolf," he said, trying to sound sufficiently respectful.

"Who?" A pause, and then a brassy sounding laugh. "Just kidding. Angie told me who you were."

Who I *was* is right, Wolf thought. I'm all past tense.

"I was wondering how things were going on my case," he said.

"Okay, let me look that up."

Wolf could hear the clicking of something that

sounded like computer keys.

"Oh, yeah," the lawyer said finally. "Nothing really new to report. I've been researching some things. Working on a new brief. Hopefully, one of these days…"

He let the sentence hang there, unfinished.

Wolf felt his frustration growing.

"I was wondering about that video evidence we recovered from the Belize incident," Wolf said. "From Soraces."

"Soraces…" The lawyer's voice hung in the air once again. "He was…"

"From that spy pen thing he had," Wolf said, feeling his patience growing thin. "There was a confession video on it from Lieutenant Cummins. Where he was being interrogated. Saying that he and the others set me up in Iraq."

"Right, right." The lawyer paused to cough. "Yeah, I have a copy and turned the original over to the FBI for authentication processing."

What the hell did that mean? And why was he turning it over to the FBI when his trial had been a general court-martial in the military?

"Shouldn't the army be involved?" Wolf asked.

"Certainly," Oz said. "But I believe in a multi-pronged attack. We're hitting them from all directions with multiple appeals. But trust me. I'm working on it."

In Wolf's experience, any time somebody used the phrase "trust me", the hairs on the back of his neck stood up.

"Anyway," Oz continued, "authenticating it is moving slower than we'd like, but the FBI is looking into the matter." Wolf could hear the clicking of more keys. "The recovery of the artifacts helped, but there's also the pending investigation of your first trip to Mexico where all those Americans were murdered."

Wolf reminded him that Franker, Mac's son in law, had been pulled off the investigation of that one.

"True that," Oz said. The use of such an obscure and senseless expression seemed grossly inappropriate coming from the middle-aged Ozmand. "The Bureau is always overly concerned about any possibilities of conflict of interest."

"So does that help or hurt our case?"

"Apples and oranges, my boy. Apples and oranges. Just keep in mind that we're dealing with the federal government *and* the US Army here. So things move at glacial speed. The best-case scenario is that we'll be getting a new trial, with what we hope turns out to be exculpatory evidence on that spy pen video. But, as I said, it takes time."

"So what am I supposed to do in the meantime?"

"Hurry up and wait. Isn't that what they taught you in the military?"

"Yeah, but I was really hoping to get my name

cleared as soon as possible."

Wolf heard the lawyer's deep chuckle once again. "Cheer up, Steve. As I told you it's a slow process. Unless you've got some pull and can petition some politician for a Presidential Pardon."

The chuckle graduated to a full laugh.

"Not likely," Wolf said.

"Then take a deep breath and let me do the job you're paying me for, okay?"

After the lawyer assured him that he'd call with any updates, Oz terminated the call.

Wolf jammed the phone back into his pocket and glanced at his watch again. It was now nineteen-twenty-five and although still light, he could sense the impending nightfall.

He debated whether to spend the night in a nearby hotel or head to Lumberton now to see his sister.

I need to do a little recon, he thought. Maybe she can provide some insight as to what's going on before I plunge into the abyss.

But it wasn't like the Jimmy-problem was going to go anywhere.

He pressed the button to open the trunk of his rental car and slung his old army backpack inside. As it landed, something spilled out of the side pocket. It was his copy of *The Tempest*.

He recalled having just gotten past the part about the shipwreck and Prospero and Miranda had just found Ferdinand right after the magical storm.

The titular tempest.

He tucked the book back in place. I hope I'm not driving into one of those.

CHAPTER 3

THE PINE TREE HOTEL
LUMBERTON, NORTH CAROLINA

Traffic had been light the night before, and the drive to Lumberton had only taken Wolf about forty minutes, but figured that it was a bit too late to drop in unexpectedly on his sister and her family. Instead, he'd gotten a hotel room and grabbed a quick meal. Finding nothing on television of interest, most of the news channels being too depressing to watch, he sought solace in *The Tempest* and kept reading the play until he fell asleep. As usual, his sleep didn't last long, and in his dream he was back in Iraq, kicking down a door and confronting a group of tangos inside, all heavily armed. As he raised his own M4 to fend them off, the scene shifted into slow motion madness, made more intense because no matter how hard he squeezed the trigger of his weapon, it would not fire. The face of the nearest tango loomed large, lips spreading apart revealing long, yellowish, pointed teeth and he pointed his AK-47 at Wolf.

And still, the damn trigger wouldn't move...

At the last possible moment before the enemy's rifle discharged, Wolf jerked awake, sweat-covered and breathless.

It was the dream. That same, recurring dream that had haunted his nights for years, even during his incarceration. The circumstances varied, but the result was always the same. For a time, when he was staying at Mac's and seeming to be getting his life together, the dream had ceased. But now, with this current situation involving his younger brother, the old ghosts had crept back.

He'd lain awake for what seemed like an eternity, trying in vain to slip back into slumber, but sleep remained elusive. The last he remembered before finally dozing off again was staring at the illuminated, digital screen on the bedside clock showing *3:09* in vivid red numerals.

When he woke up again it was morning. The red numerals now flashed *6:50*. Rising, he slipped on his sweats and went to the hotel exercise room, but it offered him little in the way of equipment, so he went outside to run. The streets held a vague familiarity for him because he'd visited the city numerous times in his youth, but a lot had changed. Rather than risk getting lost, he kept it simple: run for fifteen minutes in one direction, and then turn around and head back. By the time he got back to the hotel he'd broken a good sweat, which was all he wanted to accomplish. After a quick shower during which he washed his running clothes and wrung them dry, he checked out and asked the clerk if she had a phone book.

"A what?" the girl asked, her words muffled by the mask that covered the lower portion of her face.

"I need to find a phone number for someone," he said.

She gestured at the computer behind the check-in counter.

"Who do you want?" the girl asked, her hands poised over the keyboard.

"Pearl Fowler. Her husband's name is Frank, or Franklin."

The girl's fingers danced over the keys.

"Okay," she said. "Frank and Pearl—what kind of a name is that?"

"She's an Indian," Wolf said.

"Oh."

Wolf caught the trace of an embarrassed flush caressing the girl's cheeks.

"Sorry," she said, and read off the address and phone number.

Wolf resisted the temptation to ask her, "For what?" She was obviously a millennial and had been conditioned to apologize for slightest possibility of offending someone. Instead, he merely requested that she write it down, and she did. She stepped back over to the counter and handed it to him.

He delayed things further by going to a restaurant and eating a leisurely breakfast, leaving the spread of wet running clothes under the Toyota's back window hoping the sun would dry them out. As he lingered over his second cup of coffee, he tried to get interested in the free newspaper he'd gotten from the hotel. According to the weather report on the last page of the first section, a hurricane was slowly moving toward Florida and could possibly shift and sweep up the East Coast.

Great, he thought. *Just what I need. A real tempest to go along with the metaphorical one I'm most likely riding into.*

The waitress came by with a glass pot full of dark brown liquid and offered to refill his cup of coffee, but Wolf declined. He then glanced at his watch and knew he was procrastinating. It was already closing in on ten o'clock.

It's tiiimmme, he thought, mentally hearing the ring announcer's now-famous refrain before the big fight.

It's not a ring, he reminded himself. It's an octagon.

He got up and left a generous tip for the waitress before paying his bill. Then he went out to his rental car. His running clothes were indeed dry, and he stuck them into his backpack.

When he drove onto the street where his sister lived, he abruptly pulled to the curb at the far end of the block and stopped. It was a typical residential street full of well-maintained houses and well-kept lawns.

Quite a step up for Pearl, considering the trailer park existence from which they'd come. He was glad things had gone well for her, but did he really want to face her?

It had been what, five years? No, more than that. Closer to six.

She'd never come to see him in Leavenworth, but he'd specifically directed his family not to visit. His court-martial had been a sham and it was overseas anyway. There was no way they could have attended that one. So he'd faced it alone, just like he'd faced all his other adversities. It was the way he'd wanted it. In prison he'd gone to great lengths to deliberately keep his family at arm's length, choosing not to communicate with them other than an occasional phone call and a few letters. Being inside, even though he knew he was innocent, he'd taken refuge behind that familiar emotional wall, much in the same manner as he'd done in combat. It was the only way to survive. Weakness killed. It was all about survival mode. His stance had caused an estrangement from his family, but it was a necessary one.

Now he had to face them, but remnants of the wall were still in place.

Wolf shifted the car back into gear and slowly crept down in front of the house.

It took him a long time to put the vehicle into PARK, and once he did, he still didn't move. Instead, he just surveyed the house.

It was your basic single-family dwelling: a ranch-like wooden structure with an attached garage. A second story was set over the main section, and he was certain it had been expertly added since he'd last been there. Her husband, Frank—a nice guy as Wolf remembered, was a carpenter. In her letters Pearl had written that Wolf might consider coming to work for him upon his release.

Her letters... They'd never stopped, even though he'd seldom, if ever, written back. The idea of someone connected to the prison reading, and possibly censoring them, was revolting to him.

Pearl and Frank had two kids, a boy and a girl. They were school-aged now—ten or eleven.

What were their names again?

Paula and Frank Jr.

Paula, named after their mother.

He was glad she'd gotten that accolade. At least she had something to be proud of.

The front curtains parted slightly for an instant and Wolf heaved a sigh. She'd seen him.

I'd better get out and announce myself, he thought, before she or somebody else calls the cops on the suspicious looking Indian sitting in the rented car in a residential neighborhood. An ex-con Indian, at that.

He shut the engine off and got out and stretched. He was halfway up the walkway when the front door burst open and Pearl came running toward him, arms outstretched, calling his name, her movements suddenly somehow transforming into slow motion as she approached. She'd put on a few pounds, and looked heavier than he remembered, but then it had been a few years. Her raven-black hair was long and pulled back into a ponytail, and she wore no makeup. Still, she remained beautiful to his eyes, and a warm feeling engulfed him, tinctured with guilt and regret.

He'd waited way too long to come home.

Seconds later, he felt her pushing herself against him, encircling his neck and shoulders in an enthusiastic hug and repeating the same litany over and over.

"Oh, Steve, I'm so glad you've come back…"

Despite their familial association, Wolf felt embarrassed. An appropriate reply eluded him and for some strange reason one of the lines from *The Tempest* echoed in his mind.

Be not afeard. The isle is full of noises, sounds, and sweet airs, that give delight and hurt not.

The fact that it was uttered by Caliban, the savage monster character, made him smirk.

The monster hath returned, he told himself in mock Shakespearian fashion.

"Sorry," he said. "I should have called."

But Pearl was having none of that. She released her

embrace, stepped back, and looked him up and down.

"My God, Steve, you look great." Her brow furrowed as her gaze lingered on the row of dark stitching over his left eye. "What happened here?" Her fingers brushed lightly over the cut, touching his forehead above it.

"I forgot to duck," he said, recalling that famous line again.

Her brow furrowed and she canted her head to the side.

"You didn't get into a fight, did you?" she asked.

"Actually," he said, forcing a smile, "I did. But it's all right. I got well paid."

The furrows in her face deepened and he explained what he meant. After another moment she was holding his arm and escorting him toward the door.

"I'm so glad you're here," she repeated. "Come on. We've got a lot to talk about."

I'll bet we do, he thought, and walked beside her.

***

THE WOLF RESIDENCE
NEW SPENCERLAND, NORTH CAROLINA

Jimmy Wolf slid out of the narrow bed in his sliver of a room in the mobile home and reached for his ragged blue jeans, which he'd left in a heap on the floor the night before.

The morning, actually, he corrected as he picked them up, shook them in the hopes to get the wrinkles out, and slipped into them. He had to exhale, not take in another breath, and suck in his stomach so that he could get the front snap fastened. As it was, a dollop of flesh looped over the top section, but he was able to get his belt fastened as well. Grabbing the same T-shirt from yesterday, he brought it to his nose and smelled it.

It was sweaty, but not too bad, so he pulled that on too.

Once this thing's over with, he thought. I'm gonna buy myself some nice new clothes.

He grabbed his cigarettes from the nightstand, shook one out of the pack, and lit up. It felt good to smoke. That was the main thing he missed about being in the rubber suit when he was helping Sheridan cook up the meth. Tobacco helped him think. Leaving the cigarette pack and the lighter in his jacket vest, he stepped over to the door and opened it. It was only about a four-foot walk, the damn trailer was so small. After sliding the door into the slot, he glanced both ways in the equally small hallway and padded down to the bathroom in his bare feet. His mother and uncle were seated at the kitchen table.

Jimmy was starting a wave of acknowledgement when Uncle Fred said, "About time you got up."

Hearing that, Jimmy switched the wave of greeting into one of derision.

Him and my mother, he thought. Always on my ass. But pretty soon, I'll be outta here for good. And when they find out I got money, they'll be *kissing* my ass.

With that image in mind, he slammed the bathroom door as hard as he could. As he was urinating in the toilet, he heard his uncle shouting from the hallway:

"You lazy no-good son of a—"

Uncle Fred stopped after probably realizing that if he continued with the insult, he'd actually be calling his own sister a bitch.

Jimmy laughed and yelled back.

"That all you got to say, Uncle?"

Silence.

Jimmy flushed the toilet and side-stepped to the sink. After setting the burning cigarette on the edge of the toilet bowl, he turned on the cold water, cupped his hands under the faucet, and then splashed some of the liquid onto his face. It did little to relieve the pounding headache of his hangover. Exhaling, he repeated the ritual, rubbing his fingers over the stubble on his chin.

Indians ain't supposed to have to shave, mentally adding a bit of sarcasm as he stared at the mirror. So I won't.

He tried to laugh at his own witticism, which he knew was rather pathetic, but his head hurt too much. Everything hurt. He rinsed his mouth one more time. It didn't help.

His teeth needed brushing, too, he knew, but the inside of his mouth felt like it was covered with cotton, or something worse. He pulled at the mirror to check inside the medicine cabinet and found a bottle of aspirin with three pills in it. Shaking them into his palm, he tossed the aspirins into his mouth and lowered his face to the faucet once more. They went down, but not that easily.

Nothing was going easy this morning. The persistent pounding inside his head was seeing to that. After glancing at his wrist and seeing only hair and the light patch of skin where his watchband shielded it from the sun, he realized he'd left his damn watch on the nightstand. At least he hoped he had. He'd been too drunk to care last night. Jimmy grabbed for the cigarette and accidentally knocked it onto the floor. It landed with a hiss, having fallen into a large droplet of water that was the result of his facial splashing.

He frowned when he saw the soggy square. Leaving it where it was, he pulled open the door and went down the hallway and into the kitchen.

"About time you got up," Uncle Fred said.

"Gimme some coffee, would ya?" Jimmy said.

"Is that any way to talk to your mother?" his uncle

said.

Jimmy snorted in obvious disgust and slumped down onto one of the chairs.

His mother set a cup of coffee on the table in front of him and then sat down opposite him.

"What time did you get in last night?" Uncle Fred asked.

"Dunno." Jimmy took the coffee cup in both hands and drank some. It was hot, but not very. "Shit, put this in the microwave." He shoved the cup across the table, causing some of the dark liquid to splash onto the table.

"Hey," Uncle Fred said. "You should show some respect."

Jimmy's head was still pounding, and he needed the coffee. While looking askance at his uncle, he said, "Please" as sarcastically as he could.

Uncle Fred exhaled sharply and shook his head.

"Get off my back, will ya?" Jimmy said. "I got in late last night."

"We know," Uncle Fred said. "We heard you. What the hell time was it? Three?"

His mother reached over and placed her hand on her brother's forearm, giving her head a little shake. Jimmy could tell by her expression that she wanted him to cease and desist.

It'll save his old ass from getting pounded, Jimmy told himself, even though he had never hit the old man. His mother put the cup into the microwave and set the timer for a minute. Then she grabbed a paper towel and mopped up the spilled coffee.

Jimmy massaged the bridge of his nose while he waited and watched the cup circulating inside the microwave. The three of them sat in silence until the machine made the dinging sound, indicating that it was finished. His mother rose, popped open the door, and then set the heated cup in front of him once more.

He grabbed it and took another sip.

It was hot this time. So hot it burned his mouth.

"Shit," he muttered.

"Watch your language," Uncle Fred said.

"Go to hell," Jimmy said, and managed another, cautious sip.

"Jimmy," his mother said. "No more of that. No more fighting."

"He started it," Jimmy shot back.

Uncle Fred started to respond, but his sister held up her hand. The old man said nothing.

Jimmy felt somewhat emboldened.

Maybe she's on my side, he thought.

But a second or so later he knew different.

"We're just worried about you," she said. "You've been acting so strange lately."

He frowned. "I got a job. What more do you want me to do?"

"A job?" Uncle Fred said. "Is that what you call

it? Hanging around with a bunch of lowlifes, doing whatever they tell you to do, leaving for days on end on these errands."

"Lay off," Jimmy said. "When my music takes off one of these days—"

Uncle Fred snorted derisively. "Your *music*."

"Shut up," Jimmy snapped. He drew back in hand and balled up his fist.

"Jimmy, no," his mother said.

He worked his mouth, realizing that he couldn't hit the old man, at least not this time. Instead, slammed both hands onto the edge of the table and shoved himself backwards. The gesture caused more of the coffee to slosh over the rim of the cup.

"Go to hell," he said as he got up. "Both of you."

"Don't sass your mother like that," his uncle, said.

"I'm full growed and can do whatever the fuck I want."

"Jimmy," his mother said. "Your language."

He waved dismissively in her direction.

His uncle started to get up as well, but Jimmy took a step back, balled up his fist, and cocked back his arm.

"Stay sitting down, old man," he said, his voice a low growl, "or so help me, this time I won't hold back. I'll belt you one. Stroke or no stroke."

His uncle glared at him but did not rise.

"If I was your father," he started to say.

"But you ain't," Jimmy shot back. He blew out

another derisive snort. "Fred Stalking Bear. Big shot among the tribe members… Big shit. To me, you ain't nothing. And you ain't my dad, neither."

"Jimmy!" his mother cried out.

"Aw, hell," he said, rising. "I'm outta here."

And soon, he thought, it'll be for good.

***

THE FOWLER RESIDENCE
LUMBERTON, NORTH CAROLINA

She walked Wolf toward the still-open front door, holding his arm as if she were afraid he would some-how vanish or run away, all the while chatting about how she wished he would have called first.

"Frank and the kids are going to love seeing you," she said, pulling open the screen door.

Wolf told her he couldn't stay for supper.

"What?" Her facial expression registered surprise and disappointment. "Why not?"

"From the sound of things, I need to get home and talk to Jimmy."

Pearl compressed her lips and said nothing as she escorted him through the door. After guiding him to the nearby sofa, she told him to sit down and headed toward the archway that led to the other rooms.

The inside of the house was much as Wolf remembered it. They had a faux fireplace and a huge television screen affixed to the wall opposite the door. The floor was finely grained wood and there was an L-shaped sofa against the opposite wall. When she returned, she had two plastic bottles of ice-cold water, one of which she handed to him. Although Wolf wasn't particularly thirsty, he accepted it with a "Thanks."

"Like I said, I wish you would have called me." She twisted the cap off her bottle.

Wolf did the same. Despite his initial lack of thirst, his mouth felt suddenly dry, and the cold liquid was most welcome.

"Does Ma know you're here at least?" Pearl asked.

Wolf took a long drink and shook his head.

"I haven't talked to her," he said. He didn't want to say for how long.

"Well, let me call her then."

His sister reached into her pocket and pulled out a cell phone, but Wolf held up his hand and shook his head.

"I'd rather you didn't," he said.

"What?" Her brow furrowed. "Why?"

He didn't want to experience the angst over his neglect at not maintaining proper communication ties, especially after his release from prison.

"Look," he said. "I know I've been away for a long time, but I've come back now because of Jimmy. You can call her after I leave and tell her, okay?"

"I still wish you'd reconsider staying for dinner."

Wolf shook his head. "Can't."

Pearl regarded him for several seconds and then slipped the cell phone back into her pocket.

"Whatever you say," she said.

"Are you…" she started tentatively, "going to see Darlene?"

The question hit him like a bolo punch to the gut. Then he remembered that his sister and his ex were once good friends.

"Hadn't planned on it."

"She still lives in town, you know. I somehow seem to run into her every time I go to visit Ma." Pearl paused. "She always asks about you."

Again, Wolf didn't answer, but the conversation was making him feel uncomfortable.

"How's she doing?" he managed to ask.

Pearl shrugged. "She's okay. Moved on. Has her own life now." She sighed and stared at him, and then asked, "How did you ever let her get away?"

She left me, Wolf almost told her. But instead, he said nothing.

"Back then she called me quite a few times," Pearl said. "Asking why you weren't calling her or answering her letters. Did you write her?"

Wolf shook his head

"Why not?" Pearl asked.

"It's complicated."

"Complicated? She said you always wrote her when you were deployed. Why didn't you—"

"I told you," raising his voice, "it's complicated."

He immediately regretted his loss of control.

She seemed ready to say more, then relented and just remained silent.

How could he explain it?

When he'd been deployed, he'd had access to a computer. He could send emails, write letters, send pictures more or less freely. On the inside, it was a different story, a different world. One ruled by strength and violence. Showing any weakness, any compassion meant capitulation, degradation, or death. It had to do with mindset... Survival mode. In order to get through it, he had to stop caring about anything and everything that made him vulnerable, and that included family.

"But then again," she said, her voice taking a harder edge. "You weren't so good about writing me or Ma, either, were you?"

"Sorry, sis," he said, standing up. "It's hard to explain. I better go."

"No, please."

She made a lips-only smile, placed her hand on top of his, and recoiled slightly after brushing over his calloused and enlarged knuckles.

"Oh, my God," she said. "What happened to your hand?"

"I'm a fighter now," he said. "Professional. That's how I got this." He reached up and brushed the stitches on his brow. "But like I told you, I get well paid."

Her eyes seemed to search his face, studying the stitched cut and then searching for traces of other wounds.

Most of them aren't visible, he wanted to say.

"So what's the story with Jimmy?"

Her eyes drifted downward.

"He's fallen in with a bad crowd," she said.

"Who, exactly?"

"A bunch of low-life white guys," she said.

Her use of the word "white" was a mild surprise. Not only were both she and he half Caucasian, but her husband was as well. But Wolf knew that in troubled times, tribalism often offered a refuge.

"Anybody I'd know?" he asked.

Pearl drank from her bottle.

"I don't know," she said. "Do you remember Bob Spencer?"

The name had a distant familiarity.

"The guy that owned that used car dealership? Always making those dumb commercials on TV?"

Pearl smiled and recited the opening line from the commercial.

"Honest Bob Spencer," she said.

"King of the New Lumberton used car business," Wolf finished for her.

"Jimmy's been hanging with his son. Bobbie Junior. Along with a couple of hillbilly trailer park trash types. George Earl Mess, Willard Gibbons, and Craig Langford."

Wolf tried to put faces with the names, but the only one he could come up with was Bob Spencer Jr. He recalled a skinny, smart-ass kid with long hair hanging down around his collar.

"The Spencer boy is the only one I can remember," he said.

"His father's the mayor now."

"The mayor? The used car business must be pretty good."

"He's not only got that, but a whole lot more. Owns several more businesses."

"Honest Bob Spencer?" Wolf said. "His commercials always made him look like a horse's ass."

"He still is. But times change. He's also a state senator now. He got together with the tribal leaders a couple of years ago and got the approval by the state gaming board to put an off-reservation casino not far from the Rez. He's one of the main investors."

Wolf recalled the large Indian population in the area. His tribe had never had an official reservation designated, but when he was growing up, the Indian population all lived in one concentrated area which became informally known as "the Rez".

"Is it bringing in any money to the tribe?" he asked.

She frowned. "If it is, nothing's showing. Our tribe never had that much official standing. And, like I said, Spencer Sr. has taken over just about everything in sight. He even rammed some petition through in the capitol to get the town's name changed to New Spencerland."

"That's a mouthful."

Pearl laughed. Wolf was glad to see that.

"The people all hate it. Most everybody was against it, but Spencer supposedly had this petition showing the majority approved of the change."

"Sounds like the place is going to hell in a hand-basket."

"That's putting it mildly."

"Has Jimmy been getting in trouble?"

Her face scrunched up. "He was trying to start a career as a rock singer, but you can probably guess how successful that was. Now he's sort of out of control. Staying out all night, sleeping all day. Sassing Ma and Uncle Fred when they try to get him to straighten up."

"He got a job?"

She frowned again, more severely this time.

"If you can call it that. He works at the recycling plant, but his hours are really strange. And sometimes he'll be gone for days at a time."

"Recycling plant?"

"The textile mill closed down years ago," she said. "And that put a lot of people out of work. Then Spencer Sr. bought the place and made part of it into a recycling center. They collect garbage on one side and glass and plastics on the other. There's a big incinerator that burns the garbage and makes the whole area stink so bad it hurts to breathe." Her frown deepened and she heaved a heavy sigh. "Remember when the air was so fresh and clean?"

They sat in silence a bit longer.

"I'm surprised Uncle Fred hasn't straightened him up," Wolf said.

Pearl's face got a strained look on it.

"He's not well," she said. "He had a slight stroke last year. That's why he's been living with Ma."

He didn't know what to say. In view of what he'd just heard, it seemed foolish to offer any hope that he was going to be able to right whatever was wrong. From the sound of it, it appeared as though he was heading into one of those damn tempests after all.

CHAPTER 4

CORPORATE COMFORT INN
PHOENIX, ARIZONA

Bray checked his cell phone for messages while he waited for Maureen to get him a cup of coffee. The hotel had once provided a nice buffet breakfast, but with the COVID restrictions it had dwindled to just a couple of coffee thermoses and twin stacks of Styrofoam cups. His cell had a text from Abraham saying *Call me*. After punching the appropriate buttons, he got the lawyer's secretary on the phone. Her sultry voice told him that Mr. Abraham would be with him shortly. Maureen set the cup down in front of Bray. Powers joined them carrying his own cup.

"What's the plan?" he asked, sliding into a seat on the other side of the round table.

Bray frowned and wiggled his cell phone, indicating he was on hold.

Presently, Abraham's voice came on the line.

"You're in Phoenix, I take it?"

"Right," Bray said. "Arrived yesterday and we're getting organized."

"Good. Needless to say the old man's been pestering me already. Wants to know of any progress you've made."

Bray felt like making a smart aleck remark but decided against it. Nor did he want to tell him about the Meridian Insurance cover he'd spent the night creating. You never knew if the lawyer was surreptitiously recording the conversation. Instead, he waited for Abraham to continue. He didn't have to wait long.

"So I take it you haven't turned up anything new?"

"Working on it."

Bray heard the lawyer expel a heavy breath.

"All right," he said. "As soon as you do have something, call me. And let's start using those specials we bought, okay?"

"Roger that," Bray said, knowing Abraham was referring to the burner phones they'd purchased before he'd left. "How's that computer problem going?"

"Slow," Abraham replied. "Three down. So far, all useless bullshit."

The lawyer was referring to the laptops that Bray had obtained on the black market down in Belize. He'd made significant inquiries in all the black-market places hoping to gain possession of the missing laptop that had been taken from the trashed Von Dien estate. After he'd spread some substantial money around, he'd received a bunch of them, all purported to be *the* laptop. After smuggling them back to the U.S. and turning them over to the lawyer, Abraham had then hired an army of geeks to break into the collection of hard drives to try and see if any of them were legit. Bray had recovered twelve of them. With three down, that meant there were nine more left to analyze. Maybe something would turn up in one of them yet.

Bray set his phone down after terminating the call and picked up his coffee cup. It was only lukewarm now and tasted bitter. He set it down and frowned.

"Let's get out of here," he said, getting to his feet. He was dressed in a business suit and now slipped the jacket off and folded it neatly over his arm. Maureen was also dressed in business attire, and Powers wore a blue Polo shirt and tan dockers.

"All right," Bray said, heading toward the door. "We take our respective cars to our assigned destinations. Maureen, you hit that bail bond place that McNamara and Wolf usually work out of. Jack, you go to that gym place and check it out. See if Wolf shows up there. Maybe talk with that Reno Garth guy."

"Okay," Powers said. "What am I gonna tell him?"

"Tell him we're interested in booking Wolf for a fight back in New York."

"A fight?" Powers said. "What if he don't believe

me?"

"Make him believe it," Bray said. "At this point all we need to do is to find out where Wolf's at. And maybe get some contact information. We're just gathering as much information as we can right now."

Powers drank from his cup and simultaneously held up his left hand forming an O shape with his thumb and index finger.

"And me?" Maureen asked.

"The same," Bray said. "But wear something more provocative. Low cut to show off your tits."

She smiled demurely.

"You know," she said. "That's a pretty sexist remark."

"Yeah, right," Bray said, remembering that she'd spent the better part of the previous night in his bed. "Use what you've got to the best advantage, I always say. Keep those guys looking and their tongues will keep wagging."

"Gotcha," she said, the smile never leaving her lips. "And what you gonna be doing besides delegating?"

Bray glanced at his watch. It was getting close to his designated appointment time.

"Like I said, I've got my appointment at the FBI office downtown," he said. "I'm going to see about possibly filing a FOIA request." He stopped and felt his pocket for the flash drive. "But that reminds me. I want you to find a FedEx. We've got to print up our Meridian Insurance credentials and cards."

"Everybody's favorite," she said. "Want me to take care of that for you?"

He handed her the flash drive. "The files are on here. Buy the card stock and do a dozen of the cards for each of us. And get a receipt."

"Don't I always aim to please?"

He smiled knowing that the double entendre remark was most likely lost on the dense Powers. But that was the way it should be.

Maureen winked at him and said, "Wait for me while I go change."

She then headed back toward her room, saying over her shoulder, "I may need to do some shopping if I don't have anything provocative enough."

"Fine," Bray said, watching her ass in the tight skirt. "Just make sure you get a receipt."

As she disappeared around the corner, Powers asked, "How forthcoming you think the feds are gonna be?"

He drained his cup, crinkling it in his big fist.

"Probably not very much," Bray said, quickly moving his arm with the jacket away from any errant droplets from the crushed cup. "And watch what you're doing. I need to look professional and don't need any god damn coffee stains on my clothes, idiot."

"Sorry," Powers said.

Bray didn't reply and continued toward the front doors, which automatically whooshed open upon his approach.

He just hoped those tight-ass pricks at the Bureau would be half as accommodating.

***

U.S. HIGHWAY 41
NEAR LUMBERTON, NORTH CAROLINA

Wolf kept the window down as he drove, allowing the wind to rush in over him. He'd kept his hair military short so there was no need to be concerned about that, and the warm air was tinctured with a late-summer coolness. There was none of the stifling heat of Vegas. As he drove, he kept running the conversation with his sister over and over again in his mind, especially the part about Darlene.

How did you ever let her get away?

Besties forever, he thought.

Both of them were the same age and had been girlfriends in school. Best girlfriends. It had seemed a natural extension of things when Wolf and Darlene had started dating. Pearl had been delighted, especially since nobody in the family had cared much for Wolf's former girlfriend, Crystal Bear. This set him wondering if she was still around New Lumberton, now known as New Spencerland.

The idea of changing the name of a town to one named after yourself struck him as the ultimate in narcissism. But then again, Bob Spencer Sr. had always been a bit of a pompous ass. The long-ago TV image of the rotund figure in a Colonel Sanders-type suit hawking his vast collection of used cars flickered in Wolf's memory. So now he was the mayor... This was going to be quite an interesting homecoming. His thoughts then turned to Jimmy and how he was going to handle things.

More of his sister's words floated back to him:

He's sort of out of control. Staying out all night, sleeping all day. Sassing Ma and Uncle Fred when they try to get him to straighten up.

It sounded like his little brother's arrested adolescent development had extended beyond his teen years. Wolf wondered if he was partially to blame for that. He'd sort of been reluctantly cast in a surrogate father role, given the poor parenting their real father had provided. Wolf had purposely avoided that responsibility, first by joining the army when he did, and then by volunteering for all those deployments. He'd been running from the responsibilities, using being on foreign soil as a blockade. And then he was locked up when Jimmy probably needed him the most. Looking back now, it was clear that it had ruined his relationship with Darlene, too.

How did you ever let her get away?

In his heart he knew the answer: she was too good for him. Just like Yolanda.

He was debating how beneficial this family reunion was going to be when his cell phone rang. Wolf grabbed it and glanced at the screen.

Mac.

He answered it and raised the window so he could hear better.

"How you doing?" McNamara asked.

"I'm good. You?"

McNamara's deep chuckle resonated.

"Having a good time," he said. "Kind of reminds me of the old days on the Ho Chi Minh trail, hanging by the border of Cambodia, waiting for Charlie to come marching along so we could knock the shit out of 'em."

Mac had spent virtually his entire army career in Special Forces and had been in several wars.

"Is the border as bad as it looks on TV?" Wolf asked.

"Border? What border?" McNamara laughed. "Now you know better than to ask me that. Everything always looks worse than it is on TV."

It was Wolf's turn to laugh.

McNamara's tone turned serious.

"It's way outta control," he said. "We're just like the little Dutch boy running from one hole in the dike to another. Basically, all we're doing is trying to keep these ranchers and their personnel safe along the border down here. Just trying to scare them off, keep 'em from trashing private property mostly. Some of these boys are coming across with bad intentions. And other stuff. Those we're giving a kick in the ass back across the Rio Grande."

"Sounds pretty hectic."

"Tedious, mostly. Except for the occasional drug smugglers. We mixed it up with them a couple of times, too."

"Mixed it up?"

"Nothing big." McNamara laughed. "Exchanged a few rounds, back and forth is all."

"They're shooting at you?"

"Nothing we can't handle." McNamara laughed again. "Those fuckers can't shoot worth a damn, and once they see we've got no qualms about shooting back they know they're not dealing with some hand-cuffed government agency. The assholes fade into the mesquite and find another, easier place to cross."

"Didn't you say you were turning them over to the border patrol?"

McNamara laughed again. "What border patrol? Those poor bastards are spread so thin and are being so overworked that you can't even find one of them. It's like the wild west." He paused, and then added, "We're in the process of stocking and fueling up now, so I figured I'd take a chance and call. What's your sit-rep?"

"Just doing some recon," Wolf said. He didn't want to say that he hadn't called his mother.

"You convince you little brother to enlist?"

"I haven't arrived yet."

"What?"

"I'm still trying to sound things out, Mac."

"Well…" He sounded as if he was going to give an admonishment, but then his voice trailed off. Wolf heard him sigh, and then say, "You know, if you need any help, just ask. I'll hop on a plane and come back you up in a heartbeat."

"I appreciate that."

Mac was like a second father to him.

Wolf heard someone yell in the background accompanied by two toots of a car horn.

"Aw, hell," McNamara said. "Buck's got the Hummer all filled up and we're getting ready to shove off again."

"All right. Stay strong."

"All the way," McNamara said, using an old airborne refrain. "You, too. And keep me posted. Good luck."

Wolf conveyed the same to him and tossed the phone down on the seat. He mulled over Mac's suggestion about Jimmy. Was trying to get him to join the army a viable solution? Or the marines, maybe? The service had been a godsend to Wolf himself, but Jimmy was different. He'd always been an impressionable kid, easily led astray. Wolf knew the military would either make you or break you, and he certainly didn't want the latter to happen to his little brother.

And with my dishonorable discharge and prison record, he thought, it's not like I have anything successful to point at.

Realizing that there was nothing he could do at the

moment but speculate, he exhaled a long breath as another line from *The Tempest* came to him.

We are such stuff as dreams are made on, and our little life is rounded with a sleep.

He wasn't finished reading the play and still had to write his final paper and email it to the professor to complete the course.

The irony of the play's setting, a mystical island where the past, present and future all merged to form a paradox, and the similarities of the situation that he was driving into kept gnawing on him.

Another line came to him: *Misery acquaints a man with strange bedfellows*, and he wondered how much misery was waiting for him once he arrived in the metamorphosed town of New Spencerland.

Most likely, he thought, there'll be plenty.

***

FBI BUILDING
PHOENIX, ARIZONA

Bray sat in the air-conditioned waiting room and pushed the black-framed spectacles up on the bridge of his nose. The lenses weren't prescription. He wore them today only because he hoped they'd make him appear more business-like and less threatening. It was part of the persona he'd adopted for the role he'd decided to play, that of an overworked, bookish insurance investigator carrying out a routine assignment.

Little do they know, he thought, that I'm gathering information that will probably set one or two individuals up for a mob hit.

That both amused and unsettled him.

He was getting paid top dollar to trace this one down, so he had no room to complain, but on the other hand, Bray didn't relish the idea of being connected to a murder or two, if down the road the Don decided to carry out his vendetta. The old man had looked sick, but also cruel and mean, and the dyed mustache and goatee made him look like an incarnation of a bed-ridden Satan. Him and his quest for revenge. It was turning into a Devil's vendetta, all right.

Bray glanced at his watch. The feds were taking their sweet-ass time. He'd submitted his FOIA request over thirty minutes ago, and all they'd said was that someone would be with him shortly. The building itself was on 7th Street and set apart from other structures. Whether that was by design or merely a product of urban zoning, Bray didn't know. He'd felt trepidation upon entering the massive four-story tan brick structure. The outside windows were staggered in checkerboard fashion, giving it the aura of a gigantic chess board placed perpendicular to the sandy ground. A wrought iron fence surrounded the place, and a huge cactus was next to the horizontal plaque with the designation: *FBI PHOENIX DIVISION*. The address ran vertically along the side. All things considered, it gave off an aura of ominous methodology. The Bureau was known for its tenacity and professionalism. This wasn't a time for games or subterfuges, but he had little choice.

He debated the prudence of using his own name at this point, but this part of his investigation was legitimate and didn't tie directly to either Wolf or McNamara. He was, after all, simply trying to get a complete accounting of the death of Anthony Marco Fallotti and Dexter Von Dien. Fallotti's former legal partner had employed him as part of a life insurance policy that they were required to make good on.

Or so his cover-story went.

The door separating the waiting room and the inner offices opened, and a tall man in a blue suit stepped partially through. He had the look of an agent fresh out of the academy.

A blue suit... Didn't these tight-sphinctered assholes wear anything else?

"Mr. Bray?" the man said. "I'm Special Agent Roberts. Would you come with me?"

Bray reached up and pushed the glasses up again as he stood. When he got to his feet, he held his notebook flat against his chest like a teenage schoolgirl carrying her books.

Act the part, he told himself. Mr. Milquetoast.

The agent held the door open and motioned him through. Bray followed him down a long corridor with offices on either side. Most of the doors were closed, but Bray had the feeling that the place was teeming with activity.

Roberts stopped and gripped the doorknob of one of the closed offices. He pushed the door open and motioned for Bray to follow. The adjoining room was small; perhaps no bigger than twelve by fifteen. There was a table in the center of it and chairs on either side. Pointing to the seat on the other side of the table, Roberts walked over to the chair on the opposite side and placed both hands on the chair-back. He didn't sit down. Instead, he cocked his head at the chair on the other side of the table. The wall opposite them as one big mirror.

One-way glass, Bray thought. This is an interview room.

The hairs on the back of his neck stood up. Maybe this wasn't such a good idea after all. But another part of him relished the challenge. He was Daniel, walking into the lion's den.

Stick to your cover, he told himself.

Immersing himself in his new role, Bray tried to act significantly intimidated as he hustled himself around the table and into the chair and muttered, "Oh, dear."

Peripherally, he caught the hint of a smirk from the agent.

Good, he thought. Let them think I'm just another harmless nerd.

"The administrative aide forwarded your FOIA request to me," Roberts said. "May I ask what the reason is for your interest in this case?"

"Of course," Bray said. "I'm an insurance investigator and there was a life insurance policy for one Marco Anthony Fallotti. I've been assigned to do a comprehensive report on the accident."

Roberts said nothing, making it clear that he expected Bray to continue.

It was a good interview tactic. Use the silence so that the other person feels obligated to continue talking.

But two can play at that game, Bray thought, and said nothing more.

Finally, Roberts was forced to speak.

"Unfortunately, the matter is still under investigation," he said. "It's Bureau policy not to release any information until the case has been fully adjudicated. After that, the pertinent information will be made available at vault-dot-FBI-dot-gov."

Bray made a scrambling motion to spread his folder out on the table and then remove a pen from his pocket. Smoothing out the first sheet of paper on his tablet, he sat poised over the notebook.

"Could you please repeat that?" he asked.

Roberts did, then added, "And the full adjudication of the matter includes any appeals that might be filed, should the matter be brought before the court."

Bray scribbled on the tablet. He'd expected as much, but it was worth a shot to see if he could get any more information from this tight-assed prick. He reached into his inside jacket pocket and pulled out a small notebook and began paging through it.

"Umm," he said, running his index finger down one page and then another. "I was down in Belize last week and found the police down there most unhelpful. While I did get copies of their reports, their documents are not very professional."

"Sorry to hear that," Roberts said.

"They did say that the FBI was down there investigating, however," Bray said quickly. "Do you have reason to believe that this was something other than an accident?"

After completing his sentence, Bray looked up and stared at the other man to gauge his reaction. The agent's face betrayed nothing.

"Any time an American citizen is killed in a foreign country it becomes a Bureau case," Roberts said. "It's standard operating procedure."

"Would it be possible to speak with those agents who investigated it?" He bumped the glasses upward again for effect. "As I said, the Belize police were most unprofessional."

"Well, our agents are very busy and have a heavy caseload." Roberts smiled, but Bray detected something off balance in it. "As I told you, everything will be posted in their report. Check the website in a bit."

"But you said—" Bray stopped and emitted a scoffing sound. "Oh, but of course. You're right. With all the pressing issues you have going on, I can imagine."

He flashed an innocuous smile. "It's just that the Belize authorities said there were some other Americans down there who might have witnessed something. Would you have their names so I could follow up with them?"

Roberts started to speak but someone on the other side of the one-way glass knocked on it. The agent stiffened and excused himself.

Seems I've hit a nerve with somebody, Bray thought, and then felt a bit of a chill. He knew this could go south in a heartbeat.

After about two minutes, the door opened again, and Agent Roberts returned with another man. This one was equally young, but tall and rangy. He looked a bit more seasoned than his partner and wasn't wearing a suit jacket. The sleeves of his white shirt were rolled up to the elbow and an empty holster rode on the right side of his belt.

"I'm Special Agent William Franker," this second man said. "I was told you have some questions about an accidental death of two Americans down in Belize?"

"Yes." Bray gave the glasses one more adjustment and replayed the same dumb grin. "Were you one of the agents involved in the investigation?"

This Franker guy ignored the question.

"Do you have some identification I might see?" he said.

"Most assuredly." Bray made a fuss of setting down

his notebook, then picking it back up, then setting it down again and patting his pockets. All the while he was wondering what to do next. He'd obviously struck a nerve, but why? After patting all of his pockets and searching half of them again, he withdrew his private investigator's license and handed it across the table. Franker studied it. Roberts stood by looking stupid.

There was no doubt who was in charge here.

Franker set the identification on the table, took out his phone, and snapped a picture of it.

"Merciful heavens," Bray said, imbuing just the right amount of nervousness into his tone. "Did I do something wrong? I'm merely trying to get information for our report."

The special agent put his phone back into his pocket

"Nothing wrong?" he asked rhetorically. "I don't know. Did you?"

Bray was feeling some genuine nervousness now. He was through playing this game. It was time to get out as quickly as possible.

"I don't think so," he said.

"Who's your client again?" Franker asked.

"My client?" Bray intentionally furrowed his brow to give that concerned and confused appearance. "Why, I told you. The life insurance company." He picked up his notebook and began paging through it. "I'm sure I have it in here somewhere."

"Who's the beneficiary?" Franker asked.

There was definitely more to this than this guy was letting on.

Bray looked up, figuring the best thing to do was drop a legitimate name that could be followed up upon.

"I'm not at liberty to give that information out. Suffice it to say, I was contacted by the law offices of Mr. Jason Abraham," Bray said. It felt almost good to actually be able to tell the truth. And he knew that this reference would be a long trail to nowhere. "He was Mr. Fallotti's former law partner."

Franker absently smacked the identification into his open palm a few times and then handed it back to Bray.

"As we told you," he said. "This is still an active investigation. When the final report's ready, we'll let you know."

It had gone about how Bray had expected it would. Well, maybe a bit more intimidating. He'd learned a little, and hopefully had seemed innocuous enough that he would be no more than a blip on the FBI's radar. But this way, should his or Abraham's name come up later, they could explain their involvement with a perfectly legitimate rationale.

Insulation. But would it be enough?

"Sorry we couldn't be of more help," Roberts said, holding the door open.

I'll *bet* you are, Bray thought as he made a show of standing up.

He couldn't wait to get out of here and call Abraham.

***

HIGHWAY 41
NEW SPENCERLAND, NORTH CAROLINA

The highway ran straight through the center of town, just like Wolf remembered it, but that was the only remnant since his last visit. The sign proclaiming that you were now entering the city of New Lumberton had been replaced with a much larger version with the new moniker.

YOU ARE NOW ENTERING THE CITY OF
NEW SPENCERLAND
A CITY OF THE FUTURE WHERE
GOOD THINGS HAPPEN

Next to the big sign a decorative stone arch held another metal sign, this one with painted white letters against a pine green background.

Robert J. Spencer, Sr.
Mayor

The streetlights along the main boulevard were all affixed with similarly colored banners with alternate listings of the town's new name and the man in charge.

Mayor Spencer, Wolf thought. You've come a long way from hawking used clunkers.

He hadn't been expecting so many changes. The older section of the main street, which had once been composed of a lot of mom-and-pop stores, now had quite a few of those boarded up or with *CLOSED* signs in the front windows. The used car lot that he remembered from Honest Bob's TV commercials was still there, but much larger than Wolf recalled. Plus, several more auto dealerships had sprung up along the way, along with numerous taverns, a couple of liquor stores, and a bunch of restaurants. He immediately wondered if Saravan's was still in business. Back in the day, it had been the place to go. Flipping on the turn-signal, he headed down a perpendicular street and saw the vertical sign for the restaurant just as it had always been. Proceeding a bit farther, he passed two fast food places and a carwash. Houses and apartment buildings sprang up where he didn't expect to see anything but empty fields.

After making a left turn he crossed over a large bridge that spanned the canal. On the other side, he knew there would be the railroad yard and then the old textile factory, which Pearl had said had been changed into a recycling plant.

And not for the better.

Remember when the air was so fresh and clean? It makes the whole area stink so bad it hurts to breathe.

Just as he drove over the second set of railroad

tracks, which caused the suspension of his rental to groan and shimmy, he caught scent of the odor and understood what she'd meant. It did smell bad—like a mixture of rotting garbage, soot, and something else, almost reminiscent of a urine-like odor.

Ammonia maybe?

Either that, he thought, or somebody's been emptying their litter boxes there en masse. It sure wasn't how he'd remembered it.

That when I waked I cried to dream again.

Another Caliban quote.

But after all, he reminded himself, this monster hath returned.

He drove past the main entrance and saw another large sign.

THE SPENCER RECYCLING CENTER
KEEPING THE ENVIRONMENT SAFE FOR YOU
ROBERT J. SPENCER, CORPORATION PRESI-
DENT

A gate with a seven-foot-high cyclone fence with three strips of barbed wire running along the top bisected the expansive driveway. Some forty yards beyond that the massive red brick structure that Wolf remembered from his youth seemed to go on endlessly within the confines beyond the fencing. It had always seemed mysterious to his childhood fascinations—another world, an adult world, where men and women labored inside making who knew what. Now numerous dead trees populated the ground in between the fencing and the street, their gray, leafless limbs stretching effetely toward the blue sky.

He continued on the main road, waiting for the chance to make a U-turn.

A couple of huge garbage trucks rumbled toward him from the opposite direction, their big diesel engines emitting a high-pitched whine, their horizontal exhaust pipes spewing forth dark clouds. Both passed Wolf by and then made left turns to go into the plant. He wondered if Jimmy had a job driving one of those things. Pearl had said he worked there.

At least the kid was working.

Instead of making the U-turn, he reconsidered and proceeded straight on the thin ribbon of asphalt that now wound through some fields overgrown with tall weeds that sagged with an unhealthy torpidity. The New Lumberton Mall was a couple of miles down this same road and to the left. Wolf wondered if Spencer had changed the name of that place, too, and decided to find out. After a quick five minutes, he got his answer.

The entrance to the mall was still marked by the large, circular sign that resembled an oversized exclamation point. Inside the uppermost, circular portion, the once familiar design was still the same. It had a solid black depiction of a man in a top hat with a cane. Ringing the silhouette was *NEW LUMBERTON*

MALL. WELCOME. Both used to be lit up at night, but the silhouette and the enclosing circle looked a bit shopworn. Wolf turned onto the entranceway and noticed several large weeds had pushed their way up through the asphalt roadway. As he proceeded further, he saw the empty parking lot that surrounded the huge, X-shaped cluster of buildings perhaps a hundred yards or so beyond. The windows and entrances of the major anchor stores were boarded over, the wood looking weathered and discolored. A plethora of weeds of various heights populated the expanse.

No wonder Mayor Spencer didn't bother to change the name here, he thought. The place is long gone.

Just for nostalgia's sake he drove around the two-lane mall drive that encircled the complex. Once, during his youth, the mall had been the place to go to hang out. Sometimes they'd hold carnivals in sections of the huge parking lot or in the adjacent grassy fields. Now those fields looked as overgrown with thick weeds like the ones next to the recycling plant, only much greener. Wolf saw a smattering of wildflowers amongst the errant shrubbery. Somehow, it made him feel better. At least something of beauty had survived.

After completing his circle, he got back on the main road and headed toward town. As soon as the opportunity arose, he turned left to avoid heading by the depressing sight of the recycling center again, nor did he want to risk maybe catching sight of Jimmy. He didn't want to see his brother until he'd had a chance to talk with his mother and uncle. Maybe they could shed some light on what was going on.

More dread began to creep over him.

What if Jimmy was into booze, or drugs, or something? He knew the rate of alcoholism and probably substance abuse was high in Native American populations.

Native Americans, he thought, and smirked. Now I'm doing it.

They'd always called themselves Indians. The politically correct designation was yet another label placed on this by some liberal white man. Pat the noble savage on the head, pretend that you respect him, and demonstrate the hypocrisy by assigning to him a label he didn't conceive.

O, brave new world that has such people in it!

The Tempest again, but at least it wasn't Caliban this time. That quote was one of Miranda's, Prospero's beautiful daughter.

Speaking of beauty, he decided to drive past the Memorial Park in the center of town. It had a winding stone sidewalk, with rows of well-attended rose bushes on either side leading to a ten-foot black marble obelisk commemorating the veterans who'd died in all of the country's past wars. It had been one of the reasons he'd chosen to enlist, and he'd made it a point to go there upon returning from each of his deployments. Except the last one, when he'd been shipped off to prison instead. The place held vivid memories for him. It was the place where he'd taken Darlene right before he got down on one knee, in ceremonious fashion, and asked her to marry him.

On bended knee, he thought. What an idiot I was.

Oh, what fools these mortals be…

More Shakespeare, but not *The Tempest* this time. That one was from *A Midsummer Night's Dream*, unless he was mistaken.

How about, *To sleep, perchance to dream.*

Hamlet. That one he was sure of.

He was going to have to finish that damn paper and send it off to get his grade.

Maybe tonight, but then again, maybe not.

He still had a tempest or two of his own to get through.

***

GOLD BANQUET HOTEL AND CASINO
NEW SPENCERLAND, NORTH CAROLINA

Spence pulled his yellow Corvette into the *NO PARKING FIREZONE* spot next to his father's Cadillac. He was still feeling a slight buzz from the cocaine he'd snorted earlier, but he knew he was in full control of his faculties. Booze, pot, coke, even the meth he'd tried occasionally, never affected him that much. He was one of those rare individuals who felt he could handle anything.

The fortunes of having a superior intellect, he thought.

He sauntered over to the front entrance and waved his hand in a mock magical, abracadabra motion as the big doors slid open. The girl behind the main hotel desk saw it and giggled. Spence made a mental note to check her out later. Right now, he had a ton of stuff to do, not the least of which was this meeting with his dad and Redfox. Winking at the girl as she stood perched behind that Plexiglas shield, he caught a glimpse of the security guard out of the corner of his eye. At first, Spence assumed the guard was going to give him an admonishment about him not wearing a face mask, but the guy just waved and smiled.

Good, Spence thought. That dumb mask mandate cramps my style.

Spence continued to saunter through the lobby and turned right to head into the office section. Glancing into the casino, he saw the sparsely populated gaming tables. It was early, so the scarcity of players was understandable, and they were in the midst of an ongoing pandemic. But Spence silently wondered if the G was going to someday connect the dots and see that the amount of people frequenting the casino never matched up to the massive amounts of money taken in, compliments of Batton.

He got to the hallway where the row of offices was, pausing at the door that said CASINO MANAGER.

Instead of knocking, Spence went right in. The Native American babe that was masquerading as Redfox's secretary—he was boning her on the side, glanced up at Spence and smiled.

He'd have to make a point of checking her out, too. She was a real fox.

"My dad here?" he asked.

"They're in the office," she said and pointed toward the closed door.

Spence walked over and twisted the knob. Inside he saw Pence Redfox seated in the big leather chair behind the massive, uncluttered desk, smoking a cigarette. A half-full bottle of what looked like bourbon sat on the desk next to two small glasses of amber-colored liquid. His father, Robert Spencer, Sr., sat in the chair in front of the desk, within arm's reach of the outermost shot glass.

"Sorry I'm late," Spence said.

Redfox pulled open a drawer, and then set another glass on the desktop.

"Drink, Bobbie?" the Indian asked.

Spence frowned. He didn't like it when anybody called him "Bobbie". It was a carry-over from his youth. His parents had stuck him with that nickname.

"No thanks," he said, and took a seat in the second chair in front of the desk. "What's up?"

"We just wanted to get a status check," his father said. "Everything ready to go?"

"I'm assuming it is," Spence said. "They finished

their preparation yesterday and are packing it today. I'm heading over there now to supervise."

Bob Sr. smiled.

"That's my boy," he said.

Yeah, Spence thought. Always your "boy". I should be out in front running things already, but I guess I'm going to have to wait a little longer.

"So you'll be leaving when?" his father asked.

"I won't be leaving at all," Spence reminded him. "My guys will."

"Right." The old man beamed with fatherly pride. "You know what I meant."

Spence shot him a lips-only smile. This whole line of questioning, this damn command to appear, was nothing more than a demonstration of obedience— some reassurance to his father that things were on track, but that the old man was the one in charge. Spence felt the resentment building in his chest.

He still doesn't regard me as an equal, he thought. But that's gonna change real soon.

"Pike get here yet?" Redfox asked.

Spence shook his head. "I'm expecting a call from him any minute now."

The Indian grunted an approval.

His question irritated Spence, too. The old fart was the manager in name only... Merely a figurehead that allowed them to open the place under the title of an "off-reservation casino". What a load of crap. The real deal was Spence's father, and soon, hopefully, him, although he hadn't decided if he was going to stay after his big score, or just take off on a world tour, or something.

But how often did somebody get the chance to live in a town that was named after you?

His cell phone jangled, and he looked at the screen.

It was Pike.

Speak of the devil.

CHAPTER 5

MEMORIAL PARK
NEW SPENCERLAND, NORTH CAROLINA

Wolf looked for a parking spot along the curb on the street and saw that everything was metered. That was something new. The side street adjacent to the park offered an array of open spots, and he felt the urge to walk a bit anyway. He took out his cell phone and punched in his mother's number, but he didn't press CALL. Instead, he slipped the phone back into his pocket.

I'm not ready yet, he told himself and started walking.

He went past the old hotel, The New Lumberton Drake, and saw that it had seen better days. An orange *NOT APPROVED FOR OCCUPANCY* sticker was affixed to the glass on the front door. He and Darlene had spent their wedding night there, and he'd hoped to get a room today to avoid having to stay at the trailer. According to what his mother had told McNamara, both her brother, his Uncle Fred, and Jimmy were all staying in the family trailer. There wouldn't be much room. Just like when he was growing up.

Not a lot has changed, he thought. I'm suddenly back to where I began, only with fewer prospects and a lot more problems.

A few people strolled by, but nobody that he knew.

Continuing down the block, he saw a sign indicating the Gold Banquet Hotel and Casino was down the block. The hotel portion was the tallest building in the area by far. It had to be at least 25 stories. Wolf didn't want to take the time to count them all. Wanting to check the place out, he quickened his pace. Perhaps he could get a room there. Another sign at the next street indicated that the casino entrance was to the left. He kept going and made the turn.

The vastness of the place stunned him. Even from a hundred yards or so away, the casino looked immense. It resembled a huge domed church, with a second, block-like building adjacent to it. A flat, one-story building lay in between, with a solid overhang spanning part of the circular drive-in front.

Gambling... Every politician's answer to everything. The new religion and opiate for the masses... Until the check came due.

It was then that Wolf saw a man stumbling in the

middle of the street. His long black hair weaved from side to side with each staggering step as he headed for a red pickup truck parked at a jutting angle. The man fished in his pocket and withdrew a bundle of keys, which he promptly dropped. He took a staggering step backwards, almost toppled over, and then lurched forward. A car pulled out from the casino parking lot and whizzed past him, blowing its horn.

The guy whirled around, yelled something obscure and most likely profane at the passing vehicle, and raised his right hand with an extended middle finger.

Nobody loves a drunken Indian, Wolf thought, recalling that book title again. He hoped the guy wasn't going to get into that pickup truck.

Taking a few steps in each direction, the drunk began patting his pockets, then stopped and moved forward with halting steps to the glistening metal bundle on the pavement. He was next to the pickup now, and as he bent down, his head banged against the rear fender. Grabbing his forehead and straightening up, he delivered a punch to the shiny red metal and then howled in pain. With elongated steps, he went backwards again and almost fell, waving his arms in wide circles to keep his precarious balance.

Wolf quickened his pace, figuring maybe he could sit the guy on the curb and prevent him from getting behind the wheel.

Just then a police car shot past him. The squad car's siren emitted a split-second wail, sounding like an audio punctuation mark. The drunk's head twisted around and his face registered surprise and disdain.

A tall, lanky cop got out of the squad car. It appeared to be a one-man unit. The officer's uniform shirt was a darker blue than his pants, with a solitary stripe running along the outer seam. He squared a round-crown hat on his head and hitched his black nylon pistol belt up as he stood. His sidearm appeared to be a Glock 21.

Wolf made his way closer and figured he'd step in if things turned ugly, but he was hoping he wouldn't have to. Memories of his own father being pulled over in his pickup truck years before danced through Wolf's memory. There were more than a few nights his old man hadn't made it home until he'd stood before the judge the next morning to answer the charges of DWI and resisting arrest. Many of those times he bore a whole host of cuts and bruises. To his credit, his father had never complained about any of the beatings, only saying that he'd gotten what he had coming. Wolf always liked to imagine his dad had given as good as he'd gotten though.

Nobody loves a drunken Indian, he reminded himself again, even though his father had been primarily Caucasian and only a quarter Native American.

There I go with that Native American stuff again, he thought with a smile.

Political correctness was seeping into everything. A small crowd of on-lookers had gathered on the sidewalks on either side of the street.

The cop approached the drunk and was engaging the man in a conversation. His tone was loud and stirred a familiar memory in Wolf.

"Skip," the cop said. "What you trying to do? Get arrested again?"

The Indian shook his head and as he turned toward the voice, his legs became tangled, and he started to fall.

The cop jumped forward and caught him before he hit the pavement. Lifting him, the officer then grabbed the Indian's arms and walked him to the curb. As the policeman's face became visible, the recognition solidified.

Nick Paxton.

He and Paxton, or Pax as he was called, had grown up together. They'd played on the same football and basketball teams in high school and enlisted in the army together after graduation. The army had different plans for each of them and once they'd finished Basic, Wolf went off to infantry AIT and then jump and ranger schools, while Pax became a military policeman.

Another squad car was barreling down the block. It screeched to a halt by the two figures. A big guy, with a bigger gut, shifted himself out of the cruiser and slipped a nightstick into a ring holder. He glared at Wolf and then to Paxton and sauntered over.

"What you got, Pax?"

"Old Skip's had one too many again."

Skip was starting to protest and struggle. Paxton kept pushing the man back down, but he did so in a gentle fashion. Wolf stepped across the street and retrieved the ring of keys the Indian had dropped. Then, with slow deliberation, he approached the two figures.

"You know damn well your license is suspended," Paxton was saying. He did a quick glance over his shoulder in Wolf's direction, did a double take, and then a smile flickered on his lips. The heavyset cop turned also, and his hand dropped to his gun.

Paxton held up his hand in front of them and waved it dismissively.

"Well, I'll be damned," he said. "Steve? That you?"

"It is," Wolf said, holding up the keys. "He dropped these on the street."

Paxton looked back to the seated drunk, who was trying to rise, and then stopped. Skip grabbed his stomach with both hands, leaned to the side, and began to puke. Paxton did a quick dance-step backwards. After Skip had finished his regurgitation, he wiped his mouth with the back of his hand and collapsed backward onto the grass of the parkway.

"Aw, shit," the heavyset cop said as jumped back.

"Fuck you all," Skip said. "I'm gonna take me a nap."

Paxton seemed momentarily satisfied that the situation had reached a temporary respite. His smile widened and he stepped over to Wolf.

"Nobody loves a drunken Indian," Wolf said. He was using that book title a lot but couldn't recall who the author was. Still, it was so totally appropriate.

"We're lucky that's all it is," Paxton said. "We've got a growing crystal meth problem around here that keeps on getting worse."

"Sorry to hear that."

"Yeah, me too," he said extending his open palm. "It's about time you came back home."

The two men shook.

"Yeah," Wolf said. "I figured it was."

He didn't want to mention the true nature of his trip.

Paxton turned to the heavyset officer and said, "Glen, this is an old buddy of mine. Steve Wolf. Steve, this is Glen Cook."

Wolf held his hand out toward the other cop, who made no motion toward it.

"Wolf?" he said. "Any relation to Jimmy Wolf?"

"He's my kid brother."

Cook's head rocked a bit in acknowledgement, and he then shook Wolf's hand.

"So what's it been?" Paxton asked. "About four and a half years?"

"More than that." Wolf wondered if Paxton knew about Wolf's DD and his serving time.

But why wouldn't he know? It wasn't like it was a secret, and if he was a cop...

Paxton's left hand clapped Wolf's right shoulder.

"Man," the officer said. "You look solid as hell. I seen your last fight on TV, too. You kicked his ass."

"Hardly," Wolf said, knowing from that last statement that his recent past, and all the stigmas that went with it, were an open book around here. "I got lucky."

"What do you mean?" Paxton said. "You knocked him out, didn't you?"

"I paid for it." He pointed to the stitch-work on his eyebrow. "That guy was no pushover."

Paxton snorted and gave his head a little shake.

"The USA champ," he said. "I've been following your fighting career since you got out—" Paxton stopped abruptly, and then added. "Since I heard you started fighting."

Wolf forced a smile too, silently letting Paxton know that he knew the other man was cognizant of Wolf's fall from grace. Cook continued to stand in silent assessment of Wolf.

They stood in an awkward silence for several seconds.

"Hey," Paxton said finally. "Let me see about getting Skip home and I'll buy you lunch."

Wolf was just about to decline, but then thought better of it. Since Paxton was the law, perhaps he could give him a little bit of an insight as to what Jimmy was mixed up in of late.

"All right," he said, "but I'm buying."

Paxton started to grin when a mini yelp from a siren blasted, startling all of them.

A black unmarked police car pulled up across the street and the man behind the wheel wore an obvious frown.

Paxton muttered, "Oh, shit."

Wolf glanced at the unmarked squad. Cook emitted a low chuckle.

"You're gonna wish you had somebody in cuffs," he said.

The driver's door thrust open, oblivious to the possibility of other traffic and a large-framed man got out. His belly made Cook's overhanging gut look small by comparison. He had a blue cloth mask secured over each ear and flattened over the heavy swell of his under-jaw beneath the protruding cleft of a chin. After pulling it up, he jammed a cowboy-style hat on his head and lumbered over, his substantial belly jiggling over the leather pistol belt as he walked. His uniform had the same coloring as the other two coppers'—dark blue shirt over light blue pants, with a darker stripe running down the outside seam, but this man's badge was gold colored. As he drew closer Wolf saw that the imprint around the star said *CHIEF OF POLICE*. There was something familiar about the man's face.

"What's going on here? Cook? Paxton?" the chief asked. "And where are your masks?"

"I left mine in the car, Chief," Cook said. "But I was just leaving."

"Then get going," the chief said. His head rotated

back to glare at Paxton as Cook hurried to his squad car, got in, and drove away. The chief reached up and pulled the mask down a bit, so that it was fixed under his chin again. Then he looked at Wolf. Something seemed to flicker in his eyes.

Recognition maybe?

"Well, Chief," Paxton said. "I wasn't wearing one outside."

"You know the rules." The big head turned and spoke directly at Wolf. "Who the hell are you?"

"Chief," Paxton said, before Wolf could respond, "this is an old friend of mine."

The other man ignored him.

"I asked you a question, mister." The chief turned enough so that Wolf was able to see the man's nametag—*LANGFORD*.

Then it hit him: Ben Langford. When Wolf had left, Langford had been the area mailman.

Coming up in the world, Wolf thought, and said, "Steve Wolf. Glad to make your acquaintance."

The sneering expression deepened.

"Lemme see your ID," Langford said.

"Chief—" Paxton began.

Langford held up a big palm, indicating the matter was not open for discussion.

Wolf removed his wallet and took out his Arizona driver's license.

Langford accepted it, keyed the shoulder mic of his radio, and called the dispatcher. "Run a twenty-seven, twenty-nine on a subject," he said into the mic, and read off Wolf's information. "Run him through NCIC."

Wolf almost smiled. This is turning into quite the homecoming.

About thirty seconds later, the dispatcher came back on the air.

"Clear and valid through Arizona. NCIC clear."

Langford clicked his mic and handed the license back to Wolf.

"What are you doing here?" the chief asked.

"Visiting family," Wolf said. He resisted the temptation to ask if that was a crime around these parts but running afoul of the local law was never a winning proposition.

"You're Sam and Paula Wolf's boy, ain't you?" Langford said. It was more of a pronouncement than a question.

"That's right," Wolf said.

Langford looked him up and down and then squinted slightly as he scrutinized the stitched cut on Wolf's eyebrow. He then turned to Paxton.

"Get that piece of garbage off the street," the chief said, pointing to the slumbering figure on the parkway.

"I was just about to take him home, Chief," Paxton said.

The chief shook his head. "Take him in and toss him in the drunk tank."

"Aw, Chief, he's—"

"Public drunkenness," Langford said. "Now book him."

Paxton winced a bit and cast a quick look at Wolf.

"Need a hand putting him in the squad car?" Wolf asked.

"No," Langford said. "He doesn't."

An automobile horn sounded, and all three men turned. A vintage, gold Cadillac El Dorado convertible pulled up with a hefty looking man sitting behind the wheel.

Langford quickly straightened his posture and turned toward the vehicle.

"Hi, Ben," the man in Caddie said, his face stretching into a wide grin. "What's going on?"

Wolf recognized this one immediately. The last time he'd seen that face was on a used car commercial a good ten years ago. "Buy your next car from Honest Bob Spencer," the close-up of his round face used to say on the tube. In the afternoon light Wolf could see that Robert J. Spencer, Sr., good old Honest Bob himself, had aged fairly well. There was a little more sag to his jowls, an added bit of heft to what could be seen of his middle, concealed in a tight-fitting light-blue Polo shirt. But at least he still had all his hair, if it indeed really was his. The more Wolf looked at it, the more he started to think that maybe it had once belonged to some Korean girl. It was slicked back in the same oily, Ronald Reagan style pompadour he'd worn twenty years ago on local TV.

"Nothing important, Mr. Mayor," Langford said. "Just dealing with a couple of Indian troublemakers."

"Oh?" Honest Bob smiled. "You're not into causing trouble, are you, Steve?"

Wolf was shocked that Spencer had recognized him. They'd had only a few encounters during his youth, although Wolf had bought his first used car from the man over a decade before. Then dispatcher's voice came over the radio asking Paxton for his status. The transmission echoed over both police officer's shoulder mic radios, and from a receiver in the Caddie.

He must have heard Langford run me, Wolf thought. He's a hands-on mayor, all right.

"No, sir," Wolf answered, figuring using military courtesy would get him farther than adversarial commentary. "Just here visiting family, sir."

The mayor's smile widened.

"Excellent," he said. "You staying in the Rez, or will you be checking out our fabulous casino and hotel?"

The Rez... Pearl had used that antiquated expression too. The mayor was obviously trying to relate to all his constituents.

"But he can't go in the casino, Mr. Mayor," Langford blurted out. "I know about this guy. He's an ex-con, and him being in there's against federal law."

This further surprised Wolf. How the hell did this local yokel in North Carolina know about his military conviction? Somebody must have a big mouth. But then again, if this tub of lard was the chief of police, he could run anybody's criminal history he wanted.

But why mine? Wolf thought. And why now?

"My reputation precedes me, I see," Wolf said.

Spencer held up his hand and waggled his fingers.

"Ah, I think we can make an exception in his case," he said. "His younger brother—Jimmy, right?"

Wolf nodded.

Honest Bob made a clucking sound, the politician's grin still plastered on his face.

"Jimmy. Yeah, he works for me at the recycling plant." He made a huffing sound. "Well, for my son, Bobbie, actually. He's running the plant pretty much now. But anyway, I'll tell Pence to reserve a room for you, Steve. Stop by when you're done here and get registered."

Pence?

"Pence Redfox?" Wolf asked.

As he remembered it, Redfox had been an unofficial leader in the Rez. He was also a drunk—a semi-permanent fixture perched on every barstool in town back in the day. Was he some kind of bigshot now?

Spencer smiled. "Yeah, good old Pence. He's casino manager. Tell him I sent you."

"Thank you, sir," Wolf said.

Keep it courteous, just like in the army. And in the joint.

"Carry on," Spencer said. He shifted the Cadillac

onto DRIVE, but before hitting the gas he looked at Langford and added, "Chief, stop by my office when you're done here. I've got something I need to talk to you about."

Langford stiffened and said, "Yes, sir, Mr. Mayor."

The words seemed to come awkwardly to him. Wolf didn't think the other man had ever served either as a soldier or a law man. How he'd ended up as chief of police was a wonderment. So was the New Spencerville Police Department for that matter. In the old days, when Wolf was growing up, New Lumberton had been just a small community based around the textile mill and later the large shopping mall. The policing had been done by the county sheriff's department. But then again, a lot of things had changed since then.

Spencer took off and Langford's face resumed its belligerence. He turned back to Wolf and Paxton, lifting his arm and pointing a finger at Wolf's face.

"All right." His voice was a low growl. "Now you listen to me, jailbird. I know all about you and your dishonorable discharge and prison time. Despite what the mayor says, I'm telling you here and now, we don't put up with no troublemakers in this town. Understand?"

This time Wolf didn't answer. He was through backing off, but neither did he want to go for round two in a fight he couldn't win.

"*Understand?*" Langford growled, using more emphasis this time.

"Perfectly," Wolf responded.

The lack of reaction seemed to fluster Langford and his lower lip crept up over his upper. He began muttering as he did a half turn back toward his squad car and took a tentative step or two.

"My son served his country proudly," he said. "With honor and distinction. Left part of himself over there. Unlike someone like you who was a disgrace to the uniform."

This time Wolf had had about enough.

"If I were you," he said, "I'd quit talking about things you know nothing about."

"I know plenty," Langford shot back. "Plenty." He lifted his left hand and pointed at Wolf again. The chief's right was hovering next to his pistol. "And rest assured, I'm gonna be watching you like a hawk. A fucking hawk. You step outta line one time, even for spitting on the sidewalk, and I'll come down on you so hard your head will be spinning."

Wolf's momentary flash of anger had subsided enough that he was able to remain silent.

Langford held his stare for a few seconds more and then rotated his head toward Paxton.

"And, you," Langford said, "do your god damn job."

With that, he turned and lumbered to his squad car.

"And be prepared, Paxton," the chief called out over his shoulder. "Weather reports say that there's chance that hurricane might move up the coast and give us some storms."

After opening the door and wedging himself inside, he slammed the door and took off.

Both Wolf and Paxton watched him leave.

"Welcome home," Wolf said, thinking he now had a better understanding of how Mac must have felt returning from Vietnam as a young GI that everybody hated and blamed for doing their duty.

Paxton sighed. "Sorry about that, Steve."

Wolf shrugged. "No matter. I've been through worse. But what was that bullshit he was spouting off about his son?"

A slight frown twisted Paxton's face.

"His kid, Craig," he said. "He was in the army. Combat engineers. Lost a leg from an IED in Afghanistan."

"Shit. That's too bad." It brought Wolf back to the casualties he'd seen and suffered with, especially Spec 4 Martinez, on the last mission. The one in Iraq which spelled the end of Wolf's military career. Pete Thornton, from Best in the West, was missing a lower leg, too.

"You okay, buddy?" Paxton asked.

"Yeah," Wolf said, snapping out of the grueling reverie. "Just remembering some bad times."

"Yeah. Plenty of those."

"Too many."

"Well, it doesn't look like I'm going to be able to make lunch." Paxton gestured toward Skip, who was now snoring next to the puddle of vomit. "Maybe we could meet for a drink later on?"

"Sure."

Paxton took a business card out of his pocket, scribbled a number on the back, and then handed it to Wolf.

"Here," Paxton said. "This is my cell. Call me when you you're up for that drink. I'm working days, mostly, but that could change."

Wolf put the card in his pocket and held out his hand. Depending on how things turned out with Jimmy, Wolf doubted he would make the call.

"Great seeing you again, Nick," he said.

The two men shook and as they did, Wolf noticed a flicker in Paxton's eyes.

Still shaking hands, Paxton asked, "So why did you come back, anyway?"

His voice held an unfamiliar tone. It was something Wolf couldn't quite place.

"I told you," Wolf said. "Family."

Paxton gave Wolf's hand a little extra squeeze and grunted. He ran his finger over his nose briefly and then locked eyes with Wolf again.

"Like I told you, Steve." Paxton's brow furrowed slightly, "It's great seeing you again, but there's something you ought to know."

"What's that?"

Again, Paxton hesitated. "Darlene," he said, his eyes still locked on Wolf's. "You planning on seeing her, too?"

"Hadn't planned on it."

But the walk by Memorial Park, and the place where he'd proposed, had made him think about her.

"Well," Paxton said, "that's good. Because her and me, we're engaged. And we're going to be married soon."

Wolf didn't know why, but the news caught him like a gut punch. Still, he knew it should mean very little to him. He smiled, trying to appear as sincere as possible.

"That's great, Pax. I'm glad to hear it."

Paxton compressed his lips momentarily, and then a smile twitched his right cheek.

"I'm glad to hear you say that," he said.

Wolf again offered to help him get the slumbering drunk into the squad car.

"That'd be the last thing I need," Paxton said. "If old Chief Langford heard about something like, and I'd be working midnights for the next six months."

"He runs a pretty tight ship, huh?"

Paxton snorted and opened the rear door of his squad car.

"No comment."

"The last time I was here he was the mailman."

"Right." Paxton laughed and pointed to his trouser leg. "That's why we're all wearing these mailman pants."

It was Wolf's turn to laugh. He said goodbye and began walking down toward the casino. Maybe he could find out more about Jimmy in there.

Once again, the sad refrain from that old Willie Nelson song about returning from Vietnam played in his memory.

Welcome home.

*****

OUTSIDE THE OFFICE OF EMMANUEL SUTTER
BAIL BONDSMAN
PHOENIX, ARIZONA

A soon as he'd gotten out of the FBI building Bray had called Maureen and Powers and told them to drop everything. He told them to meet at the parking lot of the bail bondsman's office. Maureen had laughed and said she'd just finished her interview there.

"I bought a new tank top for the occasion, too," her voice purred over the phone. "I'll wait for you here."

He could hardly wait to see her in it, but knew he had to touch base with Abraham before things went any farther. Powers had already been to see Reno Garth as well. Bray bristled at their unexpected efficiency.

Who'd *a thunk* it? he asked himself.

Naturally, the lawyer didn't answer so Bray sent him a text and then called his main office. The secretary told him that she would relay his message, "as soon as Mr. Abraham is available."

And when will that be? Bray wondered.

Things weren't stacking up to his liking. The whole FBI encounter had left him with a bad feeling. Being stuck in an interview room, being watched by a second agent, the sudden interruptive knocking, and the appearance of that second agent, Franker, made him wince. Their investigation of Belize was obviously far from over, and him nosing around about the whereabouts of Wolf and McNamara was certain to raise a red flag if the Don ordered a hit on one or both of them. His gut was telling him to walk away and leave this one lie. It was getting too problematic.

But considering whom he was dealing with, could he simply walk away?

The bail bondsman's office was in a dinky strip mall, and Bray drove around the place to make sure they weren't being watched. After satisfying himself that the coast was clear, he called Maureen and asked where she was at.

"I'm in line at the Starbucks drive-up," she said. "You want something?"

"You seen Powers?"

"He's here. We're getting a snack."

He glanced over toward the other side of the lot and saw the other two rentals parked in front. "I see you. Stay there."

Bray heard the grinding sound on the burner that

indicated he had an incoming call.

Abraham, no doubt.

He terminated the call and pressed the button to accept the pending call as he drove over to them.

"What's so important?" Abraham asked. "You got something?"

"I've got something all right. A lot of suspicion. The feds are all over this business."

After a pause, Abraham muttered, "What do you mean?"

Bray gave him a quick rundown of his interview experience, culminating with his recommendation that they cease and desist.

"Cease and desist?" the lawyer said. "Why?"

"Because if this thing ends with one or both of our pigeons getting whacked, there's a neon lighted pathway right back to me," Bray said, then added for emphasis. "And to you, as well."

"So, what are you suggesting?"

"That we drop this damn thing like the hot potato it is."

"Rob," Abraham said, "forget that. These aren't the kind of people you tell no to."

It was the first time the lawyer had called him Rob.

He must be feeling the desperation, too, Bray thought.

"I tried to mask it through that life insurance angle," Bray said.

"Good. I'll have one of our underwriters draw something of the sort up. Backdate it with a bunch of phony records showing it was paid in full."

Bray felt uneasy. He stopped next to Powers and waved. Maureen came strutting out carrying a bag and a couple of paper cups in a cardboard carrying tray. The tank top she was wearing was practically translucent. And she wasn't wearing a bra. The sight of her gave him a momentary pause as well as a lascivious thrill.

"You there?" Abraham asked.

"Yeah," Bray said. He motioned for her to get into the passenger seat.

She waved and altered her course, cocking her head toward Powers for him to join them.

"Anything come from those laptops?" Bray asked.

Maureen set the tray on top of the roof and then opened the door. Her breasts jiggled provocatively with each movement. Bray had no doubt she'd left the bail bondsman stupefied.

"Nothing yet," Abraham said. "Look, just keep looking into it, but be careful. Use that cover thing you were talking about."

"Meridian Insurance Corporation. I will."

"And find out where these two jokers are. Fast. Spare no expense. All we have to do then is tell the Don and he'll turn the dogs loose."

"Yeah," Bray said. "Right."

He terminated the call just as Powers was getting into the back seat. Maureen was in the passenger seat and handed a cup to him along with a Danish wrapped in waxed paper.

"You find anything out?" Bray asked her.

"Only that those two idiots in there are a couple of perverts," she said. "They couldn't take their eyes off my boobs."

Bray couldn't blame them. He found himself grinning as well as leering at her.

"Is that it?"

"Neither one of our pigeons are in town," she said, pausing to bite into her roll. She followed up with a sip from the coffee cup. "That guy Wolf doesn't even live here anymore."

"He's relocated to Vegas," Powers said, his mouth full of partially chewed pastry. "I got the name of the gym where he's working out at there."

"Where's McNamara?" Bray asked.

Maureen picked a bit of cheese off her cleavage.

"He's down in Texas," she said, "working the border."

This didn't sound really bad to Bray. Two different areas... Split up, they'd be less formidable. And down at the border, hell, people were disappearing around there all the time. Maybe the double hits, should the vendetta call for that, would be easily conducted. And hopefully he and Abraham wouldn't be connected either. But then again, there always seemed to be more to things than what was on the surface.

"What we gonna do now?" Powers asked, spewing out some tiny particles of masticated dough.

Bray frowned.

"Cover your damn mouth, for Christ's sake," he said. "And as to your question, we're going to Vegas."

CHAPTER 6

SPENCER RECYCLING FACTORY
NEW SPENCERLAND, NORTH CAROLINA

Jimmy shut off the ignition of his Yamaha V Star, pushed down the kickstand, and tilted the front wheel so that the motorcycle canted on a slight angle to the left. He eyed Pike's huge, gleaming, silver and white Harley Davidson Road King Classic. The big man still sat on his motorcycle, fingering his gold skull and crossbones medallion. It was the size of an old silver dollar and gleamed in the sunshine. The percussive cycling of the engine served as a reminder to Jimmy that his bike, along with GEM's and Willard's Honda Rebels were just pathetic little rice burners by comparison. And Craig's trike was even worse.

But that'll change, Jimmy thought. The first thing

I'm gonna do when I get my share is go buy myself a real motorcycle. The biggest, reddest Harley David-son anybody's ever seen.

Despite his reverie, the percussive thrumming of the 1745 cubic centimeters made his already throb-bing head feel worse. The rumblings of his own 250 cc V Star had been bad enough on the way over.

Pike shut his off too but stayed astride his deluxe machine. He glanced over at the other bikes and smirked.

"It's almost a sacrilege parking mine next to these pieces of shit," he said, and took out his cell phone.

They were outside the rear, south entrance to the old textile mill. On the other side of the massive brick structure, the north side, Jimmy could faintly hear the sounds of the arriving and departing garbage trucks bringing their deliveries into the recycling plant. The odor of garbage hung in the air, and Jimmy reflected that he preferred that sweetish/sour scent to that of the acerbic, cat piss smell of the meth that he and Tim Sheridan had cooked up this past week. The comin-gling of the two was sickening.

God, he wanted this to be over with. But there was still a long way to go. And lots of risks, too. Every-thing had to unfold just right, and many things could go wrong.

"Yeah, it's me," Pike muttered into his cell phone.

"I'm there."

Jimmy could make out that it was Batton's voice coming from the phone but couldn't understand the words. The man always spoke in an overly loud tone, just like that comedian, Kevin Hart.

Pike listened and then said, "Got it, boss."

He pressed a button to terminate the call and then used the heel of his left boot to jam the kickstand down and in place. He angled the heavy motorcycle to its resting position and swung his right leg over the seat.

"Let's go see Junior," Pike said with a grin.

Pike was a big fucker, as tall, or maybe even a little taller, than GEM, but much slimmer especially around the middle. His arms were all corded muscle, too. GEM, on the other hand, had a layer of flab covering his gut, but he was a madman, especially when he'd had a taste of meth. Jimmy wasn't sure which one of them, Pike or GEM, would win in a fight but Pike always carried that massive gun underneath the Levi jacket displaying his colors and all his biker awards. The vest was so large Jimmy knew it had to be specially made to fit Pike's big frame. In addition to his *1%* hard-corps biker's patch affixed on the left-chest side, Pike had several rows of the winged motorcycle wheels with the sprouted wings coming out of the center of the spokes. They were mostly black and silver, with different colors intermixed. When Jimmy asked what they all stood for, Pike had just laughed.

"You'd cream your jeans if I told you," the big biker had said. "Someday, when you and me have some time and a couple of beers, I'll give you the low-down."

Jimmy let it go at that. He knew from what GEM and Willard had told him that many of the winged awards had to do with various sex acts, with the outer coloring around the wings representing women of different races. That was something Jimmy figured he'd explore down the road, when he was rich. Neither GEM nor Willard had any biker award ribbons on their vests, and Pike regarded both of them as nothing more than biker wannabes.

Amateurs, Jimmy thought, catching sight of the rubberized butt of the shiny stainless-steel revolver. I sure hope this thing Friday goes off without any problems

The huge gun was a Colt Anaconda, Jimmy remembered. With a six-inch barrel. Even in Pike's big hands the thing looked enormous, like fucking miniature cannon.

Pike pulled the worn Levi vest over the pistol's grip and strode forward. His engineer boots, with the big heels, made him seem even taller, and he moved with the grace of a big jungle cat. GEM's boastful brag about being able to tear off Pike's head and shitting down his neck didn't sound so plausible now.

The biker turned his head. "You coming, or what, Poncho? Little Bobbie's waiting for us."

"Yeah," Jimmy said, and quickened his pace. "But listen. My name's Jimmy."

Pike smirked. "Oh yeah? I call all Mexes Poncho."

"I'm not Mexican. I'm Indian."

This brought a deep laugh from the big biker.

"Okay, Cochise." He smoothed his hand over the solid gold skull and crossbones medallion that rode on the center of his big chest on that big-ass chain.

Jimmy didn't care for that comment, but figured he'd better leave it alone. Not only could Pike pound him into the ground with one hand tied behind him, but Bobbie would sic GEM on him if he somehow pissed Pike off and jeopardized this big payday setup scheme. He trailed behind as they walked toward the huge, brick structure. While the east side on this south end had some large, sectioned off rooms, it also had the overhead loading dock doors, like a big multi-car garage. It was ideal for surreptitiously bringing the trucks in and out.

And for cooking up the meth.

"Jesus," Pike said. "This place smells worse every time I come here."

Jimmy could agree with that. But he wouldn't have to smell it much longer.

They walked past the other motorcycles belonging to GEM, Willard, and Craig's Ridley three-wheeler. Bobbie's yellow Corvette was parked next to them, as well as Tim Sheridan's dumb-looking Nissan with the scrape along the left front fender.

He was probably driving plastered and hit something.

Jimmy wondered, with all the money the disgraced high school teacher was now making doing the cooking, why he didn't trade it in for a sharper model. Or at least get the damn fender fixed. But then again, Sheridan had a gambling problem and was probably giving a good portion of what they were paying him back to the casino. He went there faithfully to see Crystal Bear, his own kind of crystal meth.

It's like a fucking circle, Jimmy thought. Make the shit, get paid, drop the junk off in Atlanta, and bring the money back to be laundered at the casino. And then lose the money they pay you there, like Sheridan did.

But that was all about to change, at least for him, GEM, Willard, Craig, and Bobbie. They were all going to be rich this time out. And Tim Sheridan would be left holding the bag. It was something Jimmy felt a little bit bad about, but not a lot. After all, Sheridan's sister had dumped Steve when he was in prison. That had been a shitty thing to do, so that family deserved what they got. They could all go to hell as far as he was concerned.

Pike reached for the doorknob and twisted, but it was locked. He hammered a big fist against the solid metal door.

Presently it opened a crack and Jimmy saw a flicker of GEM's face. The door opened all the way and he and Pike entered. He saw the bright red and white side panel of the Rent-n-Haul twenty-foot box truck that was parked in one of the loading bays. Its retractable back door was open. Willard and Craig stood off to one side, and Bobbie was a few more feet away, an unlit cigarette dangling from his lips. Seeing that made Jimmy crave a smoke, too. Sheridan never let him smoke whenever they were mixing the shit up, or even in the building itself. But Jimmy never argued about it. There was a big *NO SMOKING* sign affixed to the wall next to them, and even though Sheridan was nowhere in sight, he'd reminded Jimmy often enough that even an unintentional spark could blow the whole fucking place sky high.

But that was going to happen pretty soon anyway.

Pike strolled over to the rear of the truck and Jimmy followed. Bobbie was on his cell phone and Jimmy could tell by the loud voice coming from the other end of the call that it was Batton again. Bobbie came over, still in conversation and extended his open palm toward Pike. The two men shook.

"In fact," Bobbie said, "your man just walked in now."

He listened some more and then handed the phone to Pike. The big biker mumbled something into it, listened, and then grunted something. He gave the phone back to Bobbie.

More loud, undistinguishable mutterings could be heard, and then Bobbie said, "Alonzo, relax. I told you. I'm the man in charge up here now. My father's just running the business end of things with the casino. Everything's cool. Believe me."

This time Jimmy heard Batton's loud reply a bit more distinctly. It sounded like, "It better be."

After more cajoling, Bobbie terminated the call and looked at them, flashing what appeared to be a nervous smile on his face.

"It's cool," he said, looking at Pike. "Everything's set. All five batches of the ice placed in vacuum-sealed containers, and then buried in drums full of coffee. And the drums have been sealed, too." He pointed toward the truck's interior. "We just finished with the first part of the load."

Jimmy saw five oil drum-sized barrels inside the rear box portion of the truck.

"We're gonna get the rest of the stuff loading in shortly," Bobbie said.

The rest of the stuff consisted of a special artificial section precisely made to resemble a wall of what appeared to be several wooden crates with containers of ammonium nitrate and propane. In reality, it was all plaster and empty metal containers set into a pre-formed plaster and vinyl façade. Artfully done, it looked very much like the real thing. It was designed to fit snugly across the back of the truck's box portion but could be removed quite easily for loading and unloading.

Pike went over to the truck, jumped up into the open box section, and felt the seals on the barrels. They were held in place by a nylon belt. After checking each one, he grunted an approval.

Jimmy glanced around. The bay next to this one was empty, but there was a long, solid floor-to-ceiling curtain barrier that was hanging from an overhead rod. The curtain was folded against the back wall. GEM walked over, grabbed it, and began walking it toward the closed bay doors. Each section had one of these long canvas curtains that could be pulled out to conceal the respective sections of the loading bays. Privacy curtains, Bobbie jokingly called them.

It was where they were going to conceal the duplicate Rent-n-Haul truck when they did the switch.

It made Jimmy nervous, and he started to sweat. He would have rather Pike not see GEM moving the curtain, even though the duplicate truck was not even parked in the building yet. It would be when they returned from Atlanta with the suitcases full of cash.

The mother lode.

"Where's Tim?" Jimmy blurted out, hoping to divert Pike's attention from the immediate surroundings.

"He's changing into his gambling duds," Craig said with a smirk.

"Going to see his girlfriend Crystal so she can take some more of his money from him," Willard added with a chuckle.

"Crystal? That foxy Indian chick?" Pike asked. "He banging her yet?"

"If he ain't," Willard said, "he better hurry the hell up."

"Why's that?" Pike said, arching an eyebrow.

Bobbie glared at Willard.

Jimmy knew that the goofball had slipped up, giving Pike an inference that something significant was in the cards. He decided to try and ameliorate the gaffe.

"Word is she's gonna be leaving town soon," he said almost too quickly.

Bobbie shifted his glaze to Jimmy.

Did I screw up? he wondered. But what was I supposed to do?

But it seemed to mollify any concern that Pike was

exhibiting. He made a clucking sound and shook his head.

"Too bad," he said. "I was sorta hoping to check that out one of these days on one of my lay-overs."

"Hell," Bobbie said. "That's no problem. I'll fix you up. Tonight, if you want."

Jimmy wondered what Sheridan was gonna say about that.

Pike's lay-overs usually only lasted a day. Two days at the most. He would come up from Batton's place in Atlanta on his Harley, check into the casino hotel, and spend the night. Then, the next day or so he'd escort the meth from here back down there, and then come back with the money to be laundered. He and GEM would follow the truck both ways as security, keeping an eye out for any cops while Jimmy and Willard would drive the truck down to Atlanta and back. But Jimmy also knew that it was part of Pike's assignment to keep an eye on him and the rest of them. "The Carolina Boys," he called them.

"I ain't so sure that coffee smell's gonna be fooling them drug-sniffin' dogs," Pike said. "Should we get stopped."

"Which is why we're also using the vacuum-sealed cans," Bobbie said. "As well as the façade."

Pike stared at the big plaster display set off to the side.

"Trust me," Bobbie said. "It hasn't missed yet, has it?"

"Only because we ain't never been stopped yet," Pike shot back. "We need to start varying this routine a bit. Some super trooper's bound to get suspicious one of these days."

"Then I'll tear off his head and shit down his neck," GEM said, walking around the front of the truck to join them.

Pike snorted. "Yeah, right. That's real smart. Kill a cop and draw more attention to us." He gave GEM a once over and squinted a bit. "Ain't you fighting tomorrow night?"

"Yeah," GEM said. "Why?"

Pike reached out and gave a quick, hard slap to the roll of flab hanging over GEM's belt.

"Looks like you been skipping your roadwork, boy. You sure you're in shape to fight?"

GEM's face puckered with an angry looking frown.

"Don't worry about me none," he said, balling up his fists. "I'm ready to tear somebody's head off and shit down their neck."

Pike grinned. "You're repeating yourself."

This seemed to infuriate GEM even more. The corners of his mouth twisted downward in a belligerent scowl. "I could start with you, right now."

Pike raised his hands, palms outward and emitted

a deep chuckle.

"Hey, big guy, relax," he said. "I believe you. In fact, you're looking so good, I may even put some money down on you tomorrow night." He then chuckled and gave a quick slap to GEM's belly again. "But then again, maybe I won't."

GEM looked like he was going to say something more, but a sharp glance from Bobbie seemed to eliminate the urge.

Oh, shit, Jimmy thought. We ain't even left yet and this whole thing's already starting to wobble.

***

GOLD STANDARD INDIAN CASINO
NEW SPENCERLAND, NORTH CAROLINA

The closer Wolf got, the more the meretricious opulence of the casino seemed to dominate and overwhelm everything. The massive hotel tower cast an ominous shadow over half of the parking lot in the late morning sunshine. And the signs in front of the place were all gold and glitter and bright, twisted neon. There didn't seem to be a lot of cars parked there, and that surprised Wolf. But it was still early in the day, and he figured that a place like this did most of its business at night.

He paused in front of the hotel entrance and saw

Honest Bob Spencer's Cadillac convertible parked in a fire zone next to the red curb. He'd left the top down in an apparent display of boldness.

Everybody in town probably knew whose car it was, so nobody messed with it.

Honest Bob's the man, Wolf thought, and reached out to pull open the glass door but the two big doors came apart with a whooshing sound and he immediately felt the coolness of the manufactured air conditioning. The lobby area was practically deserted, except for a couple of bored looking employees. One of them, a young woman who looked like she might have some Indian blood, given her high cheekbones, was behind the information/check-in desk. She wore no mask, but she sat behind a Plexiglas screen and cast a friendly smile in Wolf's direction. He was glad to see it. The predominance of masks covering everyone's face when you walked into a place had a depressing effect, which was why Wolf refused to wear one unless pushed to do so. As he moved in her direction, he caught sight of two men off to the side engaged in conversation. One was Honest Bob Spencer, looking more like a well-packed, old style army duffel bag with legs and arms and a head with somebody else's hair.

No, he wasn't anywhere as classy or as tough as a duffel bag. Wolf changed the comparison to an overstuffed laundry bag.

The other guy was a tall, slender Indian. His hair, which was snowy white, hung down below his shoulders. He wore a suit, in contrast to the mayor's light blue Polo shirt. It had to be Pence Redfox. He'd aged quite a bit since Wolf had seen him last. Back then, his hair was long, but almost all jet black.

The two were also maskless and engaged in a one-sided conversation, if you could call it that. It looked like the mayor was doing just about all the talking and Pence was doing the listening and nodding.

"May I help you, sir?" the girl behind the counter said.

"Maybe," Wolf said. "I'd like to get a room."

"Okay, sure," she said. "We've got a lot of openings. How long will you be staying?"

Wolf didn't really know. He felt like using the old airborne refrain, "As long as it takes," but he knew its significance would be lost on her. Instead, he answered, "A couple of days, but no more than a week." If he couldn't get his brother straightened out and maybe enlisted in the military in that amount of time, there probably wasn't much more he could do.

Except maybe mess things up further, he thought.

He wasn't the best of role models, and suddenly wished he'd taken Mac up on his offer to fly out and assist.

"Should we just leave it open, then?" the girl asked.

"Sounds good," Wolf said and took out his wallet. As he pulled out his driver's license and a credit card and handed it to her through a slot in the Plexiglas, he felt the presence of someone merging close on his right. Wolf automatically shifted his body away from the approach and glanced that way. It was Redfox and Spencer.

Honest Bob had the same, fatuous smile on his face that he'd flashed back at their first encounter.

"Look who's back," the mayor said. "The prodigal son returns, eh?"

Pence Redfox flashed a quick grin. Wolf noticed that the man's teeth were in terrible condition.

"You're Sam Wolf's boy, ain't ya?" Redfox asked. He held out his hand.

"Yes, sir," Wolf said, almost out of reflex now, but figuring the extra courtesy would allay any suspicions.

"Sara," Redfox said to the girl behind the Plexiglas shield. "His room's on the house."

Her eyebrows arched and she gave Wolf a reappraisal.

"Yes, sir." Her fingers danced over the keyboard and then she handed Wolf's ID and credit card back to him.

"I appreciate the offer," Wolf said, "but I'll be glad to pay."

"Nonsense," Spencer chimed in. "We take care of our hometown heroes. You served, didn't you?"

"I did," Wolf said, wondering if Honest Bob had already forgotten the disparagement leveled by the chief of police. "But—"

"No buts," the mayor said. "You earned it. Give him a suite."

"Yes, Mr. Spencer." Wolf heard the girl's fingers working the keyboard again.

"I appreciate it, sir," Wolf said.

"In fact," Spencer continued, "we could always use another Wolf on the payroll. Interested?"

Wolf wondered where this was going. He was eager to find out more about his brother's employment but seeking information from a politician was always a risky proposition.

"What type of work you talking about?" Wolf asked.

Honest Bob shrugged.

"Well," he said, "like I told you before, your brother's working for me at the recycling center." He paused and smiled. "Actually, my son Bobbie's running that show. But I do have some car dealerships in the area. How'd you feel about maybe starting off in one of them?"

"Let me think about it," Wolf said. "But I've pretty much settled out West now. I'm most likely only going to be here for a few days. Visiting my family."

Spencer clapped him on the shoulder and flashed a politician's grin.

"Okay, think it over. And in the meantime, regards to your family." Turning to Redfox, he added, "Pence, give him some complimentary chips to play, would ya?"

"Sure thing," Redfox said.

"Gotta fly." Spencer laughed. "Parked in a fire zone, you know."

Wolf doubted anybody on the police department would give the mayor a ticket.

He watched him stride off, his gait reminiscent of a horse's waddle.

"Here you go, sir," the girl behind the Plexiglas said, and handed Wolf a brightly decorated cardboard folder with the two card keys inside. "I gave you an extra key, just in case."

Wolf thanked her and wondered, just in case of what?

Redfox offered to show him the rest of the casino, but Wolf declined.

"I parked my rental down the street," he said. "I better go move it to this parking lot."

"Okay," Redfox said. "But look me up anytime. I'll be glad to okay a line of credit for you at the tables."

As Wolf walked out through the big sliding doors he wondered if they saw him as a potential sucker or a potential threat.

Keep your friends close and your enemies closer, he thought. Is that what they're trying to do to me?

The exact relationship between Spencer and Red-fox also intrigued him. The mayor had referred to "good old Pence" as the casino's manager, but Honest Bob had walked around like he owned the place. Maybe staying here was a good thing. At least it would give him a bit more of an idea of what was going on in the community of New Spencerland.

As he emerged through the doors and into the shade of the big canopy overhang, the heat of the day engulfed him. The sun was shining, but in the distance, it looked like some dark storm clouds were moving in. Then the discordant voices engaged in a less-than-harmonious conversation intruded. Wolf glanced to his left and saw a man and a woman in a rather spirited dispute in the shade of the overhang of the concrete canopy about twenty feet away. A lit cigarette waved in the woman's hand. She was long-legged and tall, with a flowing mane of ebony hair tied back into a ponytail and wearing some kind of purple and black uniform. After a second, he realized it was a dealer's outfit from the casino. There was also something familiar about her, but it took a few more movements on her part, and another second or two of mental assessment, before he placed her.

Crystal Bear.

Another pretty face from the past, and the long-ago past at that. He'd known her just about forever. Back in grammar school her father had shortened their last name to just Bear from the original Bear-Tracks. And she'd suffered the indignities of adolescent cruelty of the never-ending taunts: *Sometimes you get the Bear, and sometimes the Bear gets you.* Though the other kids used to tease her about it, but Wolf never did. They'd gone to grammar and high school together, and she'd been his first real crush, with her dark eyes and beautiful face. As she matured, she'd become one of the first girls to develop breasts, and that fascinated all the boys. Both of them being Indians, they gravitated to each other and eventually started to date. She and Wolf had been hot and heavy for a while, and then Darlene came along.

The guy looked familiar, too. It took less time to place him: Tim Sheridan, his ex-brother-in-law.

But it was the middle of the day, and wasn't he a teacher? At least that's the way Wolf remembered it the last time he'd been here. Maybe he was on his lunch hour or a holiday.

The quarrel continued, and the way they touched each other, a volatile mixture of familiarity and hostility, also had the look of textured intimacy.

"I told you, you gotta stop coming to my fucking table," Crystal said, her voice low and so angry she practically spat out the words. "It doesn't look good. They got cameras on all of us."

"But, honey—"

"Don't give me that 'honey' shit," she said. "You

want me to lose my fucking job? Like you did."

She'd always been something of a potty-mouth, even back in the day. She'd smoked back then, too.

Wolf was glad he'd never picked that bad habit up.

"Pretty soon I'll have all the money we need to get away from all this," Sheridan said.

He reached for her arm

"Yeah. Right."

She shook off his fingers, turned away, and brought the cigarette to her lips. It was only then that she obviously became cognizant of Wolf standing there watching. Recognition flickered on her features, but then her mouth drew tight, and she turned away and murmured something indistinguishable to the man. His head rotated and he glared at Wolf. Recognition flickered in his eyes, too, but he said nothing.

Wolf gave a slight nod of acknowledgment and continued walking.

A lover's quarrel, he thought, smiling himself now. Interesting that it's between my two "exes", so to speak.

He walked briskly down the sidewalk and back to where he'd parked and had almost gotten to the car when his cell phone rang. Glancing down at the number, he saw it was Reno.

"What's up?" Wolf asked.

"Hey, man. Just calling to see how the cut's doing."

"It's fine. I'll get the stitches out in a few days."

It then dawned on him that he might not be back home in that short a time. Maybe he'd have to find a doctor around here, or else try to do the dirty deed himself. But then again, his mother might be able to handle the task. All it would take would be some pointy scissors and a pair of tweezers. She'd spent a lifetime patching up his dad, with his never-ending penchant for drinking and fighting.

"Hey," Reno said, "I gotta tell you something. Something strange."

Wolf was immediately intrigued.

"What's that?"

He heard Reno sigh. "This morning I was at the gym, and I got a visit from some dude claiming to be an insurance investigator asking questions about you and Mac and Mexico and Belize."

That set off alarm bells with Wolf.

"Meridian insurance," Reno said. "But I was suspicious right away. I kept his business card."

"What did you tell him?"

Reno laughed. "Don't worry. Just the usual. CRS— Can't remember shit. At least about Mexico. I told him I didn't know nothing about Belize, either."

"What did he ask about Belize?" Wolf recalled their last time down there. He, Mac, and the rest of the crew had gone down there to rescue Mac's daughter, who had been taken hostage by Soraces and Von Dien.

"Said he was investigating some helicopter accident." Reno snorted. "I told him I didn't know nothing about it."

Reno had in fact been there when they'd shot down the chopper that had been taking off. Or, more accurately, when Mac had shot it down.

"I tried to reach out to Mac to tell him, too," Reno said. "But I can't get ahold of him. Know if he's still down in Texas?"

Wolf realized he didn't know McNamara's exact location either but decided that the fewer who knew where he was, the better.

"Not really," he said.

"Well, when you talk to him, let him know, will ya?" Reno chuckled. "And see if you can find out when he's coming back. I let him borrow my Hummer."

"Will do." He recalled Mac's previous comment about how much the relationship between him and Reno had evolved and changed over the past year or so. From bitter enemies to the best of friends.

"Hey, you back in the gym yet?" Reno asked.

"No," Wolf said. "But I been doing some roadwork."

"That's good. You can't afford to get out of fighting shape, brother. Just in case I can set up another match for you. Or hopefully a title shot. And the way things are today, it could pop up at the drop of a hat."

That was the farthest thing from Wolf's mind at the moment. In fact, he'd been debating for a long time whether or not to drop his MMA career. But then again, the idea of making one more big payday still had a lingering appeal.

"I mean," Reno said, "me and Barbie can drive up to Vegas and I can put you through some training regimes. If you want."

"Actually," Wolf said, "I'm in North Carolina at the moment."

"North Carolina?" Reno's voice was incredulous. "What you doing there?"

"Visiting family."

"Oh." After a moment of silence during which Wolf could almost picture Reno's dumbfounded expression, Reno followed up with, "So when you coming back?"

"Not sure," Wolf said. "I've got an open ticket on my return flight. My little brother's been getting into some stuff. He needs some counseling."

"Oh, okay. I got you." His tone sounded relieved. "Well, anyway, I got the license plate on that supposed insurance guy's car that was here. I had my brother run the plate and it was a damn rental. He looked into it a bit more and the guy works for a private investigation firm out of New York. Bray Investigations. You ever heard of it?"

Wolf hadn't, but the New York connection rang a bell. Von Dien and his lawyer, Fallotti, had been based in New York. With this guy asking questions about Mexico and Belize, and a helicopter accident, it sent

Wolf's danger meter into the red zone. He hoped it wasn't some old ghosts coming back to visit.

Could there be a connection?

How could there *not* be one?

This was just what he needed.

"I'll see what else my brother can find out," Reno said. "I'll try and get ahold of Mac again, too."

Wolf thanked him and promised to let him know when he was returning.

As he terminated the call, he realized he'd been talking and walking, and thus virtually ignoring his surroundings.

He was at Memorial Park again and glanced down toward the walkway leading to the place where he'd asked Darlene to marry him. He felt a sudden urging to meander down the winding sidewalk, stroll under the leafy arch on this late summer's day and visit the monument once more.

Did he want to see it again? Just for old time's sake?

Just then the wind shifted and the prevalent foul odor from the recycling center was lingering in the air.

Bygone times and bad smells, he thought. Not a good combination.

He decided not to stop.

Then he heard her voice call his name from behind him. He recognized it immediately.

"Steve."

It was a tentative offering. Someone reaching out.

He turned and saw Darlene standing about ten feet away.

"Pearl called me. Told me you'd come back."

***

PHOENIX INTERNATIONAL AIRPORT
PHOENIX, ARIZONA

Spare no expense, the man said, Bray thought as he plopped down in one of the padded black chairs and took out his burner phone. He quickly input the text for Abraham and hit the SEND button.

At airport. Going to Vegas.

It took several minutes for the reply to come back. Bray had already sent Maureen for three cups of coffee. Not that he'd sent her because of her feminine gender, but rather because he felt that Powers was so stupid that he'd probably mess the instructions up. He made a mental note to jettison the idiot the first chance he got. But of course, that might not be so prudent, considering what the big dumb guy knew regarding this latest caper. If he blabbed, it could produce complications.

His phone chimed with an incoming text message.

That was quick.

Bray smirked. *You said spare no expense, right?*

I did.

So did I.

Good, Abraham texted. *Keep me posted.*

Will do. Any news on the laptops?

Yes. Paydirt on one. Have geek working on it now.

That news amazed Bray, but then again, it probably shouldn't have. He had spread an enormous amount of cash, by Belizean standards, down in that armpit of a country. Most of it had been in the section that had all those Guatemalans who'd formerly worked at the Von Dien estate. According to what he'd found out, after the helicopter crash, the servants had systematically looted just about everything of value in the place.

Just like kids raiding a candy store. Or maybe more like the looters at Macy's during the riots last summer.

Interesting, was all he could think to type for a reply.

He wondered what the geek would find.

I'll keep you posted, Abraham texted. *You do the same.*

He caught sight of Maureen coming back with the tray of coffees and a stack of what looked like some kind of pastries.

Powers grunted an approval.

Bray glanced at his watch and saw it was getting close to noon. Not bad. They should be in Vegas in little over an hour or so. Then maybe they could run one of their quarries to ground.

The sooner the better, he thought.

CHAPTER 7

MEMORIAL PARK
NEW SPENCERLAND, NORTH CAROLINA

Darlene was still just as beautiful as Wolf had remembered. Her hair was a little blonder, but her eyes were just as blue. It had been those blue eyes that had captivated him that first time as she looked up at him. He'd never forgotten them. Not even after four, almost five years.

Five years...

If anything, she had improved with age.

She moved closer to him, and he struggled for something to say... The right words... Any words, but none came.

He stood frozen in place and found himself transported back to that dark void, where nothing else mattered except survival. It was the same place to which he'd retreated in combat and in Leavenworth. He was dreading the coming bitter questions.

Why didn't you call me more often? Why didn't you write? You never answered my letters.

But those accusations didn't come. Instead, she gave him a quick hug and then seemed to sense his mood and stepped back, an expression of uncertainty spreading over her face.

"It's good to see you," she said.

He said nothing. He was still in the void, and it wouldn't allow it.

"You're looking good," she said. Then her eyes focused on the stitches and a slight furrow appeared between her beautifully shaped eyebrows. "What happened?"

At first, he didn't know what she meant, and then it dawned on him.

The cut.

He shrugged. "Oh, nothing. I forgot to duck." He was getting a lot of use out of Dempsey's old line. "How've you been?"

"I'm fine." Her response was quick, almost reflexive. "You?"

He felt his wariness slipping away. Suddenly they were just two people who'd shared something once... In another life.

"I'm okay," he said.

"Like I said, Pearl called me."

Best friends forever.

It also explained the lack of recriminations on her part. Pearl must have clued her in, explained about the survival mode he'd explained to her. He wondered if his sister had called Ma, as well. He wouldn't put it past her, and then he felt a slight pang of guilt that he'd been in town a couple of hours already and still hadn't reached out to his mother.

Procrastination, he thought. Every fool's refuge.

"She says you're here about Jimmy," she said, as if they'd just bumped into each other and were having an innocuous conversation.

A conversation?

He had yet to utter more than a few words.

Guess I'd better rectify that, he thought, but didn't know what to say.

Should he tell her he was glad to see her? That she looked fabulous? That he understood about the "Dear John" letter he'd received in Leavenworth? That he harbored no ill will or resentment? That he was happy to hear she was starting over with someone new? That Pax was a great guy?

She smiled at him.

"You're still a man of few words, I see," she said.

Her smile brought him back. Along with her eyes, it was a feature that always enthralled him. Her teeth were so perfect.

"Yeah," Wolf managed to say, and then cleared his

throat. "I came back to see if I could talk to Jimmy. Can you give me any insight?"

The space between her eyebrows formed twin creases.

"Well," she said, "he's fallen in with a bad crowd, so to speak."

She named off the same people that Paxton had, which reminded Wolf of his earlier pronouncement: *We're engaged. And we're gonna be married soon.*

"Yeah, Nick told me," he said. "Can't say that I remember any of them. Well, maybe little Bobbie. He was always kind of a show-off, wasn't he?"

"He still is. His father too," she said, intentionally lowering her voice to mimic one of the old TV commercials. "Honest Bob Spencer, mayor of New Spencerland."

Wolf laughed. "That's a pretty good imitation. And him, I have met. He got me a comped room at the casino."

Darlene rolled her eyes and frowned.

"You're staying there?" she asked.

"The old hotel's closed down. Lots of changes since I was here last."

Her frown deepened.

"Yeah, lots of changes. And not all of them for the better." She compressed her lips momentarily, then added, "But I can't complain, especially about Mayor Spencer."

Wolf was starting to feel uncomfortable. Not only was he standing with his ex-wife, who was now engaged to his best friend, the town cop, but she and Wolf were standing very close to the very spot where he'd proposed to her. All he needed now was Pax to come riding by in his squad car. Wolf already had the big-bellied chief of police gunning for him.

He took a half a step back.

Keep it socially distanced, he thought.

"So what else can you tell me about Jimmy?" he asked.

The blue eyes drifted to the side as she apparently considered the question with much deliberation.

"Just what I've heard from Pearl," she said. "She told me she gave you the lowdown."

"More or less, but nothing specific."

"What was that phrase they used to use in all the textbooks? A minor requiring authoritative intervention? Well, he's not really a minor anymore, is he? But he's certainly in dire need of the latter. And—"

She stopped talking.

He repeated the conjunction as an interrogative. "And?"

Darlene took in a deep breath and glanced downward.

"And," she said, "I'm afraid we've both got younger siblings who need an intervention."

His thoughts immediately went to her younger

brother, Tim. Although there was only a year-and-a-half age difference between them, he was her only sibling.

"I just saw Tim over at the casino," Wolf said.

She looked up. "He wasn't gambling, was he?"

Her words were tinctured with mild desperation.

Wolf shook his head. "Not that I saw. He was talking to Crystal Bear."

"Her." The pretty mouth formed another frown. "He must have been gambling then. At her table. She works there as a blackjack dealer. Tim's got... Sort of a thing for her."

Wolf tried to assess the disapproval in her voice. He doubted it was due to any prejudice against Indians. After all, she'd married him once, hadn't she?

"I take it big sister doesn't approve?" he asked.

Her gaze shot back to him, with some sharpness to it now.

"You, of all people, should know what she's like," she said.

Wolf was somewhat taken aback, but then remembered, back when they'd first married, Darlene accused him of carrying on an affair with Crystal. He hadn't, but his pride and anger had kept him from totally denying it. That crisis in their marriage passed without further incident. Or so he'd thought. But still, after all this time why did it matter at all? It was a couple of exes ago.

"What's that supposed to mean?" he asked.

She closed her eyes, looked downward, and reached over to brush her fingertips over the back of his hand.

"Sorry," she said. "I just meant that she had a reputation of being kind of a... wild child. Back in high school. Sometimes you get the bear... Remember?"

Wolf doubted that was all she'd been implying but left it at that. Instead, he managed to pull up another quote from *The Tempest* that was rolling around in his head.

"O brave new world," he said. "That has such people in 't!"

Her eyes widened in surprise. "Is that Shakespeare?"

"Yeah. I've been taking some classes."

"Impressive," she said. "What play? *Macbeth*?"

He shook his head. "*The Tempest*."

"Wow. And I'm the one who majored in English."

He shrugged. "I've been reading the play. Have to do a paper on it, and I'll be through. But what about Tim?"

"Well," she continued. "Like I said, Tim's no angel himself. He's such a shy, sensitive type. Way too impressionable. And he sort of got in trouble before. Bad trouble."

"Tim?" Wolf felt incredulous. The last he remembered, his young brother-in-law had graduated from college and was set to be a teacher at the local high school. Then the words Crystal had spoken in the overheard argument came drifting back.

You want me to lose my fucking job? Like you did.

"He was a teacher, wasn't he? What did he do?"

It took her several seconds to muster a response. Finally, she said, "It's a little embarrassing." A couple of silent beats went by, then, "He was teaching at the high school. I was there, too. I still am. English. He taught chemistry."

"I do recall him as being pretty smart."

"Book smart, maybe. But people stupid. He had an affair with a student. It ended badly."

She left it at that, and Wolf didn't press for more details.

"Anyway," she said. "He got fired. It resulted in a town scandal. I nearly left the school because of it, but Mayor Spencer intervened. For once, I give him credit for doing the right thing. He told the school board to quietly drop the whole disciplinary matter if Tim resigned. He gave him a job at the recycling center, and supposedly paid an unspecified amount of money to the girl's family."

A payoff? For somebody else's transgression? Apparently Honest Bob had an altruistic streak a mile wide. Or did he?

It didn't make a lot of sense to Wolf, and he said so.

Darlene shrugged. "I never totally understood it

either. It was just after his election for mayor. He told Tim that everybody makes mistakes, and he wanted the town of New Lumberton to shine, not be a place noted for an unfortunate mistake."

"That's when it was still New Lumberton?"

She nodded.

The names have been changed to protect the guilty, he thought, taking liberties with an old television refrain he'd caught on the nostalgia channel.

"Anyway," she said, "I really can't complain about him. Sure, he's a bit of an ego maniac, but he went to bat for Tim and for me."

Swept the incident completely under the rug, Wolf thought. But why? What was Honest Bob's real motivation?

He felt her fingers brush his arm, then linger there.

"There I go," she said. "Being the local gossip. After Pearl called me and told me you were back, she asked me to look you up and say hello and wish you good luck."

Was that better than goodbye and good luck?

"I appreciate that," he said. "And it was nice seeing you again. You've remained as beautiful as ever."

He felt a pang of regret after uttering that last line. Was it too suggestive?

Her fingers vanished from his arm, but she smiled.

"You look good, too, Steve. And it was nice seeing you as well. If there's anything I can do to help you while you're here, just ask."

"I may take you up on that," he said. "I would offer to buy you lunch, but I really need to go out and see my mother. Looks like a storm's moving in."

She glanced up at the darkening clouds. "Yes, it does. There's supposed to be the remnants of a hurricane moving up this way."

"So I heard."

"I need to get going, too. We only had half a day at the school because tonight's teacher/parent conferences. I've got to go back and prepare."

Wolf's mind shot back to her brother's indiscretion, and he wondered how the teacher/parent conference had gone in that instance. It almost made him chuckle.

But then, he thought, who am I to scoff?

People who live in glass houses…

And actually, he was more intrigued as to why Honest Bob Spencer would go to such extensive lengths to help a disgraced high school chemistry teacher.

The memory of the powerful ammonia odor emanating recycling center drifted back to him. And Nick had mentioned a growing crystal meth problem in the area. The pieces were starting to fit.

What kind of job did Darlene's brother really have?

And Jimmy worked there, too.

Wolf felt a sudden chilling feeling. He hoped to God that his little brother wasn't mixed up in something really bad.

No, not Jimmy. He couldn't be.

Wolf knew he'd procrastinated long enough. Now it was time to find out.

The darkening clouds seemed to be more pronounced now. There was definitely a storm moving in.

***

SPENCER RECYCLING FACTORY
NEW SPENCERLAND, NORTH CAROLINA

Jimmy and Willard were struggling to wedge in place the big, artificial prefab display that looked like a floor-to-roof stack of cardboard boxes into the rear of the Rent-n-Haul truck. GEM, who was stronger than both of them put together, was standing by watching with a smirk on his face. The mock wall really didn't weigh all that much and could actually be moved without too much strain. It was more awkward than heavy, but it still irked Jimmy that GEM wasn't helping. It was like he had unofficially promoted himself to be the assistant boss, or something.

Assistant boss, my ass, Jimmy thought. That big fucker's just lazy.

Craig stood off to the side near GEM. He wasn't helping either, but he had an excuse with his leg. Plus, he was keeping a lookout for Pike and Bobbie in case they came back inside. Pike had said that he wanted to talk to him privately and they went outside.

Jimmy wondered what that was all about but knew better than to ask. At least not right now.

Willard unexpectedly dropped his end and it crashed onto the cement floor and the corner of the façade broke loose, sending the fragment spinning like an old toy top. It made a weird echoing sound.

"God dammit," GEM said. "Wait till Little Bobbie sees that."

A large section of the bottom portion had broken off as well, exposing the actual thinness of the plaster veneer on the wooden frame. It looked like a missing tooth in the front of someone's mouth.

"I couldn't help it," Willard said. "My hand slipped. But we're gonna bust it up anyway, ain't we?"

GEM glanced toward the big overhead door, which was still closed, making the inside of the bay hotter than hell.

"Yeah, but not now," GEM said. "It'll be your ass if Pike sees that."

"Shit," Jimmy said. "They're due back inside any second now."

"Relax," Craig said, hobbling over. "I've got some Gorilla Glue in my bag. I'll fix it."

"You all better move your asses then," GEM said.

Jimmy didn't like the big fat fucker. He was always

pushing people around, especially when he was high, and Jimmy suspected he was close to that now.

And you better not let Bobbie know you're sampling the product with the plan so close, he thought to himself.

He knew better than to say it out loud.

Craig grabbed his ditty bag and lumbered forward on that one good leg and his prosthesis. He got to the display and told them to lift it up onto the metal guard above the bumper. They did and Craig motioned for GEM to get him the missing part.

Oh great, Jimmy thought. Now that leaves nobody watching for Pike.

Craig twisted the cap off the Gorilla Glue and took the piece from GEM.

"Just let me make sure it fits right," he said.

Jimmy and Willard stood still holding the damn thing and watched as Craig stuck it back together. He smeared a bunch of the glue onto broken section, wedged it into place, and held it there for several seconds.

"You done yet?" Jimmy asked. He cranked his neck toward the side door to check for Pike.

The coast was still clear.

More sweat rolled down his sides.

I'm standing here like a dope, he thought, waiting for some stupid Gorilla Glue to harden, and hoping that the main meth man's biker-enforcer didn't walk back in and see that we've broke the damn thing.

After what seemed like an eternity, Craig released his grip on the broken section and gave it a tiny wiggle.

It seemed to hold fast.

"Looks good," Craig said.

"Then set it the rest of the way on up there," GEM said

They lifted it and slid it into place so that it concealed the secured barrels.

Jimmy exhaled with a sigh of relief, and not a moment too soon.

The voices that he heard told him that Pike and Bobbie had returned from outside. He heard the side door open, and the voices grew more distinct.

"Hurry up and get rid of that stuff," he whispered.

Craig frowned at him, shoved the top back on the Gorilla Glue, and jammed it into his pants pocket.

Jimmy glanced around the corner of the truck and saw that Bobbie and Pike were almost there.

"All set?" Bobbie asked, rounding the corner and smiling his knowing smile.

GEM nodded.

"Good," Bobbie said. He held his hand out toward the now affixed display. "Meet with your inspection?"

Pike glanced at it and smirked. "Meets with mine, all right. I just hope it'll hold up should we get pulled over. Who's doing the driving?"

Bobbie put one hand on Jimmy's shoulder and the other on Willard's.

"My two ace men here," he said, and gave Jimmy's trapezius muscle a little squeeze.

"Okay," Pike said, looking directly at them. "You know the route. You done it before. Me and GEM will be riding look out in the pickups. If we see any cops either sitting or coming, we'll call you, just like always. Keep it right at the speed limit both ways, especially with the load we got coming back."

Especially with the load we got coming back? That didn't seem to fit. Weren't they just carrying the suitcases full of money?

He started to open his mouth but caught a minute shake of the head by Bobbie, so Jimmy kept his mouth shut.

"All right," Bobbie said. "Since everything's cool here, let's you and me take a ride over to the casino and meet with my old man."

"Sounds like a plan," Pike said. "I'll meet you over there."

With that, he turned and began walking, but stopped.

"Hey, big man," Pike said, addressing GEM. "What time's your fight tonight?"

"Eight."

"Good," Pike said. "It'll give me a chance to eat and maybe get laid while I'm here. See you at the mall. And like I told ya, maybe I'll even bet some money on you. But I'll have to see who you're fighting first."

GEM frowned as the biker strode away.

"See you at the casino, Junior," Pike said over his shoulder. "I got to go gas up my Harley."

About forty seconds later, Jimmy heard the percussive roar of the big motorcycle's engine.

"One of these times," GEM said, "I'm gonna rip off that asshole's head and shit down—"

"Yeah, yeah," Bobbie said. "We've heard that one before. Now listen to me, all of you. We're almost home free. Jimmy, you and Willard go pick up that other truck and bring it here. And then help Craig set up his charges." He stared at Langford. "You're clear on all that, right?"

"Command detonation via cell phone," he said. "Not a problem."

"We can't afford any mistakes," Bobbie said.

Craig rolled his eyes. "Ain't gonna be none. I was twelve bravo, remember? Combat engineers."

"What I'm asking is," Bobbie said, "you're absolutely sure that this shit won't go off prematurely, right?"

Craig frowned. "Right. I told you, I know what I'm doing."

Bobbie turned back toward Jimmy. "You're going to call us when you're getting close, right?"

"Right."

Jimmy was hoping that this little rich prick wasn't

going to make them recite the whole damn plan out loud again. To head off that possibility, he quickly added, "And I'm going to email you pictures of the suitcases when we stop for gas."

"Okay, good. That's just what I was gonna remind you of. You're reading my fucking mind." Bobbie was talking fast now and that meant he was getting nervous. Or maybe he'd snorted another line of coke. Jimmy hoped to hell Pike didn't get suspicious.

"And make sure that Tim Sheridan doesn't know anything about this," Bobbie said. "Until it's time."

It had to be about the fiftieth time he'd stressed that over the last couple weeks and days.

"Relax," Willard said. "Chances are, he ain't even gonna be around. He's got his money now and he'll be too busy over at the casino spending it and trying to get into Crystal's pants."

"Good luck with that," Craig said, "if Pike's fucking her."

She was a beautiful girl and Jimmy remembered that his brother used to date her, once upon a time.

Steve, he thought. I wonder what he's doing now?

"Wait till that asshole Sheridan finds out that he's gonna get blamed for the fucking accident," GEM said with a snorting laugh.

The way he'd said "asshole" bothered Jimmy. Despite everything, Sheridan wasn't really that bad of a guy. And the way Gem said "accident" didn't sit well either. This thing was going to be a lot more than that. It was going to be a god damn explosion, for Christ's sake. A real big one.

But luckily, he wouldn't be there to see it. He was getting out of there in the first truck, and glad of it. That part of the plan was all right with him, but he was starting to be a bit concerned about Sheridan. Even though the guy always treated him like a gofer, he was always safety conscious and reminding Jimmy to make sure and wear his protective gear and not to do any of the meth. Maybe it was the teacher in the man. In any case, even though Sheridan wasn't what you'd call a friend, Jimmy still felt kind of a kinship with him. They'd worked together doing the cooking for months.

"You don't think Batton'll want to kill Tim when he hears all his money got blown up, do you?" Jimmy asked.

"He's probably gonna want to kill somebody," GEM said with a laugh.

"Just so it ain't me," Willard chimed in.

This time both he and GEM laughed.

"Relax," Bobbie said. "Pike will be in the locker room and hear the explosion and then see the fire. We'll stick with our claim that some residual gas ignited, and the place caught fire. And good old Pike'll think that all that illegal cash got burned up, then he'll report the loss to Batton. With all the dangerous chemicals Sheridan uses, they'll think it was some kind of accident. It'll all look legit. Just the price of doing business. Happens all the time in meth labs."

The closer this got, and the more Bobbie talked about it, the less sure Jimmy felt.

"It'll go like clockwork from here on out," Bobbie said. He paused and arched an eyebrow. "As long as we all stick to our plan, and that Craig here knows his stuff, and nobody else drops the ball."

"I don't drop balls," GEM said. "I smash 'em. You just watch me do that tonight. I'm feeling mean. Real mean."

For emphasis, he smacked his right fist into the palm of his left hand.

"And I do know my shit." Craig slapped to his leg. "And I ain't gonna make no mistakes. Can't afford to."

Bobbie chuckled and clapped Craig on the shoulder. "When this is over with, you'll have enough money to get a new leg made out of solid gold if you want."

The five of them stood in silence, then Bobbie pointed at Jimmy. "Which is why you're gonna take Willard over now to pick up the second Rent-n-Haul truck."

Jimmy replied with a nod. Damn, he needed a smoke something fierce.

"And you help Craig get everything set up when they get back."

"Me?" Jimmy knew his voice sounded like a whine.

Bobbie smirked. "Help him cross all the T's and dot all the I's."

Jimmy wasn't looking forward to that. The use of explosives always terrified him, dating back to firecrackers on the Fourth of July when he was a kid.

Bobbie was still staring at him. "Got it?"

This time Jimmy replied with a minute, singular jerk of his head.

"Okay." Bobbie clapped his hands. "I've got to go over to the casino with Pike and see my dad."

"Hey, what did Pike want?" Jimmy asked. "When you two went outside."

Bobbie gave him a look. He almost seemed impressed that Jimmy had caught that the biker had asked to talk privately. After a deep breath Bobbie smiled again, and this time it was a wide grin. "Well, I wasn't going to say anything right now, but you'll be finding out soon enough anyway. So I'll tell you. And it's good news." Pausing, to milk the suspense, like some side show magician about to pull a rabbit out of a hat, Bobbie let his gaze sweep over each of them. When he spoke, his voice was a whisper. "We really hit the jackpot. Pike told me that Batton's sending over a bigger amount of cash than usual to be laundered. That's what we have to go talk to my dad about now. But don't say shit about it. Got it?"

Nobody was speaking now but were all probably thinking the same thing: This meant even more money for them.

"Got it?" Bobbie asked again, in a louder tone.

"Got it," they all answered, almost in unison.

"That's the spirit." Bobbie tossed his head back and laughed. "Like I told you before… Pretty soon we're all going to be very rich men. Very rich."

And this coming from the only rich son of a bitch among the five of us, Jimmy thought. At least for now, anyway.

But until they were all home free, it was still just a pipe dream. The risk factors were high, and Bobbie seldom talked about those. Most of the time he kind of glossed over those parts. Jimmy could feel the sweat dripping down inside his shirt from his armpits as he mentally reviewed all they had to do. Everything had to go down just right, without a hitch... And then he thought about Pike and that big Colt Anaconda that he always carried.

Damn, it was going to be good when all this was over.

***

THE WOLF RESIDENCE
NEW SPENCERLAND, NORTH CAROLINA

As Wolf got to the section of town where he'd grown up, informally known as "the Rez", because it was predominately Native American, he saw that things appeared virtually unchanged. The houses, or what there were of them, all seemed to still be in a state of perpetual disrepair just like the vast assortment of mobile homes. He didn't blame this on laziness as much as he did poverty. Nobody could afford to make any upgrades. Temporary repairs were scattered throughout the scene: plywood patching, showing that weather-beaten look, tons of layered, duct tape in inappropriate places flapping in the breeze, and stacks of cement blocks set one atop another instead of permanent concrete steps. If that shiny new off-reservation casino was bringing any revenue or prosperity to the tribe, it wasn't in evidence here. The Rez looked as run down as it always had.

He slowed to a stop down the street from his mother's trailer and stared at it, thinking about the last time he'd been there. It had to have been what—more than five years? Between leaving for his last deployment and then being sent to Leavenworth. While he was still inside, his mother had written him that his father had died in an automobile accident.

Wrapped his truck around a cement porch, Mc-Namara had told him much later.

Was it because of the shame of his first born being disgraced and sent to prison?

But hell, Wolf thought. He was no paragon of virtue either.

His reflections turned to Mac again, and that PI asking questions. It didn't bode well.

We've got a lot of dirty laundry, he thought. I'm going to have to look into that when I get back. After I deal with my immediate problem: a younger brother in trouble.

Maybe real big trouble, if he was mixed up with drugs. Jimmy was seven years Wolf's junior, and of legal age. He was capable of making his own decisions. And his own mistakes.

The more things change, the more they remain the same.

He knew he could wait no longer.

Shifting the car into gear again, he crept forward until he got to the driveway. The trailer looked in even worse shape than he remembered it to be. One window was boarded over, and the wood looked weather-beaten. The railing on one side of the steps was partially broken, and the cement stairs had some gaping holes. The wooden trim around the whole place was in need of a coat of paint.

Why the hell hadn't Jimmy at least tried to make some repairs?

Had the kid turned into a real lazy ass? Or maybe he was to be on drugs after all. Wolf was anxious to find out which, hoping that it was the former rather than the latter. Laziness was a situation he might be able to deal with easier by giving his younger brother a swift kick in the ass. Addiction was another matter. But either way, he knew he was going to have to deal with it, and soon.

The beat-up old red pickup parked in front had to be his Uncle Fred's. Pearl had mentioned that Jimmy had a motorcycle now and there was no trace of one.

He must be out, Wolf thought. Or at work.

A few errant raindrops struck his windshield.

Wolf stopped, shifted into PARK, and then shut off the engine. Taking his time, he opened the door and then stretched. It was an Indian custom not to rush up and knock on the door. You had to give the other person a chance to observe your arrival and ready themselves. Or at least that's what his uncle had always told him.

Good old Uncle Fred… Almost more of a father to him than his real old man had been. Wolf had always valued his uncle's stories and wisdom, and he'd turned out better for it. It was too bad that it apparently hadn't worked out that way for Jimmy. He started toward the set of stairs leading up to the door. Glancing toward the pickup, he saw a big spider's web affixed to the front bumper. It didn't look like the truck had moved in a while. Either that or the spider was very industrious.

Before he could open the screen door and knock, the interior door whooshed inward and his mother stood there, her expression a mixture of both sorrow and joy. She looked smaller than he remembered. Tiny… frail looking… Not the strong matriarch of his memory. Her once black hair was now almost completely gray, and deep worry lines bracketed her mouth and deep wrinkles lined her forehead and the separation between her eyebrows.

"Oh, Steve," she said. "It's been so long. So long."

"I know," he managed to say. His throat felt dry and knotted up.

Stepping forward, she embraced him, and he felt a combination of happiness and dread. He felt awkward, his arms fumbling, as if he didn't know where to put them. Should he return her embrace?

He did, but gently, barely touching her at all.

Uncle Fred rose ponderously from the chair by the table across the small living room and lumbered forward, using a cane with his right hand. His left leg dragged slightly, and his left arm was cocked close to his body.

Was that the stroke Pearl had told him about? She'd said it was a mild one. This didn't look so mild.

"Nephew," his uncle said. "About damn time you came home."

Wolf felt the tears well up and his eyes ached momentarily. Luckily, the wetness seemed to be limited to just giving his eyes a wet, glossy feel.

"Yeah," he said, "about damn time is right."

CHAPTER 8

APPROACHING THE RENT-N-HAUL LOT
NEW SPENCERLAND, NORTH CAROLINA

When Jimmy was giving Willard a ride on the back of his motorcycle to get the second damn Rent-n-Haul truck the son of a bitch was giggling and trying to tickle Jimmy continuously. Finally, he pulled over to the curb and jerked the bike to a stop.

"What the fuck you doing?" Jimmy said.

Willard squeezed him tighter, in bear-hug fashion. "Just thinking on how I'm gonna spend all that money," Willard said.

"We ain't gonna be spending nothing unless we get this truck. And knock off that tickling shit, would ya?"

Willard tickled Jimmy's gut again, and then pinched his right nipple.

"Hey, cut it out," Jimmy said, swatting the other

man's hand. "You a fucking fag, or what?"

He's fucking high, Jimmy thought. This asshole must have grabbed some of the shit when nobody was looking,

"Just pretending you were Crystal," Willard said. "Okay, I won't do it again. Word."

The initial stages of a light rain were starting. Jimmy frowned, depressed the clutch, and slammed the piston down into first. He shot out from the curb and heard the screech of brakes behind him. The driver of an approaching car had slammed on its brakes and blew his horn.

"See what you almost made me do, fool?" Jimmy said.

Neither of them had on a helmet, and Jimmy had no doubt the crash would have been grievous.

Willard gave the driver of the car the finger as he drove by glaring.

"Knock that shit off," Jimmy said. "He might have a gun in there."

Willard giggled.

Great, Jimmy thought. If he wrecks the damn Rent-n-Haul on the way back, we'll really be up shit creek without a paddle.

He decided he'd do the drive back. They'd have to take the time to lower the ramp and walk his bike into the bed. Then he'd have to either lay it on its side or find some way to strap it in.

Shit, shit, shit, Jimmy said to himself.

Willard didn't molest him on the rest of the way as the rain started to come down heavier. When they got to the Rent-n-Haul place, which was owned by Bobbie's father, Jimmy pulled his bike up behind the box-truck and shut off the engine. Willard jumped off the rear of the bike and ran toward the cab of the truck.

"Hey," Jimmy called out. "Help me get this ramp lowered down."

"Come on, man," Willard said. "It's starting to rain."

"Do it. And give me the keys."

"Huh? What for? I'm supposed to drive."

Jimmy stepped over and thrust his index finger an inch in front of the other man's face.

"You're doing meth," Jimmy said. "And don't try to tell me you ain't."

"So?"

"So, you ain't driving. I am. Now get that ramp down so we can put my bike inside."

Willard seemed about to say something in protest, but Jimmy grabbed him by the collar and pulled him forward, patting his pockets until he found the key ring.

"Or do you want me to tell Bobbie what you been up to and have him send GEM over here to beat your ass?"

Willard expelled a puff of breath.

"Shit," he said, "GEM's the one that give it to me. That fucker's high, too."

"Just pull out that god damn ramp." Jimmy released his hold on Willard's shirt and shoved him toward the rear of the truck. He went to the big latch lock handle. The end of it was secured by a padlock with an elongated hasp. Beside the ignition and door key, the ring had a smaller key that was obviously for the padlock. He slid it in and twisted. The lock popped open. Twisting it from the O-shaped hole, Jimmy pulled the padlock free and then rotated the lever to release it so that the sliding door could be opened. He pushed it upward. Willard, in the meantime, was giggling as he struggled to pull out the damn ramp. Jimmy gave the overhead door a final shove and then went to help him.

He was both angry and scared. They were about to put a plan into motion to rip off a big-time meth dealer from Atlanta, and he was in the middle of it with a couple of fucking meth heads.

Could things get any worse?

He felt more raindrops hit his face and looked skyward.

Massive dark clouds seemed to be rushing towards them.

It looked like that storm they'd been talking about, the one connected to the hurricane down south, was rolling in for sure.

Or at least the start of it was.

He was feeling waterlogged already and even if he kept the bike into the back of the truck on the way back to recycling plant, he still had to drive it back home in the rain.

Could things get any worse?

***

MCCARRAN INTERNATIONAL AIRPORT
LAS VEGAS, NEVADA

Bray turned on his phone as soon as the plane had touched down and checked the messages. It looked like Abraham had tried to call the burner three times, and then had left a text on Bray's regular cell.

CALL ME ASAP

All caps, no punctuation.

Was that supposed to connote urgency?

Glancing out the window, he saw the plane was doing its slow advance toward the gate. There were too many people around for him to risk a call now. Too many inquiring ears. He decided to send his own text back to the lawyer.

Just landed. Will call shortly.

The reply came a few seconds later.

Okay. Make it soon.

Soon stretched into a solid forty-five minutes. It

took them that long to deplane, get to the baggage claim area, find the right carousal, and then make their way to the shuttle bus to the car-rental place. On the bus Bray figured he might as well chance it here because they'd sat in back and the thing wasn't half-full. He dialed Abraham's burner on his own. It rang only once before the angry sounding voice came on.

"About fucking time."

Bray emitted a soft chuckle.

"Sorry about that," he said. "What's up?"

"Plenty," Abraham said. "That damn laptop's turned out to be a goldmine."

"Oh?"

"You have no idea. But it's both a blessing and a curse."

Bray waited for the lawyer to explain or at least elucidate a bit more.

"Where you at now?" Abraham finally asked.

"On the shuttle bus to the car rental place."

"What have you got going?"

"We've got a few places and people to check out here," Bray said. "Plus, I've got my office in New York doing a credit check on both parties' credit cards. Those should tell us plenty."

"Okay, good. I'm pulling up now to see the old man, brief him what we've got."

"On the laptop?"

"Right. Some security footage that was recorded

down there." He paused and blew out a quick, heavy breath. "And it's dynamite. Raises the stakes completely. We're going to have to give it our A-game."

A-game?

Bray wasn't liking the sound of this. It implied that urgency had been raised to a new level.

"What is it?" he asked. "What does it show?"

"Later," Abraham said. "I'm pulling up there now. But suffice it to say, the old man's going to go ballistic."

***

THE WOLF RESIDENCE
NEW SPENCERLAND, NORTH CAROLINA

The three of them sat at the kitchen table drinking coffee while the rain pounded the roof of the trailer. Wolf was mostly rotating his cup, not having drunk that much, as he listened to his mother's long list of concerns. She'd launched into a litany of complaints about his younger brother and how he was out of control, an unspoken concern for her youngest imbuing each tale. It sounded to Wolf like his brother was hell-bent on self-destruction and heading there fast. The prospect of drugs shadowed every thought.

The same question still nagged him: What was the best way to handle it?

His original inclination of beating some sense into

the kid was out. He knew that would only alienate him further. Besides, it was obvious that Uncle Fred was an authority figure in Jimmy's life, and that hadn't helped rectify things. Of course, the stroke had diminished their uncle somewhat.

No, more than somewhat. More like a lot.

And from what his mother had said, Jimmy was not the least bit intimidated by his uncle. Nor was he respectful.

It angered Wolf that the kid would be so ignorant.

Across the room the steady, plunking sound echoed again in the moments of silence. A big plastic bucket was sitting about five feet away, halfway filled with water that had dripped down through what appeared to be a hole in the roof. It was a nice, round hole and Wolf pointed up at it.

"What happened there?" he asked.

His mother compressed her lips and brought her gaze down to the tabletop.

"Him and his crazy friends," she said. "They were in here playing cards one night. It was late and I'd already gone to bed. Then I heard this awful bang. I came running out of my bedroom and they were all laughing and waving their arms around. There was smoke in the air and one of them had a gun."

"They shot a hole there?" Wolf asked.

She closed her eyes, saying nothing, but the meaning was clear.

"They were all drunk, or high or something," Uncle Fred added.

Or high or something...

What was he trying to say? What was he trying *not* to say?

Wolf read between the lines.

Out of control behavior was putting it mildly. It was way past time to do something. He'd hit rock bottom after his trial and then arrival at Leavenworth. There was nowhere to go but up. He doubted that Jimmy had reached that depth yet, but from the sound of things, he wasn't that far away. Wolf wondered if the kid knew how close he was, tiptoeing on the edge of the abyss.

First things first, he thought. I need to figure out exactly what we're dealing with.

Another solitary drop plunked down into the bucket.

"Guess I better empty that before it gets too heavy to lift," Uncle Fred said, jockeying his big body forward.

Wolf placed a hand on his uncle's arm.

"Let me do that," he said, getting to his feet.

His uncle grinned.

"I was hoping you'd say that."

Wolf strode over and stared up at the hole. The bullet had gone completely through.

Should be fairly easy to patch, he thought. All it

would take is climbing up there onto the roof and then a little bit of additional patching inside.

It was something that Jimmy should have done.

He frowned as he considered how far his brother had fallen and Wolf made a mental promise that he was going to make all the necessary repairs to this place before he left. Maybe he could get Pearl's husband, Frank, to assist. After all, the man was a carpenter.

And Jimmy's going to help, too, Wolf thought. Even if I have to stand over him with a baseball bat.

He had a momentary flashback to his childhood and his father's strict and often brutal disciplinary techniques. They'd all been directed at Wolf, rather than at Jimmy. One time, when Wolf was a boy and his old man was drunk, the beating had gotten so out of control that his mother had had to cold-cock her husband with a frying pan. She'd bloodied him, but he was a tough bastard, turned on her. Wolf had tried to stop him and had gotten knocked down. It had been such an ugly scene that Uncle Fred had come over the next day for a little "heart to heart" session. Uncle Fred had been a professional boxer at one time in his youth. Wolf recalled that his father had never abused him or his mother again.

He looked over at his uncle's now twisted left arm.

A lot had changed.

Now it's my turn at bat, he thought.

After dumping the bucket into the sink and returning it to his designated spot on the rug, he looked at his mother.

"Which room is Jimmy's?" he asked.

***

GOLD BANQUET HOTEL AND CASINO
NEW SPENCERLAND, NORTH CAROLINA

Redfox and Spence were both smoking cigarettes, and his dad was puffing on one of those long, thin cigars he liked so much. Four shot glasses and a bottle of bourbon were on top of the big, empty desk. Pike, who was sitting in the outmost chair in the Redfox's office, was the only one not smoking. For a big, tough, raw-boned biker dude, this a bit out of character.

But who gives a shit? Spence thought.

"So," Pike continued, "like I was telling your son here, we got an extra heavy load coming up this time."

"How heavy?" Bob Sr. asked.

"Double what we usually bring," Pike said.

Their "usual" cargo back from Atlanta was two or three suitcases. This meant there would be six or seven this time. Each suitcase was usually a cool million. Spence watched the reactions of the other two. He'd already been briefed by Pike back at the plant.

Seven mill, he thought. Ours for the taking. Or

rather, mine.

He could barely contain himself as the visions of all that cash danced through his mind's eye. That meant $1,400,000.00 apiece if it were to be split maybe five ways. Spence was already excluding Sheridan from the equation.

Maybe giving GEM a bonus to eliminate the other three would be a viable option.

The big fucker would no doubt do it without compunction if the prospect of more money were dangled in front of him. But GEM could be somewhat difficult to control, especially with his recent propensity for the ice.

Spence continued to review the possibilities.

Was there a way to get rid of GEM, too?

He'd have to think about that. In any case, his priority would be switching the trucks and getting control of the suitcases. They all knew and agreed that they had to sit tight on the money for a while. He would give each of his toadies a bit of spending money, and then take off with the rest. Luckily, his dad had been grooming him to eventually take over the banking duties, so Spence knew how to channel the money drops into those offshore accounts. What the old man didn't know was that Spence had recently set up one just for himself.

Won't he be surprised when I don't show up for work one day, he thought. And call him from some island in the Caribbean somewhere.

He was smiling when he noticed the other three staring at him.

"Well?" his father said. "What about it? Everything set?"

Spence realized he'd allowed himself to drift right out of the conversation.

"Yeah," he said, drawing deeply on his cigarette. "Of course, it is."

He blew out the smoke.

Pike continued to stare at him now.

"What you smoking?" he asked, his tone half-serious.

Spence was a bit taken aback but covered his embarrassment with a laugh.

"Hey, we're ready as ever. We drive down make the drop, pick up the suitcases, drive it back, and then make the delivery here, via our armored car."

"And where's that at?" Pike asked. "I didn't see it in the center."

"It's parked in one of my lots," Bob Sr. said. "Inside the service center. The fewer people who see it, the better."

"Relax," Spence chimed in. "We'll have it at the plant by the time you get back."

"Right," Redfox said. "And we'll be standing by here to accept the shipment and do the laundry, just like always."

Spence could tell the Indian was half in the bag. He'd drained his glass once already and began pouring himself another.

"Anybody need a refill?" Redfox asked.

The others all shook their heads. It wasn't even dinner time yet.

"My boss just wants to emphasize that he doesn't want any slip-ups," Pike said. "This is a significant uptick in the game."

"We've got it covered," Bob Sr. said, smiling. "Don't we always?"

Pike said nothing. He still hadn't touched his drink.

All business, Spence thought. Let me see if I can loosen him up a bit.

"Did you say you were interested in that piece of Indian tail?" he asked.

Pike's eyebrows arched momentarily as he glanced over.

"Yeah," he said.

"Well," Spence said, "let's set that up then." His head rotated toward Redfox, who was sitting there with a snickering expression.

"What's that girl's name working the blackjack table?" Spence asked. "Tall, pretty, real good figure?"

"Crystal?" Redfox smirked as he shot a squinted glance at the big biker. "She the one you want?"

"She'll do," Pike said.

"Consider it done, then," Spence said. "Tonight,

after the fights."

Pike's smile was fractional.

"Appreciate it."

"Anything for Batton's main man," Spence said.

A happy biker-enforcer is a distracted biker-enforcer, he added mentally. And one that's less likely to notice our upcoming sleight of hand.

*****

SPENCER RECYCLING FACTORY
NEW SPENCERLAND, NORTH CAROLINA

Jimmy shifted the cigarette to the other side of his mouth and hit the button on the cell phone as they were approaching the back gate to the recycling center. When Craig answered, Jimmy told him they were there and to get ready to raise the overhead door. He pulled around to the frontage road that led to the eastern side of the facility. It had its own rear gate that provided a discreet entry and exit from that side of the massive building.

Mentally, he went over the plan once more. Tomorrow night he'd drive the loaded Rent-n-Haul truck in via the front gate and then hightail it around to the back of the building while GEM delayed Pike from driving right in and following. By the time the biker got around to the eastern side, the loading bay would be open, and this second truck will be in place with the dummy suitcases inside. Pike will assume that was the truck with the suitcases while Jimmy drove the real truck entirely around the building and back out the open front gate.

And then the decoy truck will get blown up.

Damn, there was a lot that could go wrong. What if Pike somehow notices this second truck before they took off tomorrow morning? It'll be concealed by that curtain, but still... Bobbie said he had everything figured out, and not to worry. It all sounded so plausible when they'd gone over it, time after time, but was it?

Just so everybody does his part right, Bobbie kept saying.

But what if somebody screws up?

The rain was falling with regularity now and the wipers were swooshing the water off with each swing. He hit the brakes and came to a stop in front of the seven-foot double set of gates.

"Go open 'em." He handed over the key to the big padlock that secured the front gate.

Willard groaned and made no move to accept it.

"Hey, man. It's raining."

"So?" Jimmy thrust the key at him again.

"How come I'm always the one that has to do the shit job?"

"Come on, move it. We got to get my bike out before I back it in, too."

"Yeah, yeah," Willard said, grabbing the key, wrenching up on the door handle, and shoving the passenger side door open. He jumped down and slammed the door hard.

"That's right," Jimmy shouted. "Break it. Then we'll really be in deep shit."

Willard shuffled toward the gate with an animated step.

Asshole, Jimmy thought. He edged through the gate as soon as Willard had shoved it open, then stopped so the high idiot could get back into the cab.

"Man, I'm got soaked." His tone sounded pathetic.

"Tough shit," Jimmy said. "And you're gonna get even more wet riding your bike home when we get done here."

Willard's face transformed with a simper.

"Hey, yeah, you're right." He giggled again.

Jimmy pulled forward and drove until he came to the second set of bay doors next to the one in which they'd parked the first Rent-n-Haul truck. He swung it around and stopped.

"Let's get my bike out of the back," he said, taking one last drag on his cigarette before stubbing it out on the window and tossing the butt to the ground.

Willard heaved a sigh and shoved the passenger side door open again.

Jimmy slipped the truck into PARK and slid out himself. Once again, he had to do most of the work pulling out the ramp because Willard was pretty much out of it.

"You're about as useful as tits on a boar hog," Jimmy said.

"Yeah." Willard chuckled. "I like tits."

"Well, you'd better get your shit straight by tomorrow night," Jimmy said. "Or else."

He saw Craig and GEM standing in the open bay watching them. Jimmy hopped up into the back and went to his motorcycle. The Yamaha lay on its side, having fallen over during the ride back.

Shit, he thought. I knew I should've secured it better.

Struggling, he managed to lift the bike up and for once was glad it was only a 500 cc instead of a big 1745 cc-sized engine like Pike's Road King Classic. He checked it over and everything seemed to be all right.

Say what you want about the Japs, he thought. But they build good bikes.

But it was still a rice-burner.

After jockeying it around a few times he got it facing the right way and straddled it so he could coast down the ramp. When he got to the bottom, stupid Willard jumped at him and yelled, "Boo!"

Jimmy reflexively backhanded him across the face.

"What you do that for?" Willard said.

Both GEM and Craig were laughing.

Jimmy walked his bike over to where the other three motorcycles were parked. He hoped Willard wouldn't crash on the way home, but that was his problem. And if he did, at this point they could probably get by without him. Plus, it would mean less of a split between the rest of them. At least the rain seemed to be ending. It had dissipated to a faint mist.

After returning to the truck, he shifted it back into gear and started backing it into the stall adjacent to the other truck.

"Come on back," Craig yelled, waving his arm in a circular motion. "You're good."

Jimmy kept backing the truck up until Craig held up his palm indicating that it was time to stop.

After shutting it off, he left the keys in it and jumped out. GEM was already pulling the huge, ceiling-to-floor canvas curtain. It would conceal this second truck when they pulled the first one out in the morning. They'd be leaving early, and Pike would most likely be staying out of the building with his chopper. But even if he did want to go inside to take a piss, or something, the curtain would do the job.

Hopefully.

But what if it didn't?

No, Jimmy thought. I can't go worrying about that. All I can do is my part and pray that the rest of it holds up.

"Hey," Willard yelled, giggling once again, the

backhand blow apparently forgotten. "Look over there. I see a fucking rainbow."

Jimmy glanced to the south and saw the band of bright colors ascending in an arch from the ground into the now clear blue sky.

Maybe it would bring them luck. They were going to need it.

"Okay, dickhead," GEM said. "I'm gonna hold your fucking head under the cold-water faucet till you sober up."

"Huh?" Willard said. "What for?"

"'Cause Craig and Jimmy got work to do, numb-nuts. Come on."

With that, GEM pulled Willard up the stairs that led to the interior of the building.

Jimmy glanced at Craig, who was already hobbling toward him with his uneven stride as he carried a large backpack.

"What's in that thing?" Jimmy asked.

"Don't ask," Craig said. "Help me load some of them canisters of propane over next to the truck."

Now Jimmy knew then why GEM had left the immediate area so fast. The big fucker was scared. Craig was going to set up the explosive charges now. There was no doubt he had all the C-4 shit that he'd bragged about stealing from the army in that backpack. The sweat started dripping from Jimmy's armpits again.

"Is that the explosive stuff?" he asked.

Craig just delivered a tight-lipped smile.

"Is it dangerous?" Jimmy asked.

"Dangerous enough that I don't want that fucking stoned idiot around. That's why I told GEM to take him outta here. Stupid shit's fucked up on something, ain't he?"

Meth, Jimmy thought. The high that keeps on giving.

"Hey, man," Jimmy said, thinking he didn't want to stick around either, "I need to go take a leak."

"This'll only take a couple of minutes," Craig said. "Now bring those canisters, would ya?"

Jimmy swallowed hard and grabbed a canister of propane in each hand. Craig directed him to place them on the ground near the underbelly of the decoy truck. He then walked to the short concrete staircase, transferred his cane to his right hand, gripped the iron banister, and started his descent. He held onto the iron hand-railing as he stepped down with a slow, practiced methodology: bad leg first, balance, then good leg placement on the step. He repeated the sequence on each one of the five stairs, and Jimmy wondered how it must feel to be missing a limb.

Damn, he was glad it wasn't him.

Or Steve, thank God, with all the deployments he'd had.

He momentarily wondered about his big brother and how he was doing. From the way he'd looked on

TV in that MMA fight, he was a super bad ass.

He must be doing great, Jimmy thought. Money, girls, new cars...

Craig made his way over to Jimmy and told him to hold up one of the canisters.

Jimmy did so and Craig removed a block of something covered with an oily skinned brown paper. There was writing along the top, but from Jimmy's viewpoint it was upside down. All he was able to distinguish before Craig ripped it off was *PROPERTY OF THE U.S. ARMY.*

Craig crinkled the brown paper into a ball and shoved it into his pocket. He then started kneading the block of the soft, waxy looking substance.

"That C-Four?" Jimmy asked, his voice barely above a whisper.

"Yep." Craig pressed the malleable compound around the upper part of the canister, as if he were crafting an art project out of modeling clay. "Go over and get that five-gallon jerrycan and bring it over here."

Jimmy saw the gas can sitting in the corner of the bay. He was glad to get away from the explosive, despite Craig's assurance. He grabbed the can, which was probably pretty close to full, and lugged it back to the side of the decoy truck. Craig began applying some of the C-4 to one side and then removed a roll of duct tape.

"Run a strand of tape around it," he said.

Jimmy felt his mouth go dry and his fingers fumbled as he tried to snag the severed end of the tape. His hands were sweating almost as much as his armpits, and he paused in his task to quickly wipe them on his pants.

Craig snorted a laugh.

"I told you not to worry," he said. "It ain't gonna go off till I tell it to."

Easy for you to say, Jimmy thought.

He stared down at Craig's gym shoes, knowing that inside the left one was an artificial foot, and wondered what that felt like.

Probably like nothing, he mentally joked. Cause there ain't nothing there.

He finally separated the strip of duct tape and pulled a section loose.

"That's good," Craig said. "Now wind it around like this." He rotated his hand around the top of the gas can. "We're gonna want to make this look like one of the propane or ammonium nitrate canisters blew up, but the gas will spread the fire real nice."

Jimmy wound the tape around the can, securing the gob of C-4.

"You see," Craig said, taking out two cell phones and holding one up in his right hand. "This baby is used as the remote control." He held up the phone in his left hand. "And this one sends the signal energizing the relay connected to the blasting cap. It's set on vibrate."

"Cell phones?" Jimmy's voice sounded reedy.

"They're perfect and convenient. They have just the right voltage and synchronization capabilities. And the vibration circuit can be addressed by phone number or function. Inside is a little, asymmetrical wheel that shakes. It's what causes the vibration feature." He popped one of the phones open and took out his knife. "You just remove the motor and connect the circuit to the blasting cap relay."

It all sounded like Greek to Jimmy.

Craig began fiddling around with more stuff and Jimmy closed his eyes. His gut was roiling, and he felt like taking off at a full speed run, and suddenly realized that if something did go wrong, with poor Craig's missing leg he couldn't get away very fast at all.

It only took a few more minutes. Then Craig said they were done.

"Good," Jimmy said. He wiped his palms on his thighs again. The underarms of his shirt were both sodden with huge half-moons of perspiration. "Let's go then."

As they stepped back Craig stood there admiring his work. He had the one master cell phone in his hand.

"Command detonation," he said, making a quick

gesture. "Just hit the button for the pre-dialed number and ka-blooie."

"Damn," Jimmy said. "Don't even play like that, okay?"

Craig laughed.

"Relax. It ain't gonna go off till I tell it to. Or at least not till Bobbie does."

And I'm glad I'm not gonna be here when that happens, Jimmy thought.

***

THE WOLF RESIDENCE
NEW SPENCERLAND, NORTH CAROLINA

Jimmy's room was a mess. His bed looked like it hadn't been made in a week. An ashtray full of cigarette butts and the remnants of a few hand-rolled joints were on the floor next to the bed. He didn't see anything that looked like a pipe, so hopefully that meant that the kid wasn't smoking anything really hard core. He'd seen drugs destroy a lot of people, but could he convince his brother of the danger? Reaching someone was both tricky and difficult, and being the disgraced soldier and ex-con, he couldn't exactly preach from the metaphorical high ground. And physical force wasn't the answer either. Beating the shit of him for messing up, and for being a disappointment to Ma, would most likely just alienate him further.

Jimmy needed someone to look up to, to show him the way. He needed a big brother more than ever now.

He checked the rest of the room, looking in dresser drawers, under the mattress, his guitar case, and in all the spots he'd seen his troops hide contraband. He'd seen some clever hiding places in Leavenworth, too.

Then he found something: a manila envelope stuffed into a slice in the mattress. Wolf pulled it out and saw it was folded, rather than sealed, and secured by three rubber-bands. It was block-like in shape and Wolf had the gut feeling it was cash. He undid the rubber-bands and opened it.

It was money, all right. Quite a bit. Mostly hundreds and fifties, he noted, as he fanned through it. He estimated it to be about six thousand. Not a bad little nest egg for a kid who worked at a recycling factory.

But what kind of work?

Wolf also wondered if he was paying Ma any room and board.

Probably not.

He considered counting a portion of it out and giving it to her, but then decided against doing that. If he were going to rebuild a relationship with his brother in order to try to talk some sense into him, it would be better to give him a bit of wiggle room. It was a substantial amount of cash, however, which meant that either the Spencers were paying him a real good wage, or he was dealing.

Maybe both.

This whole Spencerland set up was starting to stink.

As he shoved the money back into the envelope and reapplied the rubber-bands he heard what sounded like a motorcycle engine pulling into the driveway.

Jimmy maybe?

Wolf shoved the envelope back into the mattress and tucked the flap back in place.

As he was finishing, he heard the front door burst open and then Jimmy's excited voice.

"Why's the light on in my room? I know I didn't leave it on. Who's been in there?"

Wolf moved to just inside the doorway and waited.

Jimmy's voice sounded highly agitated. "You go in there?"

Wolf didn't know if he was speaking to their mother or Uncle Fred, but either way, he didn't like it. His younger brother needed to show some respect.

Swallowing his impulse to step out and grab his younger sibling by the scruff of the neck, Wolf instead moved to the door frame and said, "No, they didn't. I did."

Jimmy's jaw dropped and he stood there, mouth agape.

"Steve," he muttered. He remained frozen in place for several seconds, and then rushed forward and grabbed Wolf in an awkward bear-hug.

Once again, Wolf didn't relish the physical contact, but he endured it without comment or reciprocation.

His brother was blubbering now, asking a series of nonstop questions.

"How you been doing? When did you get here? Why didn't you call me and tell me you were coming?"

Wolf gently but firmly extricated himself from his brother's embrace. The kid's body odor was pungent, and he looked bad. He'd gained weight and a cigarette dangled from his mouth. His black hair had that long, unkempt look. He sure wasn't the bright-eyed kid that Wolf remembered.

"Hey," Wolf said. "Take it easy, will you? I haven't been squeezed that hard since my last MMA fight."

Jimmy pushed himself back.

"Yeah," he said. "I seen that one on TV. You really kicked that fucker's ass."

Wolf felt like telling him to watch his language but stopped short. It was just like training the green recruits in the army. They used profanity and bravado to try and project maturity and masculinity. It was usually a washout on both fronts. Jimmy wasn't that much different.

But still, Wolf thought, I am his big brother.

He gripped Jimmy's shoulder.

"Watch your language in front of Ma," he said.

Jimmy looked perplexed, then winced. "Come on,

Steve. You're hurting my arm."

Wolf hadn't realized he'd been squeezing so hard, but maybe that was a good thing.

"Your language," he said.

"Huh?" Jimmy said. "Oh, yeah. Sorry, Ma. Didn't mean nothing. Just sorta slipped out."

Wolf took this as a positive sign and released him. Maybe he'd be able to reach the kid after all.

Their mother just nodded, the sad look never leaving her eyes.

"I got to get supper on," she said. "You're staying, aren't you, Steve?"

"Wouldn't miss it," he said, smiling. "I've been dreaming about eating some of your cooking all day."

The lines in her face crinkled with a smile and she moved toward the small kitchen.

Wolf thought about his bank account. It had grown pretty fat with his MMA winnings and the money that he'd gotten in a payoff from Von Dien. Maybe he could use some of it to buy his mother a new place. And a new truck, one with an automatic transmission, for Uncle Fred.

"Hey," Jimmy said, shaking another cigarette out of his pack and sticking it between his lips. "I got an idea. Why don't you come with me the fights tonight?"

"The fights?" Wolf asked.

"Yeah." Jimmy flicked on a disposable lighter and held the flame to the end of the smoke. "Some local

MMA stuff. Nothing big, like what yours is, but it's still pretty cool. I got a buddy who's fighting tonight. My friends will all be there. I want to introduce you to everybody."

Wolf glanced askance at his mother and saw her wince a tiny bit at the word "friends".

The last thing that Wolf wanted to do was to watch a bunch of amateurs going at it. But on the other hand, it would also afford him a closer look at the group Jimmy was associating with and maybe get an idea as to what they were into. Plus, it might be a way to bond with him.

He felt it was a first step, but knew any bonding wasn't going to be easy.

***

THE ORLEANS HOTEL AND CASINO
LAS VEGAS, NEVADA

After checking into an adjoining, three-room-suite, Bray told the two of them to go down to the food court and grab lunch.

"It's already past lunch," Powers grumbled. "And I'm starving. All I had all day was them stupid pastries. They didn't even give us pretzels on the plane."

"Make it an early dinner then," Bray said. "We're here to work, remember?"

"You gonna be joining us?" Maureen asked. She gave him a quick wink. "Or do you want me to pick something up for you?"

Bray replied with a fractional smirk and saw that her double entendre had gone completely over Powers' head, which was good.

"I'll be down in a minute," he said, giving her a quick up and down glance. He was looking forward to being with her later. "I got to make a call first."

After they left, Bray sat down on the comfortable bed, pulled out the burner phone, and sent a quick text.

You available for a call?

Less than a minute later, the phone rang, and Bray answered it.

"Just finished with the old man," Abraham said.

"You mentioned some security video?"

"Yeah. That guy Von Dien had cameras set up all around the place. One of them picked up two males with one of them holding something that looks like a damn bazooka. He fires it and leaves a trail of white smoke in the air."

That sort of fit with what one of the Guatemalans had told Bray.

"Bazookas haven't been used since the Korean War," he said. "Must have been something else. A LAW maybe?"

"Whatever," Abraham said. "Anyway, the old man's

convinced that those two shot the helicopter down. He's upped the ante. Wants them found and surveilled until he can get a specialist out there. Got it?"

A specialist?

Bray took this to mean an assassin. Knowing the Don's penchant for overkill, he might even be sending a whole hit team.

"You there?" Abraham asked.

"Yeah," Bray said. "We're working on it."

"Well, work faster. He's already reached out to some major league players."

Players...

That had the sound of more than one. This was just what Bray had been worried about. The old Don was hell-bent of revenge now and determined to carry out his devil's vendetta to the hilt. With Bray being on record as talking to the FBI, if and when McNamara and Wolf turned up dead, both he and Abraham would be tied into the investigation. Especially if it was some gruesome, mob-style revenge-like hit.

"Look," he said. "We're going to need to separate ourselves. Get some insulation on this."

"We'll have to deal with that later," the lawyer said. "Like I told you, these aren't the kind of people you say no to. Find them. They want results."

With that, Abraham terminated the call.

Bray sat there for the better part of a minute thinking it through and considering his options.

They want results.

Yeah, he thought. And what I want is a few degrees of separation.

CHAPTER 9

THE OLD NEW LUMBERTON MALL
NEW SPENCERLAND, NORTH CAROLINA

The long-awaited family reunion dinner hadn't gone
as well as Wolf had hoped, nor was it what he expected. Although Jimmy had changed out of his sweaty
clothes, washed his hands, and combed his hair, he
still looked and smelled bad. Other than that, he was
positively garrulous at dinner, constantly asking Wolf
about what it was like being a professional fighter, as
well as a modern-day bounty hunter. The questions
all had a materialistic base, regarding how much
money could be made. Now they were approaching
the New Lumberton Mall Wolf replayed part of the
troubling conversation in his head.

"Maybe I'll be a bounty hunter, too," Jimmy said.

"Bail bondsmen are illegal in North Carolina,"

Wolf said. "Hence, no bounty hunters."

"Shit," Jimmy said. "I ain't gonna be staying around here much more."

Their mother's eyes caught Wolf's and a silent communication virtually passed between them.

I hope you can talk some sense into him, she seemed to say.

Wolf had given a minute nod.

"Maybe I'll go back with you," Jimmy said. "I ain't got nothing holding me here."

Wolf glanced over at their mother and saw her wince. The kid needed some tact. And manners.

"I wouldn't exactly say that," Wolf said. "This is our home. Always will be. I've missed it."

Jimmy shoveled some peas into his mouth and spoke as he was masticating his food.

"What's there to miss? The whole place stinks."

Wolf held his tongue, but he felt like reaching over and smacking him. His blatant disregard for the feelings of their mother and uncle was like someone jabbing a baseball bat into Wolf's stomach. How had his brother become such a jerk?

I've been away too long, he reminded himself.

He'd missed crucial years at the end of his little brother's adolescence.

When Uncle Fred had commented that Jimmy needed to find a good career, something solid, like being a plumber or electrician, the kid had scoffed.

"That's for chumps," he said.

"It's a decent way to make a living," his uncle retorted. "You might want to think about that. You may be supporting a family one of these days."

Jimmy's face scrunched up in a scowl.

"Shut up, old man. You don't tell me what to do."

That disrespectful outburst brought an instant rebuke from their mother, and when Jimmy glared at her with angry eyes, Wolf couldn't help but intercede this time.

"She's right," he said. "Now quit acting like a spoiled brat, or I'll—"

Wolf didn't finish the sentence. Getting into a family argument was the last thing he wanted. The kid's gaze swiveled to Wolf, and he saw the flash of anger and hurt.

Sighing, Wolf shook his head and looked down at his plate.

Everything I do seems to make it worse, he thought.

Jimmy said nothing for several seconds and then continued to consume the rest of his food.

"Pretty soon," he said between chews, "I'm gonna have all the money I need, and I'll be outta here."

Exchanging another quick glance with his mother, Wolf wondered what this last statement meant. He recalled the stash that he'd found in the kid's mattress. Was that what he meant by all the money he'd need? If so, he needed a reality check. But that was dependent on him developing a realistic outlook. To Jimmy's way of thinking, his stash might seem like a lot of money, when it actually wasn't.

Perception was reality.

Still, he was determined to try and straighten things out, but remained at a loss as to how to do that. Her silent gaze spoke to him again.

Now is not the time.

No, he thought. It isn't. I have to build some kind of bridge here in order to reach him.

Or at least try.

So when the rest of the meal continued in silence, Wolf finally broke it by asking Jimmy about the fights he'd talked about.

The inquiry seemed to renew him, and he began talking about the event.

"Like I said, it ain't nothing like what you do, Steve. But it's pretty damn entertaining. And my buddy GEM's the main event. He's one bad dude."

"GEM?" Wolf asked.

"George Earl Mess. We call him GEM. Don't know if you remember him, or not. He's my age. And Bobbie Spencer will be there, too. His dad's the mayor now."

"I know," Wolf said.

So agreeing to drive there in Wolf's rental was easy. Jimmy said he'd already gotten soaked on his motorcycle and there was the possibility of more rain. In the car Jimmy continued his garrulous conversation, bragging about his friends and how cool they were as the familiar sight of the mall's dilapidated sign came into view. Surprisingly, the orange and red neon lights surrounding the image of the man with the top hat and cane were illuminated.

"This is it," Jimmy said, taking out another cigarette.

"Isn't this place been closed down?" Wolf asked. "The sign's still lit up."

Jimmy laughed and lit up the smoke.

"Yeah, it is. Been closed down for about two years. But the stupid shits just boarded it up and left everything in place, even the fucking generators. All you got to do is go into the old facility engineer room and flip the big circuit breakers and the power comes back on."

"Sounds like you've got some experience doing that."

His brother chuckled and blew out a cloudy breath. "Yeah. Me and my friends been kinda running these fights every week or so. Me and Bobbie. He takes a percentage of the gate and the drinks and the bets and we kinda split it."

Kinda split it. Meaning that the rich kid probably took most of it.

"The fighters do all right, too," Jimmy continued. "They both get paid something, but the guy that wins gets the most."

"How long you been holding these things here?"

Jimmy shrugged and took another drag. "A couple of months. They were supposed to start tearing it down one of these days, but Bobbie got his dad to put a hold on that."

"Must be nice to be the mayor's son."

Jimmy snorted. "You know it, but he treats us right, though."

Wolf thought that sounded like a load of horse shit. It was more like a rich kid calling the shots with a bunch of not-so-rich friends to do the grunt work and be left holding the bag should something go wrong—a formula for making sure Spencer Jr. had all his patsies all lined up to take the fall.

"Before they were talking about maybe building the casino on this property," Jimmy said. "But they decided not to."

"We've never had an official reservation," Wolf said. "How'd they get it approved to be an Indian casino?"

"Bobbie's dad. He's not only the mayor, but he's in the state legislature, too. Got some kind of off-rez approval, or something. Anyway, it's raking in the big bucks."

Wolf turned onto the closest mall entrance drive and saw a string of other cars proceeding around the outer ring road. The old X-shaped main structure looked dark from this angle. Wolf remembered that it was composed of four big anchor stores, major retail chains, which were all connected by a large interior court with lots of smaller shops.

"The other side's where we got to go," Jimmy said. "This side's all boarded up."

Wolf wondered what the inside of the place was going to look like now. Memories of his youth, growing up and hanging out here flashed in his memory.

The opposite side of the mall had quite a few cars in the lot. The large main mall doors on this side had light spilling out from an open space. Wolf drove around and finally caught a parking spot farther away. He shifted into PARK and debated whether or not this might be a good time to try and start a meaningful conversation with his brother.

"So who are these friends of yours I'm going to meet?"

"I told you, Bobbie Spencer—Don't call him that. He hates it. GEM—He's the one fighting. Craig Langford, the police chief's son. He's a veteran like you. Lost a leg over there, so don't say nothing about that neither. And Willard Gibbons."

Jimmy unbuckled his seatbelt and opened the door.

"Ready? I can't wait to introduce my big brother, the real champ, to everybody. They're gonna shit."

Before Wolf could reply, his cell phone chimed, and he looked at the screen.

Mac.

"I got to take this," he said. "Business."

Jimmy's grin faded. "But we need to get in there now."

"You go ahead. I'll catch up." Wolf pressed the button and raised it to his ear. "Twice in one day. I feel flattered."

McNamara laughed. "You should. So how's the family reunion going?"

"Could be better," Wolf said, and told him to hold on. He looked at his brother who was still frozen in the passenger seat. "Go on ahead, Jim. I'll meet you inside. Where will you be?"

"Center court. Where that old shoe store used to be. That's where the fighters warm up."

Wolf watched Jimmy slide out of the car.

"See you inside then." His brother started walking toward the mall. "Tell the guy selling the tickets at the door that you're with me. Call me on my cell if you have any problems, okay?"

Wolf watched the kid go and reflected on how difficult it was to be to try and reach him. He wondered more about the possibility of a drug problem.

Maybe he's already lost, Wolf thought.

"Anybody home?" McNamara's voice said on the phone.

"Yeah. I'm out with my little brother. Just waiting for him to walk away."

"Oh. How's that going?"

"Slow."

McNamara was silent for a few seconds, then said, "You convince him enlist yet?"

Wolf emitted a short laugh.

"I'm not sure if that's in the cards. He's pretty undisciplined. I'm worried he might have a substance abuse problem."

"Aw, hell." McNamara was silent for a time, then added, "You need me to come out there?"

Wolf considered it. He'd always valued Mac's friendship and support, but Jimmy hardly knew the man. "Thanks, but this is something I have to handle alone."

"Well, I'm sure you'll figure something out. You always do."

Wolf said nothing. The truth was, he wasn't so sure.

"How are things down in your neck of the woods?" Wolf asked, hoping to change the subject.

"Crazy. Ron's flying the helicopter as best he can, but them cartel fuckers have a fifty-caliber set up on their side. So far, all they been doing is taunting us with it, but…"

"That sounds like a war zone."

"It is. Anyway, I need to talk to you. Something came up. Reno called me. We got somebody dogging us."

"I know. He called me too. Said some guy came by the gym asking questions. Reno said he pulled the

CRS routine."

"That ain't all. Kase says that somebody, maybe the same guy, came by the Bureau office asking about Mexico and Belize. Bill talked to him."

Bill... Wolf couldn't help but grin.

It was good to know that Mac was now on a nickname basis with his new son-in-law.

"What did your favorite son-in-law have to say?"

McNamara snorted. "Favorite son-in-law."

Wolf heard him sigh.

"Well, she could've done worse, that's for sure. And he said he didn't give the guy shit due to it being an active investigation."

"I'd still like to know what this is all about," Wolf said.

"Me too. That's where Reno came in pretty handy, and things started to come together a little bit. He got the plate on the guy's car and had his brother run it. Came back to a rental agency, and the guy who rented it works for Bray Investigative Services."

"Out of New York," Wolf said.

"You heard of 'em?"

"No. Reno told me."

"Oh, okay. I'm preaching to the choir then."

"Not really. It's too soon to be worried," Wolf said. "But we probably need to keep our guard up."

"Yep. I'm going to call Miss Dolly and warn her. I've got most of Best in the West down here with me, but I'll call Pete Thornton, too."

"Sounds like a plan," Wolf said.

More cars were filling up the parking lot.

"Look, Mac, I gotta go. My brother's hanging out with some real idiots around here."

"The marines are always looking for a few good men. Maybe you could convince them all to enlist and let some big DI straighten their sorry asses out."

"Maybe," Wolf said. The report of a fifty-caliber troubled him. "You stay safe down there, okay?"

"Will do." McNamara chuckled. "Wouldn't do to mess up Reno's Hummer. Did I tell you he loaned it to me?"

"Yeah."

McNamara sighed. "Damn, I didn't used to repeat myself so much. Guess I'm getting old."

"Nah," Wolf said, trying to think of a quick way to bolster his friend's sagging ego. "You're getting better. Just ask Miss Dolly and Brenda."

That elicited a chuckle from Mac, and they terminated the call.

Wolf slipped the phone into his pocket and followed the trail of people walking toward the open entrance doors of the abandoned mall. The reports of someone asking questions about him and Mac on their trips south of the border were troubling, but maybe it was a legitimate insurance investigation. They'd all covered their tracks well, and even the FBI seemed to be on their side now.

He caught the distinctive odor of marijuana as he walked by a girl and a guy passing a joint back and forth. The girl giggled.

I'll have to put this new development on hold until I get more information, Wolf thought.

In the meantime, it was all he could do to figure out what to do about his brother.

There were a bunch of motorcycles lined up on the sidewalk adjacent to the entrance. A yellow Corvette was parked there, too. No Cadillac convertible, though.

Maybe the mayor's not a fight fan, Wolf conjectured.

The crowd narrowed, separating into a double line, and slowed substantially as it got closer to the opening. Wolf joined the procession. As he got closer to the entrance he saw a hand-printed sign on a poster board saying, *FIGHT NIGHT. ADMISSION $20.*

At this point Wolf decided not to drop Jimmy's name to try to get in for free. The cloak of anonymity might serve him better. He took a twenty out of his wallet and paid his way. The crowd widened again and fanned out into the once-familiar mall corridor. At one time it had held a superb selection of stores and shops, but now the interior was a mishmash of boarded up windows and doors. Those that weren't covered up had large, flat sections of crushed and broken plywood lying beneath shattered panels of plate glass. The debris had been swept into numerous piles, which left the main walk-way unobstructed. The mall had two levels and from what he could see of the upper section, it appeared to be a mirror image of the first floor. There were large planters in the center of the aisle, which had once held a variety of plants. Now these two-foot brick barriers held nothing but desiccated vegetable matter, the long dead tendrils curled and yellowed in a vain for search for sustenance. Wolf looked up as the crowd neared the large center court area. The skylight above it, from what he could tell, seemed to be intact. Throngs of people were crowded around the upper-level banister and more lined the double sets of escalators, which apparently weren't activated. Cyclone fencing forming a black, cage-like octagon which had been set up in the middle of the center court on top of a three-foot high platform. A large, blue mat had been spread out beneath the cage. Off to the side a couple of shirtless men danced around in circles shadow boxing.

At least they won't be going down hard on the solid floor, Wolf thought.

His memory took him back to his youth when the mall publicized that genuine Italian marble had been imported to be laid out as the flooring of the new mall. Now several makeshift bars, consisting of more stripped plywood placed upon wooden sawhorses, had cans of beer and soft drinks sitting on their flat surfaces. Numerous coolers were in place and several men seemed to be acting as bartenders, handing out drinks in exchange for money. A third makeshift table had been set up with a chalk board behind it. Five sets of names were listed in successive order. The fighters, no doubt. Two men standing behind it were accepting cash and apparently taking bets. Other men, all wearing black sweatshirts with *SECURITY* labeled across the front of them, stood by, and each wore a holstered sidearm. Wolf recognized one of them as Glen Cook, the cop he'd seen earlier.

Cook jerked his head in fractional acknowledgement.

Wolf did the same and glanced around a bit more. He didn't see any open drug usage, other than a few people smoking pot.

The cacophony of several hundred discordant voices, all cackling and laughing and shouting, drowned out any semblance of coherence, and it was virtually impossible to distinguish a conversation more than ten feet or so away. Wolf scanned the crowd for Jimmy and then saw him standing next to a group of people. The six of them were all talking and seemed to know each other.

Jimmy's so-called friends…

Wolf assessed the group as he made his way toward them. Jimmy was laughing, with a cigarette bobbling between his lips and a beer in his hand. He took what looked like one final swig and tossed the can at an overstuffed trash container. It hit the side and bounced away. Next to him were two guys about his age, one maybe a few years older. They both had long hair and a less than pristine appearance. The leaner of the two had a cane, and Wolf immediately ascertained from the man's slight shifting movements that he was wearing a prosthesis on his lower left leg.

That must be the police chief's son, Wolf surmised.

The fellow next to him was shorter, fatter, and had a dumb, vacuous expression, looking like he'd fallen off a garbage truck. Or maybe he'd just been rolling around in one.

Two of the others were good sized individuals, one of whom had his long, blond hair bound back in a ponytail-like braid. He was wearing a Levi jacket that had motorcycle gang colors written all over it. His black T-shirt was tight across his large chest which harbored a gold skull and crossbones medallion in the center like a Superman emblem. His arms looked tan and very well-muscled. The other big guy wore a hooded sweatshirt and blue jeans. A dollop of fat bulged over the man's beltline, and he had on expensive looking gym shoes. His hair was close-cropped in a buzz-cut style.

The last of the six was shorter, with a block-like physique. His dark hair was combed in a pompadour style, and the clothes he had on spoke of money. He wore high quality sweats that looked like they'd been hand-tailored by Neiman Marcus. As his head lolled back in laughter it somehow became apparent to Wolf just who this last individual was.

Bob, don't call him Bobbie, Spencer, Jr.

Jimmy's head turned as he took a swig of beer and caught sight of his brother. A grin spread over his face, and he worked his way toward Wolf, pushing people out of his way.

"Hey, Steve, over here," Jimmy called out.

Wolf made his way over to him.

"Want a beer?" Jimmy asked, steering him toward one of the makeshift bar tables.

Wolf actually hadn't had a drink of any kind of alcohol in quite some time. It was anathema when he was training for a fight, and he also had come to dislike the feeling of lacking control and not always being at his best.

"Just a soda will be fine," he said.

Jimmy's expression told him that his little brother was surprised, but he motioned to one of the attendants next to the cooler and pointed to a soft drink can.

"That'll be six bucks," the attendant said.

"Hey," Jimmy shot back. "Screw you. Don't you know who I am? I don't gotta pay for nothing."

The man's eyes narrowed.

"Here," a booming voice said, "I'm buying for them."

Wolf saw that it was the good-sized biker dude who'd been talking with Jimmy and the group. The big man plopped a twenty onto the plywood counter and added, "Keep the change and give me another beer."

"Pike," Jimmy said. "You don't gotta do that. We ain't supposed to pay here 'cause we're with Bobbie, and he's running this."

Pike clapped him on the shoulder and winked.

"We're here to have a good time," he said. "And to watch the other guys fight, not do it ourselves." He accepted the three cans from the barkeep, handed one to Jimmy, and did a double take when he saw the non-alcoholic brand. Raising an eyebrow, Pike handed that one to Wolf.

"An airborne trooper that don't drink?" Pike said. "That's gotta be a first."

Wolf accepted the can and was certain he'd never met the guy before.

How the hell did he know I was airborne? Wolf wondered, and then realized that Pike must have caught sight of the jump wings tattoo on Wolf's right forearm—A remnant of his time at Fort Benning, right after completing jump school.

"Not tonight," he said.

"Pike," Jimmy said, "this is my big brother, Steve.

He's here visiting."

Pike's cheek twitched slightly as he offered an open palm.

Wolf shook it and felt the man's strong, calloused grip.

"You're *that* Steve Wolf?" Pike asked.

That Steve Wolf?

He popped the tab on the can and felt the mixed spray of liquid and CO_2 gas caress his hand then took a sip, not so much because he was thirsty, but more so to give himself a momentary respite.

How in the hell did this guy know so much about him?

"Yeah, he's *that* one," Jimmy said. "You heard of him, huh?"

"The light-heavyweight MMA U.S. champ," Pike added. "Who hasn't?"

Wolf smirked in a self-effacing sort of way. "A lot of people, I'd imagine."

"And an ex-ranger, too," Pike said. "Got the Silver Star, too, didn't you?"

My military record? Wolf thought. How does this guy know about that?

"I don't think I caught your name."

"Pike. Lucien Pike. Out of Atlanta."

Atlanta. That was where Jimmy was going tomorrow.

"Come on over here and meet the rest of the guys,"

Jimmy said, tugging on Wolf's arm. His brother took a quick pull on his cigarette and then drank some more beer.

As they pushed their way through the crowd Wolf was cognizant of how hot and stuffy it was in the old mall. If the air-conditioning units were still in working order, they weren't doing a very good job. Jimmy was pushing his way along. Wolf and Pike followed, walking side-by-side.

"I heard you lived out West," Pike said. "Phoenix, or someplace?"

"Vegas at the moment." Wolf took another tiny sip. He wasn't liking it that this guy, whom he'd just met, seemed to know so much about him. "How'd you know that?"

It was Pike's turn to imbibe, and he tossed down a copious amount of beer from the can. As the big man moved, Wolf caught a glimpse of the butt of a pistol in a shoulder holster on the man's left side.

"Your little brother," Pike answered after emitting a loud and extended belch. "Talks about you all the time. Say's you're some kind of bounty hunter, too."

Wolf neither confirmed nor denied that one.

Jimmy was several feet ahead of them now, waving his arm in a circular, come hither, gesture. The other four members of his spectacular network of friends stood there grinning.

"Steve," he said, "I want you to meet everybody.

This is Willard and Craig." He pointed to the dopey-looking guy and the one with the cane and prosthesis. "Craig was in the army, too."

Wolf nodded in acknowledgement.

"Always glad to meet a fellow vet," he said. "Army or marines?"

"Marines?" Langford laughed. "Not hardly. I was one of the smart ones. Or at least the army told me so."

"What was your MOS?"

"Twelve bravo," Langford said. "Combat engineers."

"Thank you for your service." He offered his hand to Langford.

Langford's smile turned into a frown. "Duty, honor, country, and all that bullshit." He shifted the cane to his left hand and shook Wolf's hand with an obvious reluctance. "It was too late by the time I realized that pursuing the thanks of a grateful nation was for losers."

A bitter man, Wolf thought, then shot a fast glance at the man's lower leg. But then again, looks like he's got a right to be.

Once again, his memory shifted to the many disabled vets he'd seen, including Spec 4 Martinez, his own squad member who'd lost a leg from the IED blast on Wolf's last ill-fated mission.

"And this is George Earl Mess," Jimmy said. "Otherwise known as GEM. He's fighting in the main event tonight."

The huge man with the buzz-cut merely stared at Wolf, not offering anything in the way of a greeting.

"Don't mess with Mess," Willard said, his face already cast with a drunken looking stupor.

"And last, but not least, Bob Spencer," Jimmy said, finishing the introductions.

"Ah, the mayor's son," Wolf said, extending his hand again.

Spencer Jr. accepted it and flashed a grin that looked about as sincere as a used car salesman's promise.

"Glad you could make it," Spencer said. "Welcome to fight night at the mall."

His hand felt as limp as a dead fish.

"Jimmy's always talking about you," he said. "Says you're a fighter as well."

"Right," Wolf said.

"Why he's the United States light-heavyweight champ," Jimmy said. "And pretty soon he'll be world champion, He can beat anybody here, with one hand tied behind his back."

GEM snorted derisively.

"Don't look so bad to me," he muttered.

Wolf caught a whiff of the man's very noticeable body odor. Even in this enclosed crowded area, where a mixture of all sorts of smells mingled with the pervasive scent of incipient decay, GEM's stench was pungently obvious.

Maybe he's going to use the funk to knock his opponent out, Wolf thought. Instead of his fists.

He'd actually fought some opponents who used their own foul smelling sweat as a secondary weapon. It was called an "in your face" offense. Wolf recalled Reno telling him a story about a boxer in the forties called Tony "Two Ton" Galento, whose legendary intentional lack of personal hygiene was purportedly known to distract his opponents and place them at a disadvantage. Even the great Joe Louis had complained about it when the two fought for Louis's title. Now, Wolf could relate most vividly.

"Hey," GEM grunted, "you hear what I said."

The man's tone was gruff, confrontational.

This bad boy was trying to pick a fight, all right.

Wolf was neither intimidated nor in the mood to be ameliorating. Still, the big idiot was one of Jimmy's friends.

"I didn't hear your question," Wolf said

The man's mouth drew into a tight line.

"I said, you don't look so bad to me."

Wolf stared back at him. It was a no-win situation. Just like in the prison yard. He offered nothing in the way of provocation except a steady and unfazed stare. Unlike this oaf, Wolf wasn't here to fight. Plus, he had Jimmy's welfare to consider. There was also something vaguely disturbing about the guy's eyes. They looked odd and unfocused, with the irises jerking with rhythmic persistence, the pupils heavily dilated.

This guy was on something.

"Hey, GEM. That's my brother, man. Leave him alone, will ya?"

The large, buzz-cut head rotated toward Jimmy. It was like a gallon bucket on a barrel.

"I'm talking to him, not you." He took in a deep breath, inflating his chest, which was massive. "Somebody gets smart with me, I tear off their head and shit down their neck."

Wolf certainly didn't want his younger brother to mix it up with this monster.

"Jimmy," he said, "back off."

"Yeah, *Jimmy*," GEM said, intentionally distorting his voice to imitate a higher pitch, "back off."

Wolf stepped forward to pull his brother back. GEM apparently took this as an act of aggression and raised his arms, his fists clenched.

"You wanna mix it up with me?"

Wolf stopped. "Not really. But if that's the way you want it…"

GEM licked his lips. "You better be careful what you say to me." His tone was emboldened, but a bit uncertain.

Having had his fill of this knucklehead's belligerence, Wolf returned the man's dead-on stare.

He imagined punching through the big man's head, feeling the jaw give under the pressure of the blow.

"Hey," somebody in the crowd yelled. "Sounds like GEM's gonna fuck somebody up before the fights even start."

A wave of hyena-like laughter rippled through the crowd.

Suddenly a chant started circulating: "Don't mess with Mess."

The rhythmic chanting seemed to spur GEM on further. "I'll rip off your head and shit down your neck."

"Aw, you need a different line," Pike said. "That one's as old as the shit in your teeth."

GEM's head rotated toward him. "Stay outta this, Pike." He looked back to Wolf.

"Hey, GEM," Bob Spencer said. "Cool it, will ya. Your chance to fight's coming up later."

"I don't like smart assholes," GEM said, turning to glance at the other man. "And like I said, this guy don't look so bad to me. I can take him."

"Looks can be deceiving," Wolf said, feeling an irritation creeping into his voice. Wolf's tolerance had reached the tipping point. The last thing he wanted was to get into a no-win confrontation in this snake pit. But he also knew, from his time in Leavenworth, that to show fear or weakness would be fatal. "So follow your friend's advice and save it for the ring."

"Sounds to me like you're pretty scared," GEM said.

"Don't mess with Mess." The repetitive chant was spreading now, growing in intensity. This one was going south in a hurry. Wolf knew he was in the middle of some very unfriendly territory. If push came to shove, it would be better to hit and move, but how far could he get with this hostile crowd closing in around him.

Wolf flashed a smile. He was almost back in the prison yard now. The line had been drawn in the sand.

"That shows how little you know," he said.

GEM stepped forward, puffing out his chest even more.

"Listen, Injun boy, mess with me and I'll tear off your head and shit down your neck, asshole."

It was the '*Injun boy*' that did it. This guy was going down now.

"You're repeating yourself," Wolf said. "Now back off."

"Or what?"

GEM lurched forward but Jimmy jumped between them.

"Hey, GEM, no. He's my brother."

GEM pushed Jimmy out of the way and snarled, "I don't give a shit."

The force of the shove sent Jimmy on awkward

goose-steps backwards. He tried to maintain his balance but fell onto his butt about ten feet away.

"Hey," Spencer yelled. "Knock it off. We got too much going on tomorrow."

The command didn't seem to affect the enraged giant, who continued to saunter forward.

Wolf moved back and raised his hands, clenching his own fists now. The crowd parted behind him, giving these two would-be combatants plenty of room.

"Don't mess with Mess."

The ridiculous chant continued to echo in the enclosed structure, growing in volume and intensity.

"Don't mess with Mess."

Here we go, Wolf thought.

Going to battle, especially in a street fight, wasn't something he relished, but after seeing the company his little brother was keeping, Wolf was now actually kind of looking forward to knocking the shit out of somebody.

"DON'T MESS WITH MESS."

"DON'T MESS WITH MESS."

The crowd's repetitive refrain seemed to ignite the odiferous monster to critical mass. "I'm gonna rip your head off—"

"You gonna talk or fight, asshole?" Wolf said, assuming a triangular fighting stance on the balls of his feet.

"GEM. God dammit," Spencer yelled again. "I told

you, knock it off."

It was obvious that GEM had a weight advantage of at least sixty pounds and from the look of him, one punch wasn't going to do it. Not with the chemical junk that was flowing in his veins.

"You forgetting the plan?" Spencer seemed almost frantic now. "Knock it off, dammit."

GEM turned toward him and snarled, "Fuck that. I'm gonna—"

Jimmy jumped forward again and collided with the bigger man's body. It was like a bug hitting a semi's windshield.

"Jimmy," Wolf called out. "No. Stay out of it."

GEM shoved the smaller man away again and started toward Wolf.

The sudden explosion of the gunshot ripping through the air sounded like a peal of unexpected thunder, snapping everyone into silence.

GEM stopped in his tracks, shaking his head, like he'd been tagged by a vicious left hook.

The odor of burned gunpowder hung in the air, mingling with the plethora of the other unpleasant odors. Lucien Pike stepped forward, a huge stainless-steel revolver with a long, six-inch vented-rib barrel in his right hand. A wisp of smoke rose from the end of the muzzle. He'd apparently fired it into one of the vacant planter boxes. Luckily, they still had dirt in them. The gunshot had reverberated inside the domed structure with such a concussive roar that it had silenced the myriad of ongoing voices, including the irritating chant.

"You heard the man, Mess," Pike said. "We got important things to do tomorrow." He grinned and added, "Besides, I'm here to see the octagon fights, and I even bet some money on you."

GEM's mouth tugged up at the corners into something resembling half a smile, but then he frowned again.

Wolf detected a bit of relief mixed in with the truculent scowl. He'd seen that type of bluster many times. It was a covering for fear. GEM was essentially a bully, and a coward at heart. Faced against somebody pretty much his own size and he'd fold up like a worn-out lawn chair.

"All right," Spencer said, his voice now coming across strident and amplified by use of a megaphone. "Now that we've got the prelim hype over with, the betting table is now closed, and it's time to get on with tonight's official festivities."

The immediate group of people standing around them dissipated, and the two half-naked men who'd been shadow boxing outside the cage walked inside. A third man dressed in a blue shirt with large sweat stains under the arms followed.

Wolf looked at Pike. "Thanks."

"No sweat." The biker smirked. "If I would've heard

that son of a bitch say that shit-down-your-neck line one more time, I'da beat his ass myself."

Wolf grinned.

"And like I told you," Pike said, "I got some money bet on that stupid lard ass, and it wouldn't do to have you lay him out before his fight. You might've hurt him."

"I would've done my very best."

Pike winked at him and said, "There's no doubt in my military mind about that." He jammed the big revolver back into its leather harness and snapped the securing strap. After giving the weapon a double pat, he then lifted the left sleeve of his T-shirt exposing a well-developed deltoid muscle with a tattoo of a black, screaming eagle's head on it. *101ST AIRBORNE* was lettered underneath it. "Besides, us airborne troopers have to stick together, right?"

All the way, Wolf thought, but he was beginning to wonder even more about this man.

CHAPTER 10

PARKING LOT

GOLD BANQUET HOTEL AND CASINO

NEW SPENCERLAND, NORTH CAROLINA

As Wolf pulled into the casino parking lot, he felt overwhelmed by frustration as he replayed the rather disastrous evening in his mind's eye. The fights, if you could call them that, had been very unimpressive and mercifully quick. With the exception of the first one, where the two lightweight opponents had danced around throwing ineffective punches and kicks, mostly not connecting, the matches had been short and brutal. After the restless crowd began showering the first two fighters with empty, crushed beer cans, the referee in the blue shirt had told them they'd better start fighting if they expected to get paid. After that, they tore into each other, and both emerged bloodied at the end. It was the only decision match. The others, including the main event with Jimmy's loutish friend, GEM, were little more than exercises in mismatched brutality. GEM's opponent was in way over his head, and the bigger man beat him unmercifully. When he fell to the mat obviously unconscious, GEM followed him down and kept right on pounding. It took the ref way too long to walk over and tap the aggressor's sweaty shoulder, and even then, he intentionally drove in a few more punches, necessitating Spencer Jr. to get on the megaphone and order him to cease and desist.

"You don't want to kill him, Mess," Spencer said, grinning the whole time.

After the megaphone command, GEM stood up and marched around the octagonal cage with his arms raised.

"There you have it, ladies and gentlemen," Spencer chimed in on the megaphone. "Living proof that you don't mess with Mess."

The crowd roared.

Wolf was disgusted. He'd seen more sportsmanship exhibited in the prison yard boxing tournaments that he'd participated in than this fiasco. When Jimmy turned to him and asked what he thought of GEM's performance, Wolf didn't reply. He felt like saying first prize should be a bar of soap and a can of spray deodorant. As far as the big man's fighting ability,

Wolf had been less than impressed. He relied totally on his size and power, which appeared to be considerable, but was diminished by his lack of effective style. GEM had lumbered forward throwing circular, roundhouse punches that you could see coming a mile away. Sure, they'd hurt you if they hit you, but the way he was telegraphing them, they were as easy to avoid as a wrecking ball.

Power, but no finesse.

With the completion of the matches, things deteriorated between him and his brother even more quickly. Jimmy had consumed numerous cans of beer and had become rather inebriated. Wolf had hoped to try and talk to him, to try to make him see that these purported friends didn't have his best interests at heart at all. But it was arguing with a drunk. The kid didn't want to leave, even though the crowd was being ushered out of the decrepit mall by security, Cook and several other men whom Wolf assumed to be off-duty police.

"I want another beer," Jimmy said. "Or maybe we can all go to the Green Temple."

The Green Temple was a town bar that was known for watered down whiskey that was a kissing cousin to embalming fluid.

Wolf had tried to get him to agree to go home, so they could maybe put on a pot of coffee and talk, but it was no such luck.

I'm arguing with a drunk, Wolf told himself, disappointed and at a loss as to how to reach his younger brother.

Surprisingly, it was Spencer and Pike who convinced Jimmy and the three others to vacate the premises and go home.

"Hey, we got a long drive tomorrow," Pike said. "And we're leaving early. You can't afford to be hung over. Word is that the hurricane gonna be moving on up the coastline and bringing a whole lotta rain and wind with it."

"Damn straight," Spencer said. "And I ain't paying you guys for doing nothing."

But, Wolf wondered, what exactly is he paying them to do?

On the drive back Wolf tried pumping Jimmy for more information as to what this long drive was all about, but the kid was evasive as all hell.

"Where you driving to?" Wolf asked.

"Atlanta. And then back up here again."

A drop off and a pick-up?

It didn't sound good. Too much like a round-circuit drug delivery.

"What are you driving?" Wolf asked.

"Truck."

"I didn't know you had a license for that."

"It's just a Rent-n-Haul box truck," he said. "A twenty-footer. Not one of them big rigs."

"What are you hauling?"

Wolf watched as best he could to gauge his brother's reaction.

The alcohol had slowed his intellect and he sat dumbfounded for several seconds, and then said, "Uh, I dunno. Some shit, or something, that Bobbie and his old man need delivered to their partner down in Atlanta."

The answer was sufficiently evasive enough to tip Wolf's suspicions over the top.

"Hey, got room for me to come along?" Wolf asked, still trying to pin him down. "I got nothing to do, and it'd give you and me a chance to catch up."

Wolf caught the tell immediately: a nervous flicker around the eyes, a twitching of the lips.

"Ah, no," his brother said. "Can't do it. Bobbie would have a fit."

"He going along?"

"No, but if he found out…" Jimmy's tongue flicked out like an exploring snake's and then disappeared. "Besides, I got Willard riding with me both ways and there's only two seats."

"Only two seats?" Wolf kept his tone moderate, free of suspicion or accusation. "Didn't you say that Pike and that guy, GEM, were going too?"

"Well, they are." The tongue wet his lips again, and then he swallowed hard. "We got more than one truck going. They're going in other cars."

"Other cars?"

"Well, pickup trucks, actually."

Jimmy's reply had been quick. Too quick. He was nervous about something.

Two more vehicles... Lookouts for the state police, no doubt.

"And what are they carrying?" Wolf asked.

His brother shrugged. "I dunno."

"How well do you know this guy, Pike?"

Jimmy shrugged emphatically. "I dunno, I told ya. I just know him, is all. He works for somebody down in Atlanta."

"Who's that?"

His brother shrugged again. "Fuck, I don't know. Bobbie handles all that stuff. I just drive."

Wolf blew out a long, audible breath. "I got to tell you this doesn't sound good."

"Huh?"

"I'd hate to see you get in trouble."

"Whaddaya mean, get in trouble?"

"Just what I said. You're into something way over your head. You think your friends are going to help you?" Wolf paused in the hope that his point would strike a chord with his little brother.

"Hey, get offa my back, would ya? I know what I'm doing."

He wasn't liking the way this was playing out, but what could he do to stop it? Knock him out and tie him up? That wouldn't work, he knew, but by the same token, he had to try something.

"Look, Jimmy, have you thought this thing through? Considered what could happen?"

"Hey, it's my fucking job, all right? My fucking life. And quit calling me *Jimmy*. My fucking name's *Jim*. Got it?"

Nobody loves a drunken Indian, was Wolf's mental reply.

Things went further downhill from there. By the time Wolf pulled up in front of the family trailer, he and his brother seemed on the verge of coming to blows, and that was definitely not something that Wolf wanted. They weren't even speaking. Jimmy wrenched the door open, jumped out, and slammed it shut. He turned and headed inside without saying another word or looking back.

Guess I could have handled that better, Wolf told himself.

But the idea of how still eluded him.

You could never win arguing with a drunk.

There was plenty of room to park in the hotel casino parking lot, and Wolf wondered about the apparent sparseness of players coming to the place. It was a weeknight, and there was the threat of some approaching severe weather. Maybe that accounted for it. The image of Jimmy driving a truck in a bad storm flashed through his mind.

Maybe it's a good thing, he thought. If he is hauling some kind of dope, what self-respecting cop's going to stop him if it's raining?

The speculation was both amusing and disconcerting: hoping for a storm to lessen the chances that his brother wouldn't get caught doing something illegal.

A storm… A tempest… Wolf smiled to himself. He still had to write that damn paper and send it in. That diversion did little to dissuade him from the immediate and overwhelming problem.

What the hell had his little brother gotten himself into?

And, more importantly, he thought, what the hell can I do to get him out of it?

Wolf saw a big, shiny Harley Davidson parked near the building in a special motorcycles only section adjacent to the overhang. It was a Road King Classic.

He wondered if it was Pike's. He remembered Jimmy going on about the man's big, mean Harley. Wolf also remembered something else.

They're going along in pickups, his brother had said about the drive down to Atlanta. Him and Willard in the truck, Pike and the big dolt, GEM shadowing them in vehicles.

Police lookouts, as he'd figured, and if for some reason the box truck broke down, whatever they were transporting could be transferred to the pickup trucks. But old Pike would be kicking himself hard if some real bad rain and winds came through here and took his motorcycle for a twirl.

That brought a smile to Wolf's face, but in spite of the biker apparently being a less than positive influence on Jimmy, Wolf had to respect that the man had military experience, and airborne at that. The 101st was a top-notch outfit.

Wolf sighed. It was too bad that Pike had fallen from grace and gotten involved in this drug stuff. Although Wolf had no definitive proof of that, at least that's the way it appeared to be shaping up.

He closed and locked the car. Walking to the main entrance he saw Honest Bob's yellow Caddie parked in the fire zone spot once again. Next to it was a canary-yellow Corvette. He'd seen that one at the mall.

Looks like a family reunion, he thought, and decided to check out the bar in the chance that he might see father and son in conversation and maybe do a bit of reconnoitering. He went into the casino. There were small groups of people gathered around the various slot machines and gaming tables. No one was wearing masks, but this didn't bother Wolf at all. It wasn't like a rectangle of cloth over the mouth and nose was going to afford the wearer any real protection. It was pure cosmetics. With his military background Wolf had been exposed to gas too many times in training and also in various situations to take the mask thing seriously. The key to survival, and wearing a protective mask, was to make sure that the rubber of the M-190 protective mask was tight and properly sealed against the skin. Thus, it was necessary to be clean shaven and not have a lot of shaggy hair either. He got a kick out of the TV shows featuring all those immaculately groomed but bearded actors playing soldiers and SWAT cops.

Television... As if it reality mattered.

Bitterness began to flood through him, and he realized he'd been focusing on this mask mandate nonsense because he didn't want to face the fact that his brother, his little brother, was in a truck driving full speed toward the cliff of oblivion. He hoped Jimmy hadn't passed the point of no return yet. Wolf hated to think of the kid getting busted and going to prison.

It was doubtful he'd survive it.

Wolf continued through the casino to the bar area, glancing around as he walked. Again, it was sparsely populated. A row of half a dozen booths lined each wall and in the middle were numerous tables and a horseshoe-shaped bar. Off to the right side he saw four figures ensconced in an isolated booth. Pence Redfox was one of them. Honest Bob, his son, Bobbie Jr., and Pike were the others. They were in what appeared to be a busy conversation.

Interesting, Wolf thought. But what good does it do me?

He couldn't very well go over and join them, nor

could he sit in a nearby booth without being noticed.

He debated the possibility of dropping a dime to the state police about a possible drug dealing operation happening tomorrow.

Bad idea, he told himself.

For one thing, all he had at the moment was suspicion. He had no legitimate proof of anything. Supposition wouldn't hold too much water, and even if the police did move on it, how would that help Jimmy? Wolf figured the kid was being used as a drug mule. Even if the cops did move in and intercepted the shipment, Jimmy would be the one taking the fall.

Wolf took a seat at the bar and ordered a beer. The bartender smiled, grabbed a stein, and stuck it under the draft spout.

He felt dejected enough to drink this one. Maybe he'd get a shot glass of whiskey to make a depth charge.

As Wolf watched the frothy head of the beer forming on top of the yellow liquid, he strained to catch any fragment of the conversation of the four men in the booth.

No luck. He was too far away. The drinks, with the exception of the one in front of Redfox, all sat apparently untouched on the table in front of them. Their voices were subdued and not audible over the din of the clanging slots and ripples of laughter and exclamations from some of the more enthusiastic players.

An attractive woman was sitting at the far corner of the horseshoe and it took Wolf a moment to realize who she was. She seemed to catch sight of him at the same instant.

Crystal Bear.

He smiled reflexively.

So did she.

Grabbing his beer, he walked over to her. This would put him farther away from the trio, but the chances of overhearing anything in this noise-filled environment was rather slight anyway. Plus, this way he might be able to keep watching them, and he wanted to talk to her. She wasn't wearing her casino dealer's uniform now. On the contrary, she had on a low-cut black blouse and a tight skirt. The blouse was sleeveless and showed off a lot of fine cleavage. As he rounded the curve in the counter, he saw that her right leg was crossed over her left, displaying an elegant glimpse of well-developed calf and what had to be an expensive, designer, high-heeled shoe. The leg bounced up and down a little as she sat there implying impatience. In front of her on the bar were an ashtray and a martini glass full of clear liquid. An olive, pierced by a toothpick, twirled between her fingers. When she saw Wolf approaching, she placed the olive into her mouth and bit it between straight, white teeth.

"Funny meeting you here," Wolf said.

She stared at him momentarily, dropped the half-eaten olive back into the drink, and took out a cigarette and held it up.

Wolf set the stein on the bar and made a show of patting his pockets, smiling and then shrugging.

"Sorry," he said, "I don't have a light."

The bartender strolled over with a book of matches with the casino imprint on it and set it down next to Crystal's drink. Wolf plucked the matches off the counter, pulled one from the paper row, and struck it on the safety-scratch pad. The match ignited with a hissing sound.

Crystal placed the cigarette between her lips, gripped Wolf's hand with her own, and leaned forward so that the tip of the cigarette was in the flame. She kept holding his hand a little longer than was necessary and he was afraid the flame would sear his finger and thumb. He took in a breath to blow it out, but she beat him to it, exhaling a sharp stream of smoke that extinguished the flame. Wolf caught some of the residual smoke as he inhaled. He pulled away and coughed several times.

"I see you still don't smoke, huh?" Crystal said.

He coughed two more times, and then shook his head.

So much for my James Bond savoir faire, he thought. Guess I should have remembered to hold my breath.

"So you finally decided to come home."

"I figured it was time."

"Time… What cruel word that can be."

"It looks like it's been pretty good to you. You look great. Still as pretty as ever."

As she smiled, he detected a slight fan of delicate wrinkles next to her eyes—the incipience of impending crow's feet.

A loud voice carried over from the booth.

"No shit?"

It was Redfox.

Honest Bob immediately laid a hand on the other man's shoulder and whispered something inaudible, glancing around. Redfox did the same.

Wolf locked eyes with Spencer Sr., but only for a moment.

Searching for something to say, Wolf said, "I heard you were working here."

Crystal picked up the partially eaten olive, placed it into her mouth, closed her lips over it. Slowly, she pulled the impaling toothpick free.

"I was wondering if you recognized me this afternoon," she said.

"I recognized you, all right. But my sister already told me you worked here."

"Your sister? Pearl?"

"Yeah."

"Figures." She tapped the cigarette on the ashtray so hard that the ember separated and fell off. Frowning, she dropped the remainder into the tray. "She never did like me, even back when—"

Crystal stopped talking and turned slightly to reach inside a mammoth brown leather purse on the stool next to her. It had some kind of intricate repetitive pattern on it. Wolf saw that it was a Louis Vuitton.

Expensive tastes.

Taking out her pack of cigarettes, she shook one loose, and held it between her fingers.

"Want to light my fire again?" she asked, her smile demure, suggestive.

Wolf struck another match and held it up for her. Her fingers curled around his hand once again, and at her touch he felt something similar to a jolt of electricity course through him and settle in his groin. It had been a long time, but not a forgotten one.

"Yeah," she said, slowly uncurling her fingers from him with a protracted lingering. "I do work here, and so what? A girl's got to find work where she can around this town. And it's not like I've got a lot of options."

She drew deeply on the cigarette and blew a stream of smoke upward through the side of her mouth, away from Wolf.

"Shit, the textile mill's closed," she continued. "Not that I'd want to waste my life doing something like that. Watching my mom and dad was bad enough. And now it's supposedly a fucking recycling factory that smells like shit warmed over. Even the fucking mall's closed."

Wolf was a bit shocked at her overuse of the eff-word, but she was, after all, a tough cookie. She was obviously in survival mode, too. Her own kind of survival. He was also intrigued that she'd said, "supposedly". There was obviously a lot more to that place than met the eye. Maybe she could give him some insight.

"I know," he said.

"And my family didn't have the money to send me to college like Darlene, your sweet little ex." Twin plumes of smoke descended from her nostrils. "How is she, by the way?"

"She's engaged."

Crystal smirked again, her dark eyes studying him for any reaction.

"So I've heard. Nick Paxton." The tip of her tongue flicked over her lips, wetting them. When she drew on the cigarette again, she left a red lipstick stain on the white filter. "He's a cop now. Who'd a figured that? He used to be quite the nerd during high school."

Wolf hadn't remembered Pax that way. In fact, he hadn't thought about high school very much at all, but it was clear she still had one foot in the past. He glanced over at the quartet in the booth. They were still talking, although things seemed to be getting close to a wrapping up stage, so he searched for a way to keep her talking. Maybe there was still a chance she could give him some insight into what was really going on.

"Want to get something to eat?" he asked. "I've heard the restaurant here is good. Maybe I could buy you a late dinner?"

"Very late," she said. "No thanks. I'm actually here on a date."

"A date?"

He glanced around, wondering if Sheridan was lurking somewhere.

"With Tim?"

The demure smile flashed again, and she gestured toward the booth on the far wall.

"That big guy over there with the blond ponytail. He promised to take me for a ride on his Harley."

Wolf looked over at Pike and saw the four men getting up from the table.

Now this is interesting, he thought. I wonder just how deep she's into what's going on?

"Going to be hard to do in that outfit," he said, appraising her tight dress.

"I've got a change of clothes in here." She patted her substantial Louis Vuitton bag. "At least all the clothes that I'll need."

Before he could say anything more, he saw her eyes

widen and her mouth gape open, forming a startled O shape.

"Shit," she muttered.

"Crystal!" someone behind him shouted. Wolf immediately glanced over his shoulder and saw Tim Sheridan's staggering approach.

"Shit, shit, shit," she said, and stubbed out her cigarette.

Wolf swirled the bar stool in a semicircle away from her and stood up, not knowing what to expect. Sheridan's face was crinkled with rage, his glare moving from Wolf to Crystal to Wolf again.

"After telling me you were sick," he said, his words slurring, "you fucking sneak off to meet *him*?"

Crystal slipped off the stool and took a few steps backward.

"I'm not meeting him," she said. "And even if I was, it's none of your fucking business."

"Like hell," Sheridan said, his head still bobbling. "I'm the one who cares about you. Loves you."

"Get away from me," she said, walking at a brisk pace on an angle away from him. "Get out of here."

Sheridan pivoted, almost lost his balance, and moved to cut her off.

"Hey," he said, "Crystal, come on. We gotta talk."

"Tim," Wolf said, "I think you need to calm down."

"Fuck you," Sheridan said. He stopped, teetered a bit, and clenched his fists as he glared at Wolf.

"Don't do it, Tim," Wolf said. "Don't even think about it."

As if debating whether or not to take a swing, Sheridan then did an exaggerated, staggering two-step and snared Crystal's upper arm. They were about ten feet away and suddenly Wolf caught sight of someone coming up fast on an intercept course. Someone big.

Pike reached out and grabbed Sheridan's right arm, swung him around, and said, "She's with me, sonny."

Sheridan released his grip on Crystal and made the mistake of balling up his left fist and trying to hit Pike. It was a clumsy, roundhouse punch and the biker swatted it away with his palm and then delivered a solid, pile-driving bolo punch into Sheridan's gut.

Wolf heard the air whoosh out of him. Pike had pivoted expertly and put his entire, good-sized body behind the blow.

Sheridan sank to his knees, both hands holding his abdomen, leaned forward and vomited, some of the expectorate splashing on the big man's heavy black boot. The biker danced back a step or two, and Wolf was afraid he was going to deliver a kick to Sheridan's face. Wolf readied himself to intercede, but Pike just took another step back, shaking his head and snorting.

The vomitus continued to dribble from Sheridan's mouth.

Crystal walked over and slapped the top of the kneeling man's head.

"You stupid shit," she yelled. "Look at what you've done. You've embarrassed me, you asshole."

Sheridan didn't look like he was in any shape to respond, either verbally of physically.

Pence Redfox strode over, looking enraged. The two Spencers were right behind him, Bob Sr. with a relaxed grin spreading on his face. His son seemed a bit more aghast.

Redfox stopped a few feet away, still staring down at Sheridan.

"You fucking idiot," he said, and then turned to the bartender and pointed. "Who let this God damn drunk in here?"

The bartender shrugged.

"Call fucking security," Redfox shouted. "And the cops, too. I want his ass locked up."

"Dad," Bobbie Jr. said.

Honest Bob Spencer Sr. winked at him and then laid a calming hand on Redfox's shoulder.

"Pence, relax," Honest Bob said. "Just a little lover's quarrel."

"Lover's quarrel?" Redfox's face was still twisted with a dominant frown. He pointed at Crystal. "You're fired, too. Get outta here."

Her eyes widened in shock. After a few seconds a tear began to wind its way down her cheek.

"I didn't know *he* would be coming here." She gestured at Sheridan. "And you told me to—"

"Dad," Bobbie Jr. said again. His voice was bordering on imploring.

His father patted him on the shoulder.

"Peeennnce," Honest Bob said, drawing out the name. "You're being way too harsh on these young folks. Besides, Tim here's my number one employee at the recycling factory. And he's one of your best customers, right?"

Wolf watched Redfox's face twitch. He nodded.

"And lovely Crystal here," Honest Bob continued. "She's a good worker, too, isn't she?"

Redfox said nothing but made an almost imperceptible nod.

"Plus, she came here tonight at my request," Spencer Sr. said. "Our buddy, Mr. Pike here wanted the pleasure of her company this evening."

The Indian's eyes shifted from the downed man to the girl and then to Pike, who stood there grinning.

"Shucks," Pike said, rubbing his fingers over his big gold medallion. "If I'da known he had such a weak constitution, I wouldn't have hit him so hard."

Sheridan was gasping now, but he was still on his knees, both hands massaging his stomach.

"All right," Redfox said. "No cops. But I want him outta here."

"I'll see about getting him home," Wolf said. He stepped over, careful to avoid the vomit, and placed both hands under Sheridan's arms, starting to lift him up.

"That's real neighborly of you, Wolf," Pike said. "But I think that boy needs to apologize to the young lady here first, not to mention cleaning his puke off of my boot."

Wolf gave Pike a sideways glance.

"Give the man a break, Pike," he said. "He's in no shape to do either."

"I don't want to talk to him anyway." Crystal wiped her cheek and stood there, a smug look on her face.

Pike's expression hardened. "Maybe you'd like to clean it off for him then."

Wolf stared at the man. "Ain't gonna happen."

"Dad," Bobbie Jr. said. His tone was laced with escalating desperation now.

"Gentlemen, gentlemen," Honest Bob said. "Let's be reasonable. You're two big tough guys. We all know that. No need for any further violence."

Typical politician, Wolf thought. Always talking out of both sides of his mouth.

Redfox whistled at the bartender, who immediately threw him a towel from behind the bar. Then the Indian strode over and thrust it at Wolf, who made no move to take it.

Pike blew out a loud burst of breath and grabbed the towel.

"No sweat, Wolf," he said, bending down and wiping off the top of his boot. "No harm, no foul."

He gave the black leather a bit of a buffing and tossed the towel down in front of Sheridan's feet. Then he looked at Wolf and smiled. "Like I said before, us airborne troopers got to stick together. Right?"

"All the way," Wolf said, leveling his gaze at Pike's eyes.

CHAPTER 11

PARKING LOT
GOLD BANQUET HOTEL AND CASINO
NEW SPENCERLAND, NORTH CAROLINA

Wolf waited under the overhang in the cool evening
air. It had the heavy, almost moist feel of pending rain.
His call to Nick Paxton explaining the situation had
been about ten minutes ago. Pax hadn't asked any
questions and said he'd be there ASAP. There seemed
to be a woman's voice in the background.

Darlene?

It made Wolf wonder if they were already playing
house.

I guess I'll find out, he thought, not that it made
any difference to him.

Sheridan, who was seated on a bench not far from
where he and Crystal had had their argument earlier,

groaned and muttered something unintelligible. He stank badly. Wolf wondered if Pike's blow had caused Sheridan to lose control of his bowels as well. From the smell of it, he had.

Wolf tried to ignore him, but Sheridan called out to him.

"Steve, why do you think she did that to me?"

His voice sounded mostly like caterwauling mixed with sobs. Wolf realized the man was crying.

"Tim," Wolf said, "get hold of yourself. You're drunk."

"I know." More sobbing made the words indistinct.

"Just sit there and take it easy. We're going to get you home."

"Home? I don't want to go home. I want Crystal. *Crystal.*" The repetition of the name was loudly emphasized. "Don't you understand?"

Wolf said nothing. After his frustrating attempt at conversation with his brother earlier, he was now running a low tolerance for dealing with drunks.

Sheridan continued to cry. "I love her." His jaw lolled open, some spittle drooling from his lower lip. "Don't you understand?"

"You'd best leave that be for the time being. Try talking to her later. Tomorrow."

"But I love her. Don't you understand? I love her."

"True loves always finds a way," Wolf said, realizing he'd borrowed the line from some sappy romance movie that he'd turned on the night before when he couldn't sleep. Then Wolf got another idea. "You work with my brother Jimmy, don't you?"

No response.

Wolf tried the question again.

"Yeah," Sheridan said.

"What type of work do you do?"

Sheridan took in a couple of shallow breaths. He didn't answer.

"Tim?"

Still no response.

Wolf debated about how far to push it. Sheridan was drunk, but it was obvious he was still straight enough to be on his guard.

He must know I'm suspicious, Wolf thought. And he might go running to one of the Spencers.

Wolf let it drop, deciding it wouldn't be good to show his hand too early. Nothing more was said between them, and Wolf was glad that at least his questions had struck some kind of nerve with Sheridan and shut him up. It also told Wolf the kind of people involved in this thing. If a couple of general questions were enough to silence a whimpering drunk, there must be a substantial amount of intimidation and fear involved. Maybe that was why Jimmy had refused to talk to him.

Easy, fast money, Wolf thought. Easy, fast danger, too.

It was getting darker, and Wolf caught the sight of some advancing headlights illuminating the now steadily falling rain. The car was a gray Lexus SUV. It turned slowly into the lot, paused, and then accelerated toward the overhang. After screeching to a halt, both front doors popped open, and Nick Paxton and Darlene got out. She was dressed in a T-shirt and blue jeans, no bra. Her breasts bounced as she ran over to her brother. Pax, Wolf saw, was also dressed in a T-shirt and jeans. Both of them wore gym shoes and no socks.

Wolf wondered what he'd interrupted.

He was both surprised that he felt a twinge of something—envy or jealousy? He wasn't sure which. This surprised him because he'd convinced himself that he was totally over Darlene, and that her relationship with Pax wasn't bothering him at all. It was easy until he saw the expression of concern on her beautiful face. She slid onto the bench beside her brother and started to hug him.

"Be careful," Wolf said. "He threw up."

And worse, he added mentally.

She seemed oblivious to his comment, pulling her brother closer despite his bad smell and soiled clothes.

"She was with another man," Sheridan said. His whimpering tone had returned. "He hit me."

"What?" Darlene said. She glared up at Wolf. "Was it you?"

"No, not him," Sheridan said, before Wolf could utter a word. "Not him."

"Who was it?" Paxton walked up to stand beside Wolf now. He made no move toward the two seated siblings.

"You know a guy named Lucien Pike?" Wolf asked.

Pax stared at him. "He's here?"

"That's his bike." Wolf gestured toward the big Harley.

"That's his?" Sheridan said, starting to get up. "I'll kill it."

Paxton side stepped in front of him, holding out both of his hands.

"You ain't gonna kill nothing," he said. "Especially something that ain't even alive in the first place."

Sheridan stopped and took in some ragged breaths. Darlene was still clinging to him now and the stench of the man was nauseating.

"Come on, Tim," Paxton said. "Let us get you home and cleaned up."

He gripped the other man's arm and he and Darlene began to walk him over toward the Lexus. Wolf stepped over and grabbed the rear door handle.

"You got a blanket or some newspapers?" Wolf asked. "You might want to spread something out on the seat."

Paxton exhaled loudly.

"Yeah, I got a tarp in the back. Hold on a second."

He went to the rear of the vehicle and raised the tailgate.

Sheridan's legs started to fold under him, so Wolf stepped over and grabbed the arm that Paxton had released. Darlene glanced at him.

"What happened in there?"

"Well," Wolf said, "I saw Crystal in the bar and was talking to her. She was waiting on her date, and your brother came in. He'd been drinking." Wolf paused. The mixture of odors emanating from Sheridan was stomach churning. "They got into a tiff. He grabbed Crystal's arm and her date showed up. Tim took a swing at the guy and got punched in the stomach pretty hard."

He paused, figuring the rest was self-explanatory. Darlene frowned.

"It wasn't my fault, sis," Sheridan said. "Honest. She lied to me. Said she wasn't feeling good tonight."

"We'll talk about it later," Darlene said.

Big sisters are something, Wolf told himself. Always protective of their younger siblings.

Paxton came from the back end with a blue plastic tarp. He squeezed between them and leaned into the back seat area. Just as he did so Sheridan made a gurgling sound, and a burst of vomit blew forth from his mouth and onto the side windows of the Lexus. Both Wolf and Darlene recoiled, but it wasn't enough to keep them totally away from the spray. Sheridan's legs seemed to weaken even more, and he started to drop. Wolf reached around and grabbed the other side of Sheridan's body and kept him from falling. It was then that he caught the glint of tears in Darlene's eyes.

After Paxton had finished spreading the covering, Wolf half-walked, half carried Sheridan to the opening and helped him into the back seat area.

Darlene ran around the car, opened the other rear door, and got in beside her brother.

"Let's take him to our place," she said.

Paxton nodded, and then quickly glanced at Wolf.

"Our place" had answered any questions he might have been considering, but he found the twinge of jealousy wasn't returning.

Maybe I've turned that corner for good, he thought.

Paxton slammed the door so hard it sent a burst of moisture from the wetness of the accumulated rain on the car.

He shook his head and snorted.

"Sorry."

"It's okay." Wolf smiled. "I need a shower anyway."

Paxton grabbed the still open front passenger door and turned to Wolf. He spoke in a low whisper. "Was he this much of a problem when he was your brother-in-law?"

Wolf's eyes quickly shot to the rear seat area and Darlene, but the windows had a heavy tint, and he couldn't discern either her or her brother.

"He wasn't around that much," Wolf said. "Too busy teaching."

"Yeah, remind me to tell you how that turned out sometime."

"I already heard."

Paxton smirked. "Well, we better get him home."

To our place. Wolf remembered Darlene's words. But he said nothing.

"Thanks, Steve, I appreciate it." Paxton held out his hand.

Wolf shook it. "Yeah, I'm glad you gave me your cell number. I just didn't expect to be using it like this."

Paxton smiled. He looked almost boyish under the now illuminated lights recessed into the overhang.

"I can follow you over and help you get him inside if you want," Wolf said.

"We can handle it." Darlene's voice sounded shrill.

Paxton's mouth puckered as he glanced over his shoulder at her. Before he could respond, Wolf cut in.

"Look, he can barely walk. You're gonna need some help. I'll just follow you over in my rental. It's parked over there."

"Nick," Darlene said, "can we get going please?"

He worked his lips some more and slammed the open front passenger door.

"I'll tag along," Wolf said. "If it looks like you're

going to need a hand getting him into the house, I'll be there. Otherwise, I'll stay out of sight." He canted his head toward Darlene in the rear section.

"Thanks, Steve."

Wolf did a quick jog over to his rental car, pressing the remote to set off its alarm in the now escalating darkness. He felt the spray of raindrops hitting him as he cleared the overhang. The glow of the flashing yellow parking lights jerked on, accompanied by the intermittent horn. Wolf hit the button again to silence it as he got to the car. He got in, started it up and saw Paxton was slowly doing a U-turn from under the front entrance overhang and moving toward the exit to the parking lot. Pulling in behind Paxton's Lexus, Wolf glanced toward the front entrance and saw Honest Bob and his namesake son both standing there staring at him. A cigarette glowed brightly in Bob Junior's hand.

Nothing like having an audience when you least need one, Wolf thought.

***

Spence watched as Wolf drove away, following the car with that idiot, Sheridan in it.

That was close, he thought, but then began to re-consider.

Perhaps he could use this little unexpected donnybrook to his advantage, or at least the fact that Pike was involved in an altercation. He could report back to Batton, after the explosion at the plant that blew up the truck, and Batton's money, that it was all because of that the idiot, Sheridan, having a hard on against Pike for fucking Crystal.

Yeah, that would work. Like icing on the cake.

He took another draw on his cigarette. Jimmy's brother, Steve, however, was beginning to be of concern. The guy was popping up in a lot of the wrong places. He'd have to lean on Jimmy a bit to find out what his brother's game was. But Spence had heard that the older Wolf was supposedly based in Vegas, or someplace, doing MMA fighting. The guy shouldn't be a major factor in anything. Probably be gone after a few days. Still, it wouldn't hurt to make sure.

Hedge my bets, he thought. So to speak.

"Is Sheridan becoming a problem?" Bob Sr. asked as he took out one of his long cigars. "We can't afford any loose cannons, you know."

"Yeah, I know," Spence said, reaching into his pocket to grab his lighter. "And he won't be. He'll get over it."

He didn't want to tell his father that the love-struck chemist was about to become a casualty of the presentation. The prick wouldn't have time to become a problem.

"This was just a minor blow-up." Spence was secretly pleased with his secret pun, knowing that the explosion reference had gone completely over the old man's head. He flicked the wheel on his lighter and held the flame to the tip of his father's cigar.

"So," Bob Sr. said, puffing to get it started. "Everything's set for tomorrow then?"

"All primed and ready to go."

Bob Sr. drew on the cigar and then blew out a stream of smoke.

"Good. Like Pike said, this is going to be a big shipment. We can't afford any mistakes."

"There won't be any."

"There better not be."

Spence just flashed a grin.

You don't know the half of it, he thought.

This was finally going to be his chance to emerge from his father's shadow. Now all he had to decide was if he was going to let the old man in on it, or not. It might be better if he knew, but then again, if he doesn't know anything, he'll be more convincing in corroborating the explanation with Batton.

Seven million bucks...

He could always call his father from the island, once everything's cooled down and he was out of here. Until then, as far as the old man was concerned, ignorance was bliss.

"Let's go back inside and get one more drink," Bob Sr. said. "A toast to our upcoming success."

"You go on in and order me whiskey soda." He took out his cell phone. "I got to make a quick call."

Bob Sr. turned and headed for the entrance doors.

Spence ruminated again about Jimmy's brother and the problems he might cause. It was better to keep him occupied. He scrolled through his numbers until he found the one he wanted.

Hedging my bets, he thought, and pressed the button.

***

RESIDENCE OF DARLENE SHERIDAN
AND NICK PAXTON
NEW SPENCERLAND, NORTH CAROLINA

Getting Tim Sheridan out of the car and into the house proved to be both messy and problematic. He'd regurgitated once again and was literally covered in vomit. Paxton told Darlene to go open the door and then asked Wolf to help him get the sobbing, semi-conscious man out of the car. The smell was horrendous.

"It'll be better to get him out of these clothes before we take him inside." Paxton handed Wolf a pair of latex gloves. He was wearing a pair.

They paused while Wolf slipped the gloves on. Paxton's suggestion and preparation told Wolf that perhaps this wasn't the first rodeo. They stopped and lowered Sheridan's now limp body to the sidewalk leading up to the front door. Darlene stood there holding the screen door open, the light from the porch light spilling over her blonde hair, which she'd pulled back into a ponytail.

"Get us a garbage bag," Pax said. "Will you, hon?"

She sighed and disappeared inside the house.

Wolf slipped off Sheridan's shoes as Paxton began unbuttoning the shirt, his gloved fingers working gingerly around the soiled material.

Wolf was struck by an ironic realization as he waited for Pax to undo the man's belt buckle.

Sheridan was being rescued and attended to by his ex-brother-in-law, and his future brother-in-law.

He left that raillery unsaid as they pulled off Sheridan's soiled pants and underwear.

"Sorta like latrine duty in Basic," Paxton said. "Ain't it?"

"Or dirty diaper duty," Wolf said.

Darlene appeared with a big garbage bag and handed it to Paxton. He held it open, and Wolf carefully rolled up the dirty shirt, pants and shoes and stuck them into the bag.

"Mind helping me carry him into the bathroom?" Paxton asked. "After we get him washed off, we got a guest room we can put him in."

"I can help," Darlene interjected quickly.

"Not a problem," Wolf said, and grabbed hold of Sheridan's legs.

Darlene compressed her lips and quickly looked away.

Paxton grabbed the upper body, and they hoisted the unconscious naked man off the sidewalk.

His breathing was sonorous now.

God watches over babies and drunks, Wolf thought. Or so they say.

***

GOLD BANQUET HOTEL AND CASINO
NEW SPENCERLAND, NORTH CAROLINA

When he got back to his room Wolf stripped his own clothes off and washed them in the sink before getting in the shower. After drying off and wringing out the wet clothes, he hung them on the shower curtain rod and sorted through his bag for some clean underwear. Although he'd brought only one pair of pants, he had an ample supply of under garments, socks, and T-shirts. He called down to the desk and asked about getting an iron and ironing board sent up, but the clerk told him that both items should already be in his room. After hanging up he did indeed find them in one of the expansive closets. The room was spacious—larger, in fact than his month-to-month apartment in Vegas.

Wolf heaved a sigh. Everything of late in his life was either hidden or transitory.

I'm going to have to figure out a more permanent plan, he thought, realizing that his current lifestyle arrangement just wasn't cutting it.

When he'd last seen McNamara he'd practically invited Wolf to move back into the above-the-garage apartment back at the ranch in Phoenix and renew their Trackdown, Inc. partnership. He had been relatively happy there after getting out of prison and starting over but moving to Vegas had seemed like a good move. He'd done it principally in the hope that he could set up something permanent with Yolanda, and he'd stayed with her for a time when he got to Vegas. But her appointment to the Metro Police Department eventually put the squelch on that. It was one thing when she was in the police academy, and he was going to school during the day and playing Mr. Homemaker in the evenings. But then she graduated. She was a cop and began actual field training.

As it turned out, cohabitation, or anything further, wasn't in the cards.

Wolf knew that ex-cons with a DD in their military records weren't a good reflection for a new, probationary police officer. She knew it, too, but hadn't said anything.

It had been his decision to move out, over her protests, and he began his stay in the monthly place. He rated it just a cut above some of his deployments. That had been a few months ago now, and he'd hoped, with the evidence he'd gotten in Belize corroborating his claim that he'd been set up, that the great Oz would have made some progress in clearing Wolf's name. The lawyer had talked a good game when Wolf had first interviewed him, now seemed to be moving in slow motion... Except when he was cashing Wolf's checks. He made a mental note to call Oz in the morning to check on things.

Oz, he thought, remembering the old movie and the scared little man hiding behind the curtain.

Maybe he'd call Mac as well... Ask him about maybe helping him with the border job. Once he got this thing with his brother straightened out.

If he could.

The rain and wind had grown heavier now, and he could hear the storm pounding away as it battered against the windows.

Another tempest.

He still had to finish reading that play and write that final paper, but that was way down on his priority list now.

All worthwhile aspirations, but first he had to deal with his brother's predicament.

He tried to figure what exactly he knew, and what he didn't know, regarding Jimmy and his less than sterling group of friends. It was a given that things were rotten in New Spencerland. Honest Bob, mayor and state legislator, controlled everything, including the police department. Wolf recalled the so-called chief's timid response when Spencer Sr. had told him to back off about keeping Wolf out of the casino.

The casino... The *off-reservation* casino.

Honest Bob was obviously calling the shots there as well. Pence Redfox was the manager in title only.

A figurehead.

A totem pole, he thought, recalling some old-fashioned Indian lore.

But that didn't change the truth. The way that Honest Bob had basically told Redfox to back off having the casino security do a job on Tim Sheridan when he threw up in the bar showed who the real boss was.

Tim Sheridan... Disgraced ex-high school chemistry teacher... Now working at the recycling center that used to be the textile mill.

Keeping the environment safe for you, he sub-vocally recited, recalling the sign in front of the place. Yeah, right.

And Jimmy worked there, too.

Wolf recalled the powerful odors emitting from the place. It was looking more and more like they were cooking up crystal meth inside. Sheridan would have the knowhow, but what was Jimmy's connection? The kid had dropped out of high school, but how much education do you need to follow instructions in a very dangerous cooking process? Jimmy was also doing some driving to and from Atlanta. Wolf grabbed his smart phone typed in *crystal meth + Atlanta* and clicked on it. The result told him all he wanted to know. The substance was a favorite of the gay community due to its purported enhancement and prolonging of sexual performance. While it did do substantial harm to the body, with numerous long-term irreversible and detrimental side effects, it remained popular. And Atlanta had a sizable gay community.

If Honest Bob and his son were producing a steady supply, and Jimmy and a few of his buddies were the delivery boys, that meant that they were reporting to somebody in Georgia. Whoever that person was, he was the money, the boss, the honcho. And the crew up here was crossing state lines, which meant they were violating federal law.

The cops here are useless, Wolf thought. But what if I could get Franker involved? Or maybe he could at least put me in contact with somebody who could look into the matter.

In the meantime, he had to try and get Jimmy out of the equation.

But how to do that?

Obviously, the kid was in it up to his neck and

thought he knew all the answers when he didn't really know squat. But he was still low level compared to the Spencers and the big boss in Atlanta. Those would be the people the feds would want to get. Maybe, just maybe, he could keep his brother out of it.

Wolf reset his phone and after a moment's hesitation, pressed the button to call Trackdown, Inc., and Kasey in particular. He didn't have her home number now that she'd moved out of the ranch, but knew she still worked the phone and computer at her dad's place during the day.

The phone rang four times and Wolf glanced at his watch, thinking it was probably way too late, even halfway across the country, for her to still be in the office.

Her voice came on the line moments later verifying his suspicion.

"You've reached Trackdown, Incorporated," the recording said. "Leave a message."

As the beep sounded, Wolf struggled for the right words. He'd never gotten along well with Mac's daughter, although she had warmed up to him a bit after they'd plucked her from harm's way down in Belize.

"Hi, Kasey," he said. "It's Steve. I need to talk to Bill about something ASAP. Off the record. Have him call me. Please."

He recited his cell number and terminated the call.

Then he got another idea. If he could convince Jimmy that the feds were investigating his little venture, and he stood a good chance of getting caught, maybe that would cause him to back out, to keep him from going along with the disreputable crowd.

It might just give me the edge I need, Wolf thought. Maybe I can talk to him, get him the hell out of here. Even if it meant physically dragging him over to the recruiter's station.

Wolf punched the button to call his brother's cell. It rang only once before going directly to voicemail.

"Leave a message," the recording of Jimmy's desultory voice said.

At the tone, Wolf made it short and sweet.

"Jimmy, it's Steve. Call me as soon as you wake up. It's important. And don't go anywhere until you talk to me first. Understand? I'll be over there in the morning before seven."

He considered adding more, but didn't want it to sound cryptic, especially if someone else might somehow hear it. Wolf texted him, too. When they next talked, Wolf figured he'd tell him the feds were onto him and he'd better back off.

This was all assuming Wolf's theory about the meth production and delivery was correct.

But how could it not be?

There were too many loose pieces that only fit together to form one picture.

It involved drugs, and Jimmy was in it up to his neck. Wolf was sure of it.

Figuring he'd done all he could, he decided to try and get some sleep. He set the alarm for six and turned out the lights to try and get some rest.

Despite his overwhelming feeling of ennui, sleep proved elusive. Wolf kept turning the situation over and over in his mind. It was just like the long nights in the army when he knew the team was going into the hot zone in a few hours. It was a feeling of temporary powerlessness. You were all adrenalized, champing at the bit, but could do nothing about it. All the moves were controlled by someone else... By the fates.

Finally, after tossing and tangling himself in the sheets, he turned on the light and reached for the remote. The big screen TV illuminated almost immediately, and he flipped through the channels, stopping on a news channel.

Two small, box-like panels consisting of the upper halves of two men in suits were superimposed on the newsreel clip of that big C-17 taking off from Karzai International Airport with the throng of people running alongside and clinging to the wheels and door. The plane continued down the runway, gaining speed, despite the desperate hangers-on. The video mercifully froze as the airplane began to lift off. The two commentators expressed their equal parts of outrage and despair. They then mentioned the loss of the thirteen U.S. military personnel, one army, one navy, and eleven marines, who'd been trying to hold the tenuous perimeter at the airport gate. Fifteen others, all marines, had been wounded in the attack.

"It's the worst single day death toll for American troops since August sixth, two thousand-eleven," one of the commentators said. "On that day the Taliban shot down a CH-forty-seven Chinook helicopter killing thirty U.S. troops, including fifteen Navy SEALS."

Why they'd abandoned Bagram Air Base in the middle of the night and not tried to run the evacuation from there, instead of downtown Kabul, mystified Wolf. Plus, the commentators went on to mention that there were an unspecified number of Americans and green card holders still in Afghanistan with no plan to get them out safely. A bungled mission, for sure, and Wolf hoped that someone would be held accountable, but he wasn't holding his breath.

They'd probably trot out a scapegoat down the line, just like they'd done in his case.

Wolf turned it off in disgust. The news had become too depressing to watch of late. He remembered Mac talking about the fall of Saigon years before. Now Wolf knew how he'd felt: Loss, disappointment, helplessness... He recalled his own deployments to Afghanistan and the people, Afghan civilians, who'd worked with him. He'd helped train some of their army's Special Forces.

They sure folded up fast, he thought. But maybe their biggest mistake was believing that we'd stick by them.

Abandonment... Betrayal... Not our country's finest hour.

He wasn't going to let the same thing happen to Jimmy.

No way.

I'm not going to abandon Jimmy, he told himself as he felt on the edge of slumber. There's no way I'll leave my brother behind.

***

Wolf's reticulating activation system, finely honed by years in the military and in prison, snapped him awake. At first, he didn't know why, but seconds later he identified the sound—the soft brushing of the door being pushed open as it passed over the thick carpeting. The hotel room was spacious: a big living room, a bathroom, and the bedroom separated from the rest by an interior door. Wolf had left it ajar when he'd gone to bed. Now he was almost certain that someone had entered.

Or had he only imagined it?

The red numerals of the bedside alarm clock showed the numerals 12:44.

Had he perhaps been dreaming?

Then he heard the subdued sounds of someone moving as silently as possible through the living room area.

He had no weapons, and was nude, except for his underpants. Lifting the sheet from his body, he slipped his legs out from under the covering and seconds later moved as quickly as he could across the room, flattening himself against the wall next to the half-open bedroom door.

Controlling his breathing to shallow intakes of air through his mouth, soundlessly, he clenched and unclenched his fists, leaving his hands free to first grab, and then strike.

How many intruders were there?

What were their intentions?

More sounds emanated from the room beyond.

Strange sounds.

A swishing noise, accompanied by something that sounded almost like a zipper being unzipped. Wolf tried to stare though the crevice between the door and the jamb but could see only the darkness of the other room.

He heard a subdued sigh, followed by the briefest sight of an undulation.

Then he caught a brief glimpse through the crevice of the door frame of a body entering the bedroom. He reached out and grabbed the shadowy form just as it passed by. Twisting, he hurled the figure forward.

Wolf shoved the door closed as his hand shot to the light switch.

The room was suddenly illuminated, and he saw the naked body of a female sprawled across his bed. She was face-down, and her long, raven-like hair was scattered across her back. Her face turned slightly, and he saw her profile, recognizing her immediately. Crystal.

"What the hell?" he said.

She gasped a few times then turned toward him, one arm, her left, crossing protectively over her breasts. Her legs scissored together quickly, and she righted herself. Her right hand shielding her pubic area.

"You really know how to welcome a girl," she said.

Nervousness twitched at her smile as she sat up and uncrossed her legs, her left hand still cupped over her right breast. Wolf saw that her pubic hair was shaved, except for an ebony stripe, like a landing strip. The image sent an erotic thrill coursing through him.

"What are you doing here?" he said, trying to conceal his utter surprise. "And how'd you get in?"

Reflexively, he turned and opened the door, peering into the dark living room. The light from the bedroom spilled into the room making things generally visible. Crystal's Louis Vuitton purse sat on the back of the sofa along with her black skirt and top. The pair of high heeled shoes, one sitting upright and the other on its side, were on the floor below. Wolf didn't see any underwear. He turned back as he heard her standing up.

She stood up straight now and dropped her arms to her side.

Her body looked magnificent, and he felt the continued erotic stimulation as she moved toward him.

"I have a master key," she said, stopping next to him now.

She was so close that he could feel the heat from her body.

"Let me get a cigarette, okay?" she asked. "I don't remember you playing so rough."

He adjusted his stance to allow her to pass by him. Her backside looked equally delicious as she walked into the living room and grabbed her purse.

For a split second he worried that she might be going for a gun.

But if she intended to shoot me, he thought, she wouldn't have taken off her clothes first.

Moments later, his rationalization proved correct as Crystal removed a pack of cigarettes and a lighter, and then jammed one of the cigarettes between her lips.

"This is a non-smoking room," he said. "There's a two hundred dollar fine."

She rolled her eyes defiantly and flicked the lighter.

"What do you care?" she said. "You're getting

comped for the fucking room, anyway, aren't you?"

"I am," he said, wondering how she knew that.

She blew a plume of smoke toward the ceiling, took another drag, and then walked toward him.

"I'll put this out in the toilet if it makes you feel better," she said.

As she brushed by, he stepped aside.

"So is a master key part of every employee's standard equipment?"

She didn't answer and closed the bathroom door.

After a few moments he heard the toilet flush. The scent of the burning tobacco still lingered in the air when she opened the door again.

They stared at each other in silence, her completely naked and him in his underwear. She'd moved so close now that he could smell the booze coming off her. Her eyes darted downward, and the demure smile returned.

"It looks like you're glad to see me," she said, moving forward. Her fingers traced over his stomach and then walked downward. "Mmmm, I don't remember you having abs like these."

"I've been doing a lot of sit-ups."

"I'll bet." She gave his crotch a squeeze.

It sent an electrical-like shock through him, but the incongruity of the entire situation hovered over him like a dark cloud. Plus, had she just come from being with another man?

He asked her about that.

She frowned.

"He was all talk and no action. Didn't even want to do any coke. I don't think he was interested in me at all." She giggled. "Maybe he's secretly gay." Another squeeze. "But I can see you're not."

He gently pushed her back.

"Crystal, I don't think this is such a good idea."

"Oh, no?" Moving closer again, her erect nipples brushed against his chest. "I do."

He grabbed her arms and pushed her back again.

"This is something that—"

"It's just the two of us," she said. "Two people who had something once, together again. I know it's not forever or anything like that, but I really need to be with somebody tonight, Steve. Please. Let me stay. I'm too messed up to drive home anyway."

"I can get dressed and drive you."

"No, just hold me. Please. Just hold me."

His mind flashed to Yolanda. Even though they'd pretty much broken up, he still had hopes that they could reconnect at some point down the road.

Crystal pressed her body against his, her arms encircling him and squeezing him tight, her cheek against his chest.

Her body felt so warm, so inviting.

"You don't want me?" she said, her voice becoming wracked with hiccupping sobs.

"It's not that," he said. "It's just that—"

She held him tighter, still sobbing. "I do whatever they tell me, but nobody really wants me. Nobody ever wants me for long."

He felt the warm flow of her tears against his skin.

Sometimes you get the Bear, he thought. And sometimes the Bear gets you.

CHAPTER 12

**THE WOLF RESIDENCE
NEW SPENCERLAND, NORTH CAROLINA**

At six the next morning Jimmy was in a virtual panic when he saw the text and then listened to his voice-mail. He'd turned the phone off last night to make sure it had a full charge, since he was going to need it today to send that email. When he heard his brother's voice on the recording it sent a chill down his spine.

Jimmy, it's Steve. Call me as soon as you wake up. It's important. And don't go anywhere until you talk to me first. Understand? I'll be over there in the morning before seven.

Shit, he knows, Jimmy thought. I don't know how he figured it all out, but he knows.

That could only mean trouble. Glancing at his

watch, he saw that it was six-fifteen—still dark out-side. They would be coming by for him any minute. If Steve showed up and caused trouble, there was no telling what could happen. In desperation, Jimmy dialed Bobbie. He answered on the first ring.

"Good to hear you're up early," he said. His voice had a cheerful ring to it, but Jimmy could tell it was forced. Bobbie was just as nervous as he was. "He's on the way."

"Huh?" Jimmy was in a panic hearing that. How did he know about Steve coming? Or was it Steve he was talking about? "Who is?"

"Willard," Bobbie said. "You forgot he's coming to pick you up so your motorcycle isn't here?"

"Oh, okay. But listen. We got trouble."

"What kind of trouble?"

"My brother's on his way over here. Or he's about to be." Jimmy considered his next words carefully. He wasn't sure how much he wanted to tell, but then he came up with something he hoped the other man would buy. "He was bugging me about coming along. For the drive, so we could talk."

"Talk? What'd you tell him?"

"Nothing. Just that there was no room."

"Soooo," Bobbie said, drawing out the word, "what's the problem then?"

Jimmy swallowed. This wasn't working. "Okay,

look, he texted me last night that he wants to see me before we leave. Wants to talk to me about something."

Silence, then Bobbie asked, "What kind of a car's he driving?"

Savage images of Steve getting ambushed on the drive over here flashed in his mind's eye.

"Why? You ain't gonna hurt him, are you?"

Bobbie's laugh sounded phony. "Hardly. I just think we need to take him out of the equation for a while. Slow him down a little. Now, he's driving a silver Camry, right?"

"Yeah. It's a rental. But how'd you know that?"

"I know everything. Never forget that."

Jimmy was stunned. Were they watching Steve?

Then he heard Bobbie's deep chuckle again.

"Don't get shook," he said. "I saw him driving it last night."

"You did? When?"

"Never mind. Just be ready. I've got Willard on the way to pick up you up now."

"But what if my brother shows up here?" Jimmy said. "Or if he goes to the recycling center, or something?"

"Relax. I'll take care of it. Now just be on the lookout for Willard. He'll be driving a green Silverado. Just be ready."

"But what are you gonna do?"

There was no reply and Jimmy said, "Bob?"

More silence. Jimmy realized he was talking to dead air.

God, he thought. I hope Steve's gonna be all right.

***

GOLD BANQUET HOTEL AND CASINO
NEW SPENCERLAND, NORTH CAROLINA

Wolf heard the alarm going off in the bedroom, and then Crystal's hand smashing down on it to shut it off. He'd gotten up earlier and run the heated iron over his pants to smooth out the residual wrinkles. Going to the bedroom door, he glanced inside and caught sight of her bare shoulder protruding from under the white sheet. She rolled over and began her sonorous breathing once more.

Looks like she requires a snooze alarm, he thought, and moved to the bathroom. He shaved and showered as quickly as he could, feeling as on edge like during his old army days, and then mentally added that it was more reminiscent of his quick and wary trips to the shower room at Leavenworth. She appeared to still be asleep as he silently dressed and left. Now it was time for another rescue, if he could swing it. A rescue of Jimmy.

Sleep had proved elusive the night before after Wolf had finally gotten Crystal tucked into bed. He'd held her and let her have a good cry before managing to extricate himself with just a quick, parting kiss and then bedded down himself on the living room sofa, replaying that old Sinatra tune about regrets, and having a few. He'd figured that in the morning he'd have some of those, but taking advantage of an old flame, who was under the influence wasn't in his DNA.

Unable to sleep, he turned on a light and finished reading *The Tempest*. By one-fifteen in the morning she was breathing sonorously, and he'd finished the play. He'd been amused by the final act, and some of the lines. Prospero's final monolog beseeched the audience to set him free with their applause, and even the malevolent Caliban had been released from his servitude and had turned over a new leaf.

I'll be wise hereafter and seek for grace. What a thrice double ass was I, to take this drunkard for a god, and worship this dull fool!

If it worked for the man monster, maybe it could work for Jimmy. He hoped that his little brother would have similar sentiments about Bobbie. Maybe his brother would see the light this morning and agree without protest to back out of the drug mule business and come with Wolf to the recruiter's office.

Hell, Wolf told himself with a reluctant smile. At this point, I'd even settle for him joining the marines.

He realized he was being overly optimistic as he jabbed the *DOWN* button several more times as he waited for the elevator, rotating his arm slightly so he could look at his watch.

0645 hours.

The timing seemed right. He doubted Jimmy would be up, much less leaving before seven-fifteen. He'd mentioned the night before that they were leaving on their trip at around eight. The drive over to the trailer would take ten minutes tops. Wolf still debated about the wisdom of his "Hail Mary" plan to confront Jimmy and tell him the authorities were on to things. That wasn't exactly true since neither Kasey nor Franker had called him back yet, but they would. It was still pretty early in Phoenix. Maybe they hadn't heard the voice message. Anyway, he'd make it clear to Jimmy that his only chance was to back out now.

Hopefully, the kid would buy it.

If he doesn't, Wolf thought. Worst case scenario, I'll go to the recycling center with him in tow and repeat the story to the Spencers. Tell them it was over.

He mulled over that contingency and figured to make it sound plausible; he could say he'd gotten a heads-up from an FBI friend. And after all, that wasn't too far from the truth. Bill Franker was a friend. Sort of anyway. And Wolf was expecting a call from him. Eventually.

The elevator doors opened, and he smiled. The car

was empty. He stepped inside and hit the button for the first floor.

It felt odd not to be getting up and doing his roadwork. It had been his almost daily routine for the past several months, ever since he'd gotten out of Leavenworth and McNamara had picked him up.

Mac... Wolf knew he was going to have to check on him, too.

He made a mental note to do that as the elevator car jerked to a halt and the automatic doors opened. The hotel lobby was empty, as was the casino when he walked past it. Wolf was feeling like things might just work out as he exited the front doors. The sky was overcast and a light, misty drizzle hung in the air.

Out of curiosity, he glanced over to the spot under the overhang where he'd waited with Sheridan for Darlene and Paxton last night. There was no trace of the second puddle of vomit that the disgraced teacher had deposited there. Even the odor had dissipated, replaced by a strong chemical disinfectant smell. Wolf caught a trace of the foul air blowing north from the recycling center, no doubt.

He noticed that Pike's big Harley was gone as well.

That he hadn't expected.

Jimmy had mentioned that Pike was going along, but in a truck. Maybe he'd left to pick it up. Wolf wondered about him and Crystal. Her description of their date had seemed rather strange, but maybe she hadn't been exactly truthful. Maybe they'd done the nasty, and Pike had kicked her out. Feeling rejected, she'd sought out Wolf.

But how had she known his room number? And how had she gotten that master key?

Too many unanswered questions. The big biker was gone, and Wolf hoped that didn't mean he was running a lap behind the group's departure. Quickening his steps, he jogged over to his rental car.

The Toyota seemed to be resting at an odd angle, one side lower than the other. He hit the remote and the car jerked slightly, displaying the blinking parking lights, and that's when he saw the rightward lean was too pronounced. Something was off.

Walking around to the passenger side, the side opposite the building, Wolf suddenly knew what was causing the tilt.

Both tires on the passenger side were flat.

***

THE SPENCER RECYCLING CENTER
NEW SPENCERLAND, NORTH CAROLINA

Jimmy watched as GEM directed Pike to pull his Harley into the loading bay area making sure he wasn't close to the decoy Rent-n-Haul truck that was also parked in the bay. The floor-to-ceiling curtain was still in place obscuring the second truck, which was parked on the far side, but if Pike went into the locker room to take a piss or shit, there was a chance he might notice it. Hopefully, they'd be driving out of here in the next couple of minutes and Pike wouldn't somehow stumble onto things. Bobbie had told them not to worry if the biker somehow did see it.

"We'll just go get another one and park it in the bay next to the decoy," he'd said. "Me and Craig will be standing by here making sure that everything's set."

Jimmy still didn't like it. There were too many variables for something not to go wrong. The plan was too complex. They should have made it simpler. The simplest was the best, because something always goes wrong. That's what Steve used to say when he was talking about the missions he was on in the army.

Steve, Jimmy thought, and worried that his brother might show up here at the last minute and try to stop him.

"Bobbie," Jimmy said, momentarily forgetting the other man's aversion to the nickname. "I mean, Spence. Can we get moving, please? I'm worried about my brother maybe showing up here. I told you he called me and wants to talk."

He didn't dare say more. Letting them know that Steve suspected something illegal was going on could put him on their hit list. Who knew what they were capable of, especially GEM, who'd already tried to pick a fight with Steve?

Bobbie smiled and took out his cigarette pack, offering one to Jimmy.

He took it and let Bobbie light it for him.

"Jimmy, Jimmy, Jimmy," he said, patting Jimmy's cheek in a patronizing manner. "I told you, I got that covered."

"What do you mean, covered?"

Bobbie sucked on the cigarette causing the ash to glow bright red, then blew the smoke out of his nostrils.

"You didn't hurt him, did you?" Jimmy asked.

"Nah. He's just gonna have a little car trouble is all."

Car trouble? What the hell did that mean?

Bobbie removed the cigarette from his mouth. "Flat tires."

That didn't sound too bad.

Jimmy drew on his cigarette. He wasn't going to be able to relax until this thing was over.

Pike was angling the front wheel of his Harley into a cocked position on the kickstand.

"You guys sure you don't want to park your rice-burners inside here too?" he yelled. "I don't mind, as long as you don't get too close to mine."

He grinned.

GEM ignored him. He'd left his Honda Gold Star

next to Bobbie's Corvette.

"Now remember," Bobbie said, leaning close to Jimmy and speaking in a whisper. "The plan. Everything depends on you getting a picture of the exact type of suitcases Batton's using. Email it to me. Got it?"

Jimmy looked over and saw Pike staring at the two of them.

They were too far away for him to have heard anything, but what if he could read lips?

Nah, Jimmy thought. That kind of shit only happens in the movies.

Pike's mouth twitched with a half-smile.

"You guys ain't gonna put your 'vette in here too?" he said in a loud voice. "Looks like there's plenty of room."

GEM's eyebrows arched in a querulous gesture. Willard's mouth was agape.

"Nah," Bobbie said. "I ain't worried about a little rain."

"A little rain?" Pike said. "According to the weather report, that hurricane's moving up the coast now and bringing a whole lotta rain and wind with it." He raised his arm and glanced at his wristwatch. "Speaking of which, we'd better get moving if we want to beat most of it."

"Right," Bobbie called out. "Saddle up."

Pike patted the seat of his Harley and walked out of the open overhead door.

"Ready, Poncho?" he said.

Jimmy felt a surge of relief that he hadn't noticed the second Rent-n-Haul truck. Or at least it didn't look like he had.

"How's your other boy doing?" Pike asked Bobbie. "I hope I didn't ruin his night, but that little fucker pissed me off."

Bobbie smirked. "I'm going to have a talk with him today. He'll be squared away."

"You'd better," Pike said as he kept walking toward the two pickups that were parked outside. GEM followed along behind him, his big gut bouncing with each rapid step.

Squared away? Jimmy wondered what that implied.

"Hey," Pike said. "I want to drive that bad boy there."

He gestured toward the black Dodge Ram 1500 Bighorn.

Willard stepped over to the Rent-n-Haul truck and reached up to open the driver's door.

"No," Bobbie said, "let Jimmy do the driving. You know the drill."

Willard frowned.

"Okay, boss."

Jimmy noticed that both he and Willard had on the same outfit—a black T-shirt and faded blue jeans. Willard's T-shirt had whitish sweat stains under the arms. Bobbie tossed each of them an olive drab boonie hat.

"Wear these," he said. "It'll make it harder to tell you two apart at a distance."

Willard slipped his on, pulled it down over his face, and giggled that silly girlish-sounding laugh of his. Jimmy knew what that meant. The fucking idiot was stoned again.

Christ, Jimmy thought. Is he even gonna be able to function?

Bobbie must have noticed it, too. He was staring at Willard now.

Pike got into the Bighorn and started it up, revving the powerful engine. GEM got into the green Silverado.

"Let's get our asses in gear," Pike shouted out the driver's door window.

Jimmy's mouth felt dry, but his hands were wringing wet.

"Remember," Bobbie said, grabbing Jimmy's arm and speaking once again sotto voce, "email me that picture."

Jimmy gave a quick nod and stepped up on the running board.

Damn, he thought. There's so much shit that can still go wrong. Awful wrong.

***

THE SPENCER RECYCLING CENTER
NEW SPENCERLAND, NORTH CAROLINA

After calling Jimmy's phone and having it go directly to voicemail after only one ring, Wolf hung up without leaving another message. He then dialed his mother's number and waited. It rang four times and then she picked up.

"Ma," Wolf said, "it's Steve. Is Jimmy there?"

"No," she said. "He got up early and somebody picked him up in a truck."

Damn, Wolf thought. I'm too late.

"Why are you asking?" his mother said. "Is he in trouble?"

"I'm not sure." Wolf hesitated, unsure of what to tell her. After all, all he really had was suspicions. "I wanted to talk to him before he left."

He heard his mother's heavy sigh.

"I know you came back here to try to talk some sense into him," she said. "But I'm afraid it's just too late."

After trying as best he could to give his mother a bit of reassurance, Wolf terminated the call and was debating his next move. A jagged cut decorated the sidewall of each flattened tire. Somebody had apparently used a knife to inflict maximum damage, rendering each tire, and the car, useless for the moment.

A delaying tactic, Wolf thought. Could Jimmy be behind this?

He was trying to convince himself that wasn't possible when he noticed a squad car pulling in the lot. As it drew closer, he saw that it was Nick Paxton behind the wheel. He waved. The squad pulled up next to him and the driver's side window retracted with electronic motorized efficiency.

"Hey, Steve," Paxton said. "Everything okay?"

"Not really," Wolf answered, pointing to the low ride of the left side of his vehicle.

Paxton craned his neck and looked at the flattened tires.

"Damn," he said. "You need a report?"

Wolf considered this. He probably would need something to show to the rental company, but right now what he needed was wheels.

Paxton glanced at the rental car's license plate and then to the MDT in his squad car. He pressed some buttons on the keyboard.

"Funny," he said, "I knew that twenty-eight sounded familiar."

"Twenty-eight?" Wolf said.

Paxton smiled. "Ten-twenty-eight. That's the radio

code for a license plate request. And one of our other officers ran it a little while ago. They're recorded on the MDT."

That piqued Wolf's interest.

"Oh yeah? What time?"

Paxton gazed at the computer screen again. "Looks like zero-six-twenty-four."

Things were starting to add up: a license plate check at zero six-twenty-four, two flat tires at zero six-forty-five.

"Let me guess," he said. "Officer Cook ran it, right?"

Paxton's brow furrowed a bit.

"How'd you know that?"

"Lucky guess." Wolf didn't want to say any more. In fact, he felt he'd probably said too much already. He didn't trust Cook, and sure as hell didn't trust Chief Langford. The verdict on Paxton was still out. Wolf didn't want to believe Pax could be in on this crooked setup.

"You ain't insinuating that Cook had something to do with this, are you?" Paxton asked.

"I'm not insinuating anything," Wolf said. "But you have to admit, it seems pretty damn coincidental."

Paxton reached to his shoulder mic.

"I'll call you a tow truck," he said.

"How about splitting the difference?" Wolf said quickly.

Pausing, Paxton asked, "What do you mean?"

"Give me a ride to my ma's place. I need to use my uncle's truck."

"Well…" Paxton released his hold on the mic and blew out a long breath. "I guess I could." The electronic door locks activated with a metallic thumping sound. "If you don't mind riding in the back of a police car."

"Been there before," Wolf said with a grin, pulled open the door, and slid onto the hard, plastic seat. He hoped it was clean but had little choice.

Beggars couldn't be choosers, and maybe there was still a chance he could catch Jimmy if he could use his uncle's truck.

Paxton called in that he was on an escort and gave Wolf's mother's address.

On the way over Wolf caught a glimpse in the rearview mirror of Paxton's eyes watching him.

"You want to tell me what's going on?" Paxton asked.

Wolf considered the request, once again wondering if he could trust his old friend, and if so, how far.

Discretion is the better part of valor, he thought, recalling another of the bard's quotable lines, but from which play he wasn't sure. *Henry V* maybe?

When Wolf didn't answer, Paxton began talking.

"Look, Steve, I know things ain't exactly been a bouquet of roses for you since you come back. I just want you to know that if there's anything I can do to help you, let me know, will ya?"

"I appreciate that, Pax."

He saw the police officer's head jerk in reply.

"I mean, I understand that you're here because of your brother hanging out with that bunch of losers. It can't be easy to watch him circling the drain like he is. But sometimes, it's all you can do. You can't live his life for him."

Wolf kept it neutral. "He's made some bad choices."

"He has. Darlene's brother, too." Paxton appeared to take a deep breath. "Is Jimmy at home? I'll help you talk to him, if you want."

Pax apparently doesn't know about the Atlanta run, Wolf thought. *Maybe he can be trusted after all.* After a moment's reflection Wolf mentally added, *Or maybe he's faking it and just shining me on.*

"Jimmy's not home," Wolf said. "I need to get my Uncle Fred's truck so I can go look for him."

"Gottcha," Paxton said, and accelerated the squad car.

As they were turning into the trailer park area, Wolf called his mother's number again and told her he needed to use the truck.

After jolting to a stop, Paxton jumped out and opened the rear door. Wolf muttered thanks and ran to the cement steps. His mother was at the screen door holding the keys. Uncle Fred was standing behind her.

"Don't know if she's gonna start, nephew," he said.

"It's been sittin' a while."

Wolf took the keys and jogged to the truck. It was unlocked and the inside cab area smelled musty. It had an ancient-style three-speed transmission stick on the column and was jammed into reverse to keep it fixed. Wolf depressed the clutch, jammed the key into the ignition, and twisted.

Nothing, not even a clicking sound.

"Shit," Wolf said.

Paxton came walking over to him.

"Don't sound too promising," he said.

Uncle Fred was now ambling toward them, leaning on his cane. In his curled left hand he had a pair of jumper cables. He gave an acknowledging nod to Paxton.

"I didn't think she'd start," he said. "I ain't been able to drive her since I had my stroke. Can't use the clutch."

"Want me to call you a tow truck?"

Wolf didn't reply and blew out an exasperated breath. He looked toward his uncle.

"How long's Jimmy been gone?"

Uncle Fred shrugged. "Probably close to forty-five minutes."

Wolf swore. The chances of intercepting him had gone from slim to none.

Paxton glanced around.

"We ain't supposed to do it," he said. "But I can

pull the squad over and give you a jump if you want."

"I'd appreciate it, Pax," Wolf said.

Paxton headed back to his squad car.

"I owe you one for last night."

Uncle Fred looked at Wolf.

"Last night?" he asked.

"Long story," Wolf said, as he slipped out of the cab and grabbed the jumper cables from his uncle's crippled hand.

After lifting the hood, Wolf was less than optimistic. There was another spider web stretching from the radiator to the engine block. The battery terminals were crusted over, and Wolf scraped them one at a time with the triangular teeth of the copper clamps. Paxton pulled up and popped the hood of the cruiser. Wolf raised it and attached the cables, positive to positive, ground to ground. He then raced around the rear of the truck and hopped into the cab again.

Please let it start, he thought, depressing the clutch.

The engine made no sound as he twisted the key.

"Maybe let it charge a little," Uncle Fred offered.

Wolf glanced to Paxton who revved the engine a few times.

The burst of the siren jolted Wolf and he scanned the nearby area for its source.

Then he saw it: the same black unmarked police car he'd seen the day before shoot into the driveway and jerk to an abrupt stop. The driver's door popped open and Chief Langford stepped out, pausing to jam his western-style hat onto his head.

"Paxton," he called out, "what the hell are you doing?"

Paxton rolled his eyes and jumped out of his car, fumbling to put on his hat.

"Just helping a citizen, sir," he said.

Langford's lower jaw jutted outward as his eyes went from person to person.

"My uncle's truck wouldn't start, Chief," Wolf said. "And he's got to go to the doctor. Officer Paxton was just—"

"Shut up," Langford said, turning back to Paxton. "You know it's against regulations to jump start a civilian's vehicle with a squad car, don't ya?"

"Yes, sir," Paxton said. "But—"

"Can it," Langford said, his mouth now twisting into an angry scowl. "Jailbird, get them damn cables off of there."

"Jail bird?" Uncle Fred said. "This man's a veteran. A war veteran. Won the Silver Star."

"Yeah," Langford said. "Well, to me he's nothing but a low down, good for nothing deserter. Served time and got a dishonorable discharge. Why my son, Craig—"

"Your son's a piece of shit," Uncle Fred said. "He was one of 'em that shot a hole in our roof and never even offered to pay for it."

"The hell you say," Langford shot back.

"It's true, you son of a—"

"Uncle Fred," Wolf said, cutting him off. He turned to chief. "Look, Chief, I heard about your son, and I feel bad for him. As a fellow vet, I consider him a brother in arms."

Langford raised his hand, his index finger extended, and thrust it in Wolf's direction like a bird's beak pecking at a tree.

"You ain't fit to shine my boy's shoes."

He paused and waited for a reply. When there was none, he dropped his hand and rotated his head toward Paxton. "You're fired. Go to the station and turn in your star and equipment."

"Chief," Paxton said, "you can't do that."

"I just did. Now move." Langford swung his substantial body in a semi-circle and began traipsing back to his black unmarked.

"You ain't nothing, Langford," Uncle Fred yelled. "I remember when you were just the mailman, and not a good one at that, before Honest Bob stuck that police badge up your ass and it come out the other end."

If Langford heard the comment, he didn't let on. He sandwiched himself into the car, slammed the door, and seconds later peeled backward in reverse. After jolting to a stop, he dropped the transmission into drive with a loud thump.

Paxton looked deflated.

Wolf reached out and placed a hand on the other man's shoulder.

"Pax, I'm sorry."

Paxton shook his head. "Ain't your fault, Steve. It's been a long time coming."

"He's a bitter man," Uncle Fred said. "May the Great Spirit watch over you, Paxton. And may the evil *uktena* stalk old man Langford's sorry ass for the rest of his days."

"Ook-tan-nay?" Paxton said.

"A Cherokee devil man," Uncle Fred said.

"Cherokee?" Wolf said. "You're not Cherokee."

Uncle Fred shrugged. "Hey, if you're going to borrow a demon to throw out a curse, theirs are as good as any."

Paxton flashed a weak looking smile.

"He's just a lot of talk," he said. "Knows he can't fire me unless he takes it before the police and fire commission."

Wolf wondered if his friend was just trying to put on a brave face. Any police and fire commission in this town would most likely be appointed by Honest Bob Spencer, so how impartial would they be. But he said nothing.

"I been wanting to spend more time with Darlene anyway," Paxton said. "Maybe we'll make the move over to Lumberton and I'll apply for the PD there."

Yeah, Wolf thought. Just a brave face.

He gave Paxton's shoulder a squeeze.

"Let me know if there's anything I can do."

"Me too," Uncle Fred said.

"Well," Paxton said, forcing a smile. "Why don't you give that key one more turn and see if this thing'll start?"

Wolf hopped back into the truck's cab. He depressed the clutch and twisted the key.

The engine made a whining sound and then kicked over. It sounded rough but ran steadily.

"It's a sign," Uncle Fred said. "The Great Spirit is with us."

I hope so, Wolf thought. But a sign of what?

CHAPTER 13

**THE ORLEANS HOTEL
LAS VEGAS, NEVADA**

Bray sat at the hotel room's desk and waited for the burner phone to ring. Inside, the air-conditioning was keeping the temperature at a very comfortable seventy degrees. Outside, the sun was beating down and he knew from the television news report that the high temps were going to reach one-hundred-and-eight by mid-afternoon. It was probably in the high nineties already and it wasn't yet six a.m. But it was nine o'clock in New York, and he knew the call would be coming any minute now.

Caught in purgatory, he told himself. Waiting for them to come calling and lure him through the gates of hell.

Only hell in this case didn't have anything to do with the soaring thermometer in Vegas. The ultimate thermometer was being controlled by a bed-ridden Mafioso in Long Island, New York.

These aren't the kind of people you say no to. They want results.

Yeah, Bray thought. They want results, but I'm damned if I do, and damned if I don't deliver.

He knew that when the feds eventually tied him and Abraham to the inevitable assassinations of McNamara and Wolf, the Don wasn't going to want anybody who could turn government witness and implicate him and the family.

He didn't know whether to laugh or cry that his credit checkers in New York had turned the trick and located both quarries. Now he had to report this to Abraham.

The hole was getting deeper.

Right on schedule his burner rang, and he picked it up.

It was Abraham's number, all right. Bray let it ring two more times before pressing the button to accept it.

"It took you long enough." The lawyer's tone sounded gruff. Was he feeling the pressure as well?

"Yeah, well, I've got some good news."

"Tell me," Abraham said.

"My credit checkers in New York. They've located both of them."

He heard the lawyer chuckle.

"Outstanding. Where are they?"

"Wolf's in North Carolina. A motel called the Shamrock near Fayetteville. At least he was the day before yesterday."

"Huh? What kind of bullshit is that? The day before yesterday? Do you have any idea how much pressure I'm under to get results? The old man is breathing down my neck about this. Or rather, he'll got a couple of *goombas* to do the breathing. And it ain't pleasant."

Bray felt like telling him that nothing about this thing was going to be pleasant. The Don would hold them responsible for finding, or not finding, their quarry. And if they did find them, they'd be drawn into some kind of mafia hit job. And McNamara's son-in-law was in the FBI. He had to educate Abraham to the imminent dangers of the quest.

"I can imagine," Bray said. "But listen—"

"No, *you* listen. You know where that McNamara guy is?"

"He's in Del Rio, Texas. Him and a bunch of his Best in the West buddies are staying at a place called the Suncrest Motel."

"Texas?"

"He's doing some border security stuff."

"Border security? Is he with the feds?"

An idea suddenly occurred to Bray. It was a good time to broach the subject.

"Yeah," he said. "As a matter of fact, he's working with them. Catching illegals."

Abraham was silent for a moment, and then said, "Hmm, this complicates things a bit, doesn't it?"

"That's exactly what I've been trying to tell you. McNamara's son-in-law's with the FBI. And I've since found out that he was one of the agents that interviewed me when I went in with that FOIA request. You think he's not going to be crawling up both of our asses if his father-in-law turns up dead?"

Abraham was silent.

Bray found some humor in that: a fucking lawyer who was at a loss for words.

Finally, he broke the silence.

"That's what I been trying to tell you all along. This whole thing could end up drawing us into a real predicament with the feds on one side and the Don and his people on the other."

The lawyer grunted.

"All right," he said finally. "You keep digging. They've already got a specialist on his way to meet you. You've got to pick him up at the airport."

"What? Who is it?"

"He goes by the title of the Clipper. I'll text you

his flight info. And in the meantime, find out exactly where that Wolf guy is."

"Did you hear what I been telling you?"

"Just do it."

Bray realized that Abraham had ended the call.

This was going from bad to worse.

***

SPENCER RECYCLING FACTORY
NEW SPENCERLAND, NORTH CAROLINA

Wolf circled the recycling plant as best he could, but he knew it was a fruitless gesture. The front gate was closed and locked, and a big sign was posted saying that the place was closed for the day. Too much time had gone by. His brother and the rest of them were long gone by now. He still wanted to check though. Reviewing his options, he debated getting onto the freeway south and trying to catch up to the caravan. They would most likely be easy to spot. Jimmy had said that he was driving a twenty-foot Rent-n-Haul truck. Knowing those things, top speed wouldn't be too far over seventy and they'd have to stop for gas at least a couple of times. He glanced at the odometer of the truck and saw it was just shy of two hundred thousand. And the needle of the gas gauge was below empty.

"Gas gauge don't work," Uncle Fred had said before Wolf had taken off. "Better put a couple bucks worth in it before you do too much driving."

Wolf had done so, and the needle hadn't budged.

So giving chase wasn't an option.

What was? They were few and far between.

It was like being trapped on the ropes while your opponent was delivering blow after blow to your sides and temples. The feeling of utter helplessness, which Wolf hated more than anything, kept gnawing at him.

The recycling plant was huge and had a half-asphalt, half-macadamized road circling the place. It was also surrounded by a high cyclone fence with three strands of barbed wire running along the top. Besides the front gate at the main entrance, which was closed, there was a secondary gate on the eastern side of the building. A frontage road gave a perpendicular access to the main highway. Wolf pulled onto the frontage road and drove up to this second gate. It was secured by a chain and heavy-duty padlock. Beyond the fencing the asphalt road gave way to an expansive cement driveway that led to a series of large overhead doors on this side of the building.

It was a loading dock area. Probably where they once transferred all the textile materials to and from the trucks in the old days.

Wolf shifted into neutral and let the pickup coast up to the gate. He noticed three motorcycles and a yellow Corvette parked perhaps fifty feet or so from the big overhead doors. It appeared to be the same one he'd seen in the fire lane in front of the casino. Bobbie Junior's car. The motorcycles looked like two Hondas and one three-wheeler.

Jimmy's friends' bikes. His brother's Yamaha was still parked at Ma's trailer. She'd said somebody'd picked him up in a green pickup truck.

Wolf noticed two men come out of a side door adjacent to the closest overhead door and start walking toward the parked vehicles. One walked with a noticeable limp.

V.I.P. progeny, Wolf thought. Chief Langford's son. The other was Bobbie Jr.

Wolf wasn't crazy about them seeing him, so he stepped on the clutch and brought the stick up and back to shift into reverse. The gears meshed only after a sustained, ratcheting grinding sound before the transmission caught and the truck shot backwards. Wolf glanced at each side mirror to gauge his progress backing up, and then caught sight of Bobbie Jr. and Craig Langford, both watching him.

He wondered if he was far enough away so that they wouldn't recognize him.

***

"Hey," Craig said. "Ain't that Jimmy's uncle's truck?"

Spence had caught sight of it, too, but he was focusing on who it was behind the wheel.

Jimmy's brother, Steve.

Cook had texted earlier that it was mission accomplished disabling the rental car, as instructed. Wolf had somehow beat-feet over to his mother's place and borrowed the truck.

Resourceful, but ultimately a day late and a dollar short. The caravan had left almost an hour ago, and even if Wolf had gotten wind of where they were going, he'd never catch them in that piece of crap.

Jimmy had mentioned that he only thought his brother had figured something out and was trying to talk him out of going. That could be a problem down the road, but most likely not.

When the explosion this afternoon knocks the shit out of this end of the meth and laundering business, Spence reminded himself, all of Steve Wolf's suspicions and concerns won't be worth a cup of warm spit. And I'll be on my way to riding high on some beach in the Caribbean with a beautiful babe on each arm.

He saw the old beat-up truck on its backward trek up the frontage road come to a stop at the highway juncture.

Spence didn't know if Wolf was still watching, but he figured what the hell. He raised his arm and waved to him.

***

THE ESTATE OF ALZONO BATTON
ATLANTA, GEORGIA

The drive to Atlanta had gone even more smoothly than the last one. They'd had to stop for gas twice and had a little over a quarter tank left. Jimmy estimated that many stops on the way back would give him the time he needed to snap that picture and email it to Bobbie.

"Man," Willard said as he stared out the windshield at the sumptuous mansion beyond the huge, wrought-iron gate. "Would you look at this fucking place?"

It was indeed impressive, with a ten-foot brick wall around the whole perimeter. Jimmy figured it had to be patrolled. The long asphalt driveway ran alongside an expansive green lawn, and the house itself, perhaps a hundred yards away, looked like some kind of hotel. It looked big enough to have a hundred rooms. The multi-car garage, as big as some houses, was off to the side with a dozen or so cars of all varieties. Jimmy had seen them on the last trip as he drove by. And he also remembered that in the back was a swimming pool with all kinds of luscious babes lounging around in bikinis. A lot of them were topless.

But this time Jimmy was more interested in looking at the rifles the two security guards had slung on their shoulders. He'd seen them before on previous trips, but somehow looked different. Scarier. The guns looked like those assault rifles they talked about on TV. Probably the same kind that Steve carried in the rangers. Hard black plastic stocks and handles, and a huge, curving clip that probably held fifty or sixty rounds. Maybe even a hundred.

He didn't know, but he was certain Steve would.

Steve...

I shoulda waited for him this morning, he told himself. Waited to talk to him.

Maybe, once this thing was over, he and his brother could take off somewhere and reconnect.

Me doing my music, Jimmy thought, and him training for his next big fight.

Yeah, once this thing was over with.

But they still had a long way to go before that happened.

He could feel the sweat dripping from his armpits again. His hands were so wet they were leaving swatches of moisture on the hard plastic of the steering wheel.

Pike was in front of them in the black Bighorn talking to the gate guards. One of them went inside the brick shack next to the big stone pillars by the iron gate. It looked like he was talking on the phone.

This guy Batton's got more security than Fort Knox, Jimmy thought. And we're gonna be ripping him off.

Suddenly, he had to take a piss real bad.

Real bad.

The one guard in the gate shack leaned out the door and said something that Jimmy couldn't hear. Pike turned and whistled and waved. Then he got back into the Bighorn as the big iron gate slowly opened.

"Okay, let's go," Willard said with a gleeful tone in his voice. "Let's go. I wanna be *riiiiccch*."

Great. The fucker still hadn't come down from the god damn meth.

"Shut up," Jimmy said. "You want one of those guys to hear you?"

Willard shook his head and emitted a giggle.

Christ, Jimmy thought. It'll be a miracle if this thing goes off without a hitch.

He followed Pike's truck up to the house. Glancing in the mirror, he saw that GEM's green Silverado was behind them. Jimmy wondered if GEM was high, too. God, he hoped not. If it was one time that everybody needed to be sharp and on top of things, it was now.

Pike slowed as he made a soft left onto the cobblestone drive in front of the house. Another security guard, a big white guy, came out of nowhere and waved them over toward the garage.

"Oh, goodie," Willard said, rubbing his hands together. "Maybe we'll get to see some of them naked babes by the pool."

"Batton catches you looking," Jimmy said, "he'll make you wish you hadn't."

Willard stuck his tongue between his lips and made a sputtering sound.

"Aw, what's he care? The bitches ain't nothing but hoes anyway, right?"

Jimmy didn't answer. He was finding Willard's behavior less and less tolerable.

Pike pulled behind the garage and kept going. Jimmy followed and they came to a stop in the center of the long structure. One of the big overhead doors began to fold upward into the building. The guard motioned for them to pull inside. Pike drove in first, followed by Jimmy and then GEM. Inside it was well lighted and the immediate area around them was empty. Jimmy glanced around and saw several of Batton's fine cars parked down at the other end. It gave Jimmy the eerie feeling of being caught in a trap.

A side door opened, and Batton stepped in, followed by a trio of black guys. Two white guys in security guard uniforms stepped out as well and one waved his arm for the caravan to stop. The overhead door behind them began to close.

This is it, Jimmy told himself.

He shifted the truck into PARK and pulled up on the door handle. Before he opened it, he grabbed Willard's arm.

"Quit fucking around," he said in a low voice. "You try any of your stupid bullshit and you're liable to get us killed."

"Ooooh," Willard said with a sarcastic lilt to us voice, "I'm scared. Real scared."

"You better be." He pushed open the door.

Pike was already out of his car and doing some kind of ritualistic handshake with Batton. He wasn't a real big guy and he kind of reminded Jimmy of Kevin Hart—not real big, but tough looking. Talked like Hart, too, always using an exaggerated, loud tone of voice. The two brothers with him looked mean as hell. One was around five-ten and wearing a black T-shirt that showed off a huge set of arms that were packed with veins and knotted muscles like Pike's. The other was taller, about six feet, and wearing a long sleeve black sport jacket, despite the heat and humidity. Jimmy was sure that the second guy was packing, too. There was something about him, his eyes, mostly, that sent chills up Jimmy's spine. He looked like he'd slit your throat without blinking his eyes.

"Hey," Batton said in his loud, deep voice, "my biker white boy comes through, right schedule."

His grin was wide.

"Don't I always?" Pike said, grinning back at him. He turned to Jimmy and the others. "Get the stuff out of the truck and put it where Mr. Batton tells you."

GEM, who'd gotten out of his truck and approached them, grunted. Without a word, he turned and went to the back of the Rent-n-Haul truck. He was always the one holding the keys. Jimmy and Willard followed. GEM slipped one of the keys on his ring into the padlock securing the latch. It popped open. After slipping the hasp free, GEM did a quick look both ways and then handed the keys to Jimmy.

"For the gas stop," he whispered.

Jimmy took the ring and jammed it into his pocket, hoping that none of Batton's minions would be suspicious.

GEM shoved the door upward making the display visible.

"Get up there and lift it down," he said.

Both Jimmy and Willard scrambled up on the loading gate. Willard grabbed at the display and pulled. It came loose and he almost fell off the back of the truck. The display twisted and made a cracking sound as it began to split down the middle. Jimmy tried to make it look like he was making a motion to grab it, but let it tumble down toward GEM. He stepped away and let it fall, smashing into several jagged pieces as it hit the floor.

Everything was going according to Bobbie's plan.

Pike jumped over to lend a hand and they pulled it off to the side.

"God dammit!" Pike said, glaring at Willard. "Now look at what you done."

"Hey, it wasn't my fault," Willard said.

GEM reached over and grabbed Willard's calf, squeezing it until the other man cringed.

"This is no good now," Jimmy said. "Where can we toss it, Mr. Batton?"

"I don't want that shit left here," Batton said. "You take it back with you and dump it at your place in Spencerville, or whatever the fuck you call it."

Jimmy and GEM exchanged glances. This wasn't exactly the way it was supposed to go down. They were supposed to leave the broken display here to facilitate Jimmy snapping the pictures at the gas stop. And when they got back, there'd be no time to load the broken façade into the decoy truck.

But it'll get blown up anyway, Jimmy thought. They'll probably find nothing but fragments.

Maybe it could still work.

"Now get my barrels off the motherfucking truck," Batton said. "And then load up them suitcases."

He swung his arm toward a stack of seven, hard-shell, gray-and-blue suitcases stacked in the corner.

Jimmy looked over to them and wondered how much money was inside each one.

Even one of them was probably enough to make

him rich.

"What you lookin' at, boy?" one of the black guys said to Jimmy. "Get your ass movin'."

He and Willard went into the box area and began loosening the canvas cables that held the barrels in place.

"I don't like that motherfucking display being broke," Batton said. "Maybe I better cancel this shipment."

Oh no, Jimmy thought. That'll ruin everything.

"Boss," Pike said, "don't worry about it. I'll make sure they drive nice and slow and obey all the speed limits. And even if they do get stopped, it's not like some narcotics sniffing dog's gonna alert on some suitcases. There's no drugs in 'em."

"That's true," Batton said. He pursed his lips as his head moved up and down with a little rocking motion. "But just in case, I'm sending the Reaper along with y'all."

Jimmy stiffened. It was bad enough having to worry about fooling Pike, but another guy too? He looked at Willard, who seemed practically oblivious in his meth-laced haze, and then to GEM who seemed equally nonchalant.

The stupid fuckers. Both of them with their heads wired up their asses. This could ruin everything.

"The Reaper?" Pike said. "What, you don't think I can handle it?"

Batton clapped the other man on the shoulder and winked.

"Hey, now listen. You my main man and you and your biker buddies are my number one white boy distributors." Batton squeezed Pike's meaty deltoid. "But the Reaper's blood. Understand?"

The big biker shrugged. "Whatever you say, boss." He turned to the black guy in the sport jacket. "Okay, Reaper, I'll buy you a beer when we get to Spencerland."

The taller of the two black men grinned, displaying a gold tooth in the front of his mouth. He placed his hands on his hips and stared up into the back of the truck. As the lapels of the sport coat got pushed back, Jimmy could see that the guy wore two guns, one under each arm in a twin shoulder rig. Both were black, semi-automatics.

The man's dark eyes were the coldest, cruelest looking things Jimmy had ever seen.

***

THE WOLF RESIDENCE
NEW SPENCERLAND, NORTH CAROLINA

Wolf had managed to get the bullet hole in the roof of his mother's trailer patched just before the rain got heavy again. Feeling at a loss to do anything as far as the Jimmy situation was concerned, he'd decided to do some much needed repairs. The pickup's battery seemed to be holding a charge, so he drove it to the Home Depot and picked up what he needed. The bullet had made a nice, round hole inside, and a serrated exit hole outside. Having no ladder, Wolf stood on one of his mother's kitchen chairs to first fill the inner hole as best he could with some silicone and then taped over it. The painting could wait.

The outside required a bit more ingenuity, since he had no ladder, and a kitchen chair wasn't going to do it. He ended up backing the truck up to the side of the trailer, finding enough sturdy plastic boxes to throw together a makeshift elevated platform, and then climbed up on top of the trailer's roof. It was precarious and reminded him of one of those old plastic crate stack challenges that had been rampant on YouTube during mid-summer. Wolf had considered those people pretty stupid for climbing up on those haphazardly stacked boxes, but now found himself doing something equally reckless. Luckily, the squared-off edge allowed him to get a bit of a grip and he pulled himself on top. It seemed sturdy enough to hold him, but he still moved gingery on all-fours. Then the rain transformed from an occasional spray of droplets to a substantial and steady downpour. Staying spread out on the roof, he crawled over to inspect the damage. The exit-hole was somewhat larger than the entry one and surrounded by an array of jagged metal shards. But given that the top of the trailer was made of aluminum, Wolf was able to pound it down and smooth it out. Then he inserted two new strips of metal under and over it and secured them by wedging them in place, after which he began to seal the entire thing with a healthy pasting of Flex-Seal. The stuff was advertised on TV as being waterproof, so this would be a good test.

The repair work was going easier than Wolf had expected until the tube of sealant ran short.

Why is it I can never just make one trip to the hardware store, he though as he began to make his way back toward the edge.

The rain was really coming down now and rather than lower himself over the side and onto the stack of crates and risk slipping, he crawled beyond the truck's tailgate, gripped the edge, and swung his legs down the side. After dangling against the wet metal for a few seconds, he pushed off and dropped the remaining six feet or so to the ground. The hard surface of the cement slab sent a wave of pain surging upward through his feet and up to his knees, which he likened to a hard-landing parachute jump. Of course, back then he'd had the advantage of wearing jump boots, not gym shoes, but the pain passed after a moment. His mother opened the door and motioned to him.

"Steve, you're soaked. Come inside."

"In a minute, Ma," he said. "I've got to move Uncle Fred's truck."

"Well, your phone's been ringing."

That piqued Wolf's interest. Maybe it was Jimmy calling. Maybe he was in trouble.

Or, Wolf thought, it could be Mac or Yolanda or even the Great Oz.

Leaving the truck where it was, he ran around to the front door and skipped up the steps to go inside.

His mother was standing there with a towel. Uncle Fred was busy spreading some old newspapers on the floor next to the table.

"Stand on these, nephew," he said. "I don't feel like mopping up your drippings."

Wolf stepped onto the papers and then took the time to dry himself off. When his hands were sufficiently dry, he picked up his phone and scrolled to the Missed Calls section.

The listing said *Trackdown Inc.*

It had to be Kasey. He pressed redial.

She answered with a crisp tone.

"Kasey, it's me. Steve. Missed your call."

"No problem," she said, her tone warming ever-so-slightly. "I missed yours last night. Bill and I had a parent-teacher's conference at Chad's school. Sorry it took me so long to get back to you."

It sounded like Special Agent Franker was stepping into the role of stepfather pretty well.

Good for him, Wolf thought. Every kid needs a father figure.

"I didn't check the messages until this morning," she said. "And Bill had already left for work. What is it you need to talk to him about?"

Wolf considered telling her but decided against mentioning anything about drugs and federal involvement in front of his mother and Uncle Fred.

"Just something I needed his advice on," Wolf said. "Do you have his cell or work number?"

She read off both to him and he scrambled for a piece of paper and pen.

"Thanks," he said after repeating them back to her. "I'll give him a call."

"Okay." Her tone sounded tentative. "But it might be better if you waited until he gets home. Maybe like seven, our time. He's on the bank robbery detail now and probably won't be able to talk."

Or appreciate me calling, Wolf thought.

"Okay," he said. "No problem. Just have him give me a jingle when he has time."

"Will do." Her tone was still imbued with hesitancy. "Have you heard from Dad lately?"

"No. Why?" He automatically tried to recall when he'd last gotten a call from Mac.

"Usually, he calls me first thing in the morning, but today he didn't."

"I talked to him the other day. He said he was with

Buck and the boys down in Del Rio and they were having a good old time."

"Yeah, that's pretty much what he told me, too, but I'm still a bit worried. I've been trying to reach him this morning, but there's no answer."

Wolf didn't like the sound of that and couldn't help but feel a slight twinge of guilt that he hadn't accompanied McNamara on his latest venture.

One mission at a time.

After assuring Kasey that he'd try to reach out to her father as well, he terminated the call and set the phone down.

"Is Big Jim all right?" his mother asked.

Wolf canted his head slightly indicating uncertainty.

"I'm sure he is," he said. "If anybody's a natural born survivor, it's Mac."

"He is at that," Uncle Fred said. "Kept your dad and me outta harm's way during Desert Storm a couple of times."

That reminded Wolf that both his uncle and his father had served with McNamara during one of his many wars, which was all the more reason to get this Jimmy problem settled and tag up with Mac again. He glanced out the window and saw that the rain had let up a bit.

Uncle Fred pointed to the ceiling. "Looks better, but it's still leaking a little bit."

"Yeah, I know," Wolf said as he headed for the door. "I'm going to have to revisit the hardware store."

Outside, the rain had ceased, for the most part, but there was still a mixture of swirling mist and cold wind blowing up from the south. As Wolf got behind the wheel, he felt the unpleasant jab in his foot of the protruding crowbar sticking out from under the seat. He kicked the tool further underneath and twisted the key again.

The engine made a couple half-hearted groans and ceased.

Wolf groaned. Not again.

He checked the battery gauge. It was in the red again. He'd have to call for another jump. Glancing at his watch, he saw that it was fourteen-oh-four. Jimmy was most likely on the road somewhere. Wolf hoped for the best on that and made a mental promise to try and talk some sense into his little brother as soon as he got back.

And I'll have to get a new battery for Uncle Fred's truck, he thought.

Then something occurred to him.

Why not just buy him a whole new truck? One with an automatic transmission so he could drive again. Wolf certainly had enough money in the bank to buy one outright.

And maybe I should think about doing something for Ma, too, he thought. So far, all that I've accomplished here is alienating my kid brother, losing track of Mac, getting one of my old friends fired from his police job, and passing up a chance to get laid by an old girlfriend.

Of all of them, the last one was somewhat bittersweet.

Regrets, he thought. I have a few ...

***

ANCHOR TRUCK STOP
INTERSTATE 20
NEAR DILLON, SOUTH CAROLINA

It's time, Jimmy thought, figuring he couldn't afford to wait any longer. He'd tried to call Bobbie several times, but he never answered. They'd stopped for gas twice already on the way back, once in Madison, Georgia, and just outside Columbia, South Carolina. Now they were coming up on Dillon and Jimmy knew this would be his last chance. Both Pike and that Reaper guy had been right on his ass both of those times. If he wanted to get those pictures taken and emailed to Bobbie, he had to make it now. In another hour and a half, they'd be pulling into New Spencerland, and Bobbie and Craig had to make sure they had the right style suitcases and that they were set up in the duplicate truck the same way they were in this one.

But he worried about the broken façade, too. What if Pike or the Reaper checked the decoy truck and saw that the broken pieces weren't there? The black Bighorn was about a hundred yards or so in front of him. He checked the side-view mirrors for any signs of the black Charger that the Reaper was driving.

It looked clear. For now, anyway.

He swung over into the right lane and angled onto the exit ramp as he called Pike and told him they needed to stop for gas. He'd purposely waited until Pike's lead truck had almost passed the freeway exit before pressing the button on the burner phone. It rang two times as the Bighorn sailed past the exit and Jimmy steered onto the ramp.

Pike answered with two questions.

"Is that you getting off? Where the hell you going?"

"Gas," Jimmy said. "And we both gotta piss."

He glanced in the side-view mirrors again and tried to see if GEM was following him off. He didn't see him, nor did he see the black Charger, which gave him a slight feeling of relief. That guy gave Jimmy the creeps.

"Shit," Pike said. "Thanks for the fucking advance notice, Poncho. Now I'll have to find a place to turn around. Wait at the gas station for me."

"Will do," Jimmy said and hung up.

Willard had that half-assed smile on his face.

"Smile for the camera," he said. "Click, click."

Jimmy merely shook his head in disgust. He couldn't wait to be free of this idiot. GEM and Bobbie, too. Pretty soon he was going to be far, far away.

With his newfound money.

The tall sign advertising the truck stop loomed about three hundred yards away.

As he accelerated, Jimmy thrust the phone to Willard, who fumbled, dropping it onto the floorboards.

"Call GEM and tell him we're getting off to get gas," Jimmy said.

"And snap those pictures," Willard said. "Don't forget."

"I ain't planning on it. Now call him."

Jimmy sped as fast as he dared toward the gas station section of the truck stop, checking the mirrors again. If the Silverado and the Charger had exited, he didn't see them.

Maybe, with a little luck, he'd be able to pull this part off.

He recalled those dark, foreboding eyes leveled at him in the garage.

"Glad we're stopping," Willard said. "Gotta piss."

"You call GEM?" Jimmy said, with an angry inflection in his voice.

"Yeah, yeah." Willard picked at the numbers and then put the phone to his ear. Moments later he said, "Hey, man, we're stopping for gas and to take them pictures. Okay?"

After what Jimmy took to be an acknowledgement from GEM, Willard said, "Okay, see ya."

He hung up before Jimmy could intercede.

"Dammit," Jimmy said. "I wanted you to ask him about the Reaper."

"What you worried about? GEM can take that skinny fucker. Break him in half."

"Yeah, right. That guy's got two guns."

"So? Bobbie's got a gun, don't he?"

"He ain't here. And so does Pike."

"Well, I'll bet Craig's packing." He flashed a moronic looking smile. "You forgetting about that night at your mom's trailer?"

Jimmy didn't bother to mention to this moron that Craig wasn't here, either. His mind flashed back to them horsing around, and Craig's gun going off and blowing a hole in the ceiling of the trailer.

I'm gonna have to give her some of my money to get that fixed, he thought.

He twisted the wheel and turned into the gas station, checking the mirrors one more time. Instead of going straight into the first set of pumps, he swung around the building and then came in from the opposite direction. That way he figured he could see any approaching vehicles and the rear section of the truck would be out of sight to them.

So far there was no sign of the Charger.

"I'm gonna go piss," Willard said.

"Not yet, you're not. Get the nozzle set up in the gas tank first." He thrust out the credit card Bobbie had given him. "Use this."

"Come on, man." Willard's face drooped. "I told you, I gotta piss. Bad."

"And I got to open up the back before anybody sees us, you dummy," Jimmy shouted, opening the door. "The pictures, remember?"

He jumped down and literally ran to the back, glancing around. The coast still looked clear. The latch was locked with that thin-hasp padlock, and he pulled out the ring of keys GEM had given him earlier. Sorting through them, he found the right one and inserted into the lock. It popped open and he slid it out, then pulled up on the latch and lifted the rear door, stopping its upward progression at about three feet.

Glancing in both directions, he put his foot on the metal rung below the tailgate and crawled through the opening of the partially raised door. Inside the box was hot and stuffy as hell. His calf brushed against the stacked and broken display. In a way, not having to remove it saved him some time, so it had been a good idea to "unintentionally" damage it. But he wished they'd been able to leave it in Atlanta, as planned. The seven suitcases sat against the wall, still secured by the nylon straps. Jimmy pulled out his own phone and held it up. It was dark and he could barely see to press the right buttons.

"Hey, Jimmy," Willard yelled. "The pump's running. I can't hold it anymore. I'm going in."

Idiot, Jimmy thought. He's as useless as tits on a boar hog.

He fiddled with the phone some more.

Finally, the buttons illuminated, and he snapped two pictures, the flash lighting up the interior with a burst of light each time. He did one over-all shot and one close-up. Checking to make sure they were good enough, he stuck the phone back into his pocket and then scrambled back to the opening and went down on all fours to get back out. As he was sliding his upper body out, he caught sight of a pair of shiny black shoes and black pant-legs.

The Reaper was standing there casting a baleful look at him.

Where the hell had he come from? And how much had he seen?

"What you doin' in the back there?" The man's tone was low and ominous. The front of his jacket was open, and Jimmy could see the handles of the two pistols. His throat went dry.

"I—" He could barely get any words out. "Was just checking on something."

"Checkin' on what?"

"Sounded like something was flopping around back there," Jimmy said. "I wanted to make sure the load was secure, is all."

The other man stared at him and then gestured for him to lift the door.

"Are you kidding?" Jimmy said. "What if somebody's watching? They'll see."

"You best be doin' what I say, little man, 'fore I bust cap up your ass."

Jimmy tried to swallow but didn't seem to have enough spit left in his mouth. He gripped the bottom of the door and lifted. It rolled upward a few more feet.

"See?" Jimmy said. "Everything's cool."

The black man told him to raise the door higher and get back into the box.

Oh, God, Jimmy thought. He's gonna kill me.

"Please, no," he muttered.

"Do it, motherfucker."

The black man's eyes glowed like twin pieces of anthracite, dark and unfathomable.

Jimmy scurried up into the back of the truck and the Reaper followed, making the climb with alarming ease. He shoved Jimmy farther inside, and then took out his phone, using it as a flashlight. After surveying the seven suitcases, he snapped a couple pictures and then shoved Jimmy toward the rear opening again.

"Down," the Reaper said.

He let Jimmy jump first, then followed, landing with panther-like grace.

Gem and Pike suddenly appeared. Pike had a questioning look on his face.

"What's going on?" he asked.

"I caught this little white motherfucker sneaking into the back of the truck." His hand shot up and gripped the lower portion of Jimmy's face, pinching his cheeks and mouth, forming a fish-like appearance.

"Hey," GEM said, "let him go."

"You want some too, fat boy?" the Reaper said.

GEM took a step forward and puffed out his chest.

"Hey, I ain't scared of you none."

The Reaper released his grip on Jimmy and dropped his hand to mid-chest level. The butt of one of his handguns in the shoulder rig became slightly more visible.

"Well, *white mo-ther-fuck-er,*" he said, enunciating each syllable with an exaggerated distinction. "If you ain't, you oughta be."

His lips parted, showing his gold tooth in front as he reached his right hand inside his sport coat.

"Hey," Pike said in a forceful tone. "Cool it, all right? We're almost there and this ain't getting us nowhere. Next thing we know the cops'll be on our asses."

After a few more seconds GEM's tongue flicked out and ran over his lips. He seemed to shrink back a step.

The Reaper snorted a laugh.

Pike's eyebrows raised and he looked at Jimmy.

"What were you doing in the back of the truck?"

"I heard something bouncing around when I was driving. Must've been that broken display thing."

Pike turned to the Reaper. "How'd it look?" Pike asked the Reaper.

"Tape's all still in place."

"Good," Pike said. "Now close this fucking thing up. And let's gas up too and get moving."

Tape's all still in place. What did he mean by that?

After Pike and the Reaper went to gas up their cars, GEM leaned close.

"I shoulda ripped that nigger's head off," he said, working his mouth again, "and shit down his neck."

"Yeah, right," Jimmy said. "The fucker's got two guns."

"I ain't scared of him."

"Whatever," Jimmy said. He felt the knot in his stomach tighten some more.

"You get the pictures?" GEM asked, leaning closer.

"Yeah. Now go gas up your ride, will ya?"

GEM puffed up his chest again.

"You don't tell me what to do, understand?"

"Yeah, sorry, GEM."

As GEM walked away Jimmy extended his middle finger but kept it down by his leg.

My brother would've kicked your ass last night, he thought.

The flow-latch of the gas pump had long since shut off the gas flow. Jimmy removed the nozzle, stuck it back into the pump, and replaced the gas cap. He then got back into the cab and pulled his cell phone from his pocket. He started the engine and pulled away from the pumps. Willard was still inside the station. After stopping at the edge of the building, Jimmy checked the two pictures he'd snapped. Not real good, but they looked passable. On the close-up he saw what the Reaper had been talking about. Sections of duct tape had been stuck over the metal seams. You'd have to take them off or cut them to open the cases. Batton had never done that before.

I'd better tell Bobbie about this, Jimmy thought.

He went to his Internet and typed in *DUCT TAPE ON SUITCASES* and sent the pictures to Bobbie.

Something slammed against the side of the truck and Jimmy jerked with a shock. The passenger door popped open, and Willard looked up at him with that stupid grin of his.

"Scared ya, didn't I?"

"You stupid fucker."

"You get 'em?" Willard asked. "The pics?"

"Yeah," Jimmy said, feeling the knot in his stomach growing tighter.

Suddenly he had to take a piss, too.

Real bad, but he had to call Bobbie first. He dialed and it rang seven times and went to automatic voicemail.

Shit, Jimmy thought, and hit the redial button.

This time it rang only twice before going to voice-mail.

Jimmy glanced in the mirror and saw Pike's truck approaching. The Silverado and the Charger were falling in line behind it. At some point GEM was supposed to pull in front as they got near the recycling plant, but now, with the Reaper tagging along, the pucker factor had increased exponentially.

His phone's ringing startled him. He was gratified to see it was Bobbie.

"Got 'em," Bobbie said. "Nice going."

He was talking about the pictures, but that wasn't what Jimmy wanted to tell him about.

"Hey, wait," Jimmy said. "We got a problem. Batton sent some bad-ass black dude with us this time. He's following along in a Dodge Charger."

"Shit," Bobbie said. "Why didn't you tell me this before?"

"I tried to, but I ain't had time to call. I didn't want to take the chance of them seeing me talking on my phone."

"Good thinking," Bobbie said. "Who is this new player?"

"The call him the Reaper, or something," Jimmy said. "He's one of the scariest looking guys I ever seen."

Bobbie was silent for several seconds and then asked, "This dude's driving a Charger?"

"Yeah. A black one."

"Just like him," Willard yelled.

Jimmy frowned at him. "Will you shut up?"

Pike was slowly driving past the cab of the truck now and Jimmy didn't want the biker to see him on the phone.

He quickly put the phone down by his leg, let Pike drive by and stop. Jimmy pressed the button to put Bobbie on speaker and said, "You still there?"

"Yeah. What's going on?"

"Pike was driving past. I got you on speaker now."

"All right," Bobbie said. "This is a new complication, but we can handle it. Here's what I want you to do. Now listen up."

Jimmy listened.

CHAPTER 14

SPENCER RECYCLING FACTORY
NEW SPENCERLAND, NORTH CAROLINA

The lab still reeked of stale cat piss, but soon it would all be gone.

Spence glanced at his watch and then wiped his palms on his thighs trying to dry them off. It was getting close to crunch time. They were five and goal, with two downs left, and with the last-minute adjustments that had to be made, the pressure was getting to him.

But only a little bit, he told himself.

They were set to arrive in a matter of minutes now. He waited for Jimmy to call to confirm that they were almost there. He took out his cell and held it in his hand, ready to answer on the first ring.

"Hey, do that outside, okay?" Craig cautioned,

glancing over at the C-4 and detonators he'd just finished setting up. "It would be rare, but there's a slight chance that the frequency from your cell might set it off prematurely."

Spence felt a chill go through him.

"What the fuck?" he said. "I thought you told me they won't go off until I make the calls."

"They shouldn't." Craig was sweating now.

Maybe he wasn't quite as good as he claimed to be. After all, a mistake in Afghanistan had cost him his leg.

Spence put the phone back into his pocket and reviewed the final modifications he'd outlined to Jimmy and GEM. The felicitousness of his last-minute changes made him feel good, like a master quarterback calling a new play that would overcome a setback and win the game. But he was still a tad nervous. Maybe he needed a little snort to make him feel extra sharp. And he deserved it. After all, he needed to do everything he could to win, because winning was everything.

He walked into the hallway, out of sight of Craig, and removed one of the chemical folds from his pocket. No sense letting the hired help know he was going to snort up. Once he'd rolled the bill, a hundred-dollar bill for luck, and snorted it, he felt the coinciding burn and euphoric rush as he pinched the top of his nose.

After a moment's appreciation, he mentally reviewed his new adjustments to the plan.

GEM was to call Pike and tell him that there was a road closure ahead and that he was going to have to take the lead. Once he was in front of Jimmy, they would proceed by a somewhat circuitous route to the front gate of the plant. GEM was to pull over and let Jimmy be the first in line when they pulled up to the gate, and then use the Silverado to block the roadway. And then GEM would take his sweet-ass time walking up to unlock it. Once he motioned Jimmy through, GEM was to drop the keys, or do whatever the hell else he could to delay Pike and the guy in the Charger from immediately driving in.

"Stall the damn truck out, or something," Spence had told him. "Just block that entranceway for a good minute, or so."

That would give Jimmy, driving fast, the chance to proceed around to the south end of the plant and be out of sight. He'd have to stop to drop Willard off at the bay doors, who was supposed to make it look like he'd just backed the Rent-n-Haul truck into the bay. And he and Craig would have already pushed back the curtain from around the decoy truck.

Once Pike and this new player, the Reaper, were inside the bay, Jimmy could swing around the other side of the building and go back out the front gate and proceed to the mall.

When Pike and GEM go into the locker room, he reminded himself, I make the command detonation.

Both the Reaper guy and Tim Sheridan will die in the twin explosions.

One in the bay, and the other in the lab.

Spence glanced at the sliding steel chain-link door of the supply cabinet. Through the holes he could see that Sheridan was slumped in there and still out cold. Twin trickles of blood wound their way down the side of his face from the several open cuts where they'd bludgeoned him into unconsciousness.

Time to take one for the team, Tim.

He looked at the charges that Craig had set up just outside the cage. It was attached to some ammonium nitrate packages that would make a nice, big bang.

Instead of one command detonation, Spence would have to do two, but it should work.

I'm just going to step outside and have a smoke, he imagined himself saying to the Reaper. *Care to join me?*

If he did, fine. One press of the button and the calls would go through in succession. First the lab, to take care of Sheridan, and then the bay, which would look like a tragic aftermath. Pike and GEM would be safe enough in the locker room, probably, but if not, that was all right, too.

Another couple casualties of war, he thought. The war on drugs.

That made him grin.

He was two command detonations away from all

that money ...

"Let's go to the bay and wait for them," Spence said. "We got to make sure the right bay door's open and that curtain's pulled back."

"Go ahead," Craig said. "I want to check on these connections one more time."

"Better you than me." He turned to take one more look at Sheridan who was still out.

Bye-bye, Timmy, Spence thought. Stay just as you are, and you'll never know what hit you.

***

HOME DEPOT
NEW SPENCERLAND, NORTH CAROLINA

It had taken what seemed like forever for the damn tow truck to arrive, and the guy had charged him way too much for the jump. Wolf revved up the engine for several minutes hoping to give the battery a charge that would hold this time, but he wasn't optimistic. Since the last one had stayed for only an hour or so, this time he employed Uncle Fred to come along.

"What am I gonna do?" His uncle asked. "With my left leg the way it is, I can't use the clutch."

"I'll leave it in neutral and you can keep the gas going with your cane."

Uncle Fred grinned. "Sounds like a plan, nephew."

Wolf was glad that he'd taken him along and given him a chance to feel useful. Maybe things were starting to come together, at least a little bit. Now, as he waited in line at the checkout with more Flex Seal, a can of white paint, and a roller, he wondered if his luck would continue when Jimmy got back. Wolf also pondered his next move.

It was about a four-and-a-half hour drive each way. They'd apparently left at around zero-seven-fifteen, which meant they should be back between sixteen and seventeen hundred, depending on how long they spent in Atlanta. If they were dropping off crystal meth, they'd probably want to make it as quick as possible. Coming back could be another matter. He doubted they'd be bringing anything back. Or would they?

It was hard to figure without knowing all the facts, but one thing was certain: If his brother made it back without any problems, Wolf figured to confront him with the accusations head-on. Tell him that he'd notified the FBI or the DEA or somebody about what had been going on here and give Jimmy the choice of continuing with his sordid activities or going to see the recruiter.

It was a Hail Mary play, but what other choice did he have?

His turn finally came, and he set the can of Flex Seal on the belt by the electronic scanner.

"Are you a veteran, sir?" the girl behind the Plexiglas screen asked.

The question surprised him, and he wasn't sure how to answer. He'd served all right, with distinction, been in combat, taken fire, and gotten decorated. But he was also the unjust recipient of that DD, and an ex-con.

"Yeah," he said. "How'd you know?"

The girl smiled and pointed at his airborne tattoo.

"My dad has one like that," she said. "You get a ten percent discount."

Wolf thanked her as he paid and then winked at her.

"Tell your dad I said thanks for his service. From one airborne trooper to another."

As he walked outside, he heard Uncle Fred continuing to rev the motor with his cane.

Maybe things were going to turn out all right after all.

***

SPENCER RECYCLING FACTORY
NEW SPENCERLAND, NORTH CAROLINA

Everything was going according to plan as GEM pulled ahead, replacing Pike in the Bighorn, and laced his way through a maze of side streets on their way to the ultimate rendezvous. Even the weather had cooperated, with the rain sweeping down on the last part of the journey and suddenly stopping, being replaced by the sun. Then, with a sudden intrusiveness, both Willard and Jimmy's private phones sounded with alerts.

"Hey, man," Willard said, looking at his. "Looks like there was a bunch of tornadoes that hit all around us, from here on up to Lumberton and to the south as well. Sure glad they didn't touch down here."

"Yeah," Jimmy said, turning off the windshield wipers. "Now call Bobbie and tell him we're almost there."

Willard played with his phone and in a moment more, Bobbie's face-time image appeared.

"Put me on speaker," he said.

Willard held the phone by the dashboard.

"We're almost there," Jimmy said, taking control. "GEM's in the lead, and I'm running right behind him."

"Okay," Bobbie said. "Good. Are Pike and the other guy still behind you?"

Jimmy checked the side-view mirror and caught a glimpse of both the Dodge truck and the Charger.

"Yeah, they're back there."

"Now this is what you're going to do." Bobbie's words were coming fast now. Faster than normal.

Probably just did a line not too long ago, Jimmy

figured.

He wasn't too crazy about a coked-out guy calling the shots. There was too much of a chance for a screw-up.

"You listening?" Bobbie asked. "This is crucial."

"Yeah," Jimmy said.

"All right. GEM already knows to let you be first in line at the front gate. He's gonna veer off to the side and let you pass him on the frontage road. Then he's gonna pull in back of you at a diagonal angle that'll block Pike and the other guy."

"The Reaper," Willard said. "Bad ass brother."

"Whatever," Bobbie said. "Now listen, this is crucial."

That was the second time he's told us that, Jimmy thought.

"GEM's gonna take his sweet ass time," Bobbie said. "He's gonna be parked behind your truck and walk up alongside to open the gate. When he throws the one side open, you drive through right away. He's gonna drop his ring of keys, look for 'em, and then walk real slow back to the Silverado, which is still blocking the entrance, get it?"

"Yeah," Jimmy said.

"Okay," Bobbie said. "Now this is the crucial part. You drive at fast clip around the east side of the building, and when you make the corner to head for the bay here, drop off Willard and high-tail it around to the north side so that you're outta sight, understand?"

"This is pretty much the same as our original plan," Jimmy said.

"I know," Bobbie said. "The main gate in front's already open. The chain's just looped through and not locked. So you just drive on around the building and go out that way. Make sure you turn right so you don't drive past us here. Willard, you hop up into the decoy truck and act like you just backed it in."

It sounded good, but Jimmy was still having some misgivings.

"What if they ask where I'm at?" Jimmy said.

"They won't," Bobbie said. "And if they do, I'll tell 'em you went to take a shit or something."

"But then Pike won't see me when he goes into the locker room."

He wasn't liking this as much as he was a few seconds ago, but at least he would be long gone when the explosion ripped through the place.

"It'll work. You guys got it?"

"Yeah." Jimmy glanced at Willard, who nodded.

"Repeat it back to me," Bobbie said.

"Aw, come on," Jimmy said. "We ain't fucking kids."

"Just do it." Bobbie's voice was stern.

After a sigh, they both recited what their forthcoming actions would be.

"Okay, good," Bobbie said. "This'll go down just like clockwork."

"It'd better," Jimmy said. "We're almost there now."

GEM pulled onto the road and then off to the side, sticking his arm out the window to motion for Jimmy to take the lead.

He pulled ahead and saw the front gate about fifty yards ahead. As he pulled around the Silverado Jimmy saw that the weather had cooperated too. Not only had they missed those twisters, but there was standing water on both sides of the macadamized roadway. No way that the Reaper could drive around the Silverado once it was blocking the road. The Bighorn, maybe, but not the low-riding Charger. Coming to a stop about ten feet in front of the gate, Jimmy checked his mirrors again.

The roadway was too straight for him to be able to see the other vehicles, which had to be directly behind him.

The sweat was pouring off him now, under both arms and down his face from his hair. His hands were so slick he worried that they'd slip off the damn steering wheel. GEM's bulky image appeared in the driver's side mirror. He was hustling up toward the front, the key ring laced through his fingers and jiggling against his hand.

Come on, Jimmy thought. Come on.

He turned to Willard, who was also sweaty looking. "You ready?" Jimmy asked.

"I'm cool."

GEM was pulling the chain through the metal framework now. Jimmy took his foot off the brake and stepped on the gas as soon as GEM shoved the one side of the gate open. He jumped aside as Jimmy drove through.

Here we go, he thought. The point of no return.

***

Spence watched Willard jump out to the truck as Jimmy slowed down just enough. Willard hit the ground and fell, rolling in the muddy gravel. Spence ran forward and helped him up. He was covered with brown water and little pieces of gravel.

"That fucker didn't even stop all the way to let me get down," Willard said, his mouth twisted into an angry scowl.

"We'll deal with that later," Spence said, glancing toward the north end of the building.

No sign of the Silverado yet. He looked the other way and saw the brake lights of Jimmy's truck flash the instant before he made the turn. Then the truck was out of sight.

Okay, he thought. Wait, wait, wait.

"Hurry up," he said to Willard. "Get in the other truck. Make like you just backed it in."

Willard brushed at his clothes as he began walking toward the decoy.

"Hustle, dammit," Spence called. He swiveled his head toward the plant's corner again and saw the Silverado rounding the corner. The Bighorn was right behind it, followed by the black Charger he'd been hearing about.

"Move your fucking ass," he yelled. "They're almost here."

That spurred Willard to double-time it. He hopped up into the cab and got behind the wheel.

The two pickups and the car pulled up and Spence stepped out onto the roadway and directed them to park next to his Corvette and the two motorcycles. His heart felt like it was beating a mile a minute now, and he regretted ingesting the coke. He almost wished he had some Valium or something to slow his metabolism down a bit. Craig was still nowhere in sight.

Where the hell was he?

Spence, his back to them, took out the command detonation phone, dialed the number, and stuck it back into his pocket.

All he had to do was to press the send button.

Pike was out of the truck and walking over to him now, glancing around.

Did he suspect something?

GEM was ambling along behind him, and the black guy they'd described as the Reaper had gotten out of the Charger and was also walking over.

Spence forced himself to grin and shot a glance

over his shoulder to check where Willard was and to see if Craig was there as well. No Craig, but Willard was hurriedly exiting the truck.

The shitbird's scared of being around the explosives, Spence thought.

In truth, he wasn't exactly comfortable standing where he was at the moment either. The overhead bay door was open behind them and the floor-to-ceiling curtain had long since been retracted. There was that nice, big open space, and Pike's Harley.

Spence took a closer look at the Reaper and saw what Jimmy meant when he'd described him as one of the scariest looking black guys he'd ever seen. The man was pure malevolence.

"Keys are in it," Pike said, thrust an extended thumb back toward his right shoulder as he looked at Willard. "What the hell happened to you?"

Willard shrugged and smiled nervously.

"Fell down."

The Reaper was staring at him, and then looked at the truck.

"Where's Poncho?" Pike asked.

"He's getting the security van for the casino delivery."

They had a Transit 250 van specially painted to look like the ones used by the security company to make the drop-offs of chips and other materials.

"Why don't you guys go get changed?" Spence said.

Pike was looking uneasy. He glanced around again.

"Yeah," GEM said. "Let's go change. I gotta take a shit anyway."

The Reaper walked past all of them and over to the Rent-n-Haul truck in the bay. He looked at the cement pavement, and then to the truck. After glancing back at them, he extended his finger and rubbed it over the side of the hood, then turned and walked back. Craig had just appeared inside the bay and was walking this way as well, but his slow gait put him far behind the black man.

There was suddenly a gun in the Reaper's hand. He leveled it in front of Bobbie's face.

"What you trying to pull, motherfucker?"

Bobbie felt his heart freeze. He could barely take a breath.

"What do you mean?" His voice sounded like a whimper.

"Hey, Reaper," Pike said. "What—"

"Shut up, Pike," the Reaper said. "That's not the fucking truck. We been driving in the rain and there's no wet tire tracks on the pavement. The hood's not even wet. Not hot, neither."

He grabbed Spence's shirt and pulled him forward. The sudden movement caused his right arm to bump his side.

Oh shit, he thought. I hit the phone. I hope—

A second later a blast occurred inside the large

building, followed by another blast scarcely a millisecond later. Craig suddenly vanished from sight, tossed like a ragdoll in a windstorm as flames burst out of the open bay door, along with a massive expulsion of dark, acrid smoke. The concussive wave barreled over them, driving Pike and GEM down to the ground. Spence's face was slapped by searing heat and his knees buckled, his consciousness leaving him as an all-encompassing blackness enveloped everything.

***

THE WOLF RESIDENCE
NEW SPENCERLAND, NORTH CAROLINA

Wolf had been up on the roof once more applying the last coating of Flex Seal to the repair when he heard the explosion. He involuntarily glanced up and saw the column of black smoke rising against the now azure sky. It had come from the eastern section of town and his higher-than-normal vantage point allowed him to extrapolate the approximate location.

The recycling plant? Wolf then felt a sudden chill.

Meth labs were notorious for being unstable. And if Sheridan was the Spencers' meth cook, his penchant for alcohol might have made him less cautious. Glancing at his watch, he saw it was closing in on eighteen hundred. Time enough for his brother to have returned from Atlanta. He smacked the lid on the can, stuck it in the plastic bag, and stripped off the pair of gloves he'd purchased for the dirty work. Below, Uncle Fred's braced cane was still idling the motor. Wolf slipped over the edge of the trailer roof and landed on the tailgate, hoping he wouldn't hit a rusted-out spot and continue on through.

He didn't.

Now, if his luck held, he'd find out that his brother wasn't hurt by the explosion.

Oh please, Lord, Wolf silently recited as he hopped over the side rail and grabbed the driver's door handle. Please let Jimmy be all right.

CHAPTER 15

THE NEW LUMBERTON MALL
NEW SPENCERLAND, NORTH CAROLINA

Jimmy had heard the explosion on his way out the front gate. It seemed a bit too early, but sticking to the plan, he'd kept going. Now, almost an hour or so later, he sat in the darkness, shivering despite the still balmy temperature and the seclusion of the closed off area. He was safely ensconced in the cleared-out section of the loading bay for the old Berglander store. In its heyday, it had been one of the big four major anchor stores of the mall. Now, it was nothing more than a hollowed our shell, but at least the overhead bay door still worked. As long as the generators were going strong, that is.

He heard something scurrying along the wall and shone his flashlight toward the noise. Two beady little eyes stared back at him for a moment, and then disappeared.

A fucking rat.

The place gave him the creeps, but his position was no doubt less precarious than that of Bobbie, GEM, Craig, and Willard. He wondered how they'd made out. The explosion had gone off quicker than he'd expected. He'd barely had enough time to drive out the gate, but he didn't look back. He couldn't afford to. If Pike or the Reaper had seen him, it would have been all over. As it was, he wondered now if they'd had any trouble convincing them that Batton's drug money had been blown to bits in the explosion.

But calling Bobbie now to check was out of the question. Not only was it against the specific instructions of the plan, but it could alert Pike and the Reaper to his presence. As far as they probably knew, he was lost in the chaos of the explosion somewhere in the plant. After all the times Sheridan had warned him about the dangers, it had finally come true.

Poor old Mr. Sheridan, he thought. He's going to have to find a new occupation now, and he ain't gonna be able to go back to school no more.

Jimmy tried to force out an accompanying laugh but couldn't. After all, he and Sheridan were once related. Sort of.

But he'll find something else, Jimmy told himself. And if he doesn't, it's no concern of mine.

The big civil defense siren that he'd heard before

had now ceased. It had been blasting for a good half hour. He imagined that the fire department was probably still doing a search and rescue mission looking for anyone who might have been trapped inside. That would probably take another hour or so at least. When they didn't find anybody, and they broke away from the scene, Bobbie would no doubt call saying the coast was clear. They'd come pick him up and unload the suitcases.

But then what?

The more he ruminated about it, the more logical it seemed that he should remove them himself and stash them somewhere inside the mall. That way should anyone somehow stumble upon the Rent-n-Haul truck, they wouldn't find it full of a drug kingpin's illegal cash.

Another couple of rats scurried in the darkness making little screeching sounds.

Jimmy took a cigarette out of his pack and lit it.

I've got to remove the suitcases and stash them somewhere, he thought.

Now it was all about safeguarding the Benjamins, until he got the all-clear from Bobbie.

***

Blackness enveloped him as he awoke and found it hard to breathe. Spence tried to move his arms but couldn't.

Oh, fuck, he thought. I'm paralyzed.

But then he realized that he wasn't. He lay on his right side, and could feel his arms, his legs, his hands… They were tingling with a constant beating of pain, needles going in and out, like when your foot fell asleep.

His legs were bent and crushed up against his chest, and his hands were behind his back.

Tied up… He was tied up.

And in some kind of small compartment.

Taking as deep a breath as he could manage, he held his eyes closed for several seconds, hoping that when he opened them he'd see something, anything, but he didn't.

Slowly, he began to explore with his fingers. They were inquisitive tendrils brushing over some rough surface.

No, not a roughness, a coarseness.

A carpet.

He tried to stretch a little and his head banged against something hard.

Metallic hard.

He was in a car trunk.

Spence swallowed and tried to convince himself to be calm.

What had happened leading up to this?

What was the last thing he could remember?

The Reaper pulling a gun, grabbing him, and then

the blasts, the two of them.

The image of Craig going pell-mell off that little concrete walkway in the bay…

Was he alright?

Doubtful. With his missing leg he couldn't move very fast. He'd most certainly been caught up in the blast zone.

GEM and Willard? They'd been between him and the explosion. Pike had too, and the fucking Reaper…

Suddenly he heard a voice, faint at first, and then growing louder, more distinct.

"How the fuck do I know?"

Silence.

Had he imagined it?

Then, "I know, I know. He was all bloody and shit. Looked dead. And I had to bust caps into two of them other motherfuckers. I wasn't about stick around and wait for no five-oh to show up."

It was the Reaper. He must be talking on a phone.

"Yeah, got him in the truck. He all right. For now."

Me, Spence thought. He's talking about me.

"Okay, how soon 'fore you get here?" Pause. "Un-huh." Another pause. "Un-huh. You want to talk to him?"

Spence heard a clicking sound and the night sky appeared between two sections of metal. The trunk lid opened, and he looked up into the face of the Reaper. The man had a gold inlay on one of his upper front teeth.

"Mr. Batton wants to talk to you, sucker," the Reaper said.

He held the cell phone down against Spence's left ear.

"Listen here, you motherfucker," Batton's loud voice said. "I'm on the way to see you and I'm almost there. When I get there, you better be ready to tell me what you done with my fucking money. Understand?"

Spence tried to reply but couldn't. He felt a warm trickle in his crotch.

Oh, my God, he thought. How did this all go so wrong?

***

EMERGENCY WAITING ROOM
MERCY HOSPITAL
NEW SPENCERLAND, NORTH CAROLINA

Wolf watched as Nick Paxton led Darlene, who was crying, to a chair on the other side of the room and gently guided her into it. He stood beside her, not looking Wolf's way at all. Paxton's face was taut.

Must be bad news about her brother, Wolf surmised.

Across the way a uniformed officer, that guy named Cook, stood next to Chief Langford, who was weeping into his cupped hands. The chief was in civilian clothes and ropes of snot hung from between his fingers.

Bad news about his son, perhaps?

Honest Bob Spencer stood there as well, his face dour, his hand on the chief's shoulder.

Wolf continued to sit in silence, waiting. All that he was told, upon arriving at the ER was that they had brought several victims in from the explosion. The names were being withheld pending positive identification and notification of next of kin. He'd repeatedly asked if one of them was Jimmy Wolf but was told they could neither confirm nor deny anything at this point.

"If you want to have a seat, sir," the hospital security guard had said, "we'll let you know as soon as possible."

That had stretched into more than an hour now. Darlene and Paxton had arrived, along with Chief Langford. They'd all been ushered into an anteroom beyond the Emergency Room retracting doors and had emerged devastated and distraught.

Maybe no news is good news, Wolf thought. He tried to call Jimmy's cell again, but it went directly to voicemail after one ring. Either he had it turned off, or he'd blocked Wolf's calls.

The doors slid open, and Wolf perked up, but then relaxed as he saw it was a nurse pushing someone out in a wheelchair. A moment later, he saw it was Pike. He had a bandage around his head and his right arm, which was also bandaged, in a sling. A plastic bag with his possessions sat in his lap. His head swiveled around as he seemed to catch sight of Wolf and signaled the female nurse to stop.

"I'll just get up now," he said.

"But, sir," the nurse said, "we have to physically escort you out in a wheelchair."

Pike lifted his feet off the oval-shaped metal rungs and jammed his big boot heels onto the floor. The wheelchair came to an abrupt stop.

"Sir," the nurse started to say, but Pike was already standing. He turned and thanked her and headed over toward Wolf, carrying the bag with his left hand and pulling his right arm free of the sling.

"Hey," Pike said. "I need to talk to you."

The nurse, obviously frustrated at the violation of protocol, twisted the wheelchair around and headed back through the sliding doors.

Wolf got to his feet.

"Looks like you went twelve rounds with the heavyweight champ," he said.

"Something like that." Pike glanced over toward the chief and patrolman, then grabbed Wolf's arm and said, "Come on over here for a minute."

"Hey, I'm trying to find out word about my brother."

"He ain't in there." Pike pulled off the head gauze exposing a section of shaved skin on the back of his skull lined with a track of dark stitches. "He wasn't at the place when it went up."

"He wasn't?" Wolf felt relieved but confused. "What the hell happened out there?"

Pike continued toward the exit, still holding Wolf's arm.

"Come on. I'll tell you."

They walked outside and into the coolness of the early evening air. Pike stopped and looked around. Nobody was around. There were numerous cars, including a marked police car, parked along the extended driveway.

"I need your help," Pike said. "That bozo in the uniform in there has my gun in the trunk of his squad car."

Wolf smirked. "Sounds like a safe place for it."

Pike didn't smile.

"I need you to help me get it back."

Wolf arched an eyebrow.

"Sorry, but that sounds like a problem above my paygrade."

Pike stared at him for a time, and then spoke in a low, even tone.

"Listen, Steve, I'm the best chance—no, make that the only chance, your brother has of getting out of this without doing hard time."

It was Wolf's turn to scrutinize the other man. Confusion, mixed with supposition raced through him.

"Exactly what do you mean by that?" he asked.

Pike took in a deep breath.

"I'm a federal agent. I've been working this Spencer/Batton thing for the better part of a year now."

The words hit Wolf like the series of repetitive jabs.

"We both know your brother's into this up to his eyeballs. And right now, there's a good chance he's going to end up dead."

That was like a follow-up left hook to the gut.

"Dead?"

"Right," Pike said. "Him and his group of idiot friends here have bitten off way more than they can chew. But you already had that figured, right?"

Again, Wolf remained silent. This was a lot to process.

"I'm the best shot Jimmy has to staying out of prison," Pike continued. "He's just a small fish. Plus, he hasn't killed anybody. Yet."

"What are you saying?" Wolf managed to say.

"That if he shows us where the drug money him and his buddies ripped off is, and he's willing to testify, I'll do my best to keep him out of prison."

"Do your best?"

Pike held up his hands, palms outward.

"I'm being straight with you. You know the drill."

"Yeah, I do. And I know what those kind of promises are worth."

Pike frowned. "Look, I read your file. I know you got a raw deal on that Iraq thing."

"What?"

Pike gave his head a dismissive shake.

"Just fucking listen, okay? I researched everybody's family in my investigation, including Jimmy's. Now I need your help. I know you were a ranger, and one hell of a good one. I need you to help me get my gun and maybe back me up. You can talk to your brother, right?"

"Wait a minute," Wolf said. "If you're a federal agent, you can call in backup. You don't need me."

Pike's frown deepened.

"Listen, Steve, I don't know if you heard, but that hurricane dotted the entire coast and areas east of here with a bunch of tornadoes. Roads are down, flights are cancelled, and all that shit. I got no backup." He glanced back toward the ER. "And I sure as hell can't depend on the local police force here. That chief and the mayor are both in on it."

"In on what?"

Pike licked his lips. "I'll tell you, but first I gotta know. You gonna help me, or not?"

Wolf mulled over the question, then nodded. "I'm in."

"All right. Here it is. Mayor Spencer and his son

have been laundering money through the Indian casino for a very bad dude named Batton down in Atlanta. He supplies crystal meth to the community down there. The Spencers have also been supplying the stuff to him as well. We've been delivering it via rental trucks."

Wolf nodded again. It was pretty much as he had figured it.

"So today, instead of dropping the money to be laundered at the casino, like they were supposed to, Spencer Jr. and his crew staged an explosion to make it look like the money got blown up. It didn't, and their scheme didn't work."

"What's the rest of it?"

"I have a real strong suspicion that your brother absconded with the drug money. It's the only answer. When I was laid out there back at the scene, I overheard one of Batton's boys on the phone. Batton smelled a rat and took his plane up to Fayetteville just before the storms hit. He's on his way here now. I need to get that dough back to bring this case to a prosecutable conclusion, not to mention finding your brother before they do."

"And just how we gonna find him?"

Pike's lips parted in a smile.

"That'll be the easy part." He reached into the bag and withdrew a gold skull-and-crossbones medallion. "I placed a geo-locator on that truck. All I have to do is call up for the coordinates." His smile disappeared. "Now you with me, airborne?"

"All the way," Wolf said.

Pike's grin reappeared.

"Good." He dug in the plastic bag and took out his cell phone. "Now go get that fat ass cop out here so I can get my gun out of his trunk."

"And then what do we do with him?"

Pike shrugged. "We can leave him handcuffed in the back of the squad, I suppose."

"If we can't trust the local police, how long do you think it'll be before they'll be on our asses?"

Pike raised his eyebrows.

"Good point. And?"

"I've got a crowbar in my uncle's truck over there. It'll take us less than thirty seconds to get into that trunk, and they won't be any the wiser. For a while."

"Okay."

"And," Wolf said, "I think I know one member of the local PD that we can trust."

***

The trunk lid opened again, and Spence caught another fleeting glimpse of the now velvety night sky before the sudden, piercing brightness of the flashlight beam all but blinded him.

"Spen-cer, Jun-i-or," the loud voice said from the

other side of the light, pronouncing each syllable with emphatic distinction.

Spence felt the cold, hard barrel of a pistol being pressed against his forehead.

"Did you really think your little white privileged ass was gonna be able to rip me off?"

"It wasn't me," Spence said. It was all he could think of.

The gun barrel drew back and then rapped back hard against his nose. He grunted in pain.

The gun lifted away from his face and then suddenly he felt it probing his groin.

"How'd you like it if I blow your fucking balls off?" Batton said. "One at a motherfucking time."

"No, no," Spence said. "I know where the money's at. I'll take you there. Word."

"Your word ain't shit to me."

An eerie silence hung in the air for several seconds and Spence anticipated a bullet ripping through his genitals.

"Smells like the motherfucker pissed himself." That was the Reaper's voice.

Spence shuddered.

I'm going to die, he thought. In the worst possible way.

"I'll tell you where it's at. I'll take you to it."

More silence that seemed like an eternity passed, the powerful beam still shining in his eyes.

Then Batton's voice came out of the darkness: "You better, bitch. You better."

The trunk lid slammed down again.

**

THE NEW LUMBERTON MALL
NEW SPENCERLAND, NORTH CAROLINA

Jimmy had finally finished secreting the seven suitcases in the old Thom McCann's Shoe Store. There was just enough space behind the long counter to hide three of them. The other four he placed in the small, upstairs stock room. He'd toyed with the idea of maybe putting them all up there, but decided it was better to have two locations.

Don't put all of your eggs in one basket, he thought, remembering the old cliché.

After finishing things off by stacking as much junk on top and around the suitcases as he could find, he was satisfied, but his mouth and throat felt grainy. The dust from the accumulated detritus of old crumbling ceiling tiles, broken shelves, and scores of empty cardboard shoe boxes had left a peculiar taste in his mouth.

He walked out of the vacant store and lit up another cigarette. He'd flipped the switch in the engineering room to turn on the power so he wouldn't trip or fall down the metallic escalator stairs, even if it meant lighting up both the interior and the outside sign lights. Hopefully, nobody driving out this way would think anything of it.

He mulled over maybe turning them off, but he didn't want to sit in the dark again.

His phone told him it was now eight-fifteen.

Where did the time go?

And, more importantly, where the hell were Bobbie and the others?

They were supposed to come pick him up by now. He was essentially trapped here. After all, he couldn't very well be seen driving around in that Rent-n-Haul truck.

Maybe I should call him, he thought, but then decided against that.

The rules had been set, and Bobbie had everything covered.

Or did he?

Jimmy looked at his phone again and was reconsidering when he heard something at the far end of the place. The main doors that they always used. Tossing away the cigarette, he crouched down by a planter box and waited.

Damn, he thought. Why didn't I turn off those lights?

More sounds emanated from the other end. Sounds of people walking, their shoes skittering debris across the garbage-littered marble floor.

Was it Bobbie and the others?

Man, he hoped so. He considered calling out to them but waited.

Let them call out first. Bobbie had told him to wait in the loading bay of Berglander's. Would he be pissed that Jimmy wasn't there, that the suitcases were moved?

Maybe they'd checked the loading bay already and found he wasn't there.

He took a deep breath and was going to yell when a voice beat him to it.

"Jimmy, it's me. Spence. Where you at?"

Good. It was Bobbie. Maybe now they could get out of there.

"I'm over here," he said, standing and shouting. "What the hell took you so long?"

Bobbie came into full view, but he was walking funny, taking baby steps. And his tan Dockers had a big stain on the crotch. His hair was messed, and his face was ashen.

And then the Reaper stepped out from behind a jagged section of broken paneling and pointing a gun.

Oh, shit, Jimmy thought.

***

After the three of them had stopped at Paxton's house to get two handguns and his twelve-gauge shotgun, he'd driven Pike and Wolf to the old New Lumberton Mall. Pax had agreed to go with them and supply the weapons.

"I'm technically suspended," he said with a grin. "So the only thing I can do is make a citizen's arrest."

Wolf figured his friend was glad to get away from that ER. He'd told them that the four bodies at the scene were Craig Langford, George Earl Mess, and Willard Gibbons. Langford had been killed in the explosion, and the other two had been shot to death. Two rounds to the chest, and one to the head for each.

"Mozambique style," Pike said. "That sounds like the Reaper."

"How many guys does this Batton guy usually bring with him on something like this?" Wolf asked.

Pike shrugged. They were pulling into the mall now. The outside signs were glowing in the ambient darkness just like the other night. The oversized neon figure of the gentleman seemed to be tipping his hat to them.

"My guess would be five. His plane—a Learjet, has a crew of two, and he usually has three bodyguards. Of course, one of them is the Reaper."

"Let's plan on getting in there and finding Jimmy and the money before he gets here then," Paxton said.

Wolf was thinking the same thing.

"One more thing," Pike said. "Batton and his boys usually wear Kevlar vests."

"Vests?" Paxton said. "And I had to turn mine in to the station."

"Too bad," Pike said. "We could've used it. I'm riding bareback, too."

"No time to worry about that now," Wolf said. "Cut your lights and do a circle. Let's see if we can spot any cars."

Paxton turned off his lights and continued on the outer ring road.

***

Jimmy felt the second round whiz by him as he ran. Only that he'd stumbled slightly while running had saved him from getting hit.

"You can run," Batton called out in his stentorian voice, "but you can't hide."

Jimmy's breathing was ragged.

What the hell had happened? How had they gotten here and how had they found him?

Bobbie, he thought. He gave me up. That means they catch me, I die.

Glancing over his shoulder, he got to his feet and sprinted as fast as he could down the litter-strewn corridor. He knew he had to get back to the loading bay. Use the truck to escape. It was his only chance.

But how fast could he go in with a truck, when they had a Charger. Maybe more.

Still, it was his only chance for now.

Another bullet ripped by him.

Diving onto the hard marble floor, he rolled and then crawled through the broken lower portion of a store entrance. Scrambling into the dark interior, he tried to get his heavy breathing under control. He couldn't afford to be loud. They'd hear him.

He saw an indented section along a wall where rows of clothes had once hung. Flattening his body against the inlet wall, he cowered there still breathing hard.

And then he heard the crunching sound of shoes stepping on broken glass. Jimmy tried to hold his breath, but he couldn't. He inhaled trying not to make any more noise.

The crunching was getting closer.

Swallowing, he cupped his hand over his mouth and held it there, not allowing himself to breathe.

The crunching stopped.

He waited.

Nothing.

Maybe they'd passed.

His chest burned and an eclipsing blackness swarmed in front of his eyes.

No longer able to suppress it, his exhalation came out in a furious rush, and he coughed.

Gasping, he straightened up, ready to run.

But then a powerful hand grabbed him, and something hard clipped him on the temple. His knees sagged, but the powerful hand held him up. His eyes opened wide as a flashlight beam from somewhere cut through the darkness and he could see the dark, grinning face of the Reaper.

"Hello, little man," the Reaper said. "Now it's time to quit playing and take us to that money."

***

The crowbar had come in handy once again as they'd used it to pry off the boards blocking off the upper-level side door entrance that had once led to the security guard offices. The sound of the shots added urgency to their pace.

Hopefully, we'll have the high ground, Wolf thought.

The cars they'd spotted had been parked by the lower-level entrance.

Outnumbered, outgunned, and them with Kevlar vests, Wolf assessed. But at least we have the element of surprise.

The three of them moved quickly, keeping as quiet as they could, while still surveying the lower level. As they approached the center court area, a loud voice could be heard.

Wolf glanced back to make sure the others had heard it too.

Pike, holding that massive Colt Anaconda, gestured that he was moving to the left side. Paxton, with his twelve-gauge and handgun, pointed to the center. That left the right for Wolf. He had Paxton's off duty snub nose thirty-eight. Not much good for distance, but better than nothing.

The plan was for Pike to try and distract them. For all Batton knew, Pike was still one of his boys. It could buy them a few extra seconds to get into position. Wolf flattened out and did a low crawl to the edge of the upper landing. Three-foot-high glass paneling, topped by a six-inch wooden banister, lined the upper level. Below, Wolf could see seven figures, five of whom were standing in a semi-circle. Jimmy and Spencer Jr. were on their knees in the middle. The standing men all had weapons—handguns.

All semi-autos, with high-capacity magazines, no doubt.

And he saw that each of them was also wearing a vest.

Pike's Anaconda held six before a reload, as did Wolf's snubbie. Paxton had four rounds in his shotgun magazine and one in the pipe. But he'd told them they were all birdshot shells, not rifled deer slugs. Wolf saw Pax lay the shotgun down and pull out his Glock 21. It was .45 caliber and had twelve rounds in the magazine. With one in the chamber that gave Pax lucky thirteen.

At least Wolf hoped they would be lucky.

"Now," Batton shouted from below in a loud voice.

"Since y'all have betrayed me, I will give you one chance, and one chance only, to show me where my money is at. Do you understand?"

His words echoed against the empty walls.

Wolf crawled to the escalator and began the bumpy descent on his back, almost like going under a barbed wire fence and figuring it would allow him a quicker pop-up time if he had to rise and shoot. Each sharp, serrated stair edge seemed to cut into the exposed flesh of his arms and bite through the thin fabric of his T-shirt. He was about halfway down when he heard Batton yell again.

"Where is it? Where's my fucking money?"

"Jimmy," Spencer Jr. said, his voice sounded broken and wracked with sobs. "Tell him. Tell him."

"And then what?" Jimmy yelled back. "He'll kill us both for sure."

The kid's tough, Wolf thought.

"No, he won't," Spencer Junior's voice was a pathetic whine. "He promised me. He won't."

Wolf heard Batton laugh.

"Last chance, Jimmy," he said. "I'm going to count to three."

After a few seconds' delay, Batton spoke in a loud voice.

"One."

More silence. Wolf debated whether to take a quick peek but decided not to risk it. He slid down another metal stair.

"Two."

Wolf tried to quicken his pace. He was just beyond the halfway point of the escalator now.

"Three."

Silence, and then the blast of a shot, simultaneously accompanied by a sharp, shrieking cry.

Wolf recoiled. He didn't want to give up his position, but he had to know if Jimmy had taken that round. He rolled onto his side, then looked over the edge of the escalator.

Spencer Jr. lay twitching on the floor, a pool of bright crimson spilling out of the wide exit wound on the back of his head.

"Oooh," Batton said, "that sucker got his brains all over you, Jimmy. Now tell me, where's my money?"

He placed the barrel of his gun against Jimmy's forehead.

"You don't tell me now," Batton said, "I'm gonna have the Reaper here start at your fucking feet and work his way on up."

"Hey," Pike called out from above. "Looks like you started the party without me."

The five of them looked up as Pike walked to the edge of the escalator.

He's exposing himself to give us a chance to get in position, Wolf thought, and cocked back the hammer of the little thirty-eight.

"Pike!" Batton said. "What you doin' here?"

"I'm a federal agent," Pike shouted, bringing the Anaconda up. "Drop your guns. You're surrounded."

Batton's eyes widened, and then he smiled.

"Fed-er-al agent." He shook his head. "You never know who's gunning for you, do you?"

He whirled and fired up at Pike who fired back.

One of Batton's boys jerked and then straightened up and shot again.

Kevlar, Wolf thought. Looks like he took that one in the vest

The big Anaconda roared again and this time the thug fell forward, the back of his head split open.

Wolf's ears were ringing and figured Jimmy's were, too, but he shouted anyway.

"Jimmy, get down."

Bringing his gun over the edge of the escalator, Wolf rested his arms on the hard rubber handrail, and squeezed the trigger twice aiming for the assailant's left side. It was difficult to determine where the rounds struck, but the man grimaced and dropped. The Reaper fired a round up at Pike, and then swiveled and fired another one at Wolf. He heard the bullet smack into the heavy chrome paneling on the other side of him. Wolf centered his aim at the Reaper's throat and squeezed off two more rounds. The lanky gangster did a stagger-step and then collapsed. Paxton was standing and firing over the banister in the upstairs center with no cover. Pike shot three more times and two more of Batton's minions fell.

This seemed to be a cue for Batton, who took off running.

Wolf yelled and vaulted over the edge of the escalator. The drop was more than he expected, maybe fifteen feet. Luckily, he landed in the planter box. It was full of dirt and cushioned his fall somewhat. A round zipped by him, and he ducked, and then sprang from the box, returning fire.

As he jumped over the brick edge on the far side of the planter box, he saw Batton turning and zeroing in on him. Wolf raised his arm and fired without aiming. Batton jerked slightly, like he'd been hit in the side, flashed a wicked grin, and raised his pistol once more.

Another vest hit, he guessed.

He squeezed the trigger and felt it hit on an empty shell casing.

Batton leveled the gun directly at him and Wolf realized he was caught in the open without any cover. What seemed like a millisecond later, a blast roared. A hole suddenly appeared in the center of Batton's forehead accompanied by an effusion of red mist bursting forth from behind his head. The gun tumbled from the drug lord's hand, and he did an awkward pirouette to the floor.

Wolf glanced to the side and saw Pike advancing, the big Colt extended forward in front of him, a wisp of smoke curling upward from the barrel.

Wolf nodded thanks and Pike smiled.

"Like I told you before," he said, "us airborne troopers got to stick together."

EPILOGUE

ONE WEEK LATER.
LONE STAR MOTEL
DEL RIO, TEXAS

"I got good news and bad news," Abraham's voice said over the burner phone.

The lawyer sounded rather ebullient. Figuring the good must be outweighing the bad, Bray asked for that news first.

"We've both been officially fired by the Fallotti family."

"What about the Cutter? He's here and—"

"Listen, everything, from this moment on, is on hold. The Don died last night. His son, Carlo, is taking over. He's a legitimate businessman and not old school at all. Smart, too. He knows the FBI's involved and doesn't want to bring the family under any more scrutiny."

This struck Bray as fortuitous, even though they'd already gone to a lot of trouble to run McNamara and Wolf to ground.

"Okay, so what's the good news?"

"Our employment's been picked up by another interested party."

This stunned Bray. Another interested party? What the hell did that mean?

"Who?"

Abraham emitted a short laugh. "Von Dien's nephew. Says he'll pay top dollar for a complete and thorough report, which we already have."

Bray smiled. This was indeed good news. He and Abraham could continue to milk this gig, and now they didn't have to worry about being under the control of some organized crime nut case. The Devil's vendetta was on hold.

"What do you need me to do now?" he asked.

"You break camp and come back to New York," Abraham said. "Leave the Cutter and your team down there in place, all expenses paid. We need to regroup and have a business meeting with our new employer. Who knows, maybe he'll fly us both out to his island."

Lolita's Palace, Bray thought. AKA Paradise Island.

That would be something. And from the sound of

it, this nephew had a lot of dough to spread around.

"Sounds good," he said. "I'll be on the first plane back."

Things were looking up, in more ways than one.

***

ARMY RECRUITING OFFICE
LUMBERTON, NORTH CAROLINA

Wolf sat in the brand-new red pickup truck, with the automatic transmission, that he'd bought for Uncle Fred, and reflected on how big a hit his bank account had taken in the past week. But still, life was good. No, actually it was pretty great.

The afternoon sunshine beat down warm on his arm, and he couldn't help but reflect on how beautiful the day looked.

No trace of any storms.

No tempest.

He still hadn't managed to write that damn paper and email it to his professor but reminded himself that he could only handle one tempest at a time.

He peered through the window and could see Jimmy going over his test scores with the uniformed sergeant. The guy was an E-7 and looked pretty squared away. Wolf had decided to stay outside rather than go in with his brother, lest any association to him and his bad record be connected. And he was glad he did, reflecting on the call he'd just gotten from Yolanda asking when he was coming home.

Home. That was how she'd put it.

It had filled him with hope and renewed his sense of purpose. Still filled with optimism, he was getting ready to call the Great Oz to light a fire under his lazy ass, when his phone rang again. He looked at the screen and saw it was McNamara's number.

"Hey," Wolf said. "How are things down at the border?"

"Like trying to build a sandcastle during high tide," Mac said. "We're thinking about heading out for some R and R before the next wave. You're welcome to join us."

"Let me think about it," Wolf said.

"Okay, you do that." After a few seconds pause, he asked, "So how'd you make out with your little brother?"

"Good," Wolf said, glancing in the window once more. Both Jimmy and the E-7 seemed to be smiling. "We're at the recruiter's now."

"Outstanding," McNamara said. "I knew you'd bring him around, straighten him out. Who was it said that you can't go home again?"

"Thomas Wolfe, I think."

"Another Wolf, huh?" Mac laughed. "Well, I'm glad you proved him wrong. We couldn't afford to leave your kid brother behind."

"Damn straight," Wolf said.

Leave no man behind, he added mentally.

Especially Jimmy.

"Okay," he said. "I thought about it. Where should I meet you for that R and R?"

A LOOK AT BOOK SIX:
DEVIL'S BREED

Nothing ever goes as planned...

That's what Steve Wolf is starting to believe after
a carefully planned appeal to clear his name—an appeal his high-priced lawyer assured him was a slam-
dunk—mysteriously disappears from the Military
Court of Appeals docket.

Disappointed, Wolf considers joining his friend
and mentor, Big Jim McNamara, down at the border
doing security work. But when a federal agent unexpectedly reenters Wolf's life with a proposition, he's
hard-pressed to refuse. All Wolf has to do is assist in
an undercover operation by pretending to be asso-
ciated with a hard-core motorcycle gang called the
Devil's Breed, and his appeal will be back on track.
There's just one catch—the mission is to stop an international human trafficking and drug ring that is

controlled by a powerful Mexican cartel and led by an enigmatic and legendary figure known as El Tigre. To complicate matters more, Wolf must accomplish all of this while being stalked by a foe from his past.

On a sudden collision course with murder, kidnapping, and disaster, Wolf finds himself in a race against time and a question plaguing his mind—will he risk it all to save the life of a man who once saved his?

COMING OCTOBER 2022

ABOUT THE AUTHOR

Michael A. Black is the author of 36 books and over 100 short stories and articles. A decorated police officer in the south suburbs of Chicago, he worked for over thirty-two years in various capacities including patrol supervisor, SWAT team leader, investigations, and tactical operations before retiring in April of 2011.

A long time practitioner of the martial arts, Black holds a black belt in Tae Kwon Do from Ki Ka Won Academy in Seoul, Korea. He has a Bachelor of Arts degree in English from Northern Illinois University and a Master of Fine Arts in Fiction Writing from Columbia College, Chicago. In 2010 he was awarded the Cook County Medal of Merit by Cook County Sheriff Tom Dart. Black wrote his first short story in the sixth grade and credits his then teacher for instilling within him the determination to keep writing when she told him never to try writing again.

Black has since been published in several genres including mystery, thriller, sci-fi, westerns, police procedurals, mainstream, pulp fiction, horror, and historical fiction. His Ron Shade series, featuring the Chicago-based kickboxing private eye, has won several awards, as has his police procedural series featuring Frank Leal and Olivia Hart. He also wrote two novels with television star Richard Belzer, I Am Not a Cop and I Am Not a Psychic. Black writes under numerous pseudonyms and pens The Executioner series under the name Don Pendleton. His Executioner novel, Fatal Prescription, won the Best Original Novel Scribe Award given by the International Media Tie-In Writers Association in 2018.

His current books are Blood Trails, a cutting edge police procedural in the tradition of the late Michael Crichton, and Legends of the West, which features a fictionalized account of the legendary and real life lawman, Bass Reeves. His newest Executioner novels are Dying Art, Stealth Assassins, and Cold Fury, all of which were nominees and finalists for Best Novel Scribe Awards. He is very active in animal rescue and animal welfare issues and has several cats.